NEW STORIES
FROM THE SOUTH

The Year's Best, 2007

NEW STORIES
FROM THE SOUTH

The Year's Best, 2007

Selected from U.S. magazines by
EDWARD P. JONES with KATHY PORIES

with an introduction by Edward P. Jones

Algonquin Books of Chapel Hill

Published by
ALGONQUIN BOOKS OF CHAPEL HILL
Post Office Box 2225
Chapel Hill, North Carolina 27515-2225

a division of
WORKMAN PUBLISHING
225 Varick Street
New York, New York 10014

Introduction by Edward P. Jones. Copyright © 2007 by Edward P. Jones.

"Goats" by Rick Bass. First published in *The Idaho Review*. Copyright © 2006 by Rick Bass. Reprinted by permission of the author.

"A Season of Regret" by James Lee Burke. First published in *Shenandoah*. Reprinted with permission of Simon & Schuster Adult Publishing Group from *Jesus Out to Sea: Stories by James Lee Burke*. Copyright © 2007 by James Lee Burke.

"The Ice Garden" by Moira Crone. First published in *TriQuarterly*. Copyright © 2006 by Moira Crone. Reprinted by permission of the author.

"Ghost Town Choir" by Joshua Ferris. First published in *Prairie Schooner*. Copyright © 2006 by Joshua Ferris. Reprinted by permission of the author.

"The Safe" by Tim Gautreaux. First published in *The Atlantic Monthly*. Copyright © 2006 by Tim Gautreaux. Reprinted by permission of the author.

"Fourteen Feet of Water in My House" by Allan Gurganus. First published in *Harper's*. Copyright © 2006 by Allan Gurganus. Reprinted by permission of the author.

"Hollyhocks" by Cary Holladay. First published in *Five Points*. Copyright © 2006 by Cary Holladay. Reprinted by permission of the author.

"At the Powwow Hotel" by Toni Jensen. First published in *Nimrod*. Copyright © 2006 by Toni Jensen. Reprinted by permission of the author.

"Life Expectancy" by Holly Goddard Jones. First published in *The Kenyon Review*. Copyright © 2006 by Holly Goddard Jones. Reprinted by permission of the author.

"Beauty and Virtue" by Agustín Maes. First published in *Ontario Review*. Copyright © 2006 by Agustín Maes. Reprinted by permission of the author.

"Dogs with Human Faces" by Stephen Marion. First published in *Epoch*. Copyright © 2006 by Stephen Marion. Reprinted by permission of the author.

"One Day This Will All Be Yours" by Philipp Meyer. First published in *McSweeney's*. Copyright © 2006 by Philipp Meyer. Reprinted by permission of the author.

"Jakob Loomis" by Jason Ockert. First published in *The Oxford American*. Copyright © 2006 by Jason Ockert. Reprinted by permission of the author.

"Which Rocks We Choose" by George Singleton. First published in *The Georgia Review*. Copyright © 2006 by George Singleton. Reprinted by permission of the author.

"Story" by R. T. Smith. First published in *Prairie Schooner*. Copyright © 2006 by R. T. Smith. Reprinted by permission of the author.

"Bela Lugosi's Dead" by Angela Threatt. First published in *Gargoyle*. Copyright © 2006 by Angela Threatt. Reprinted by permission of the author.

"A Terrible Thing" by Daniel Wallace. First published in *The Georgia Review*. Copyright © 2006 by Daniel Wallace. Reprinted by permission of the author.

"Unassigned Territory" by Stephanie Powell Watts. First published in *The Oxford American*. Copyright © 2006 by Stephanie Powell Watts. Reprinted by permission of the author.

CONTENTS

Edward P. Jones

INTRODUCTION
New Stories from the South — 2007

When in the late afternoon of life, you go off onto a path never imagined — if raised by people who know the true value of things — you do not forget those who first gave bread and sustenance. Of the stories in my first collection, *Lost in the City,* one first appeared in *Callaloo,* and another in *Ploughshares.* After the other stories in *City* were written and collected with the first two to make a whole book, no one, except *The Paris Review,* thought enough of them to publish another one.

Being on this unexpected path has proven to be a busy thing, but we should never discard our good raising; doing so puts you in risk of becoming one of those creatures slithering through life without values. So when Kathy Pories, this series' editor, asked if I would choose the stories for 2007, the busy me initially said no, but the other me remembered that no other annual anthology but *New Stories from the South* and the Pushcart Prize reprinted my story from *The Paris Review.* The story, "Marie," was about a fairly uneducated old woman who, even after many decades of life in a city, still could not forget the Southern values of right and wrong she had inherited as a child and a young woman. I am here now because it meant something to have that story anthologized. I am here because I cannot forget *Callaloo* and *Ploughshares* and *The Paris Review*. They, like so many literary journals, say yes to us when others say no.

Hither and yon, they still debate whether Washington, D.C. — where I was born and came to know what is true and what is not so true — is a part of the South. It might well be that that debate is why I have never stood up straight and asserted that I was a bona fide son of the South. I'm in the room, but I'll stand in the corner for the evening, if it's all the same to you. And that is another reason I first said no to choosing the stories for this book.

Still, so much is about the heart, wherein the soul dwells, and so maybe my heart, when all the standing in the corner is done, doesn't care if Washington is north or south of the Mason-Dixon line. The heart knows enough to make me create a character who is called upon in a story to assert, with great authority, that the South is "the worst mama in the world . . . and it's the best mama in the world." The heart knows that just about every adult — starting with my mother — who had an important part in my life before I turned eighteen was born and raised in the South. They — the great majority of them black and the descendants of slaves — came to Washington with a culture unappreciated until you go out into the world and look back to see what went into making you a full human being. A culture defined by big things, by small things. By food (from greens to pigs' feet and tails to black-eyed peas on New Year's Day). By superstition (resting your clasped hands on the top of your head shortens your mother's days on this Earth; "my word is my word until the day I die"). By speech ("fetch"; "yonder"; "a month of Sundays" — and a phrase my mother was particularly fond of using: there were, she would say, so many awful problems in the world that could be cured by people simply doing the correct and proper thing, "but that would be too much like right").

Black people passed this culture on to me, but once I discovered Southern literature I learned that much of it was shared by whites, whether they wanted to admit it or not. I read Richard Wright and Truman Capote and Wendell Berry and Erskine Caldwell and a whole mess of other writers and came upon white people who, in their way, were also just trying to make it to the next day. *Dear Lord, reach down and gimme a hand here.* Those fictional white people lived in a world that was not alien to me. And yet growing up in D.C., I had known no Southern whites, except for the ones on television. As I read, I felt I knew far more about that world of people than I did about those people who lived in cities in the North, who lived, as I did in D.C., with concrete and noisy neighbors above and below and a sense that the horizon stopped at the top of the tallest building. It does not matter where Washington fits on the map; I was of the South because that was what I inherited.

None of that afforded me anything special in choosing the stories in this book. In many instances, I knew it was the South right away because I recognized the landscape, I recognized the voices, I knew the trials and tribulations. Like the story here about a wealthy white Virginia family — so closely related to ones in Faulkner — weighed down by the past, by emotions that cannot be tamed. Or the one about two young men determined to become rich by buying one calf at a time and creating a cow and bull empire.

A few times, there were worlds that I knew were the South because the author told me so. One story in this volume takes place in the north of the Midwest, but the man at the center of the story, like me, had his character forged in the South; the place, I feel, is in his blood. And in several stories, the land of the South has become hardly different from places in the North — a horror of malls and high-rises built and inhabited by people who, no matter what they say, really do envy New Yorkers. One story unfolds among the one-story, low-income dwellings of Richmond. Another takes two Jehovah's Witnesses, schooled the same as their sisters in the North, into alien territory in North Carolina; those two women could be knocking on any door in America, but in that story the territory is quite specific. And still another story has a son watch his father's emotional wasting away in an area where neighbors have not been taught, like once upon a time, to know and care about each other. But the neighborhood is not the father's problem; the new West Virginia, however, is.

What did help me, ultimately, is what I learned early in life about the artistry of storytelling, often from people who could not read or write. They hadn't read James Baldwin or Elizabeth Spencer or Anton Chekhov, but they knew, as those writers knew, how to entertain on the way to their point, and perhaps that is, at the close of the day, what it is about. You will find here one or two stories that might seem to meander, but you shouldn't wander away: Southerners, I've found, might seem to take the long way to get from A to Z (a result, maybe, of having all those porches and living in weather that doesn't always encourage taking it fast, getting straight to some point). But each place along the way is, in the end, crucial to the story.

I should confess that I did not feel I could choose any story that seemed to have been built solely around some anecdote, a story of one note, as it were. And there were several very worthy such stories by very talented writers. But we are all slaves to the little bit that we know, and while those stories may have captured me for the moment, I did not hold them in my heart the way I did, for example, the one about the woman and the convict, whose duty is to kill dogs. Or the one about the basketball coach, drowning in a pool of love. To be sure, I grew up appreciating anecdotes and jokes, the momentary entertainment. But now, for something to claim me long after the last sentence, I need a sense that the world, for even one character, has shifted, whether to a large or a tiny degree, as I do when I read Richard Wright's collection *Uncle Tom's Children*. Or Capote's "A Tree of Night" and "Miriam." Please take note in these pages of the way the world shifts for that group of junkyard men. A big shift. Or the smaller shift with the woman in the trailer park.

Volumes like this one are of course always subjective. (I am now far more sympathetic to those who did not publish or reprint me long ago.) No doubt some reader will have come across some story that should have been included here. I understand that. But I have tried to do my best to pick stories that are not, to use some of William Faulkner's words, about the glands, but about the human heart. What helped me most, in the end, was whatever I have accumulated over the years of reading and taking to heart the stories written by people whose work will last. It could be that I read them and learned it all wrong, but I think my heart was in the right place.

I am ever so grateful to Kathy Pories, the editor of this series and my guide, who read hundreds of stories, far, far more than I read. Her eye is sharper and keener than my own. You have my word.

With that, I'll step out of the way, for here are eighteen men and women, who are standing in their own corners of the South, waiting to tell you something.

Rick Bass

GOATS

(from *The Idaho Review*)

It would be easy to say that he lured me into the fields of disrepair like Pan, calling out with his flute to come join in on the secret chaos of the world: but I already had my own disrepair within, and my own hungers, and I needed no flute call, no urging. I've read recently that scientists have measured the brains of adolescent boys and have determined that there is a period of transformation in which the ridges of the brain swell and then flatten out, becoming smoother, like mere rolling hills, rather than the deep ravines and canyons of the highly intelligent: and that during this physiological metamorphosis, it is for the boys as if they have received some debilitating injury, some blow to the head, so that, neurologically speaking, they glide, or perhaps stumble, through the world as if in a borderline coma during that time.

Simple commands, much less reason and rules of consequence, are beyond their ken, and if heard at all, sound perhaps like the clinking of oars or paddles against the side of a boat heard by one underwater, or like hard rain drumming on a tin roof: as if the boys are wearing a helmet of iron, against which the world, for a while, cannot, and will not, intrude.

In this regard, Moxley and I were no different. We heard no flute calls. Indeed, we heard nothing. But we could sense the world's

I

seams of weaknesses — or believed we could — and we moved toward them.

Moxley wanted to be a cattle baron. It wasn't about the money — we both knew we'd go on to college, Moxley to Texas A&M, and me to the University of Texas — and that we'd float along in something or another. He wanted to become a veterinarian, too, in addition to a cattle baron — back then, excess did not seem incompatible with the future — and I thought I might like to study geography. But that was all eons away, and in the meantime, the simple math of cattle ranching — one mother cow yielding a baby, which yielded a baby, which yielded a baby — appealed to us. All we had to do was let them eat grass. We had no expenses, we were living at home, we just needed to find some cheap calves. The money would begin pouring from the cattle, like coins and bills from their mouths. With each sale, we planned to buy more calves — four more from the sale of the fatted first one, then sixteen from the sale of those four, and so on.

I lived in the suburbs of Houston, with both my parents (my father was a geologist, my mother a schoolteacher), neither of whom had a clue about my secret life with cattle (nor was there any trace of ranching in our family's history), while Moxley lived with his grandfather, Old Ben, on forty acres of grassland about ten miles north of what were then the Houston city limits.

Old Ben's pasture was rolling hill country, gently swelling, punctuated by brush and thorns — land which possessed only a single stock tank, one aging tractor, and a sagging, rusting barbed-wire fence that was good for retaining nothing, with rotting fence posts.

Weeds grew chest-high in the abandoned fields. Old Ben had fought in the First World War as a horse soldier and had been injured repeatedly, and was often in and out of the V.A. clinic, having various pieces of shrapnel removed, which he kept in a bloodstained gruesome collection, first on the windowsills of their little house, but then, as the collection grew, on the back porch, scattered in clutter, like the collections of interesting rocks that sometimes accrue in people's yards over the course of a lifetime.

Old Ben had lost most of his hearing in the war, and some of his nerves as well, so that even on the days when he was home, he was not always fully present, and Moxley was free to navigate the rapids of adolescence largely unregulated.

We began to haunt the auction barns on Wednesdays and Thursdays, even before we had our driver's licenses — skipping school and walking there, or riding our bikes — and we began to scrimp and save, to buy at those auctions the cheapest cattle available: young calves, newly weaned, little multicolored lightweights of uncertain pedigree, costing seventy or eighty dollars each.

We watched the sleek velvety gray Brahma calves, so clearly superior, pass on to other bidders for $125, or $150, and longed for such an animal; but why spend that money on one animal, when for the same amount we could get two?

After parting with our money, we would go claim our prize. Sometimes another rancher offered to put our calf in the back of his truck or trailer and ferry it home for us, though other times we hobbled the calf with ropes and chains and led it, wild and bucking, down the side of the highway, with the deadweight of a log or creosote-soaked railroad tie attached behind it like an anchor, to keep the animal — far stronger, already, than the two of us combined — from breaking loose and galloping away unowned and now unclaimed, disappearing into the countryside, our investment now no more than a kite snatched by the wind.

We gripped the calf's leash tightly and dug in our heels, and were half hauled home by the calf itself. In the creature's terror it would be spraying and jetting algae-green plumes of excrement in all directions, which we would have to dodge, and were anyone to seek to follow us — to counsel us, perhaps, to turn away from our chosen path, still experimental at this point — the follower would have been able to track us easily, by the scuffed-up heel marks and divots of where we had resisted the animal's pull, and by the violent fans of green-drying-to-brown diarrhea: the latter an inauspicious sign for an animal whose existence was predicated on how much weight it would be able to gain, and quite often the reason these marginal calves had been sent to the auction in the first place.

Arriving finally at Moxley's grandfather's farm, bruised and scratched, and with the calf in worse condition, we would turn it loose into the wilderness of weeds and brambles circumscribed by the sagging fence.

We had attempted, in typical adolescent half-assed fashion, to shore up the fence with loose coils of scrap wire, lacking expertise with the fence stretcher, and in some places where we had run out of wire we had used the orange nylon twine gathered from bales of hay, and lengths of odd-sorted rope, to weave a kind of cat's cradle, a spiderweb of thin restraint, should the calf decide to try and leave our wooly, brushy, brittle pasture.

We had woven the fence with vertical stays also, limbs and branches sawed or snapped to a height of about four feet, in the hopes that these might help to provide a visual deterrent, so that the curving, staggering, collapsing fence looked more like the boundaries of some cunning trap or funnel hastily constructed by Paleolithics in an attempt to veer some driven game toward slaughter.

We had money only for cattle or fence, but not both. Impulsive, eager, and impatient, we chose cattle, and the cattle slipped through our ramshackle fence like the wind itself—sometimes belly-wriggling beneath it, other times vaulting it like kangaroos.

Other times the calves simply went straight through the weakened fence, popping loose the rusted fence staples and shattering the rotted, leaning fence posts and crude branches stacked and piled as barricades. Sometimes the calves, fresh from the terror and trauma of their drive from auction, never slowed when first released through the gate at Old Ben's farm, but kept running, galloping with their heads lowered all the way down the hill, building more and more speed, and they would hit the fence square on.

Sometimes they would sail right on through it, like a football player charging through the paper wrapped between goalposts before a football game, though other times they would bounce back in an awkward cartwheel before scrambling to their feet and running laterally some distance until they found a weaker seam and slipped through it not like anything of this world of flesh and bone, but like magicians, vanishing.

When that happened, we would have to leap on the old red tractor, starting it with a belch and clatter that inevitably frightened the calf into even wilder flight; and with Moxley driving the old tractor flat out in high gear, and me standing upright with a boot planted wobbly on each of the sweeping wide rear fenders, riding the tractor like a surfer and swinging a lariat (about which I knew nothing), we would go racing down the hill after the calf, out onto the highway, the tractor roaring and the calf running as if from some demon of hell that had been designed solely to pursue that one calf, and which would never relent.

We never caught the calves, and only on the rarest of occasions were we ever even able to draw near enough to one — wearing it down with our relentlessness — to even attempt a throw of the lariat, which was never successful.

Usually the animal would feint and weave at the last instant, as the tractor and whizzing gold lariat bore down on it, and the calf would shoot or crash through another fence, or cross a ditch and vault a fence strung so tightly that as the calf's rear hoofs clipped the fence going over, the vibration would emit a high taut hum, which we could hear even over the sound of the tractor.

It was like the sound of a fishing line snapping, and by the time we found an unlocked gate to that pasture, the calf would have escaped to yet another field or pasture, or might be down in some wooded creek bottom, reverting to instincts more feral and cunning than those of even the deer and turkeys that frequented those creeks; and we would scour the surrounding hills for all the rest of that day — sometimes mistakenly pursuing, for a short distance, a calf which might look like ours, until that calf's owner would come charging out on his own tractor, shouting and cursing; angling to intercept us like a jouster.

Old Ben fell too ill to drive, and then began to become a problem while Moxley was in school; he had begun to wander out into the same fields in which the rogue calves had been released, and was similarly trying to escape his lifelong home, though he was too feeble to bash or batter his way through the patchwork fence, and instead endeavored to climb over it.

Even on the instances when he made good his escape, he snagged his shirt or pants on a barb and left behind flag-size scraps of bright fabric fluttering in the breeze, and we were able to track him that way, driving the roads in his old station wagon, searching for him.

Sometimes Old Ben lay down in a ditch, trembling and exhausted from his travels, and pulled a piece of cardboard over him like a tent to shield him from the heat, and we would pass on by him, so that it might be a day or two before we or a neighbor could find him.

Other times however Old Ben would become so entangled in his own fence that he would be unable to pull free, and when we came home from school we would see him down there, sometimes waving and struggling though other times motionless, quickly spent, with his arms and legs akimbo, and his torn jacket and jeans looking like the husk from some chrysalis or other emerging insect: and we'd go pluck him from those wires, and Moxley mended his torn jacket with the crude loops of his own self-taught sewing; but again and again Old Ben sought to flow through those fences.

There were other times though when Old Ben was fine, fit as a fiddle; times when the disintegrating fabric of his old war-torn mind, frayed by mustard gas and by the general juices of war's horror, shifted, like tiny tectonic movements, reassembling into the puzzle-piece grace his mind had possessed earlier in life — the grandfather Moxley had known and loved, and who loved him, and who had raised him. On those occasions, it felt as if we had taken a step back in time. It was confusing to feel this, for it was pleasant; and yet, being young, we were eager to press on. We knew we should be enjoying the time with Old Ben — that he was not long for the world, and that our time with him, particularly Moxley's, was precious and rare, more valuable than any gold, or certainly any rogue cattle.

On the nights when the past reassembled itself in Old Ben and he was healthy again, even if only for a while, the three of us ate dinner together. We sat on the back porch feeling the Gulf breezes, coming from over a hundred miles to the southeast, watching the tall ungrazed grass before us bend in oceanic waves, with strange little gusts and accelerations stirring the grass in streaks and ribbons, looking briefly like the braids of a rushing river; or as if animals-in-hiding were running along those paths, just beneath the surface and unseen.

We would grill steaks on the barbecue, roast golden ears of corn, and drink fresh-squeezed lemonade, to which Ben was addicted. "Are these steaks from your cattle?" he would ask us, cutting into his steak and examining each bite as if there might be some indication of ownership within; and when we lied and told him yes, he seemed pleased — as if we had amounted to something in the world, and as if we were no longer children. He would savor each bite, then, as if he could taste some intangible yet exceptional quality.

We kept patching and then repatching the ragged-ass fence, lacing it back together with twine and scraps of rope, with ancient twists of baling wire, and with coat hangers; propping splintered shipping pallets against the gaps, stacking them and leaning them here and there in an attempt to plug the many gaps. (The calves ended up merely using these pallets as ladders and springboards.)

In his own bedraggled state, however, Ben saw none of the failures. "That's what being a cattleman's about," he said — he, who had never owned a cow in his life. "Ninety-five percent of it is the grunt work, and five percent is buying low and selling high. I like how you boys work at it," he said, and he never dreamed or knew that in our own half-assedness, we were making so much more work for ourselves than if we'd done the job right the first time.

After we got our driver's licenses we used Ben's old station wagon — he was no longer able to drive — and after getting him to bed, and hasping the doors to his house shut, as if stabling some wild horse, and latching the windows from the outside, we left the darkened farmhouse and headed for the lights of the city, which cast a golden half-dome high into the fog and scudding clouds.

It was a vast glowing ball of light, seeming close enough that we could have walked or ridden our bikes to reach it: and driving Ben's big station wagon, with its power steering and gas-sucking engine, was like piloting a rocket ship. There were no shades of gray, out in the country like that: there was only the quiet stillness of night, with crickets chirping, and fireflies, too, back then — and the instrument panels on the dashboard were the only light of fixed reference as we powered through that darkness, hungry for that nearing dome of city light. The gauges and dials before us were as nearly mysterious to us as the instrument panel of a jet airplane, and neither Moxley nor I paid much attention to them. For the most part, he knew only the basics: to aim the car, steering it crudely like the iron gunboat it was, and how to use the accelerator and the brakes.

And after but a few miles of such darkness, there would suddenly be light, blazes of it hurled at us from all directions — grids and window squares and spears of light, sundials and radials of inflorescence and neon; and we were swallowed by it, were born into it, and suddenly we could see before us the hood of the old Detroit iron horse that had carried us into the city and swallowed us, as the city, and Westheimer Avenue, seemed to be swallowing the car, and we were no longer driving so much as being driven.

All-night gas stations, all-night grocery stores, movie theaters, restaurants, massage parlors, oil-change garages, floral shops, apartment complexes, dentists' offices, car dealerships — it was all jammed shoulder-to-shoulder, there was no zoning, and though we had seen it all before in the daytime, and were accustomed to it, it looked entirely different at night — alluring, even beautiful, rather than squalid and chaotic.

The neon strip fascinated us, as might a carnival, but what ultimately caught our imagination on these night sojourns was not the glamorous, exotic urban core, but the strange seams of disintegrating roughness on the perimeters: pockets toward and around which the expanding city spilled and flowed like lava: little passed-by islands of the past, not unlike our own on the western edge. We passed through the blaze of light and strip malls, the loneliness of illuminated commerce, and came out the other side, on the poorer, eastern edge, where all the high-voltage power grids were clustered, and the multinational refineries.

Here the air was dense with the odor of burning plastic, vaporous benzenes and toluenes adhering to the palate with every breath, and the night-fog sky glowed with blue, pink, orange flickers from the flares of waste gas jetting from a thousand smokestacks. The blaze of commerce faded over our shoulders and behind us, and often we found ourselves driving through neighborhoods that seemed to be sinking into the black soil, the muck of peat, as if pressed down by the immense weight of the industrial demands placed upon that spongy soil — gigantic tanks and water towers and chemical vats, strange intestinal folds and coils of tarnished aluminum towering above us, creeping through the remnant forests like nighttime serpents.

Snowy egrets and night herons passed through the flames, or so it seemed, and floated amidst the puffs of pollution as serenely as if in a dream of grace; and on those back roads, totally lost, splashing through puddles axle-deep and deeper, and thudding over potholes big enough to lose a bowling ball in, Moxley would sometimes turn the lights off and navigate the darkened streets in that manner, passing through pools of rainbow-colored poisonous light and wisps and tatters of toxic fog, as if gliding with the same grace and purpose as the egrets above us. Many of the rotting old homes had ancient live oaks out in front, their yards bare due to the trees' complete shading of the soil. In the rainy season, the water stood a foot deep in the streets, so that driving up and down them was more like poling the canals of Venice than driving: and the heat from our car's undercarriage hissed steam as we plowed slowly up and down these streets.

We were drawn to these rougher, ranker places at night, and yet we wanted to see them in the full light of day also; and when we traveled to these eastern edges during school, while taking a long lunch break or cutting classes entirely, we discovered little hanging-on businesses run out of those disintegrating houses, places where old men and women still made tortillas by hand, or repaired leather boots and work shoes, or did drywall masonry, or made horseshoes by hand even though there were increasingly few horses and ever more cars and trucks, especially trucks, as urban Texas began the calcification of its myths in full earnest.

Places where a patch of corn might exist next to a ten-story office building, places where people still hung their clothes on the line to dry, and little five- and ten-acre groves in which there might still exist a ghost-herd of deer. Ponds in which there might still lurk giant, sullen, doomed catfish, even with the city's advancing hulk blocking now partially the rising and setting of the sun.

Through such explorations, we found the Goat Man as surely and directly as if he had been standing on the roof of his shed calling to us with some foxhunter's horn, leading us straight to the hand-painted rotting-plywood sign tilted in the mire outside his hovel.

BABY CLAVES, $15, read the sign, each letter painted a different color, as if by a child. We parked in his muddy driveway, the low-slung station wagon dragging its belly over the corrugated troughs of countless such turnings-around, wallowing and slithering and splashing up to the front porch of a collapsing clapboard shed-house that seemed to be held up by nothing more than the thick braids and ghost-vines of dead ivy.

Attached to the outside of the hovel was a gerrymandered assemblage of corrals and stables, ramshackle slats of mixed-dimension scrap lumber, from behind which came an anguished cacophony of bleats and bawls and whinnies and outright bloodcurdling screams, as we got out of the car and sought to make our way dry-footed from one mud hummock to the next, up toward the sagging porch, to inquire about the baby claves, hoping very much that they were indeed calves, and not some odd bivalve oyster we'd never heard of.

We peered through dusty windows (some of the panes were cracked, held together with fraying duct tape) and saw that the rooms were filled with tilted mounds of newspapers so ancient and yellowing that they had begun to form mulch.

An old man answered the door when we knocked, the man blinking, not so much as having been just awakened but as if instead rousing himself from some other communion or reverie, some lost-world voyage. He appeared to be in his sixties, with a long wild silver beard and equally wild silver hair, in the filaments of which fluttered a few moths, as if he were an old bear that had just been roused from his work of snuffling through a rotting log in search of grubs.

His teeth were no better than the slats that framed the walls of his jury-rigged corrals, and, barefooted, he was dressed in only a pair of hole-sprung, oil-stained, forest-green workpants, on which we recognized the dried-brown flecks of manure-splatter, and an equally stained sleeveless ribbed-underwear T-shirt that had once been white, but which was now the color of his skin, and appeared to have been on his body so long as to have become like a second kind of skin — one which, if it were ever removed, might peel off with it large patches of his original birthskin.

The odor coming from the house was quite different from the general barnyard stench of uncleaned feces, and somehow even more offensive.

Despite the general air of filth and torpor radiating from the house and its host, however, his carriage and bearing was erect, almost military — as if our presence had electrified him with hungry possibility; as if we were the first customers, or potential customers, he might have encountered in so long a time that he had forgotten his old patterns of defeat.

When he first spoke, however, to announce his name, the crispness of his posture was undercut somewhat by the shining trickle of tobacco drool that escaped through some of the gaps in his lower teeth, like a slow release of gleaming venom.

"Sloat," he said, and at first I thought it was some language of his own making: that he was attempting to fix us, tentatively, with a curse. "Heironymous Sloat," he said, reaching out a gnarly spittle- and mucus-stained hand. We exchanged looks of daring and double daring, and finally, Moxley offered his own pale and unscarred hand.

"Come on in," Sloat said, making a sweeping gesture that was both grand and yet familial — as if, horrifically, he recognized in us some kindred spirit — and despite our horror, after another pause we followed him in.

Since all the other rooms were filled with newspapers and tin cans, Sloat's bed had been dragged into the center room. The kitchen was nearly filled with unwashed pots and dishes, in which phalanxes of roaches stirred themselves into sudden scuttling escape as we entered. The rug in the center room was wet underfoot — the water-stained, sagging ceiling was still dripping from the previous night's rain, and on the headboard of the bed there was a small fish bowl, filled with cloudy water, in which a goldfish hung suspended, slowly finning in place, with nothing else in the bowl but a single short decaying sprig of seaweed.

The fish's water was so cloudy with its own befoulment as to seem almost viscous, and for some reason the fish so caught my attention that I felt hypnotized, suspended in the strange house — as if I had become the fish. I had no desire to move, nor could I look anywhere else. All of my focus was on that one little scrap of color, once bright but now muted, though still living.

I glanced over at Moxley and was disturbed to see that he seemed somehow invigorated, even stimulated, by the rampant disorder.

So severe was my hypnosis, and so disoriented were both of

us, that neither of us had noticed there was someone sleeping in the rumpled, unmade bed beside which we stood: and when the person stirred, we stepped back, alarmed.

The sleeper was a young woman, not much older than we were, sleeping in a nightgown only slightly less dingy than the shirt of the older man — and though it was midafternoon, and bright outside, the girl's face was puffy with sleep, and she stirred with such languor that I felt certain she had been sleeping all day.

She sat up and stared at us as if trying to make sense of us, and brushed her hair from her shoulders. Her hair was orange, very nearly the same color as the fish's dull scales, and Sloat stared at her in a way that was both dismissive and yet slightly curious — as if wondering why, on this particular day, she had awakened so early.

She swung her feet off the bed and stood unsteadily, and watched us with unblinking raptness.

"Let's go look at the stock," Sloat said, and we could tell that it gave him pleasure to say the word *stock*.

The three of us went through the cluttered kitchen and out to the backyard — it surprised me that there were no dogs or cats in the house — and the girl followed us to the door but no farther, and stood there on the other side of the screen. Her bare feet, I had noticed, were dirty, as if she had made the journey out to the stables before, but on this occasion lingered behind, as if perhaps made shy.

Sloat was wearing old sharp-toed cowboy boots, his thin shanks shoved into them in such a way that I knew he wasn't wearing socks, and he walked in a brisk, almost fierce line straight through the puddles and troughs toward the stables, as if he enjoyed splashing through the muck and grime, while Moxley and I pussyfooted from little hummock to hummock, sometimes slipping and dipping a foot in one water-filled rut or another. Foam floated on the top of many of the puddles, as if someone, or something, had been urinating in them.

Sloat pushed through a rickety one-hinge gate, and goats, chickens, and other fleeting, unidentified animals scattered before his explosive entrance. Sloat began cursing and shouting at them, picked up a stick and rat-tat-tatted it along the pickets to excite them further, like a small boy, and as if to demonstrate their vigor to their potential buyers.

A pig, a pony, a rooster. A calf, or something that looked like a calf, except for its huge head, which was so out of proportion for the tiny body that it seemed more like the head of an elephant.

"I buy them from the Feist Brothers," he said. "The ones that don't get sold at auction. They give me a special deal," he said.

The animals continued to bleat and caterwaul, flowing away, flinging themselves against the fences. Some of them ran in demented circles, and others tried to burrow in the mud, while the goats, the most nimble of them, leapt to the tops of the little crude-hammered, straw-lined doghouses and peered down with their wildly disconcerting vertical-slit lantern-green eyes as if welcoming Moxley and me into some new and alien fraternity of half-man, half-animal: and as if, now that Moxley and I were inside the corral, the goats had us exactly where they wanted us.

Moxley had eyes only for the calves, thin-ribbed though they were, dehydrated and listless, almost sleepwalkerish compared to the frenzy and exodus of the other animals. Six of them were huddled over in one corner of the makeshift corral, quivering collectively, their stringy tails and flanks crusted green.

"Which are the fifteen-dollar ones?" he asked, and, sensing weakness, Sloat replied, "Those are all gone now. The only ones I have left are thirty-five."

Moxley paused. "What about that little Brahma?" he asked, pointing to the one animal that was clearly superior, perhaps even still healthy.

"Oh, that's my little prize bull," Sloat said. "I couldn't let you have him for less than seventy-five."

Between us, we had only sixty-five, which in the end turned out to be precisely enough. We had no trailer attached to the back of Old Ben's station wagon, but Sloat showed us how we could pull out the backseat, lash it to the roof for the drive home, and line the floor and walls of the station wagon with squares of cardboard, in case the calf soiled it, and drive home with him in that manner. "I've done it many a time myself," Sloat said.

The girl had come out to watch us, had waded barefooted through the same puddles in which her father, or whatever his relation was to her, had waded. She now stood on the other side of the gate, still wearing her nightgown, and watched us as Sloat and Moxley and me, our financial transaction completed, chased the bull calf around the corral, slipping in the muck, Sloat swatting the calf hard with a splintered baseball bat, whacking it whenever he could, and Moxley and me trying to tackle the calf and wrestle it to the ground.

The calf was three times as strong as any one of us, however, and time and again no sooner had one of us gotten a headlock on it than it would run into the side of the corral, smashing the would-be tackler hard against the wall; and soon both Moxley and I were bleeding from our shins, noses, and foreheads, and I had a split lip: and still Sloat kept circling the corral, following the terrified calf, smacking him hard with the baseball bat.

Somehow, all the other creatures had disappeared — had vanished into other, adjacent corrals, or perhaps through a maze of secret passageways — and leaning against one of the wobbly slat walls, blood dripping from my nose, I saw now what Sloat had been doing with his wild tirade: that each time, as the calf rounded a corner, Sloat had pushed open another gap or gate and ushered two or three more nontarget animals into one of the outlying pens, until finally, the calf was isolated.

Sloat was winded, and he stood there gasping and sucking air, the bat held loosely in his hands. The calf stood facing the three of us, panting likewise, and suddenly Sloat rushed him, seemingly having waited to gauge when the animal would be midbreath, too startled or tired to bolt, and he struck the calf as hard as he could with the baseball bat, hitting it on the bony plate of its forehead.

The calf neither buckled nor wobbled, but seemed only to sag a little: as if for a long time he had been tense or worried about something, but could now finally relax.

Sloat hit the calf again quickly and then a third and fourth time, striking it now like a man trying to hammer a wooden stake into the ground; and that was how the calf sank, shutting its eyes and folding, sinking lower: and still Sloat kept striking it, as if he intended to punish it or kill it, or both.

He did not stop until the calf was unconscious, or perhaps dead, and lying on its side. Then he laid his bat down tenderly, as if it were some valuable instrument, and to be accorded great respect.

The Goat Girl watched as if she had seen it all before. Sloat paused to catch his breath and then called to us to help him heft the calf quickly, before it came back to consciousness, though we could not imagine such a thing, and I was thinking at first that he had just stolen our money: had taken our sixty-five dollars, killed our calf, and was now demanding our assistance in burying it.

The Goat Girl roused herself finally, and splashed through the puddles of foam and slime, out toward the car in advance of us, as if intending to lay palm fronds before our approach. She opened our car door and placed the scraps of cardboard in the car's interior, for when the calf resurrected.

"How long will he be out?" Moxley asked.

"Where are you taking him?" Sloat asked, and I told him, west Houston — about an hour and a half away.

"An hour and a half," said Sloat, whom I had now begun to think of as the Goat Man. He shook our proffered hands — cattlemen! — and told us, as we were driving off, to come back soon, that he had a lot of volume come through, and that he would keep an eye out for good stock, for buyers as discerning as we were, and that he would probably be able to give us a better break next time.

Moxley slithered the station wagon out to the end of the drive — the Goat Man and Goat Girl followed — and Moxley stopped and rolled his window down and thanked them both again and asked the girl what her name was.

But she had fallen into a reverie and was staring at us in much the same manner as the calf had after receiving his first blow; and as we drove away she did not raise her hand to return our waves, nor did she give any other sign of having seen or heard us, or that she was aware of our existence in the world.

Driving away, I was troubled deeply by the ragtag, slovenly, almost calculated half-assedness of the operation; and on the drive home, though Moxley and I for the most part were pleased and excited about having gotten another calf, and so cheaply, I was discomforted, could feel a rumbling confusion, the protest that sometimes precedes revolution, though other times leads to nothing, only acquiescence, then senescence. I could see that Moxley did not feel it, however; and sensing this, I felt weaker, and slightly alone.

The calf woke up when we were still an hour from Ben's ranch. The calf did not awaken gradually, as a human might, stirring and blinking and looking around to ascertain his new surroundings, but awoke instead explosively, denting a crumple in the roof immediately with his bony head. He squealed and then began crashing against the sides of the car's interior so violently, and with such a clacking of hoofs, that we were afraid he would break the glass and escape; and his frenzied thrashings (unable to stand to his full height in the back of the car, and instead crawling), reminded me of how, hours earlier, the calf had been rounding the makeshift corral.

We attempted to shoo the calf to the back, swatting at him with our hands, but these gestures held no more meaning for the bull than if we had been waving flyswatters at him, and his squeals transformed to full roars, amplified to terrifying proportions within the confines of the car. At one point he was in the front seat with us, having lunged over it, and in his flailings managed to head butt me, and he cut Moxley's shins so deeply with swift kicks of his sharp little hoofs that they were bruised and bleeding, and he nearly ran off the road — but then the calf decided it preferred the space and relative freedom of the backseat, and vaulted back over the seat again and into its cardboard lair, where it continued to hurl itself against the walls.

As the Goat Man had foreseen, and as a symptom of the ailment that had caused it to not be bid upon in the first place at the regular auction — the auction that had preceded the mysterious Feist Brothers obtaining him — the calf in its fright began emitting fountains of greenish, watery diarrhea, spraying it midwhirl as if from a hose, so that we were yelling and ducking, and soon the interior of the car was nearly coated with dripping green slime: and though panicked, we were fierce in our determination to see this thing through, and we knew that if we stopped and turned the calf out into the open, we would never capture it again.

Somehow we made it home, and in the darkness of the new evening, with fireflies blinking in the fields, we drove straight out into Old Ben's pasture, ghostly gray weeds scraping and scratching against the sides of the wagon with an eerie, clawing keen that further terrified the calf: and when we rolled down the tailgate's window, he leapt out through the window into that clean sweet fresh night air; and this calf, too, we never saw again, though the residue of his journey, his passage, remained with us for weeks afterward, in cracks and crevices of the old station wagon, despite our best scrubbing.

Old Ben fell further into the rot. Moxley and I could both see it, in his increasing lapses of memory, and his increasingly erratic behavior — and though I had perceived Moxley to be somehow more mature than I — more confident in the world — I was surprised by how vulnerable Moxley seemed to be made by Ben's fading.

Ben was ancient, a papery husk of a man — dusty, tottering history, having already far exceeded the odds by having lived as long as he had — and was going downhill fast. Such descent could not be pleasant for Old Ben, who, after all, had once been a young man much like ourselves. His quality of life was plummeting, even as ours, fueled by the strength of our youth, was ascending; did

Moxley really expect, or even want, for the old man to hang on forever, an eternal hostage to his failed and failing body, just so Moxley would have the luxury of having an older surviving family member?

We couldn't keep him locked up all the time. Moxley had taken over control of the car completely, took it to school each day, and hid the keys whenever he was home, but Old Ben's will was every bit as fierce as Moxley's, and Ben continued to escape. We often found him floating in the stock tank, using an inner tube for a life vest, fishing, with no hook tied to his line, flailing at the water determinedly.

He disappeared for a week once, after rummaging through the drawers and finding the key to the tractor, which he drove away, blowing a hole through the back wall of the barn. We didn't notice the hole, nor the fact that the tractor was missing, and it was not until a sheriff called from Raton County, New Mexico, asking if Moxley knew an elderly gentleman named Ben, before we had any clue of where he was. We skipped school and drove out there to get him, pulling a rented flatbed on which to strap the tractor, and he was as glad to see us as a child would have been; and Moxley, in his relief, was like a child himself, his eyes tearing with joy.

All through that winter, we continued to buy more stock from the Goat Man: knowing better, but unable to help ourselves, and lured, too, by the low prices. Even if one in ten of his scour-ridden wastrels survived to market, we would come out ahead, we told ourselves; but none of them did, they all escaped through our failed fence, usually in the very first afternoon of their freedom, and we never saw any of them again.

We imagined their various fates. We envisioned certain of them being carried away by the panthers that were rumored to still slink through the Brazos river bottoms, and the black jaguars that were reported to have come up from Mexico, following those same creeks and rivers as if summoned, to snack on our cheap and ill-begotten calves, or claves, as we called them. We imagined immense gargoyles and winged harpies that swooped down to snatch up our renegade runaway crops. We envisioned modern-day cattle rustlers congregating around the perimeter of our ranch like fishermen. It was easy to imagine that even the Goat Man himself followed us home and scooped up each runaway calf in a net, and returned with it then to his lair, where he would sell it a second time to another customer.

Or perhaps there was some hole in the earth, some cavern, into which all the calves disappeared, as if sucked there by a monstrous and irresistible force. Any or all of these paranoias might as well have been true, given the completeness of the calves' vanishings.

With each purchase we made, I felt more certain that we were traveling down a wrong path, and yet we found ourselves returning to the Goat Man's hovel again and again, and giving him more and more money.

We ferried our stock in U-Haul trailers — and across the months, as we purchased more cowflesh from the Goat Man — meat vanishing into the ether again and again, as if into some quarkish void — we became familiar enough with Sloat and his daughter to learn that her name was Flozelle, and to visit with them about matters other than stock.

We would linger in that center room — bedroom, dining room, living room, all — and talk briefly, first about the weather and then about the Houston Oilers, before venturing out into what Moxley and I had taken to calling the Pissyard. We learned that Flozelle's mother had died when she was born, that Flozelle had no brothers or sisters, and that Sloat loathed schools.

"I homeschool her," he said. "Go ahead, ask her anything."

We could have been wiseasses. We could have flaunted our ridiculous little knowledge — the names of signatories to various historical documents, the critical dates of various armistices — but in the presence of such abject filth, and before her shell-shocked quietude, we were uncharacteristically humbled. Instead, Moxley asked, almost gently, "How long have you had that fish?" and before Flozelle could answer, Sloat bullshitted us by telling us that the fish had been given to his grandmother on her wedding day, almost a hundred years ago.

"What's its name?" I asked, and this time, before Sloat could reply, Flozelle answered.

"Goldy," she said proudly, and a shiver ran down my back. If I had known what sadness or loneliness really felt like, I think I might have recognized it as such; but as it was, I felt only a shiver, and then felt it again as she climbed up onto the unmade bed (the bottoms of her bare feet unwashed and bearing little crumb-fragments) and unscrewed the lid to a jar of uncooked oatmeal she kept beside the bowl, and sprinkled a few flakes into the viscous water.

Moxley was watching her with what seemed to me to be a troubled look — and after she had finished feeding the bloated fish, she turned and climbed back down off the lumpen bed, and then we filed out through the kitchen and on out into the Pissyard to go look at, and purchase, more stock.

Back before Ben had begun falling to pieces, Moxley and I had sometimes gone by my house after school to do homework and hang out. My mother would make cookies, and if Moxley was still there when my father got home from work, Moxley would occasionally have supper with us. But those days had gone by long ago, Ben now requiring almost all of his waking care. I helped as I could, doing little things like helping clean up the house. Whenever Ben discovered that he was trapped, he would ransack the house, pulling books down off of shelves and hurling his clothes out of his drawer; once, he rolled up the carpet and tried to set the end of it on fire, as if lighting a giant cigar: when we arrived at the farmhouse, we could see the toxic gray smoke seeping from out of the windows; and rushing inside, we found Ben passed out next to the rug, which had smoldered and burned a big hole in the ply-wood flooring, revealing the gaping darkened maw of basement below, with the perimeter of that burned-out crater circular, like a caldera, having burned so close to Ben that his arm hung down into the pit; and all the next day we hammered and sawed new sheets of plywood to patch that abyss. For a few days afterward, Ben seemed contrite, and neither misbehaved nor otherwise suffered any departures from sentience: as if such lapses were, after all, at least partially willful.

I helped cook dinners, and some nights I stayed over at their farmhouse and helped make breakfast, and helped Moxley batten down the doors and windows before leaving for school. Knives, scissors, matches, guns, fishhooks, lighter fluid, gasoline, household cleaners — it all had to be put away. Moxley had tied a hundred-and-fifty-foot length of rope around Ben's waist each night, so that if Ben awoke and went sleepwalking, wandering the dewy hills, he could be tracked and reeled in like a marlin or other sportfish.

The farmhouse was a pleasant place to awaken in the morning — the coppery sun rising just above the tops of the trees, and the ungrazed fields lush and tall and green, with mourning doves cooing and pecking red grit and gravel from the driveway — and the interior of the house would be spangled with the prisms of light from all the little pieces of glass arrayed on the windowsill, Ben's shrapnel collection. The spectral casts of rainbow would be splashed all over the walls, like the light that passes through stained glass windows, and there would be no sound but the ticking of the grandfather clock in the front hallway, and the cooing of those doves, and the lowing of distant cows not ours. Moxley and I would fix breakfast, gather our homework, then lock up the house and leave, hurrying toward school.

I had some money from mowing lawns, and Moxley was pretty flush, or so it seemed to us, from Ben's pension checks. As much from habit now as from desire, we made further pilgrimages to Sloat's corrals, that winter and spring.

And following each purchase, upon our return to Ben's ranch, sometimes our new crop of sickly calves would remain in the pasture for a few days, though never longer than a week, after which, always, they disappeared, carrying with them their daunting and damnable genes, the strange double-crossed combination of recessive alleles that had caused the strangeness to blossom in them in the first place — the abnormality, the weakness, that had led to the unfortunate chain of circumstances that resulted in their passing from a real auction to the Feist Brothers, who would sell them for dog meat if they could, and then to Sloat and a short life of squalor, and then to us, and to whatever freedom or destiny awaited them.

Ben caught pneumonia after one of his escapes. (He had broken out a window and crawled through, leaving a trail of blood as well as new glass scattered amidst his windowsill-sparkling shards of glass from fifty years earlier; we trailed him down to the pond, his favorite resting spot, where he stood shivering waist deep, as if awaiting a baptism.) Moxley had to check him into the hospital, and after he was gone, the silence in the farmhouse was profound.

Moxley was edgy, waiting for the day when Old Ben would be coming home, but that day never came; and although it had been clear that Ben's days at home were numbered, the abyss of his absence still came as a surprise, as did Moxley's new anger.

We continued with our old rituals, as if Ben was still with us — cooking the steaks on the back porch grill, and buying cattle — but the ground beneath our feet seemed less firm.

With Old Ben's last pension check, Moxley and I went to a real auction, and bought a real calf — not one of Sloat's misfits, but a registered Brahma — a stout little bull calf. And rather than risking losing this one, we kept it tethered, like a dog on a leash, in the barn. It was not as wild as Sloat's terrified refugees, and soon we were able to feed and water it by hand: and it grew fatter week by week. We fed it a diet rich in protein, purchasing sweet alfalfa and pellet cubes. We brushed it and curried it and estimated its weight daily as we fatted it for market. And it seemed to me that with some success having finally been achieved, Moxley's anger and loneliness had stabilized, and I was glad that this calf, at least, had not escaped. It was a strange thought to both of us, to consider that we were raising the animal so someone else could eat him, but that was what cattlemen did.

As this calf finally grew fatter, Moxley seemed to grow angry at the Goat Man, and barely spoke to him now when we traveled out there: and though we still went out there with the same, if not greater, frequency, we had stopped purchasing stock from the Goat Man, and instead merely went out into the Pissyards to look. After having purchased the calf from the regular auction, Sloat's offerings were revealed to us in their full haplessness, and we could not bring ourselves to take them at any price; though still, we went to look, almost morbidly curious about what misfits might have passed through his gates that week.

Moxley asked Flozelle out on what I suppose could be labeled a date, even though I was with them. I wanted to believe the best of him, but it seemed to me that it was a meanness, a bedevilment. Moxley still had the same aspirations — he was intent upon going to school and becoming a vet — but the moments of harshness seemed to emerge from him at odd and unpredictable times, like fragments of bone or glass emerging from beneath the thinnest of skin.

The three of us began to ride places together once or twice a week, and for a while, Flozelle fascinated us. She knew how to fix things — how to rebuild a carburetor, how to peel a tire from its rim and plug it with gum and canvas and seat it back onto its rim — and sometimes, out in the country, we stopped beside the fields of strangers and got out and climbed over the barbed-wire fence and went out to where other people's horses were grazing. We would slip up onto those horses bareback and ride them around strangers' fields for hours at a time. Flozelle knew how to gentle even the most unruly or skittish horse by biting its ears with her teeth and hanging on like a pit bull until Moxley or I had climbed up, and then she'd release her bite-hold, and we'd rocket across the pasture, the barrel ribs of the horse beneath us heaving: the expensive thoroughbreds of oilmen, the sleek and fatted horses farting wildly from their too-rich diets of grain.

She had never been to a movie before, and when we took her, she stared rapt, ate three buckets of popcorn, chewing ceaselessly through *Star Wars*. She began spending some afternoons with Moxley out at his farm, and helping him with chores — mowing with the tractor the unkempt grass, bush-hogging brush and cutting bales of hay for our young bull. She showed us how to castrate him, to make him put on even more weight even faster, and she set about repairing the shabby, sorry fence we had never gotten around to fixing properly.

The calf, the steer, was getting immense, or so it seemed to us, and though he still was friendly and manageable, his strength concerned us. We worried that he might strangle himself on his harness, his leash, should he ever attempt to break out of the barn, and so not long after Flozelle had completed her repairs on the fence, we turned him out into the field, unfastening his rope and opening the barn doors, whereupon he emerged slowly, blinking, and then descended to the fresh green fields below and began grazing confidently, as if he had known all his life those fields were waiting for him, and that he would reach them in due time.

I had the strange thought that if only Old Ben could have still been alive to see it, the sight might somehow have helped heal him, even though I knew that to be an impossibility. He had been an old man, war torn, and at the end of his line; no amount of care, nor even miracles, could have kept him from going downhill.

To the best of my knowledge, Flozelle did not shower, as if such a practice might be alien to her or her father's religious beliefs. In my parents' car, I drove up to the farm one warm day in the spring, unannounced, and surprised Moxley and Flozelle, who were out in the backyard. Moxley was dressed, but Flozelle was not, and Moxley was spraying her down with the hose — not in fun, as I might have suspected, but in a manner strangely more workmanlike, as one might wash a car, or even a horse; and when they saw me, Moxley was embarrassed and shut the hose off, though Flozelle was not discomfited at all, and merely took an old towel, little larger than a washcloth, and began drying off.

And later, after he had taken her home — after we had both

driven out to Sloat's and dropped her off, without going inside, and without going back into the Pissyards to look around, I asked him, "Are you sleeping with her?" — and he looked at me with true surprise and then said, "I am," and when I asked him if she ever spent the night over at the farmhouse, he looked less surprised, less proud, and said yes.

What did it matter to me? It was nothing but an act, almost lavatory-like in nature, I supposed — workmanlike and without emotion, if not insensate. I imagined it to be for Moxley like the filling of a hole, the shoveling in of something, and the tamping down. It was not anything. He was doing what he had to do, almost as if taking care of her; and she, with all the things the Goat Man had taught her, had fixed his fences, had repaired the old tractor, the barn.

She had not led him down any errant path, nor was his life, nor mine, going to change or deviate from our destinies as a result of any choices made, or not made. She was like fodder, was all. We were just filling the days. We were still fattening up. We were still strong in the world, and moving forward. I had no call to feel lonely or worried. We still had all the time in the world, the world was still ours, there was no rot anywhere, the day was still fresh and new, we could do no wrong. We would grow, just not now.

Rick Bass is the author of twenty-three books of fiction and the forthcoming memoir *Why I Came West,* to be published in spring 2008. He was born in Fort Worth, Texas, grew up in Houston, and went to school at Utah State University. After working as a biologist in Arkansas and a geologist in Mississippi and Alabama, he moved to Montana's Yaak Valley, where he has been active for twenty years in the efforts to designate the last roadless lands in the Yaak Valley as wilderness. For more information on this cause, contact info@yaakvalley.org.

NICOLE BLAISDELL

*T*hough I like to consider myself a short story writer and therefore of necessity occasionally in possession of various skills employed in that craft, such as imagination, it is with some degree of professional discouragement that I realize and acknowledge the disturbing percentage of this story that was not the yield of a vivid imagination and didn't just germinate from dusty reality and then take off into its own flight but instead has as provenance and then path a significant amount of not just truth but indeed fact.

There was such strangeness, such rot and richness, going on in Houston in the years I spent growing up there that looking back now at many of the events and incidents in which I found myself, it is hard to imagine a participant in those events not becoming a writer, or some other form of storyteller. There is still rot and cultural disintegration going on in Houston, as elsewhere in the South—still plenty of decay and fragmentation to be observed and experienced—but there is more growth, too, now, whereas in those days, the 1970s, I think the newness had not yet fully arrived. Senescence was still king: and how could a young person's eye not be drawn, with horror, to such a process, such a natural phenomenon?

As a young person in Houston, I remember also often being possessed— seized—by the certitude that every day held a story waiting to be discovered, and experienced; that that world, and that time, was overbrimming with story, and that my friend Kirby and I, driving down the road, could stop at any house, any building, knock on the door, go inside, and witness, or extract, a story. There can be no finer aptitude, I think, for developing a sense of story—such story-confidence—and I was extremely fortunate to find myself in the midst of such a falling-apart time; one moribund culture, disintegrating. The Old South not so much giving way to the New South as, instead, to the No South. Rugged and/or pastoral individualism and eccentricity would—for better or worse and in the blink of an eye—become nothingness. A macabre nation of corporate zombies was marching toward us from the horizon, but we could not see them yet. Money was their God, but we did not know it yet.

In Texas, then, in those days, I was becoming a writer long before I was aware of desiring to become a writer. The place and the time, back then, shaped it in me. It was, and remains, a way of processing the various intersections between experience and imagination. In those early days, so strange was *the cultural mayhem, last gasps going on all around us, that again, little imagination was needed, and at that age—in childhood—every experience was new.*

The Goat Man—like so much else around us—was not long for the world. Even then, we realized it. Even then, we recognized story when we saw it, when we drove past its muddy yard, when we knocked on its door.

James Lee Burke

A SEASON OF REGRET

(from *Shenandoah*)

Albert Hollister likes the heft of it, the coldness of the steel, the way his hand fits inside the lever-action. Even though the Winchester is brand new, just out of the box from Wal-Mart, he ticks a chain of tiny drops from a can of Three-in-One on all the moving parts, cocks and recocks the hammer and rubs a clean rag over the metal and stock. The directions tell him to run a lubricated bore brush down the barrel, although the weapon has never been fired. After he does so, he slips a piece of white paper behind the chamber and squints down the muzzle with one eye. The oily spiral of light that spins at him through the rifling has an otherworldly quality about it.

He presses a half dozen .30-30 shells into the tubular magazine with his thumb, then ejects them one by one on his bedspread. His wife has gone to town with the nurse's aide for her doctor's appointment, and the house is quiet. The fir trees and Ponderosa pine on the hillside are full of wind, and a cloud of yellow dust rises off the canopy and sucks away over his barn and pasture. He picks up the shells and fits them back in the cartridge box, then puts the rifle and the shells in his closet, closes the door on them, and drinks a glass of iced tea on the front porch.

Down the canyon he can see the long roll of the Bitterroot

Mountains, the moon still visible against the pale blueness of the sky, like a sliver of dry ice. He drains his glass and feels a terrible sense of fatigue and hopelessness wash through his body. If age brings wisdom, he has yet to see it in his own life. Across the driveway, in his north pasture, a large sorrel-colored hump lies in the bunch grass. A pair of magpies descend on top of it, their beaks dipping into their bloody work. Albert looks at the scene with great sorrow on his face, gathers up a pick and a shovel from the garage, and walks down the hillside into the pasture. A blond Labrador retriever bounds along behind him.

"Go back to the house, Buddy," Albert says.

The wind makes a sound like water when it sharks through the grass.

Albert had seen the bikers for the first time only last week. Three of them had ridden up the dirt road that splits his ranch in half, ignoring the PRIVATE ROAD sign nailed to the railed fence that encloses his lower pasture. They turned around when they hit the dead end two hundred yards north of Albert's barn, then cruised back through Albert's property toward the paved highway. They were big men, the sleeves of their denim jackets scissored off at the armpits, their skin wrapped with tattoos. They sat their motorcycles as though they absorbed the throttled-down power of the engine through their thighs and forearms. The man in the lead had red hair and a wild beard and sweat rings under his arms. He seemed to nod when Albert lifted his hand in greeting.

Albert caught the tag number of the red-haired man's motorcycle and wrote it down on a scrap of paper that he put away in his wallet.

A half hour later he saw them again, this time in front of the grocery store in Lolo, the little service town two miles down the creek from his ranch. They had loaded up with canned goods and picnic supplies and sweating six-packs of beer and were stuffing them into the saddlebags on their motorcycles. He passed within three feet of them, close enough to smell the odor of leather, unwashed hair, engine grease, and wood smoke in their clothes. One of them gargled with his beer before he swallowed it, then grinned broadly at Albert. He wore black glasses, as a welder might. Three blue teardrops were tattooed at the corner of his left eye.

"What's happening, old-timer?" he said.

"Not much outside of general societal decay, I'd say," Albert replied.

The biker gave him a look.

Five days later, Albert drove his truck to the Express Lube and took a walk down toward the intersection while he waited for his truck to be serviced. It was sunset, and the sky was a chemical green, backdropped by the purple shapes of the Bitterroot Mountains. The day was cooling rapidly, and Albert could smell the cold odor of the creek that wound under the highway. It was a fine evening, one augmented by families enjoying themselves at the Dairy Queen, blue-collar people eating in the Mexican restaurant, an eighteen-wheeler shifting down for the long pull over Lolo Pass. But the voices he heard on the periphery of his vision were like a dirty smudge on a perfect moment in time. The three bikers who had trespassed on his private road had blundered onto a young woman who had just gotten out of her car next to the town's only saloon.

Her car was a rust-eaten piece of junk, a piece of cardboard taped across the passenger window, the tires bald, a child's stuffed animal inside the back window. The woman had white-gold hair that was cut short like a boy's, tapered on the sides and shaved on the neck. Her hips looked narrow and hard inside her pressed jeans, her breasts firm against her tight-fitting T-shirt. She was trapped between her car and the three bikers, who behaved as though they had just run into an old friend and only wanted to offer her a beer. But it was obvious they were not moving, at least not without a token to take with them. A pinch on the butt or the inside of her thigh would probably do.

She lit a cigarette and blew the smoke at an upward angle, not responding, waiting for their energies to run down.

"How about a steak when you get off?" the man with the red beard asked.

"Sorry, I got to go home and wash out my old man's underwear," she said.

"Your old man, huh? Wonder why he ain't bought you a ring," the man with the beard replied. When he got no response he tried again. "You a gymnast? 'Cause that's what you look like. Except for that beautiful pair of ta-ta's, you're built like a man. That's meant as a compliment."

Don't mix in it. It's not your grief, Albert told himself.

"Hey fellows," he said.

The bikers turned and looked at him, like men upon whom a flashbulb had just popped.

"I think she's late for work," Albert said.

"She sent you a kite on that?" the red-bearded man said, smiling.

Albert looked into space. "Y'all on your way to Sturgis?"

The third biker, who so far had not spoken, stuck an unfiltered cigarette into his mouth and lit it with a Zippo that flared on his face. His skin looked like dirty tallow in the evening light, his dark hair hanging in long strands on his cheeks. "She your daughter? Or your wife? Or your squeeze on the side?" he said. He studied Albert. "No, I can see that's probably not the case. Well, that means you should butt out. Maybe go buy yourself a tamale up at the café. A big, fat one, lot of juice running down it."

The bikers grinned into space simultaneously, as though the image conjured up shared meaning that only they understood.

Walk away, the voice inside Albert said.

"What's wrong with you fellows?" he asked.

"*What?*" the bearded man said.

"You have to bully a young woman to know who you are? What the hell is the matter with you?" Albert said.

The three bikers looked at one another, then laughed. "I remember where I saw you. On that ranch, up the creek a couple of miles. You walk up and down the road a lot, telling other people what to do?" the bearded man said.

The young woman dropped her cigarette to the ground and used the distraction to walk between the bikers, onto the wood porch of the saloon.

"Hey, come on back, sweet thing. You got a sore place, I'll kiss it and make it well," the biker with black glasses said.

She shot him the finger over her shoulder.

"Show time is over," the bearded man said.

"No harm intended," Albert said.

"You got a church hereabouts?" the man with the black glasses said.

"There's a couple up the road," Albert said.

The three bikers looked at one another again, amused, shaking their heads.

"You're sure slow on the uptake," the bearded man said. "If you go to one of them churches next Sunday, drop a little extra in the plate. Thank the Man Upstairs he's taking care of you. It's the right thing to do." He winked at Albert.

But the evening was not over. Fifteen minutes later, after Albert picked up his truck at the Express Lube, he passed by the saloon and saw the three men by the young woman's car. They had pulled the taped cardboard from the passenger-side window and opened the door. The biker with the beard stood with his feet spread, his thighs flexed, his enormous phallus cupped in his palm, urinating all over the dashboard and the seat.

Albert drove down the state highway toward the turn-off and the dirt road that led to his ranch. The hills were dark green against the sunset, the sharp outline of Lolo Peak capped with snow, the creek that paralleled the road sliding through shadows the trees made on the water's surface. He braked his truck, backed it around, and floored the accelerator, the gear shift vibrating in his palm. The note he left under the young woman's windshield wiper was simple: "The Idaho tag number of the red-haired man who vandalized your car is — " He copied onto the note the number he had placed in his wallet the day the bikers had driven through his property. Then he added, "I'm sorry you had this trouble. You did nothing to deserve it."

He walked back toward his truck, wondering if the anonymity of his note was not a form of moral failure in itself. He returned to the woman's car and signed his name and added his phone number at the bottom.

On the way home the wind buffeted his truck, powdering the road with pine needles, fanning geysers of sparks out of a slash pile in a field. In the distance he saw a solitary bolt of lightning strike the ridgeline and quiver whitely against the sky. The air smelled of ozone and rain, but it brought him no relief from the sense of apprehension that seized his chest. There was a bitter taste in his mouth, like copper pennies, like blood, a taste that reminded him of his misspent youth.

It takes him most of the afternoon to hand-dig a hole in the pasture in order to bury the sorrel mare. The vinyl drawstring bag someone had wrapped over her head and cinched tight around her neck lies crumpled and streaked with ropes of dried saliva and mucus in the bunch grass. The undersheriff, Joe Bim Higgins, watches Albert fling the dirt off the shovel blade onto the horse's flank and stomach and tail.

"I checked them out. You picked quite a threesome to get into it with," Joe Bim says.

"Wasn't of my choosing," Albert replies.

"Others might argue that."

Albert wipes the sweat off his forehead with the back of his forearm. The wind is up, channeling through the grass, bending the fir trees that dot the slopes of the hills that border both sides of his ranch. The sun is bright on the hills and the shadow of a hawk races across the pasture and breaks apart at the fence line. "Say again?"

"In the last year you filed a complaint because some kids fired bottle rockets on your property. You pissed off the developers trying to build a subdivision down on the creek. You called the president a draft-dodging moron in print. Some might say you have adversarial tendencies."

Albert thought about it. "Yes, I guess I do, Joe Bim. Particularly when a lawman stands beside my dead horse and tells me the problem is me, not the sonsofbitches who ran her heart out."

But Joe Bim is not a bad man. He removes a shovel from his departmental SUV and helps Albert bury the animal, wheezing down in his chest, his stomach hanging against his shirt like a water-filled balloon. "All three of those boys been in the pen," he says. "The one who hosed down the girl's car is a special piece of work. His child was taken away from him and his wife for its own protection."

Then Joe Bim tells Albert what the biker or his wife or both of them did to a four-month-old infant. Albert's eyes film. He clears his throat and spits into the grass. "Why aren't they in jail?" he says.

"Why do we have crack and meth in middle schools? The goddamn courts, that's why. But it ain't gonna change because you get into it with a bunch of psychopaths."

Albert packs down the dirt on top of his horse and lays a row of large, flat stones on top of the dirt. He cannot rid himself of the images Joe Bim's story has created in his mind. Joe Bim looks at him for a long time.

"How's the wife?" he asks.

"Parkinson's is Parkinson's. Some days are better than others," Albert says.

"You're a gentle man. Don't mess in stuff like this," Joe Bim says. "I'll get them out of town. They're con-wise. They know the hurt we can put on them."

You have no idea what you're talking about, Albert says to himself.

"What's that?" Joe Bim asks.

"Nothing. Thanks for coming out. Listen to that wind blow," Albert says.

Before his retirement he had taught at the state university in Missoula, although he did not have a Ph.D., and had managed to publish several novels that had enjoyed a fair degree of commercial success. Early on he had learned the secret of survival among academics, and that was to avoid showing any sign of disrespect for what they did. But in actuality the latter had never been a problem for him. He not only respected his colleagues but thought their qualifications and background superior to his own. His humility and Southern manners and publications earned him a tenured position and in an odd way gave him a form of invisibility. In the aftermath of the most bitter faculty meetings, no one could remember if Albert had attended the meeting or not.

In truth, Albert's former colleagues, as well as his current friends, including Joe Bim Higgins, have no idea who he really is.

He never speaks of the road gang he served time on as a teenager, or the jails and oil-town flophouses he slept in from Mobile to Corpus Christi. In fact, he considers most of his youthful experience of little consequence.

Except for one event that forever shaped his thinking about the darkness that can live in the human breast.

It was the summer of 1955, and he had been sentenced to seven days in a parish prison after a bloody, nose-breaking brawl outside a bar on the Texas-Louisiana line. The male lockdown unit was an enormous iron tank, perforated with square holes, on the third floor of the building. Most of the inmates were check writers, drunks, wife beaters, and petty thieves. A handful of more serious criminals were awaiting transfer to the state prison farm at Angola. The inmates were let out of the tank at 7 AM each day and allowed the use of the bull-run and the shower until 5 PM, when they went back into lockdown until the next morning. By 6 PM, the tank was sweltering, the smoke from cigarettes trapped against the iron ceiling, the toilets often clogged and reeking.

The treatment of the inmates was not deliberately cruel. The trusties ladled out black coffee, grits, sausage, and white bread for breakfast and spaghetti at noon. It was the kind of can where you did your time, stayed out of the shower when the wrong people were in there, never accepted favors from another inmate, and never, under any circumstances, sassed a hack. The seven days should have been a breeze. They weren't.

On Albert's fourth day a trailer truck with two huge generators boomed down on the bed pulled to a stop with a hiss of airbrakes and parked behind the prison.

"What's that?" Albert asked.

"This is Lou'sana, boy. The executioner does it curbside, no extra charge," an inmate wiping his armpits with a ragged towel replied. His name was Deek. His skin was as white as a frog's belly, and he was doing consecutive one-year sentences for auto theft and jailbreak.

But Albert was staring down from the barred window at a bean-pole of man on the sidewalk and was not concentrating on Deek's words. The man on the sidewalk was dressed western, complete with brim-coned hat, the bones of his shoulders almost piercing his snap-button shirt. He was supervising the unloading of a heavy, rectangular object wrapped with canvas. "Say that again?" Albert said.

"They're fixing to fry that poor sonofabitch across the hall," Deek replied.

The clouds above the vast swampland to the west were the color of scorched iron, pulsing with electricity. Albert could smell an odor like dead fish on the wind.

"Some night for it, huh?" Deek said.

Without explanation, the jailer put the inmates into lockdown an hour early. The heat and collective stink inside the tank were almost unbearable. Albert thought he heard a man weeping across the hall. At 8 PM the generators on the truck trailer began to hum, building in velocity and force until the sounds of the street, the juke joint on the corner, and even the electric storm bursting above the swamp were absorbed inside a grinding roar that made Albert press his palms against his ears.

He would have sworn he saw lightning leap from the bars on the window, then the generators died, and he could smell rain blowing through the window and hear a jukebox playing in a bar across the street from the jail.

The next morning the jailer ran a weapons search on the tank and also sprayed it for lice. The inmates from the tank were moved into the hall and the room in which the condemned man had died. The door to the perforated two-bunk iron box in which he had spent his last night on earth was open, the electric chair already loaded on the trailer truck down below. When Albert touched the concrete surface of the windowsill, he thought he could feel the residue from the rubber-coated power cables that had been stretched through the bars. He also smelled an odor that was like food that had fallen from a skillet into a fire.

Then he saw the man in the coned hat and western clothes emerge from a café across the street with a masculine-looking woman and two uniformed sheriff's deputies. They were laughing — perhaps at a joke or an incident that had just happened in the café. The man in the coned hat turned his face up into the light and seemed to look directly at Albert. His face was thin, the skin netted with lines, his eyes as bright and small as a serpent's.

"You waving at free people?" a guard said. He was a lean, sun-browned man who had been a mounted gunbull at Angola before he had become a sheriff's deputy and a guard at the parish prison. Even though the morning was still cool, his shirt was peppered with sweat, as though his body heat created its own environment.

"No, sir."

"So get away from the window."

"Yes, sir." Then he asked the question that rose from his chest into his mouth before he could undo the impulse. "Was that fellow crying last night?"

The guard lifted his chin, his mouth down-turned at the corners. "It ain't none of your business what he was doing."

Albert nodded and didn't reply.

"Food cart's inside now. Go eat your breakfast," the guard said.

"Don't know if I can handle any more grits, boss. Why don't you eat them for me?" Albert said.

The guard tightened the tuck of his shirt with his thumb, his expression thoughtful, his shoulders as square as a drill instructor's.

He inhaled deeply through his nostrils. "Let's take a walk down to the second floor, get you a little better accommodated," he said. "Fine morning, don't you think?"

Albert never told anyone of what the guard did to him. But sometimes he smells the guard's stink in his sleep, a combination of chewing tobacco and hair oil and testosterone and dried sweat that had been ironed with starch into the clothes. In the dream he also sees the upturned face of the executioner, his skin lit in the sunshine, his friends grinning at a joke they had brought with them from the café. Albert has always wanted to believe this emblematic moment in his life was regional in origin, born out of ignorance and fear and redneck cruelty, perhaps one even precipitated by his own recklessness, but he knows otherwise.

Albert has learned that certain injuries go deep into the soul, like a stone bruise, and that time does not eradicate them. He knows that the simian creature that lived in the guard and the executioner took root many years ago in his own breast. He knows that, under the right circumstances, Albert Hollister is capable of deeds no one would associate with the professor who taught creative writing at the university and whose presence at a faculty meeting was so innocuous it was not even remembered.

To the east the fog is heavy and white and hangs in long strips on the hills bordering Albert's ranch. When the early sun climbs above the crest, it seems to burst among the trees like a shattered red diamond. From the kitchen window, where he is drinking coffee and looking down the long slope of his southern pasture, he sees a rusty car coming up the road, its headlights glowing against the shadows that cover the valley floor. One headlight is out of alignment and glitters oddly, like the eye of a man who has been injured in a fight. The passenger window is encased with cardboard and silver duct tape.

The girl from the saloon knocks at his front door, dressed in colorless jeans and a navy-blue corduroy coat. She wears a cute cap and her cheeks are red in the wind. She is obviously awed by the size of his home, the massive amounts of quarried stone that support the two top floors, the huge logs that could probably absorb a cannon shell. Through the rear window of her vehicle, he can see a small boy strapped in a child's car seat.

"I wanted to tell you I'm sorry about what happened to your horse," she says.

"It's not your fault," Albert says.

Her eyes leave his, then come back again. He thinks he can smell an odor in her clothes and hair like damp leaves burning in the fall. He hears his wife call to him from the bedroom. "Come in," he tells the girl. "I have to see to Mrs. Hollister. She's been ill for some time now."

Then he wonders to himself why he has just told the girl his personal business.

"We're on our way to Idaho. I just wanted to thank you and to apologize."

"That's good of you. But it's not necessary."

She looks down the pasture at the frost on the barn roof and the wind blowing in the bunch grass. She sucks in her cheeks, as though her mouth has gone dry. "They got your name from me, not from the undersheriff."

In the silence he can hear his wife getting up from the bed and walking toward the bathroom on her own. He feels torn between listening to the young woman and tending to his wife. "Run that by me again," he says.

"One of them was my ex-husband's cellmate in Deer Lodge. They wanted to know your name and if it was you who called the cops. They're in the A.B. That's why I'm going to Idaho. I'm not pressing charges," she says.

"The Aryan Brotherhood?"

She sticks her hands in the pockets of her jacket and balls them into fists, all the time looking at the ground. Then Albert realizes she has not come to his home simply to apologize. He also realizes the smoke he smells on her clothes and person did not come from a pile of burning leaves.

"My boss is gonna send me a check in two weeks. At least that's what he says. My boyfriend is trying to get one of those FEMA construction jobs in New Orleans. But his P.O. won't give him permission to leave the state. I have enough money for gas to Idaho, Mr. Hollister, but I don't have enough for a motel."

"I see," he replies, and wonders how a man of his age could be so dumb. "Will fifty dollars help? Because that's all I have on me."

She seems to think about it. "That'd be all right," she says. She glances over her shoulder at the little boy strapped in the car seat. Her nails look bitten, the self-concern and design in her eyes un-disguised. "The saloon will be open at ten."

"I don't follow you," he said.

"I could take a check. They'll cash it for me at the saloon."

He lets her words slide off his face without reacting to them. When he removes the bills from his wallet and places them in her hand, she cups his fingers in her palm. "You're a good man," she says.

"When are they coming?" he asks.

"Sir?"

He shakes his head to indicate he has disengaged from the conversation and closes the door, then walks down the hallway and helps his wife back to her bed. "Was that someone from the church?" she asks.

During the night he hears hail on the roof, then high winds that make a rushing sound, like water, through the trees on the hillsides. He dreams about a place in South Texas where he and his father bobber-fished in a chain of ponds that had been formed by sheets of twisted steel spinning out of the sky like helicopter blades when Texas City exploded in February of 1947. In the dream wind is blowing through a piney woods that borders a saltwater bay hammered with light. His father speaks to him inside the wind, but Albert cannot make out the words or decipher the meaning they contain.

In the distance he hears motorized vehicles grinding up a grade, throttling back, then accelerating again, working their way higher and higher up the mountainside, with the relentlessness of chain saws.

He wakes and sits up in bed, not because of the engines but because they have stopped — somewhere above his house, inside the trees, perhaps on the ridgeline where an old log road traverses the length of the canyon.

He removes the rifle from his closet and loads it. He disarms the security system and steps out onto the gallery, in the moonlight and the sparkle of frost on the bunch grass. His hands and uncovered head and bare feet are cold. He levers a shell into the chamber, but releases the hammer with his thumb so that it cannot drop by accident and strike the shell casing, discharging the round. The fir trees are black-green against the hillside, the arroyo behind his house empty. The air is clean and smells of pine and snow melting on the rocks and wood smoke from a neighbor's chimney down the canyon. In the whisper of the wind through the trees he wants to believe the engine sounds in his dream are just that — the stuff of dreams. Far up the hill he hears a glass bottle break on stone and a motorcycle roar to life.

Inside the topmost trees three separate fires burst alight and fill the woods with shadows. The sound of motorcycle engines multiplies and three balls of flame move in different directions down the ridgeline. Inside the house, he calls 911, and through the back window he sees the silhouette of one rider towing a fireball that caroms off the undergrowth, the points of ignition fanning down the slope in the wind. "What's the nature of your emergency?" the dispatcher asks.

"This is Albert Hollister, up Sleeman Gulch. At least three men on motorcycles are stringing fires down my ridgeline."

"Which way are they headed?"

"Who cares where they're headed? The wind is out of the southwest. I'll have sparks on my roof in a half hour. Get the goddamn pump trucks up here."

"Would you not swear, please?"

"These men are criminals. They're burning my land."

"Repeat, please. I cannot understand what you're saying."

His voice has wakened and frightened his wife. He comforts her in her bed, then goes outside again and watches a red glow spread across the top of the valley. The summer has been dry, and the fire ripples through the soft patina of grass at the base of the trees and superheats the air trapped under the canopy. A sudden rush of cold wind through the timber hits the fire like an influx of pure oxygen. Flame balloons out of the canopy and in seconds turns fir trees into black scorches dripping with sparks. He can hear deer running across rocks and see hundreds of bats flying in and out of a sulfurous yellow cloud that has formed above the flames. He connects a hose to the faucet on the back of the house and sprays the bib of green grass on the slope, his heart racing, his mouth dry with fear.

By noon the next day the wind has died and inside the smell of ash is another odor, one that reminds him of the small room on the third floor of the parish prison where a man was strapped down in a wood chair and cooked to death with thousands of volts of electricity. Joe Bim Higgins stands next to Albert in the south pasture and stares up the hillside at the burned rocks and great stands of fir that are now rust-colored, as though stricken by blight.

Joe Bim blows his nose into a handkerchief and spits into the grass. "We found a sow and her cub inside a deadfall. The fire was probably crowning when they tried to outrun it," he says.

"Where are they Joe Bim?" Albert asks.

"Just up there where you see that outcropping." He tries to pretend his misunderstanding of Albert's question is sincere, then gives it up. "I had all three of them in a holding cell at seven this morning. But they got an alibi. Two people at their campground say they was at the campground all night."

"You cut them loose?"

Joe Bim is not a weak man or one who has avoided paying dues. He was at Heartbreak Ridge, and one side of his face is still marbled from the heat-flash of a phosphorous shell that exploded ten feet from his foxhole. "I can't chain-drag these guys down the highway because you don't like them. Look, I've got two deputies assigned to watch them. One of them throws a cigarette butt on the sidewalk — "

"Go back to town," Albert says.

"Maybe you don't know who you're real friends are."

"Yeah, my wife and my blond Lab, Buddy. I'd include my sorrel, except the two of us buried her."

"You're like me, Albert. You're an old man, and you can't accept the fact you can't have your way with everything. Grow up and stop making life hard for yourself and others."

Albert walks away without replying. Later, he spreads lime on the carcasses of the bears that died in the fire and tries not to think the thoughts he is thinking.

That night, during a raging electrical storm, Albert leaves his wife in the care of the nurse's aide and drives in his pickup to the only twenty-four-hour public campground on the Blackfoot River in Missoula County, his lever-action rifle jittering in the rack behind his head. It's not hard to find the three bikers. Their sky-blue polyethylene tent is huge, brightly lit from the inside, the extension flaps propped up on poles to shelter their motorcycles. Lightning flickers on the hillside, across the river, limning the trees, turning the current in the river an even deeper black. The smell of ozone in the air makes Albert think of the Gulf Coast and his youth and the way rain smelled when it blew across the wetlands in the fall. He thinks of his father, who died while returning from a duck-hunting camp in Anahuac, Texas, leaving Albert to fend for himself. He wonders if this is the way dementia and death eventually steal upon a man's soul.

Down the road he parks his truck inside a grove of Douglas fir trees that are shaggy with moss and climbs up the hill into boulders that look like the shells of giant gray turtles. He works his way across the slope until he can look down on the bikers' campsite. In the background the river is like black satin, the canyon roaring with the sounds of high water and reverberated thunder. The flap of the bikers' tent is open, and Albert can see three men inside, eating from GI mess kits, a bottle of stoppered booze resting against a rolled sleeping bag. They look like working men on a summer vacation, enjoying a meal together, perhaps talking about the fish they caught that day. But Albert knows their present circumstances and appearance and behavior have nothing to do with who they really are.

They could as easily wear starched uniforms as they do jailhouse tats. Their identity lies in their misogyny and violence and cruelty to animals and children, not the blue teardrops at the corner of the eyes or the greasy jeans or the fog of testosterone and dried beer-sweat on their bodies. These are the same men who operated Robespierre's torture chambers. They're the burners of the Alexandrian library, the brownshirts who pumped chlorine gas into shower rooms. They use religions and flags that allow them to peel civilizations off the face of the earth. There is no difference, Albert tells himself, between these men and a screw in a parish prison on the Louisiana-Texas border where a guard frog-walked a kid in cuffs down to an isolation area, shoved him to his knees, and closed the door on the outside world.

The rain looks like spun glass blowing in front of the open tent flap. The biker with the red beard emerges from the opening, fills his lungs with air, and checks his motorcycle. He wipes off the frame and handlebars with a clean rag and admires the perfection of his machine. Albert levers a round into the chamber and steadies his rifle across the top of a large rock. The notch of the steel sight moves across the man's mouth and throat, the broad expanse of his chest, the hair blossoming from his shirt, then down his stomach and scrotum and jeans that are stiff with road grime and engine grease and glandular fluids.

In his mind's eye Albert sees all the years of his youth reduced to typewritten lines written on a sheet of low-grade paper. He sees the paper consumed by a white-hot light that burns a hole through the pulp, curling through the typed words, releasing images that he thought he had dealt with years ago but in reality has not. In the smoke and flame he sees a stretch of rain-swept black road and his father's car embedded under the frame of a tractor-trailer rig; he sees the naked, hair-covered thighs of a former Angola gunbull looming above him; he sees the axe-bladed face of a state executioner, a toothpick in his mouth, his eyes staring whimsically at Albert, as though it is Albert who is out of sync with the world and not the man who cinches the leather straps tightly to the wrists and calves of the condemned. Albert raises the rifle sight to the red-bearded man's chest and, just as a bolt of lightning splits a towering Ponderosa pine in half, he squeezes the trigger.

The rifle barrel flares into the darkness and he already imagines the bullet on its way to the red-bearded man's chest. The round is copper-jacketed, soft-nosed, and when it strikes the man's sternum it will flatten and topple slightly and core through the lungs and leave an exit wound the size of Albert's thumb.

My God, what has he done?

Albert stands up from behind the boulder and stares down the hillside. The bearded man has taken a candy bar from his pocket and is eating it in the light from the tent flap while he watches the rain blowing.

He missed, thanks either to the Lord or the constriction in his chest that caused his hand to jerk or maybe just to the fact he's not cut out of the same cloth as the man he has tried to kill.

Albert grasps the rifle by the barrel and swings it against a boulder and sees the butt plate and screws burst loose from the stock. He swings the rifle again, harder, and still breaks nothing of consequence loose from either the wood or the steel frame. He flings the rifle like a pinwheel into the darkness, the sight on the barrel's tip ripping the heel of his hand.

He cannot believe what happens next. The rifle bounces muzzle-down off the roof of a passing SUV, arcing back into the air with new life, and lands right in front of the bikers' tent.

He drives farther down the dirt road, away from the bikers' camp, his headlights off, rocks skidding from his tires into the canyon below.

When he gets back home, he strips off his wet clothes and sits in the bottom of the shower stall until he drains all the hot water out of the tank. His hands will not stop shaking.

The rains are heavy the following spring, and in May the bunch grass in Albert's pastures is tall and green, as thick as Kansas wheat, and the hillsides are sprinkled with wildflowers. In the evening whitetail and mule deer drift out of the trees and graze along the edge of the irrigation canal he has dug from a spring at the base of the burned area behind his house. He would like to tell himself that the land will continue to mend, that a good man has nothing to fear from the world, and that he has put aside the evil done to him by the bikers. But he has finally learned that lying to oneself is an offense for which human beings seldom grant themselves absolution.

He comes to believe that acceptance of a wintry place in the soul and a refusal to speak about it to others is as much consolation as a man gets, and for some odd reason that thought seems to bring him peace. He is thinking these thoughts as he returns home from his wife's funeral in June. Joe Bim Higgins is sitting on the front steps of his gallery, the trousers of his dress suit stuffed inside his cowboy boots, a Stetson hat balanced on his knee, a cigarette almost burned down to a hot stub between two fingers. A pallbearer's ribbon is still in his lapel.

"The old woman wants me to invite you to dinner tonight," Joe Bim says.

"I appreciate it," Albert replies.

"You never heard no more from those bikers, huh?"

"Why would I?"

Joe Bim pinches out the end of his cigarette, field-strips the paper, and watches the tobacco blow away in the wind. "Got a call two days ago from Sand Point. The one with the red beard killed the other two and an Indian woman for good measure. The three of them was drunk and fighting over the woman."

"I'm not interested."

"The killing got done with an 1894-model Winchester. Guess who it's registered to? How'd they end up with your rifle, Albert?"

"Maybe they found it somewhere."

"I think they stole it out of your house, and you didn't know about it. That's why you didn't report it stolen." Joe Bim folds his hands and gazes at the hillside across the road and the wildflowers ruffling in the wind.

"They killed an innocent person with it?" Albert asks.

"If she was hanging with that bunch, she bought her own ticket. Show some humility for a change. You didn't invent original sin."

Albert starts to tell Joe Bim all of it — the attempt he made on the biker's life, the deed the sheriff's deputy had done to him when he was eighteen, the accidental death of his father, the incipient rage that has lived in his breast all his adult life — but the words break apart in his throat before he can speak them. In the silence he can hear the wind coursing through the trees and grass, just like the sound of rushing water, and he wonders if it is blowing through the canyon where he lives or through his own soul. He wonders if his reticence with Joe Bim is not indeed the moment of absolution that has always eluded him. He waits for Joe Bim to speak again but realizes his friend's crooked smile is one of puzzlement, not omniscience, that the puckered skin on the side of his face is a reminder that the good people of the world each carry their own burden.

Albert feeds his dog and says a prayer for his wife. Then he drives down the dirt road with Joe Bim in a sunset that makes him think of gold pollen floating above the fields.

James Lee Burke was born in 1936 in Houston, Texas, and grew up on the Louisiana-Texas coast. Over the years he worked as a pipeliner, land surveyor, social worker, newspaper reporter, and U.S. Forest Service employee. He also taught at the University of Missouri, the University of Southwestern Louisiana, the University of Montana, Miami-Dade Community College, and Wichita State University.

Burke published his first short story in 1956 and wrote his first published novel, *Half of Paradise,* between the ages of twenty and twenty-three. Over the years he has published twenty-six novels and two collections of short stories. His stories have appeared in *The Atlantic Monthly, The Best American Short Stories, New Stories from the South, The Southern Review, The Antioch Review,* and *The Kenyon Review.* His novels *Heaven's Prisoners* and *Two for Texas* were adapted as motion pictures.

Burke also managed to go thirteen years during the middle of his career without publishing a novel in hardcover. During that period his novel *The Lost Get-Back Boogie* received over one hundred editorial rejections. Later, after it was published with Louisiana State University Press, it was nominated for a Pulitzer Prize.

Burke's work has received two Edgar awards for Best Crime Novel of the Year. He is also a Guggenheim fellow and has been the recipient of an NEA grant.

He and his wife of forty-seven years, Pearl Burke, who is originally from mainland China, have four children and divide their time between Missoula, Montana, and New Iberia, Louisiana.

*F*or me, *"A Season of Regret" deals with generational attitudes. My ongoing temptation is to think of the era in which I grew up as a more virtuous one. But the truth is probably otherwise. Albert Hollister is a good man as out of place in the present as he was in the past. The electrocution that took place in the parish prison where he served a short sentence was conducted with societal consent. The executioner in the story probably* *had the same instincts as a serial killer, but he was subsidized by the state. Redemption for Albert comes in the realization that he is not like the men he has loathed for a lifetime.*

Unfortunately his redemption is of a kind that will probably never be collective in nature. But at a certain age, one no longer contends with the world.

Moira Crone

THE ICE GARDEN

(from *TriQuarterly*)

I

You could see it in her eyes, he told me — her gaze was more translucent, more liquid. What he wanted me to see was the proof she was better. And I was trying to see it.

She came from the past, from a time when people could be more exaggerated, he said. Yet she would catch up. She could be modern, his Diana, now that she was home from the hospital. She would live with us again, be our mother. It seemed to me to be all he talked about.

In part, she was more willing to please. She did things she'd never done before. First week home, she went to the beauty parlor, let strangers take off half a foot of her hair. They tugged on her head, wrapped her platinum locks around rubber sticks like crayons. When she came home in a taxicab — they weren't letting her drive — I thought she looked pitiful, like a startled poodle. But to my father she was lovelier than ever. And because that was true, things would be all right. He promised me. He believed.

During the second week she was back, I heard him arguing about the treatment with Dr. Blaine. "They gave her shocks up there. Was that necessary? Was it?"

Shocks were like being struck by lightning on purpose, I knew that.

"You signed the papers, Connor. It had to be," the doctor said. "Look at this straight on, would you?"

"Of course I will," my father said, his chest filling.

Right before Labor Day, she even tried to make iced tea the way Aunt C had done it. Aunt C, that she'd "sent packing" in the spring — is how Mother referred to the way Aunt C had to leave. It wasn't quite like that. Someone else had to pack for Aunt C that day she left. She couldn't pack for herself after what happened.

My mother drew me into the kitchen. She smelled wonderful up close, a scent that surrounded me, entranced me. I'd forgotten. "You have to help me, Claire," she said.

I was only ten, but I knew how. I told her to use eight bags in two cups of boiling water. Once you had the concentrate, you put in the sugar. That was the way Aunt C had done it. Then you diluted it with water and ice. She did what I said, as if she were the little girl. But when she actually tasted the tea, she grimaced and stuck out her tongue and bit it. The sweetness hurt her teeth. She said that in Fayton they drank tea sweeter than they did in Charleston where she grew up. But she was going to do things "The Fayton Way" from now on. "The way your daddy likes things," she paused, swallowing again, shaking her head. "So, this is how your daddy likes it?" There was a certain face she made, as if the whole world was hard as could be to be in. She made me feel that way too, when she looked like that. After she asked me that question, she began to pour the entire pitcher of bronze liquid into the white sink.

But I said, please, please, let me have some. As if just because my mother made it, I would like it.

It was worse than the pure Coke syrup we had to drink when we had colds. Even so I took it right down, to please her. Then I gave some to Sweetie my baby sister who actually did like it. Our mother said Sweetie didn't have sense. She always said that about Sweetie, or something worse. She never did stop doing that.

September. Dora Cobb down the street was turning five. Her parents, Tulip, her father, and Isabel, her mother, were having an open house for the grown-ups along with the birthday party. It was a big step, to try out the public. I told Sweetie I had the heebie-jeebies, but she didn't know what I was talking about.

As soon as we walked into the Cobbs' wide bungalow, I couldn't take my eyes off my mother, and neither could anyone else. She was more amplified than other people — rounder, taller, blonder. She had bigger, prettier eyes. She looked slightly like Marilyn Monroe, actually, but her features were finer — none of them were pudgy or girlish or soft. My mother also had talent. She used to play the piano, very well. But my father said it got her riled, all that pounding, so since she'd come back, she'd given it up, too, at his urging. He claimed this was a wonderful sign.

I knew she missed Chopin. The music calmed her down, especially the sonatas that swung from hard to soft, from high notes in cascades down to low ones. When she played the piano she hummed, which made it seem she was content. So I did believe that something beautiful could cure her, if only temporarily. I held out that hope, for the most part. I still believe in the cure of art, in a way. But at that time, when I was a child, I trusted that my father was right: it wasn't going to be Chopin for my mother. It was going to have to be something else.

In Fayton, other grown-up women wore shirtwaists, or flat wraparound skirts, or, if they were daring, Capri pants, with oxford shoes or tiny flats. They all dressed more or less alike: Cheryl Sender's mother Olive, my friend Lily Stark's mother Eunice, Isabel Cobb, who always took the most care about her appearance, which my mother said was too conventional. Knowing what to wear was very much at the center of things then, in a way I think people cannot conceive of exactly anymore. The crucialness, I mean, of looks. I like to think that since those days we've backed away a bit from that, given women something else to do besides "look," which really means, "be looked at." But sometimes it feels as if it's only gotten worse.

She wore a party dress to the party, not sportswear. When she sat down and tried to chat with other mothers, she didn't use a couch the way other people did. She had a more interesting way of doing it, of tucking one leg under the other, of spreading out her skirt. As if the couch were all hers, as if no one else in the room even mattered. And I was proud of her for this in a way, this abandon: when I was with my mother, no one else *did* matter, not really.

It was the world to me to sit on her big skirt on the Cobbs' couch, and sink into her side. It would have been fine if we'd been alone. Or perhaps, even better, if we'd been up on a stage on that couch, or in a live tableau in a department store window: Mother and Daughter in party dresses, something to behold.

But at the Cobbs', I knew I had to keep my ears open. I had to be there, I couldn't just be on view. I knew that other people existed, and that the way my mother had of telling the truth upset them. Once in the past, she had told a woman her baby was yellow and asked why. She once told Dora Cobb's father Tulip that his brother Honey ought to be sent away because his mind was feeble. It probably was true but nobody said it.

During this particular birthday party, she sipped tiny sips from her cup, and nibbled on the small corner of the huge white cake Dora's grandmother made, and hardly said a word.

Isabel Cobb, whose black hair was all curly around her head, so she had "piquant looks," according to my mother, faint praise, said to her at one point, "Diana, I just think that hairdo is perfect, just perfect."

"Oh, is that what you think, Isabel?" she said back.

Like my mother, I didn't agree with Isabel, actually, but at the same time I knew my mother should have acted grateful. That was the thing that you did in public. I didn't correct her, but I knew that was a difference between myself and my mother: I knew it, if I was with people and I said or did something wrong. My mother didn't know, or didn't care. I have never been sure: she's been gone so long now there's no way to find out. Most of the time now, in most of my moods, I assume it was the latter. But I don't always think that.

When we got home from the party that day, she exploded. It was a great effort, controlling herself at the Cobbs', she told me. Other women looked at her funny. I knew what other women meant by how they looked at her. They regarded her with awe and worry, at once. But I didn't say that. I didn't want to hurt her.

"Isabel was making fun of my permanent," she said. I said, no, no, no, she wasn't. But then my mother pulled at her hair, and I could see her scalp getting red. I couldn't stop her. This was one of those times when she didn't feel pain at all, when she was so in her own world she couldn't even imagine the idea of pain, anybody's, when she took the side of the demon who hated everybody, her self most of all. I grabbed her hands finally, but not before she pulled patches right out of her scalp. Two clumps of blonde, there on the parlor Persian carpet. I grabbed up the hair and threw it in the trash: it would trouble my father so much to see it. But I couldn't do anything about her head, the horrible little spots of bleeding.

"It isn't working, and I don't see why it should," she went on when I got her in the kitchen. Got her to sit down. "They all dress like miniature, unhealthy men, as if they have something to prove."

She was a little better then. I'd made her some coffee the way she liked it: black as tar, and hot, and she said to me, "Listen, don't you do that, dress like that. You could be pretty. And you should dress to be pretty because what else is there?" She gave me her shallow laugh. "Have you had a single thought about your complexion today?"

I had heard this before, as long as I could remember, how my whole life would be decided by how pretty I turned out to be. And I had to concern myself with my complexion, my skin, my weight, my clothes, my posture, every day even now, in fourth grade. I didn't know then if she meant this was good or bad, that you had to think about these things so much. I suppose you could say she was a person who advocated for a condition she only barely endured: the condition of being obsessed with one's exterior, one's beauty. I almost knew it was not a life she always liked, the one that beautiful got you, the one that staying beautiful created for you. She complained about all the taxing routines: sunbathing, pin-curling her hair, doing her nails, refusing to eat this or that because it made you fat, doing her eyes and her lips over and over and over in a single day. Yet she never wavered in these rituals. She insisted on the sovereignty of good looks in all things. My father insisted upon it too. He was the one who had the absolute faith, the unwavering conviction in her beauty. He was the true devotee.

I cannot recall her ever saying I was, or would be, "a beauty." She hinted sometimes to me that this might happen, that I might wake up and when I looked in the mirror, it would have come to me, my special beauty, but she wouldn't tell me for sure, if, or when it was coming. So I was always, then, waiting, in anticipation, for that word, for that power. I would lie down in bed sometimes and have fantasies about things I knew nothing of — boys, movies, back seats — and I would always begin them by saying, "On this night in the future, when I am beautiful . . ." Then I would describe to myself exactly what I would be wearing — sportswear, expensive sportswear, usually, but occasionally I would dare to imagine a real party dress with a wide skirt and a cinched waist, the kind my mother looked gorgeous in. I'd conjure myself in such a dress. But I was never sure that it would happen, that the night when I turned beautiful would ever come. In a way that whole year I was suspended, in waiting, I think sometimes, and then I tell myself not to think that.

After I gave her the hot coffee that day, after I listened to her rant about the Cobbs', she invited me into her huge closet to show me her grand dresses, the formals, the ones for real dances. Tulle underskirts, no straps. She asked me to stuff the crinolines into old hose, so they would keep fresh for the next party. She insisted these dresses had to be preserved, although she hardly went to those parties anymore, the kind where there was a huge dance band, white tablecloths, rum and Coke, and dinner.

I was close to her on the closet floor. Her tuberose perfume was especially strong. The job was like forcing blooms back into buds. When we were done, the stuffed hose were scattered about like fat, severed legs. She didn't put them back on the shelves above the hangers. I wished she would, they bothered me. She started to tell me stories. What things were like back when she was happy during the war, when those officers flocked to her. I had heard these before: romantic stories very like the ones I made up when I was going to sleep. Not one suitor, two or three or more. I could listen to her forever, I thought.

But when I went to bed, the tuberose scent surrounded me, and I didn't know if I could breathe. It kept me up for hours, until finally I had to take a shower to get rid of it. I was afraid someone would come find me, shout at me to go to bed. Ask me what I was doing. Find me out.

I still stayed up, after the shower, wrapped in a towel under the blanket after bathing, listening to the night radio. Little radios, transistors, were brand new then, and I could take one with me to bed, let it talk to me on my pillow. I loved that. There was a hurricane in the Atlantic, I remember, and I couldn't sleep until I heard it had made a turn, that it had gone out to sea.

My father didn't ask much of her. Most of the time she could do whatever she pleased. As long as it was nothing much, that is: lounging, getting dressed, doing herself up, talking to the maid, telling her what to do. He was absent a lot — at the office all day, as that was where a white lawyer from a good family, in a small Carolina town, was supposed to go. But it was also true that he was the only one who watched at all, who kept things, as Aunt C said when she was still around, "Afloat." Or that's what I believed then, of course, that he was the source, the steady one, the solid man. There was some sort of family boat that could always sink, but he would save us, wouldn't he? My baby sister and I were the cargo, the ones who could fall out, but he would never let that happen. He was supposed to be the one who kept us in.

•••

I heard my parents talking on the side porch in early October. My father was asking my mother to pay more attention, take on more responsibility. Since she was well now, he said. She was well, except that she'd pulled out her hair that one time, I thought. But that permanent had fallen, and she had her loose movie star hair again, held back from her wide and impressive brow, with little fancy bobby pins. And I hadn't ever mentioned her fit after the Cobbs' party. I thought of it as just a lapse, an error, and she had told me not to, to keep her secret. I held all her secrets, then. Every one.

"You are letting things get out of hand," he said to her. He was talking about the household, about what should be bought at the grocer's, what kind of meat loaf should be made, what sort of desserts. "Sidney doesn't know what you want. You have to tell her. Talk to Isabel Cobb, get some ideas."

"I have nothing to say to Isabel Cobb," my mother answered. "I don't have any small talk. I never have. Small talk is as far as she goes."

It was true, I thought, listening. Nothing was small to my mother. Why should anything be? I thought.

"I try, do you have any idea how hard?" she added.

"But you criticize everybody. Never see the good. Look at them as if they should have come from Charleston."

Fayton wasn't like Charleston, where she came from. The thing about Fayton was that everybody knew everybody else. You didn't live only your life, you lived the whole town's life. In cities people didn't do this. In cities — Aunt C had told me, she was from one — people lived by themselves, or families by themselves. She had told me I was lucky because I had the town, my friends, my teachers, the neighbors' mothers, and Sidney, our maid. That all of them would keep me safe, and raise me. She told me that the day she left. She stopped to tell me that even in the midst of all her trouble.

"I don't want you to be anything, or make any small talk," my father pleaded. "I want you to be happy, is that so hard, Diana?"

I could have told him the answer to that. But this was back in the days when I would tell him things, and he wouldn't even know I was speaking, he was so focused on her. I would tell him the same truth right now: for some people being happy is too much to ask.

Aunt C was the last of his family she turned her back on. She was a widow, with no children of her own, from big Washington, as we called it, because there was also a little Washington, the one up near Elizabeth City, North Carolina, near the Albemarle Sound. She came after Sweetie was born, because Sweetie was just too much trouble, my mother said. The year she spent with us was the best year of my life so far.

Aunt C knew what we needed. She listened to us and played games with us and read to us and made food we liked. We *were* hers, and we wanted to be hers.

I heard Aunt C speak to my father frankly once not long before she had to leave: "I don't want to hear it, Connor. I've heard it. It was a war, and she was beautiful. And you had to have her. Well now you have her. So what are we going to do? Don't lie to me. Don't lie to yourself. The children deserve more. I don't care what you want to believe. It doesn't matter what you *hope*."

I recall there was a long silence, after that. I don't recall my father having an answer, after that.

A few days later our mother said Aunt C was stealing our love, which belonged by blood to herself. Only to her. She shouted at all of us, including my father. After some resistance, he must have decided to believe her.

I didn't understand how Aunt C could be a thief.

Two days later, he came knocking on my bedroom door early in the morning, to tell me that Aunt C was hurt, though she would get better. But she wasn't staying. When I asked what happened, he said she stumbled on the stairs, on one of Sweetie's shoes.

One of her soft little shoes, I thought. Soft as a sock, I thought. How was that, I thought.

Outside in the hall, I heard Aunt C crying behind the closed door of her little room. When I tried to go in, she said, "Go away, go have breakfast. You can't see me like this." She said she'd be fine. She said my father should leave. "Tell him to go on, what is the use of him? Let him go off to the office." He did go a bit later — he seemed ready to do that, eager, in fact. As if things were fine, as if things weren't about to sink.

"How did you fall?" I asked Aunt C when I returned to her room with some bacon, after a breakfast where my mother only stared at me, wouldn't speak.

I thought Aunt C would smell the bacon — she loved it — and open the door, but she still wouldn't let me in. "Is that what they told you downstairs? That I fell?" she asked.

I pushed my way in then. She was still in her old lady nightgown. Swiss made, like mine, with a bib, and sleeveless. She was darkly bruised on the neck and wrist. She was drenched, and weeping. I thought, how much water could be in her? Even her hair was wet, and not from a shower, from sweat. It was terrifying to see a woman that old that you loved, crying like a girl at school. She smelled a fright, like iron mixed in with lavender. Her one arm was covered with a shawl. She wouldn't lift it to let me see the worst places, where her shoulder had been wrenched, where she'd been thrown down, where the arm had nearly been pulled from the socket.

"Will you do something for me?" she said in a tiny voice. "Call Cheryl Ann. Tell her I have a little job for her, will you do that for me?"

I did what she asked, using the upstairs hall phone, and then returned, sat on the edge of the bed watching Aunt C on the vanity bench, and waited for Cheryl Ann Sender, a neighbor girl in junior high school. She lived down at the end of the block.

That's when Aunt C told me how I could trust my place, my town, and the people around me, my father, too, she said, "Although sometimes he's too idealistic, darling." My mother called from the hall outside the room, "Don't help her. Come to me, Claire. Don't you see what she's been doing? What a liar she is?"

Aunt C reached over and put her good arm around me. I didn't pull away even though I knew I should. Finally my mother went downstairs to play music.

Cheryl Ann was the oldest girl on the street. My mother had already designated her a beauty, but I didn't despise Cheryl Ann for that. I worshipped her. After my mother had stopped hanging around in the hall, and started pounding out Chopin, I sneaked down to let Cheryl Ann in. Cheryl and I helped Aunt C go out the back way, on the servant stairs. Sidney saw us, told me my mother said I wasn't to leave the house. All by herself, Cheryl took Aunt C to the hospital where they put the cast on. That's when Dr. Blaine got involved. Later that day, Cheryl Ann came for Aunt C's clothes. She packed them all up in two plaid suitcases.

It was all over by six. Aunt C was gone in a taxicab with Cheryl, straight from the hospital. She left on the night train, so shaken she could hardly walk.

The next day, Dr. Blaine came by the house and spoke to my father in the library, and said it had to be. My mother had to go to the hospital. He didn't say what kind. I heard that later, when Sidney was talking on the phone.

The hospital for people not right in the head.

There were big state hospitals then, with nice grounds, which were peaceful, some of them — people lived in such places for years, their whole adult lives. Families could take a person there and drop them off. That was, to their minds, the solution, although my father never thought in those terms, I don't think, of a problem and a solution. He had hope. It was always a sweet idiot hope that things would be something else, not what they were. Sort of presto, like that. I tried to correct for it, and also, I half believed him, but young as I was, I knew he didn't have it quite right. I didn't want to know it, though.

These other families didn't feel terribly guilty about it. They didn't wrack their brains, when they dropped someone off. I've been told stories since, ones that don't end like this one does.

These big asylums were condemned and shut down later, and such people were put out to be with the rest of us, in grim apartments, and so forth. But there was, in the past, another way of doing things, and in a sense, people could go on.

They put my mother in a red brick building up near the state capitol. Her room had barely any furniture, there were tight white sheets and a thin blanket on the bed, which had a hard metal frame — silver, cold. She was there all summer with no air-conditioning, just a box fan. My father took me to see her once. He didn't take Sweetie. My mother didn't want to see Sweetie, he said. That didn't seem to bother him.

When we got to the hospital, she cried and asked why we wouldn't let her come home. And I cried too, a great torrent of tears, for I felt several things. I felt as if I were in some way the cause of her being there. Because her fight with Aunt C, her attack on Aunt C, was what had caused her to come, and Sweetie and I were the issue in that fight. I felt enormous loss with Aunt C gone, as well. I felt terrible loneliness. Nothing was all right that summer. Nothing.

My solution was to insist that I stay, keep my mother company. I could lie down next to her, and she wouldn't have to be by herself. I will cure her, I thought, I can. I liked to think I had powers, somehow, that I could do it, all alone. I needed to think that, I suppose. Somehow at the time it must have been a help.

She said she had no one to talk to. I saw that was true. The people in the lounge on her floor were horrible: they picked their noses and beat on the table with their palms when they laughed at the Red Skelton skits on TV.

My father said I couldn't stay, and then he sent me into the hall with those crazy people. He closed the door, and spoke only to my mother, in low tones. I believed also that, inside there, he was kissing her over and over, and I didn't want them kissing in that white blank room with that cold metal bed, I didn't, I wanted them to stop. I wanted to be taken home, if I couldn't spend the summer in that white room with my mother, lying down beside her on taut hospital sheets. I certainly didn't want my father in there. Sweetie my baby sister was at home, and nobody watched Red Skelton at home. When my father came out of the room he rushed quickly past the people by the TV, and the nurses, and he pulled me down the hospital stairs and outside and into the car, but he didn't say what the matter was. He didn't speak to me at all, as a matter of fact, the whole ride, which was not unusual, but on that particular trip I especially wanted to know what he was feeling. By custom, for my mother always rode in the front seat, I rode in the back, so I was behind him, not with him, even though she wasn't there. He changed the stations over and over on the radio, but as soon as he found a game he liked, and he'd heard a few plays, the sound would start to drift, and he'd have to try again, to find another announcer amidst all that static.

That part of the Carolinas was no radio paradise: there were places the stations couldn't reach even at night, when Fort Wayne, Indiana, and KDKA Pittsburgh could get to almost everyone on the planet it seemed, except to us. He never asked me what I wanted to hear. I was not, it didn't seem, a real person to him then. Later, I was, but not then.

I don't know what they said to each other that day in the hospital, not really. I believe they were kissing, but they were also talking. Children never know the true nature of the private negotiations between their parents, the intimacies, but it doesn't seem right, in a way, does it. Since the souls of children are the product of those struggles, their lives are the concrete result. Children should have complete access to their parents' intimate lives, you might argue, they should burrow in and watch them, see it all. But then the whole picture tumbles down, doesn't it, then all the scenery and the facades collapse. And then what: probably what we really don't want to know.

June, July, and August, Sidney had long hours. There was no one else to watch us. I loved her, but she didn't know what we wanted, the way Aunt C knew. Sidney had a life of her own, and moods, and she was distracted by the troubles she had with her man Raoul, who often got into fights, or other sorts of troublesome business down at a place called the Golden Parrot. I always thought of it as the only nightclub in Fayton, and it seems that they had liquor there, although Fayton was a dry town in a dry county. But somehow everything that happened there happened to people who were drinking.

I do remember that she told me about the blues, that summer, and what to do with them. She must have seen something in me: I was not entirely in a good way that summer, or that fall, for that matter. I was becoming a little odd, a little separate, I could feel it, although I felt no power to stop it. Sometimes when children came up to me and said something about my family, I burst out into a sweat, and I ran to a grown-up. I'd had words with Lily Stark, my neighbor two years younger, whom I had played with the most — I could have no more to do with her. The teachers always took my side, for I was Claire McKenzie and I was somehow already special. That was becoming my defense in life — that I was superior, exceptional, unlike the others, the rabble.

After I came back from seeing my mother, Sidney told me I had the blues, that I'd had them for months, in fact, since the business with Aunt C, since my mother was sent away. Sidney had been shy with me before, but that day she took pity, I suppose.

"When they come you just shout them down in your mind, taunt them, say, 'Hello what you got for me today? Think I can't take it?' Like that, she said, and they scat."

"They do?" I said.

"Well, sometimes they scat," she said, then she kissed me, which was rare. She smelled of baby powder, and bergamot. She was slender, straight, young, and tall. "Maybe not every last little bit," she amended. And I started practicing, shouting down the blues in my mind. I did it all summer. I did it for years. It is effective, up to a point.

And then, late August, when my mother came home, my father

said, "Isn't this wonderful? She's cured." When he said this he was looking very handsome. And I couldn't think of anything better than having a beautiful mother in the house. In a part of myself I believed it too, that she was cured. That everything would be fine, fine, now that we had her back. Now that I had a mother.

I wouldn't be eleven for several months. In certain ways, not all, I was still simple.

The third Monday in October, Sidney left a pot of grits unwashed in the sink when her ride home came to get her, and my mother started screaming. The next day it was chilly, and Sidney wore a sweater to work which was unbuttoned three down from the neck. When I showed her, for I was very conscious at all times of what everyone was wearing, Sidney buttoned herself right back up. She said the sweater must have shrunk in the wash. It was a thick knit, with a wide band at the bottom. Because of her long waist, it didn't go all the way down to her skirt. But she had something underneath that, a cotton shirt. No skin was showing, not a bit.

Later that day after Sidney fixed herself, my mother told me to watch her, because she knew Sidney secretly wanted to go out with my father. "What was she doing all those months when I was gone?" she asked me.

"Nothing," I said. "Cleaning."

"What do you know?" she said. "What are you?"

To me the idea was completely absurd. Sidney was a young colored woman, I thought, that was the awful word we used, always, we said "colored." And where was she going to go with my father if they went out? Nowhere. The Golden Parrot was only for colored people as far as I knew, and maybe the white sheriffs who came to rough the customers up.

Black and white people couldn't do anything together in the world that I knew of, except black people could work for white people and white people could sell black people things on time, or arrest them. For the way we lived, what I had seen, this was the entire truth. It was as if my mother were saying that at night trees get up and walk around, to say my father would take Sidney somewhere on a date, and she would want to go. Yet I had to listen.

My mother could see the doubt in my face, but then she explained, her long lashes lowering, that these things happen in the real world, outside of Fayton, and then she mentioned Charleston.

As soon as she brought that city up, she sounded the way Sidney and her friend Zachary who preached did when they were at the kitchen table discussing Abraham or Moses or Methuselah or King David. My mother seemed to think everyone in the world knew the names of people in Charleston, and, like people in the Bible, all they had done was of great importance. Gilbert Crane, for example, left his wife and children for a high yellow concubine, she said, and took her to Barbados.

I never found out if Gilbert Crane was my uncle, or my cousin, or my great-grandfather, or no relation at all. I still don't know what century any of this happened in. She'd never taken us to Charleston so we could get the history straight.

I changed the subject away from Gilbert Crane and his misdeeds. I asked her if we could go down and show everybody Sweetie. It might be nice to take a trip, I thought. Maybe we could see the beach. Maybe the ocean would calm her, the way Chopin did. And it might make her feel better about Sweetie, to see her people fondling her, saying she was a pretty baby, was what I was really thinking. It wasn't that far to Charleston. The way my mother talked, it was in a foreign country.

"My people would eat you and Sweetie for breakfast," she snapped. "You have no idea." She had a husky voice, for she was smoking a lot those last days: Parliaments, or Bel Airs, and sometimes her voice and smoke were in my mind almost exactly the same sad, low thing. Sometimes when I heard it I cringed. I did just then. I didn't want to be that kind of daughter, the kind who cringes at her mother's voice.

My mother's family were Huguenots, I had been told. Even much later, when I was in my teens, if I heard the word, I thought of big, blonde, Southern cannibals. Munching on young girls for breakfast, with muffins. Big teeth sinking into slender ankles, dainty pinkies flying up, "Is it a 'she'?" they'd ask, for I knew that in Charleston they ate "she-crabs," especially. Knowing the sex of something was a prerequisite to the delight of consuming it, apparently, in Charleston. He-crabs weren't as tasty, somehow.

In truth my mother's kin were dark trollish people with bug-eyes, whom I never felt comfortable around, not for a second. I met them at her funeral, later that year, right before Christmas.

They seemed to have almost nothing in common with her, and they saw her as a stranger among them, a platinum swan among crows, an inexplicable anomaly. As far as I could tell from an early age she had been sacrificed for her gifts, despised for them, as well as paraded around, pampered, forced into a kind of false perfection, exploited. They all "adored" her, they told me. She was their precious, their gorgeous one. "And spoiled," they said. "You ever seen spoiled?" As if that were the delight of her, and why she was a menace, both. They had once had money and they had come down out of it, they hinted. But this was all very vague in 1959. People had erased their old lives by buying ranch houses, by having many cars, and doing a lot of moving around, but there were references to old mansions, to streets in Charleston, to rot and beetles and high water that had come for these assets over the years, and left them in ruins — left them, in their hearts, utterly desperate people. Or perhaps they had always been desperate. It seemed as if they were all standing in front of a vast gulf in the earth, something gaping open. They were terrified I would see it. When they spoke to me one shoved himself in front of another, so I wouldn't see the chasm behind them, and they marched toward me, one trying to out-explain the other, concealing the awful truth that would not leave them, that they were terrified I would see. One did not have to see it. It was enough to see how they felt about it.

My mother wanted to fire Sidney. Through the late fall, night after night, they fought about it. My father insisted Sidney had no designs. He wanted her to stay on. I felt the same way but no one asked me. There was too much to do without her. My mother wasn't good at certain things. I had seen her try, but she couldn't do them, nobody had ever shown her. She was used to the world doing for her. She couldn't sort Sweetie's tiny clothes, for example. Or clean up the nursery. She was no good at cooking — she knew absolutely nothing about it. Even iced tea was a struggle, that was proven. I wanted to weigh in, but of course I couldn't. Even if I had spoken, they would not have been able to hear me.

They settled it that Sidney could only be there when he was out of the house. My father said that was how my mother wanted it. And that was how it would be. This seemed reasonable to him, something we could do, put up with.

They took up this plan right after Halloween. I still wasn't sleeping well. It wasn't the perfume anymore. It was noise, my parents arguing. I stayed up late, listening to Fort Wayne, Pittsburgh, Havana on stormy nights, WABC in New York City. A fall chill came on suddenly that week, Arctic air, swooping down into the Carolinas, the weathermen said. There was no in-between, just Indian summer heat, then a hard frost. The trees hardly had time to change. In a few days, some were blaring color, and as quickly, bare. This will be the pattern this year, they said. Hot, then freezing cold, they said.

In the end, the winter took us by complete surprise, which was why the wood was so brittle in the storm, in December, people said, why the damage was so severe.

I woke the Saturday before Thanksgiving to the sound of Sweetie crying. It seemed far away, almost in another world, but that could happen in that house. There were seven bedrooms, two parlors, a library, a butler's pantry, two staircases, a sleeping porch, and a room just for the piano, which was locked.

I went to the nursery, but Sweetie wasn't in her crib. The bathroom next to it was empty. As I got closer to my parents' bedroom, way down on the other end of the hall, I heard water running, but no Sweetie. Mother must be taking a bath, I thought. So Sweetie got into something, I thought. But where did she get to?

My parents' room had a big sky-blue chenille bedspread and heavy curtains. There was a chaise lounge, peacock satin, with little fleurs-de-lis in the pattern, where my mother spent much of her life with her cigarettes. The bed was unmade, but no one was in it. She usually slept late: for her to be up on a Saturday before nine was a surprise. Then, it was silent, I even thought I had dreamed Sweetie's crying for a moment.

But I heard her again. A different sound, like a goose. Honking. I wondered was she in the hall, caught on something. I was afraid of the bath because my mother would shout at me for sneaking up on her in there. And she must have been in there, for the water was pounding away.

Sweetie screamed again, and so I had to venture in. First there was the vanity room, with two sinks, and a wide mirror. The tub was in a room beyond that. I turned toward it, sure I would see my mother's naked body, which was smooth and wonderful, under bubbles. I had seen it before, how perfectly white she was. I had seen her high breasts through the steam.

But I found Sweetie in the bath, by herself, on her back, naked, and red as a kidney bean. She was flapping her arms, and her little mouth was opening and closing. The water was up to her ears, and rising. I grabbed her up by the arms, and then I almost dropped her on the tile floor. She was so heavy, and slippery. But once I got her head over my shoulder, which changed the distribution of the weight, she stayed put for a while and I managed to get a towel around her. Sweetie was a thick, heavy baby I loved to be close to. Even squirming across my body like that, her lungs wide open screaming, there was something wonderful about holding her. Everybody was supposed to want a lusty baby like Sweetie.

Struggling down the hall with her, I saw my mother below, standing on the first landing looking out the stained glass window. She was wearing a satin quilted robe, and had a cup of coffee in her hand. I knew that this act, the one she had just committed, of leaving an eighteen-month-old alone in a high tub with the water running, was terribly wrong, and was no accident. But how could that be, I corrected myself. How could she leave Sweetie in the bath? Sweetie must have got in there some other way. Although I knew no other way. It was a big, deep tub with feet, and walls too high for her to climb in or out.

My mother must have heard us coming, Sweetie honking in my arms, but she did not turn around to see us. When I got down to the landing, I saw her eyes were veiled even though they were open, and she finally said, as if surprised, "What? Oh you have that thing. She never stops complaining." Then she paused, and I thought I saw a flash of something that frightened me: a glance like frost. She said, "Good of you. So good of you."

Then she looked out the window again. She said in a moment, recovering herself, "Come see, honey, the trees, through the stained glass, come."

I went. I gave Sweetie my thumb so she would stop screaming, but she didn't. My mother acted as if I weren't holding anything in my arms.

At the window, nevertheless, I fell into mother's world, immediately, willingly. How could I believe my mother capable of such things and still live, still go on? I just looked out the window and tried very hard to forget, to reimagine what I'd just seen, to focus on the lovely leaves drifting down, visible through the old, wavy glass. Burgundy red maple leaves, drifting down, ever so slowly.

I was doing very well. And my mother was, perhaps, training me, showing me something, about how she dealt, really, with the world, something she wanted me to know, and I was ready to receive it, to believe in it, I must have been. She was my mother, and this was something she wanted me to have, a gift from her. The gift of reverie. And then she said, "What did you say?"

"I didn't say anything," I said. I hadn't.

"I heard you, what did you say?" she asked again. She was loud, she had to be, over Sweetie, who was still wailing from fright, although my mother completely ignored that.

"I didn't say a word," I said. "I promise."

"I better not hear you," she said. "I better not in this life, you know what's good for you?"

I said, "No ma'am. No ma'am." There was nothing else I could say. I had very few choices with her, and besides, I had to take Sweetie somewhere, get her dry and dressed.

That night, I started a new routine: I pretended to go to sleep at eight, but then, when everything was quiet, I got up. I pushed my bed against the wall — this was hard to do without scraping the floor, but I did it slowly, gliding it with towels under the feet. Then I went in the nursery. I took Sweetie up out of her crib, and put her on the bed between myself and the wall so she wouldn't roll out. I slept like that until first light. Then I got up and put her back, and moved my bed to the center of the room. By then I was usually too awake to go back to sleep. I sat by the window, and waited, with a certain dread, for the house to come alive again, for my mother and father to wake up, for us to get on, as the phrase goes, with our lives.

II

It started coming down one morning in December about six. I noticed it after I put Sweetie back, and then later, when I was watching Sidney out the window. She was waiting for my father to pull out of the drive so she could come in and fix everybody else breakfast. The trees were leafless by then so a person could have a view of the sidewalk from across the street. I was looking at all the houses, trying to gauge if our neighbors knew what my family was doing to Sidney. The ice was transparent. You had to sort of believe in it to see it.

On the way to school, I felt the coldest, windy air, air that made you swallow first and close your eyes, because it didn't seem true. I liked a misty, secret cold. It seemed a great chance, to have a real winter, like the children in the readers had. It felt as if something we'd always been promised was finally being delivered.

I loved school. I loved the cloakroom, the construction paper, the poles you had to use on the windows to open them because they were so high, the stout widows who were our teachers, Mrs. Horn, Mrs. Bailey. I loved it more lately than ever. Once we took off our scarves and caps and mittens and thick coats, it was just a December morning. I didn't worry about Sweetie even.

Soon as class started, I was let out to paint a mural on paper on the bulletin board in the cafeteria. I was known for my paintings, already. Since first grade I'd been doing them in tempera. Whatever the season asked for: witches, cats, hearts, cherry trees, wise men, bunnies. Around holidays I hardly spent any time in class. The teachers all thought I was too smart to need lessons anyway. Nobody had noticed I'd been falling behind since Aunt C left in May. I didn't have my times tables past six. I couldn't study, especially for the last few weeks. I'd been worrying about Sweetie, and doing things Sidney didn't have time for now under the new rules.

I was working on a scene of children sitting on the floor by a tree, a mother above them with a real smile on her face, and a big open book in her lap. The father was looking on with great interest. Behind them was the Christmas tree. These were smooth pink people like the characters in the Dick and Jane books, or in the family TV shows. The mother looked a lot like my mother — her hair, her big eyes. But I remember thinking I couldn't draw someone as pretty as my real mother. Her beauty was too mysterious to capture, to even try. There was no point — she was so far past me.

After a while the first graders came in for lunch. They were all talking about the "stuff outside" — discussing whether it was snow or ice or sleet. I prayed for snow because I'd never really seen a good layer of it. And I thought how I might take Sweetie out and pull her on a garbage can lid with a rope tied to it. She'd go far, she'd slide down hills, we'd sled pure across town,

Around one thirty the principal Mrs. Taylor announced school was let out. The highway department said the roads were freezing up. The cafeteria ladies let me phone home. Asking what the problem was, my mother said Isabel Cobb had called, and offered to fetch me along with the other children. My mother still wasn't driving — Dr. Blaine was against it. So I waited out on the sidewalk next to Bit Cobb, a wild boy, who was throwing wet iceballs, wanting to put them down our shirts, and his sister Dora, who was in kindergarten, who wouldn't let go of my leg. She was afraid of ice. Lily Stark was there too, smiling at me. Mrs. Cobb came in her big old Cadillac and stuffed us all in the back seat. Even though she went fifteen miles an hour, the car skidded twice, and we all slid in the back from side to side. There were no seat belts then. Lily squealed and giggled. I couldn't help it, so did I. When she got to Winter Street, Mrs. Cobb said she was glad we were all alive, but we were still laughing.

At home I found my mother in the living room with the drapes drawn. The heat was on high, and she was wearing a shirtwaist with no sweater. She looked lovely, flushed, and pink. I wanted to hug her, but first I searched around for Sweetie and found her in the playpen.

My mother said, "Is it that bad? I let that bitch Sidney go home. She begged. I told her not to come back. Ever."

"You fired her?" I asked. I couldn't bear it.

"What good was that hussy?" she asked.

I wasn't supposed to answer.

I knew this voice, this old, nothing-is-good-today voice. Hearing it this time, my shoulders rose up, I breathed more shallowly. To myself, I said, "What do you have for me today?" As Sidney had taught me. But my mother looked at me as if she could hear what went on underneath my breath. In a way I wanted her to know. I knew she ought to know my life, she ought to be inside it. But I was afraid she'd hear what I said, how I yelled at my blues the Sidney way, how I worried about Sweetie now, how I sneaked her into my bed at night. In some way there is no escaping a mother, even when she isn't there.

Sweetie charmed me that day, I remember. Sidney had dressed

her up really pretty before she left. She had on her scuffed white shoes and her corduroy smock, the yellow of the inside of a pound cake. Fat cheeks.

My mother said, "Look at those bugeyes, she's so plain."

To my mother, love that didn't follow from beauty was somehow flawed, awry. If she saw a couple on the street and the woman wasn't beautiful, she asked my father what was the man doing with her? Did the woman have money?

I confess I felt it a flaw in my own makeup sometimes, how I didn't make a judgment about Sweetie's looks before I fell in love with her. But I had no choice, I didn't care. Besides, she had that tiny little mouth.

My mother said this storm better turn to snow, which was bad enough, but it would be worse if it stayed ice. The trees, she said, the ice takes the trees.

I had no idea what she meant.

She said it happened in Charleston in the thirties, and she went on, telling me how bad things could get. After a while I had the thought my mother was very brave, compared to other people. Because it was so hard for her to live, knowing all she knew, feeling all she felt, as disappointed as she was, as confused and jealous. My mother needed beauty to keep her going. There was just no other way for her. She could never get enough. I must be just like her, I thought, then I thought, no.

Drafts were seeping into the rooms, I started to notice. And after a while her words were drowned out by a certain tick-tick-ticking, loud as an orchestra of clocks. "Where is he?" she asked about my father. "Why doesn't he care?"

I knew that he cared.

"I know he can't drive, he doesn't have his chains on," she said.

Chains, I thought. Like the ones on the ghost in the *Christmas Carol* Mrs. Horn just read to us. That my father might own chains like those seemed completely true to me, in some way. But I didn't know why my mother would mention it now.

It was five o'clock, and I wanted to take Sweetie with me and watch *Sky King* with all my heart. It was about Penny, who had no mother, whose father saved somebody every week in his airplane. My mother had things to ask me, though. I tried, but I didn't know many answers. Finally she let me go, said I should "Go see what that Sidney creature left in the oven."

I walked to the back den where we kept the TV in a cabinet. I could hear the dizzy ticking outside as I went — it was stimulating, interesting, after the heaviness in the living room. I told myself I was happy. Very, very happy, in fact. School had let out early. There would be none tomorrow, everybody said.

I could see out those diamond-paned windows that the twilight was coming soon, and it was greenish. The twigs and buds on the nearest trees were gleaming. Icicles were forming on the eaves of the house. Everything seemed dipped in glass. Like varnishes, and glazes do to paintings, and china, the ice brought all the beauty out, made things more precious somehow. As if everything in the world were getting polished. So it would be prettier. I wanted to show my mother. But she'd asked me to look in the oven.

It sounded like a huge giant cracking his knuckles just beyond the back steps. The whole kitchen shook. A great thud, then.

The overhead light died. Out the window I saw our one apple tree, a pockmarked favorite of woodpeckers, had fallen. Aunt C had told me once it was half-dead. I thought of an old soldier keeling over in battle. Then I heard my father's voice, and ran to it.

He was standing in the first parlor, in front of my mother. His cloth coat had white flecks on it, and he had taken off his felt hat. He was medium tall, with a round head, his hair thin. He had been very good-looking ten years before, but his features were pliant and small, and the thickness of his face was taking over, his nose and eyes sinking in. Yet I still thought him then the handsomest man on earth.

He was talking to my mother about the country house, where my grandmother lived until she died. It was on a small farm that bordered Sweet Creek. We still owned it. We rented it out furnished when we could find a tenant. It was empty that fall, and next door to the county power station. The house was on the trunk line, he said. There was just one empty field standing between the power station and our house.

I didn't know what that was, the "trunk line." Ice and trunks made me think of Hannibal with his elephants, that Mrs. Horn had told us about.

The stove was gas there. There were fireplaces, he said. Our house in town had been modernized, and we had electric heat, so we had no hope here. We could cook there, he said. It is an idea, he said, but he wasn't sure it was a good one because of the roads. The farm was two miles outside of the city limits. He said we could be stranded out there, so, on balance, he wasn't sure.

"Let's go," my mother said. "Let's get out of here," in a tone that meant there was no way around it. And he didn't hesitate. He solemnly nodded. I saw that it seemed to fulfill a great wish that he had, that she would make a decision. That she would be the one whose wants were there for him to answer.

After stuffing the trunk of the old round blue Ford with blankets and towels and cans and baby clothes, we pulled out of the drive, and edged toward the darkening street. The wheels, which were where the chains were, it turned out, were chiming. I was in the back seat, looking at my mother's pale profile, her high, extraordinary brow.

The town was very dark, but not blue, instead, green — what is called phthalo green in a paint box. I felt a glory in it that night, an atraction — something close to excitement, but higher pitched, more rarefied.

There were no streetlights, and the only houses with any lights at all were those of poorer people on the outskirts of town, on the other side of Sycamore Street, the ones that still used kerosene. The streets were lovely, so dark, the only lights the ones glowing in the windows. They were old-fashioned, not rich and modern like us, and used propane in a tank to cook with, and coal, or heating oil, and they were all doing fine, my father pointed out as we drove by. "Mother, the irony of it," he said.

I was in the back, staring at the two of them: my father with his fading handsome face, my mother in her soft curls, and a beret — the only hat she had for the cold — set on her head at an angle, just so. I knew my mother could walk into a room and people would say in their hearts: somewhere there must be perfection in this world, this crumbling world, if creatures like her can still be produced. I knew they thought that, looking at her. I still thought it sometimes, too.

I wondered that night as we drove out there, how long I would have to wait on my beauty, my real beauty. How long I would have to wait to know my fate. But at the same time I could also wait forever, staring at my mother. I still found her irresistible, the way people who didn't know her found her. I fell in, under her spell. In one part of my heart, all I wanted in this life was to look at her and look at her and look at her. My own mother. I wouldn't want her to do anything, or say anything. Just to be there on view, the way she was in the front seat of the car, the ice-filtered glow from the last streetlamps illuminating her wide and open and porcelain face.

My father was also wearing his hat, so his eyes were obscured, but he turned once. It interested me how boyish he looked. He was addressing my mother as "Mother." Later, I would remember this ride out, and how it was the last ride like that anywhere, and I would recall the hope I still had, especially when my father called her "Mother." A boundless, whirling feeling, without end, without even the knowledge of an end. That is what I was feeling that night. That was the kind of thing I could still feel, directly.

When we got to the old house, my father unlocked the door and showed us into the foyer, and reached for the light. It came on, pinkish yellow, incandescent — this seemed so miraculous. My mother shouted out with actual, rare joy, "At last." Her mood heightened everything, the way a mother's mood was supposed to do.

Heaven, I believe I thought. This will be heaven. We can start over, fresh.

The old TV came on, I was delighted to see. A Zenith, a tiny screen, set up in a box with a phonograph on top, fabric across the speakers on the front.

My father went to the stove in the kitchen at the rear, turned the knob, tried to light the pilot. He sniffed. No gas. He went outside then, through the side door that led to a brick-paved mudroom. Coming back, he said the line into the house was still there. The gas must have been turned off. The last tenant hadn't been gone that long, so he was surprised.

"It's a valve, go turn it on — worry about the company later," my mother said. "It might freeze over by morning."

"Well where is it?" he asked her.

He must have known, somewhere, that she wouldn't know the answer to a question like that. But he listened to her. He needed to, he couldn't help himself.

"Somewhere in the ground by the road," she said. "It must be." It was a country place, set in at least a quarter if not half a mile from the highway. The property was ten acres across the front. The valve could be anywhere, but she was right, it was near the road, so the workmen could adjust it without driving up to the house.

By then my father was setting up an old hot plate beside the use-less stove. It was starting to heat, turn orange. He spread his palm above it. "Yes'm, right away, right this minute." But I knew he wasn't going out into the freezing dark. He was rebelling against her, finding his little outlet, I could see that.

My mother looked at me as if to say, "What's that about?" She seemed like anybody's mother, irritated by her husband's obsti-nacy, wanting allies. I thought her wonderful, at this moment. The way he did, I suppose.

We ate the roast we'd brought, what Sidney had cooked. This was fun, we were camping out. But we weren't going to start any fires in the fireplaces. There was no wood. My father said that was a job for the morning: flues to open, chimneys to look at, broken branches outside to chop. He seemed to be looking forward to these jobs. It was already eight thirty. We'd go to bed. The house was cold and not that many rooms had lamps. We put what supplies we had in the refrigerator and my father set Sweetie and me up in the back room, by the TV.

He seemed happy that night. He seemed so certain of us all that night. I was certain too, that we were fine, afloat. Or almost certain.

Then they went upstairs to the main bedroom.

I lay under a quilt for close to an hour. Sweetie beside me on the wide old couch, something from the nineteen forties. I was listening to the noise outside. We couldn't get any TV stations by then, just static. The show was outside. Branches breaking, shattering ice exactly like shattering glass, loud as a war in a movie. The noise was amazing, catastrophic. I was so tired I was dreaming awake, watching marching giants falling in the forest, one, then another, then another.

Later, in the patches of silence between the sounds of crashing trees, I heard them talking through the grates in the ceiling. I felt invaded. I didn't want to know those tones anymore. I could feel them like little claws in my chest. I shouldn't have been so happy, I chided myself. Then these things wouldn't hurt so much.

"You can just try, you can. You have tried. But I can see now," he said.

My mother said, "What do you think you can see?"

My father said, "That you are giving up. That you are going down. That you don't care."

"God, what else do I do but care?"

She did care, I thought. It wasn't easy for her, I thought.

"You are giving up," he told her again. "Why? Why?" pliant, begging. There was something in his tone I hadn't heard before. A sinking in, a sense that they were nearing the bottom, the falling off point.

I told myself the things I was always telling myself: that she was trying. She just wasn't that good at life. She had to learn. We were all going to show her. I tried to resurrect my optimism from a few hours before: perhaps not this fall, but tonight, surely tonight, we would start over, and she would learn. But then there was more crashing outside, more giants tumbling in the forest. They wouldn't stop. I couldn't stop them.

When I woke, sometime later, I didn't know how much later, the room had a strange glow to it. It had gotten very cold, and the sconce in the hall was off — it had been on when we went to bed. So the power was gone here, too. The night now was just the night. Our plan, her plan, was wrong, had failed.

Yet I couldn't help a certain, secret thrill in me. A curious thrill that didn't have anything to do with anybody else. The crashing had ceased. My parents weren't talking. Nobody was talking. The night was able to shut down one time, not bothered by all that buzzing, buzzing around. Talking, worrying, making plans, fixing what was wrong. Listening to see was someone crying or hurt, where Sidney was, where Sweetie was, who was angry, who was calm, was my father home yet. The empty quiet was precious to me. I couldn't hear anything but Sweetie's baby breathing. Which was all I wanted to hear, which was the best sound in the world.

I remembered years before, the first time I'd felt the same, or something like it. The calm, I mean. I must have been about six. This was before Aunt C. My mother had gone for a walk, but she hadn't come back. Not for hours. All afternoon, she was gone, and it was just Sidney and I in the house, and an everything-is-all-right kind of silence. I remember I sat in the parlor and looked at the clouds, how they passed over the sun, and every time one came, and the parlor darkened, I told myself the clouds were hours, visible, and gentle, and lumbering. We wondered where she was, Sidney and I did, but we were just wondering, in an idle, lilting, way. At other times we'd called my father, and let him know, and he'd gone out looking, but this time we didn't tell.

A deputy sheriff found her, brought her back like a stray. She had gone out of town past the tobacco fields south of Fayton, past the wooden homes with the pinwheels in the yards and the tar-paper-covered barns and shacks, the poor people's farms. He'd found her on a red clay bank beside a single lane road, he said.

Lying there in the emerald dark, I remembered how she looked when she was returned to us. Captured like a wild thing, coming in and stomping on the pleasure of the afternoon, destroying it. She didn't want to be with us, I knew it, even then.

I knew that living lacked mostly all savor for her, except when she was in one of her rages, or humming to Chopin, or when she first saw something beautiful. She especially liked things so extreme in their beauty you might call them spectacular or ugly. Beauty like that. Nothing else. Nothing in between. And nothing sentimental. Beauty did hold her. She was desolate without it. But mostly she did not find it. The kind she needed was very, very rare. Practically, you would think, impossible. Sometimes I think I have spent my whole life since trying to find that rare beauty for her, the kind she needed. She left me with her craving for it.

From above, I heard her say, "I will not. I won't." It seemed especially final to me.

And my father said, "Well then that does it."

And my heart sank. Heaven had been so close that night.

"Now, in the middle of the night?" she asked.

My father saying, "Yes, yes." He wanted to go back. He felt we'd be too isolated. Back to the house in town.

"I'd rather die," she said. "I would. I would rather die. Do you hear me?"

That is what she said. He heard her. So did I.

"I would rather die than go back to that house."

She said it three times.

When I got up about five, I could see my breath. Sweetie was still sleeping, making tiny baby snores. I went into the bathroom to try to flush, but it didn't work. Pipes frozen. So things were worse. I wrapped her in a blanket and found the room behind the kitchen, the one with the brick floor. From there, I looked out upon my grandmother's old formal garden, in that first light.

The sides of the garden were still defined by boxwoods not trimmed in years, but they grew very slowly, so they still held their shape. In the center was an oval bed of tall, hard-leafed camellias, pinker than any roses. Each was coated in ice, hard as china flowers. At the back there were two beds for bulbs with brick boundary walls two feet high, and beyond that, a stand of dwarf pines, weighed down by ice: green princes bowing for me, I thought.

Past all that, something spectacular. I could only catch a glimpse. Open land, which was the clearest blue-white, a dazzling splendor of ice. It was the brightest world I had ever seen. It was almost too bright to see. I felt pierced by the part of it that was visible, and I longed to go into it, to see it all.

I heard my mother then, coming up behind me. She said, "This place is lost. All the trees will have to come down. Come over here, look." She pointed out the grove of pecans at the back of the house, the ones with the sweetest meats. There used to be a whole line of them. A seventy-five-year-old grove, good bearers, now desperate amputees. She showed me the ugly mess, the destruction the storm had brought. I almost said to her, *but look at that field to the east, that pure field of ice. If you want to see something beautiful, you'll come see that, with me.*

I was going to say it. In fact, I think everything would have been different, this would be a very different story if I had said it, if she and I had taken a walk through it, but when she touched my shoulder, came near me with her tuberose scent, I pulled away. I cringed. I went looking for my father.

In the shallow fireplace in the downstairs parlor, using wood from freshly fallen trees, that was too wet, that bled reddish sticky sap, he was trying to start a fire, and getting nowhere. Sweetie was on the rag rug in front of the thing, having the last of the milk. "Well this is it," my mother said. "There is no way out."

She seemed to enjoy saying that, taunting him.

On the transistor radio I heard there was no school from way up in the mountains all the way to Myrtle. In the Piedmont of the state, in the stately part of the state — those dignified places as I thought of them then, with winding roads and slight hills — they had snow. Fayton didn't rate that. Fayton was just a federal disaster area.

Later on, my father found two men from a mile up the road to help him move the car, which had frozen where he'd parked it. They gave him some sand in bags, a great treasure, and they pried his Ford from the ice. He came in after, around ten, red in the face from his exertions, his long walk, to announce that he'd heard there was coal to be had, and that the main highway was passable.

He said he was taking me.

He never took me, before, like that.

It occurred to me that if I went somewhere with him, if I was alone with him, I might do the right thing for once and he would see me.

But also, I couldn't be gone so long without Sweetie.

"I might need some hands," he said to my mother, justifying himself. He had his sand, he said, and flattened cardboard boxes. He might need help putting these under the tires if we got stuck. For traction, he said, looking at me.

"You will not take Claire, are you mad?" my mother said. "All kinds of dangers are out there — power lines, treacherous streets, thieves."

"It's Fayton," he said. "What are you talking about? Let her come. Christ." The same rebellion from the night before.

"No I won't let you take her," she said.

"I am," he said, in the way that meant he was. He hardly ever used that tone with her, but there he used it. She shut up. I noticed that, and it satisfied something in me.

"Make her sit in the back seat," my mother said.

"Why?" he asked.

"It's safer when you have a wreck," she said.

He said fine, I would be in the back seat.

"It's okay. I'll stay," I said. "I'll stay." I didn't want to go without Sweetie.

"Listen, you come, Claire," he said. "Go get your car coat and some gloves, you have gloves?"

When I was in the back room, bundling up, my mother came to me and said, "Tell me what he does. Tell me where he goes. Who he talks to. He doesn't tell me. He lies. He always lies."

"Of course," I lied.

I checked on Sweetie before I left the house. She was sleeping under a thick quilt, on the floor in the parlor between pillows. I told myself she'd make it.

"If you are late, I'm calling the highway patrol," my mother proclaimed as we walked out the door. "Do you hear me?"

I heard her, but I didn't answer her. Neither did my father, which thrilled me.

When I got outside to trek toward the car, the frigid air bristled in my nostrils. There was an alarming, emergency scent in the air. Like a constant panic. I knew it was the sap of all the broken trees, especially the evergreens. The pine pitch, the smell of green. It was inescapable, it pounded in my head. It was a scent that said something, like that iron with lavender in Aunt C's room said something. *Pay attention. Don't drop your guard.*

As soon as he closed the door on my side, I wanted to climb out of the car, and go back to the house, because of Sweetie, but I wanted to be with him, too.

My father inspected the chains, which were still attached to the tires. And then he got in, and we started to roll, clanking along like escaped prisoners, slowly, noisily, around five miles an hour. In spite of all, I couldn't contain the joy of this ride, the thrill of taking off like that with him. The danger of it, too.

On the other side of the cinder block Pentecostal church, about a mile down the road, was a grocery. This was a country store beside a slaughterhouse I heard my mother once tell Sidney not to buy at. She said it wasn't clean like the IGA, but my father stopped there because, he said, "It's open. We can't be choosy." It was the first thing he'd said since we'd left the house.

I had never seen him grocery shop. I wished Sidney were with me. I thought she would laugh.

First he got cereal and paper towels and paper plates and a huge bag of boiled peanuts. I followed behind him and grabbed candy. This didn't bother him at all — he didn't seem to know that candy was different from food.

Then he thought of Sweetie, and he turned into the aisle with the little jars. Anything with a Gerber face on it, that goofy baby, he put it in the basket. She could eat food from the table now — this had been true for months, but I didn't say anything. It was amazing to watch what he did, how he thought. I was hardly ever alone with him, except at church, and there he never said anything but the prayers.

We swung by the meat, and he took a look: a butcher appeared and waved his hands back and forth. He meant to say, the cooler is out, forget about meat. I bent down toward it, and I knew at one whiff the contents were rotting.

My father went to the left, and grabbed some bags of dried beans. I wondered if he even knew what to do with poor people's food.

Someone said, "Well, Connor, remind you of the Depression?"

"Just the same," he said and a smile crossed his lips. "Except I can buy the butter beans."

His accent was thicker than normal, I noticed. He sounded like one of the boys at school who wore blue jeans, which were country. The boys I thought about.

We neared the back of the store. There must have been six or seven men sitting around smoking, by a stove that squatted in the middle of the floor, a stamped metal plate below it and another up at the ceiling where the pipe went through the roof. When I had been in this place once with Lily Stark and her family's maid, Pauline, the stove had been half-hidden by bread displays and potato chip racks, and covered with dust. But today it was resurrected, wiped down, and stoked with wood. The people around it were so hot they were sweaty.

I took a Baby Ruth and just started eating it. I prayed he wouldn't see. But then he did see, and it didn't matter to him. Not one bit. He was too distracted by the business around the stove. He knew everyone's name. He shook a few hands. They started in on practical matters: the coal, if there were enough on hand for all who needed it, and wood, who still sold wood in half cords, and could you get to the people with firewood in an old Chevrolet with chains.

I marveled at the sound of his voice, the way it moved around words when he talked to people, as if there was pleasure in them by nature alone. And at the way he cleared his throat to change the subject, the way he whispered something to an old man and made him grin. It occurred to me that if I hadn't been there with him, reminding him of his errand, he would have stayed until nightfall.

Someone with an apron told me I could wash down the candy I stole with milk. It was bound to spoil soon — I could have as much as I wanted, free. While I was getting a carton, I heard my father make a noise I'd never heard. I wasn't sure what was wrong with him. When I ran back — drinking from the spout like a common person, but I didn't care — I saw he was sitting beside an old man in overalls and rubber boots and he was laughing. It wasn't his high light laugh he did around Mother, the one he used for Jack Benny on TV. It was very deep. It was the warmest thing he had ever done in my presence. I sat on the floor and watched him listen to the old men who had storm stories and Depression stories and kept telling, over and over, versions of the same one — how one froze, how one starved, how one thawed, how some, not all, came out alive.

Finally, after I'd had a quart of milk and two Baby Ruths, and taken a few for the ride — and he'd filled up on peanuts he hadn't paid for yet, and wouldn't — he looked away, said we had to go. It was maybe three thirty. The cold was coming back to stay the night, we both could tell it. The sky was getting almost pink. Above that, a layer of green, hovering, as if in wait.

This time I got in the front seat. He forgot to tell me not to. I felt so special sitting there, next to him. I would feel that way with him many more times, all the rest of my girlhood. When I grew up, I held onto this specialness. It is very hard to let go of.

We drove slowly through the ways of the town. These were fresh, blue-green frozen paths, carved out of downed trees, draped power lines, between the old shoulders of ice-covered Fords and Dodges and Chryslers, parked or abandoned cars that hadn't been moved, and now couldn't be. It was strange to be rolling along when everything else was so still. To me the whole world had stopped so we could get a perfect view.

We came to a place I knew of but had never been to. Bryer's coal yard. He worked here once, as a boy, loading coal onto wagons, he said. He'd never told me about his boyhood before, I knew very little. Filthy work, he said, smiling.

There was a huge bonfire in the yard, and thirty or forty people were standing in a sort of line, on the white blue ice. There was the slightest dusting of snow underfoot, under the ice layer. I had never seen much real snow, so this was a thrill, another miracle. We were on the north side of town, the neighborhood between downtown and the old rail station that hardly saw a train anymore. But the train to Washington, D.C., still came through, the train Aunt C took.

I looked at the station, as we turned in and parked a good distance from the fire.

Nobody would let me go to see Aunt C off. Sidney held me back, told me my mother said Aunt C was a bad woman. Cheryl Ann went in a cab with her to the station, and then followed her right into the train car, sat her down, got her bags stored away. Aunt C was in so much pain, she screamed anytime anything touched her elbow, the one in the cast, Cheryl Ann told me later. Even if it were the softest thing that touched it — the headrest of the train seat, the conductor's sleeve, she winced.

My mother had broken Aunt C's arm in two places. She had torn the top of it almost out of the joint at the shoulder. Cheryl had told me. I knew that, but I didn't like to stay with it. But I did know it. I knew what she'd done to Sweetie, too, or tried to do. I was still the only person on earth who knew that.

It was easy to spot Sidney among the milling crowd, tall and elegant in her plaid coat with huge silver-colored buttons. I walked right over to her; I couldn't bear the thought she wasn't coming back. But then, when I was close to her — she looked so pretty, energized by the cold — I remembered what my mother told me, and I ordered myself to be vigilant.

"We will talk about yesterday," my father said. "When we come back. We aren't home. We're out at my mother's old place." It was then I realized it had been just yesterday that the storm came. It seemed forever ago. We had left one house, and settled into another, and I had so much hope, but then they had started in at it again, and my mother had said she would rather die. And now we were stranded, although for a few hours, my father and I had escaped. So many things to have happened. This had only been twenty-four hours, but it felt like a concentrate of my whole life, with a slightly happier ending than the one I used to foresee, the one right now, where I was in that coal yard with my father, him holding my hand, which was bare. For I had left my gloves in the car.

I felt very old looking back like this, grown-up, seeing things in some kind of perspective — and for a moment I believed I was going to have a new life, that must be the reason I saw everything as containing the signs, of coming toward a conclusion. It is a habit I still have — finding meanings in things that may not have them. I know it is dangerous to bury motives in every chance event, set them around in a story, waiting to explode. When in the first place, things happened, just happened. To come up with reasons for everything gives a single person too much power. And I have been trying to stop doing that.

The truth is, that afternoon, I also thought of my mother, and my mission. I know I looked at Sidney's face to see if she was in love with my father.

"You all gonna freeze out there?" Sidney said.

"Four fireplaces, coal, I don't think so," he said.

"Sweetie okay?" she asked me this. For of course, Sweetie.

"She's with her mother, she's fine," he said, clearing his voice. And in a certain way that was new I could feel the lie of it that he had to always tell, could see how it lowered his eyes, turned them darker, not so light gray. I felt horrible for him. I wanted to leave. We had to leave. I did realize that. Of course. This might be heaven, but we didn't live here. We were stranded out at that house. We were gathering coal to bring out to that house.

All through the frozen streets on the way home, I stared out at the stalled cars, like statues, under collapsed branches, covered in treacherous ice. I thought of what I wanted, which was to get home, but also to never go home, to stay with my father forever in town, and to get back and give Sweetie some of the milk I'd stolen, maybe a piece of a candy bar. I wanted so many different things, I wanted nothing. I didn't want to be anywhere. I wondered where I could go, wanting that. I opened the last Baby Ruth I had and started pulling the peanuts out of it, so Sweetie could eat it without choking. But in the cold of the car, my gloveless fingers were too stiff and the candy was too hard, and then it dropped on the floor by the front seat, and that seemed the most terrible thing I'd ever done, dropping that candy, taking this ride with my father. I never should have come. I was sure something had happened to Sweetie.

In the hall when we got there, my mother held a match up to his face, and then to mine, and said nothing. She was a wreck: her blonde hair matted, no lipstick, no eyebrow pencil. She frightened me. She was so mad she could spit.

It was bitter cold in the house by then. I could not believe we were inside. I looked around, immediately, for Sweetie. My father put the coal in the grate, in the shallow fireplace in the front parlor. He wadded up the grocery bags, and lit them.

Eventually, there were a few hot places in the room. I thought my mother's fury was over, she'd been silent so long. My father went upstairs to try to light another fireplace. My mother had forgotten about dinner, or had never had a thought of it. I got up to fetch the milk for Sweetie.

My mother followed me out into the hall, grabbed me by the arm. It wasn't gently. I felt my heart tighten, like a fist in a box.

"Tell me something," she said.

I tried to pull away.

"What did you and he talk about?" She was hard on me. She talked to me the way she talked to Sidney. She hadn't done that before.

"He used to work in the coal yard," I said. "He told me that. When he was a boy."

"What did he say about me?" she asked.

"Nothing." Knowing exactly how that would anger her. "Did he ever tell you that?"

"Say nothing, ma'am, who do you think you are talking to?" and for a moment her lips turned in, became very small. It was almost like a trick, how she made herself so ugly that night, "Why did you keep him so long? What did you tell him?"

"I didn't tell him anything. Ma'am," I said.

"I saw you riding in the front seat," she said.

"I wanted to see things," I said. I waited a very long time. Then I said what she wanted, "I'm sorry."

"You aren't sorry," she said. "You say ma'am you hear me? You have that right? Even when you are lying like a little bitch you say ma'am."

I waited again. Now my heart was moving around in my chest. It had come out of the box. I didn't say ma'am. I didn't say anything. I was against a wall, so she couldn't push me down. I thought of that.

"Well, Little Girl?" she said, mocking.

"Yes, ma'am," I said finally.

"You know what's good for you?" She raised her hand.

Something just as hard as her words was about to force itself out of my mouth. I didn't even know what it would be, only that it would be terrible, but my mother turned and stomped up the stairs, calling to my father, saying, "What you gonna do about that child how she talks back, Connor? Why in hell don't you do something ever? Do you have any idea what I have to live with? How spoiled she is?"

"What, Diana?" he said, in his coaxing way, in his way when he wanted to calm her. In his pliant, yearning way. He didn't say I was okay, or Sweetie. He didn't say he loved us. I thought he should have said so.

When she was gone, I was shaking.

I got the baby milk, and crawled under the thick afghan in the parlor, one my grandmother had made, and I pulled Sweetie in with me.

For a long time we lay on the settee, staring at the fire. Praying they would go to bed. I must have slept some. When I woke again the fire my father had made was only embers, and the parlor was getting too cold. I could hear car tires spinning on the ice. Out the parlor window, I saw my mother lit by the car's headlights. She was standing in transparent booties that covered her high-heeled shoes — the only boots she had — she had no practical clothes. She was in two coats — a fancy mohair, and over it, one of my father's for the rain. She was yelling at him, "What are you going to do then? What? You are leaving? You are going where?"

My father, "Don't you trust anybody?"

"Why don't you do something useful like turn on the gas? Find the valve, it's under a cover in the damn ground."

"I'm trying to get this thing parked. So I can get it out in the morning if it thaws. If we need something." The car wasn't moving. He was digging deep ice grooves under the tires. The grinding made a great noise, the engine revving up again and again, not getting anywhere. It was as if it were winding over and over and over again in my own body. I could not ignore it, or them.

That is why I decided to walk with Sweetie to the small mud-room on the other side of the kitchen. It was at the back of the chimney, not up on pillars like the rest of the house. There were two doors, opposite each other, the one to the outside, and the one that led to the kitchen. Both doors had glass lights. The screen doors were in a corner: they'd been taken down. Earlier that day, I had discovered it was warmer — the sun had come in, and heated the bricks on the floor, on the back of the chimney. In the morning there would be the beautiful view, the garden, first, and beyond it, the bright, brilliant field.

But I could still hear my parents outside. My father: "When have I ever not tried? When? To do the best by you? When? How?" My mother: "Turn it on, that's all I ask. You just want to get away. Take them, I don't care. GO."

There was that word in my consciousness. Gas. My mother had been yelling about gas, in the frozen yard with my father. "All right, all right, for Christ's sake," he shouted back. The car door slammed. She was silent. His steps, marching away in the noisy ice.

When I woke up the second time, I smelled fierce smoke. Then I saw it coming for us. I don't know why, but the feeling I had was not surprise. It was a kind of recognition, that was all: here it is, it has come, something like that.

Out of instinct, I covered Sweetie's nose. Then I crawled on the floor toward the doorway that went into the house. I could look through the kitchen down the corridor to the parlor. Smoke was creeping through the hallway toward us, flowing like a flood into the kitchen, and rising. I could see this because of the light of the fire, beyond, in the parlor. I didn't think to close the door to the smoke, to the kitchen. I left it standing open.

I stood to look out the glass lights of the door to the outside.

There I could see the garden. I tried to open it, but it was as if some pressure from beyond it held that door closed, some pressure ten times as strong as my body. I threw myself against it, over and over. Sweetie was on the floor by my feet, the smoke moving at us, rolling in from the kitchen.

I know I looked back and saw my mother's figure walking, not running, not crawling, in the hall beyond the kitchen. I heard her for the first time: "Sweetie? Claire? Where are you? Where did you go?"

Just as I was going to answer, a sweeping-in draft closed the door that led to her. And the outside door swung in and the glass panes in it crashed. The force that closed one door opened the other. The fire, pulling in air. Our way out was clear. I tumbled with Sweetie over the sill a few steps into the garden. Then I paused, and stood holding her.

She was limp and dear as a doll, and not on fire. And I was not on fire. We both could breathe.

I ran with her to the far end of the garden and put her down in one of the old flower beds with a brick border that would fence her in. Then I looked back and faced the house. All the downstairs rooms were involved; the parlor was burning. The kitchen was still all right, but darkening. The smoke cleared for a moment when the flames pulled up with the new air.

That's when I saw my mother a second time within. She was a shadow, stumbling. It was clear she didn't know the way out, or couldn't see her way to it. If she'd just get down on her knees, I remember thinking, she might have a chance. She is so proud, I remember thinking. I did think all those things, those normal things. *She won't crawl, and she should.*

Later they told me that happens in fires, people lose their minds in smoke, can't make a simple decision. That this can't be helped. No matter what they know. No matter who calls to them, tells them what to do.

But the fact which is mine, and always will be mine is this: she called me.

"Claire? I can't see. Connor? Claire!"

I felt something hitting my head and face just then: icicles melting off the trees above me in the fire's heat, crashing down on the frozen camellias, the coated boxwoods. Solid shards catching light, dazzling — crimson, cadmium, oranges, even flame-blues. Reflecting the fire, and cold, gloriously cold.

I didn't answer her.

Turning, ducking my head, I glimpsed the open field past the garden. The one that had been too bright to see in the morning. The moon was shining on it, and above I saw the clearest, most extraordinary sky. All was luminous and purple-blue. An entire field of ice, under a river of stars, and beyond it all, at the horizon, broken trees like brushstrokes, the slightest, whispered difference, between sky and earth. I bent down under the dwarf pines, took a few steps into that field, for it was beautiful. My mother would love to see this, I know I thought that. But then I thought something else: it belongs to me, just that gesture, that self-encompassing gesture, and is that evil or is it natural. I still don't know.

It felt as if the ice came up to me. It crept from the ground to my slippers, then to my calves in my leggings, then my nightdress and my car coat, and my grandmother's afghan that I was still gripping around my shoulders. It covered me, a transparent gleaming. And for a few moments, moments that mattered, of course, I could only stare out of the ice all round me, at the ice around me. I couldn't move, or save my mother, even call to her. I was just part of that cold place. And in some way, as just myself, I didn't actually exist. I had existed to save Sweetie, but Sweetie was saved, and now I was that pure beauty. As I remember it, I was filled with a mysterious calm, full of charm, of distance.

There was a kind of inevitability to things after: how my father came up to me later, wretched with all his sorrow, and fell on his knees, declared me for all intents and purposes, his new queen. How I saw he had to have one, and even pitied him. How we were in some ways happier, after, in our grief, than we had ever been with her. How that became our terrible secret.

I usually tell all this with an eye to its music, its hard, just, chords, its Chopin — I am still in that ice garden. It is once I turn, for I am still trying to, trying to have feeling in life the way other people do, that I lose that eye.

When I come back to myself and take a look, the house has no doors, no windows. It is only burning light, against the sky. A thing that can take a body whole, for fuel. A thing that could melt the trees, the ground, the sky, the stars, but it doesn't. I would rather die than resist, but I stay apart. At the same time I don't know what kind of girl I am saving. I believe my mother knows, she must know. I am part of her, and I want her to tell me.

But she is always out of reach. She is always in there, burning.

Moira Crone is the author of a novel and three books of stories, including *What Gets Into Us* (2006), where "The Ice Garden" also appears. She has received grants from the NEA, the Bunting Institute of Harvard-Radcliffe, and the ATLAS program of the Louisiana Board of Regents. Her stories have appeared in *The New Yorker, Mademoiselle, Image, Shenandoah,* and in many other magazines. "The Ice Garden" won the Faulkner Wisdom Prize for Novella in 2004. She lives in New Orleans and teaches at Louisiana State University in Baton Rouge, where she directed the writing program from 1997 through 2002. This is her fifth appearance in *New Stories from the South.*

*T*his story was slow to develop — at one time I had written a much longer version, which included a frame story about the character Claire, living in Boston, working as an artist, with a new baby of her own. She has a breakdown. It was in a novel that I worked on in the early nineties and finally turned into the cycle What Gets Into Us. *Parts of it are* *as old as my earliest attempts to write — I went through an ice storm like the one in the story when I was about fifteen, on a farm in Eastern North Carolina, and wrote those scenes when I was in college. In the end, it was a leap to create the voice of an adult who had endured such a mother and such a catastrophe — who could now tell this story of her younger self holding her baby sister in the light of the fire that ended her childhood. I think I had to reach a certain maturity and clarity to make that leap, to really trust that Claire could have survived, that we could hear her speak.*

Joshua Ferris

GHOST TOWN CHOIR

(from *Prairie Schooner*)

One day Lawton was with us at the picnic and the next day he came to the trailer with his boom box and sang along with "What Have You Got Planned Tonight, Diana?" Not a good song. She was trying to ignore him at the sink, but he was outside with his foot up on a milk crate and he was singing. She did the same she does when she's mad at me, threw dishes into the water and banged the pans around. But with Lawton, she also stuck up her middle finger in the window and the look on her face said it was the end of good times. *"What have you got planned tonight, Diana?"* he sang, though my mom's name is Sheryl. *"Would you consider lying in my arms?"* "He doesn't give a *fuck* what I have planned," she said to me. "He just wants his records back." I didn't know what was happening. She was working on about six months of dishes that I was finding all over for her, with things on them I never remembered eating. I found Ball jars under her bed. "What *is* this, Bob — a spatula? You can't let these things sit." "Mom," I said. "Why are you mad at Lawton?" She opened the window above the sink and her figurines fell into the water. "Because I got an expiration date on my stupidity!" she screamed at him. *"I love you more than ever now, Diana. I'm sure you're the reason I was born."* Then she popped the screen out. One after another, she threw at him all the things we eat on. All the Ball jars. She threw butter

97

knives. "Mom!" Then she moved to the doorway, to aim better. "Those are our dishes!" "I hate your ugly *face!*" she cried at him.

Lawton was laughing a little with his buckteeth. He did have an ugly face. His mustache moved like a centipede. He was watching the kitchen things collect all around him, until he got pelted on the collarbone with an I ♥ FLORIDA mug. He quit singing *like that* and just looked at her. Then he picked up his boom box and his milk crate and carried them away.

Dishes were all over the lawn. She walked out after he left and put everything in a lawn-care trash bag. Then she did the same with the dishes that were still inside the trailer. "What are we going to eat on?" I asked. One bowl with oatmeal left in it, she held it over the bag and the spoon stayed stuck. "Bob," she said. "You *have* to rinse."

He came back later that night, knocking on our windows and calling her bitch and cunt and slut and whore. She was going to give his records back till he did that. People were looking out from their doorways doing nothing, because only for like a murder does anyone in Big Coppitt Key call the police.

Day after she throw that mug at me, her boy come by early on with his balls and toys and all manner of adolescence, and I got to holler at him from the sofa, "You cain't come around here no more." "How come?" he says. "I like it here." "Go on," I tell him. "Sing it somewhere else." Then, don't even ask — just climbs the two cinderblock stairs, enters the trailer and sits on the recliner like it's family hour. I got to remind myself to put a door on. "You not hear me, boy?" Seems he don't when he goes grabbing for my lighter. The boy does not tire of grabbing. If it is colored or shaped, he is sure to take it up and give it a toss or a flick. "Can I light a cigarette for you?" he asks. "Give me that, son," I say. "You're gonna let the whole house on fire." I have more than once expressed to his momma the need for a restraint of some kind — be it medical, or an old-fashioned collar. "Where were you born?" he asks. "Where was I born?" I take a seat myself on the sofa and light up a cigarette. "I was born in Kentucky," I tell him, "or else I was born in Arkansas." "You don't know which one?" "Tough to say," I tell him, "when you got memories of them both." "Well is your first memory in Kentucky," he says, "or Arkansas?" "My first memory? Shit, that's easy — we'd gather on a porch, and somebody'd ask for a little Wild Bill Wills and the fiddler would take it from there." "Who's Wild Bill Wills?"

Who's Wild Bill Wills, he asks me. It's such ignorance as this reminds me just who it is I'm talking to. He's got a talent in life, and that's making people talk. "Listen, boy. You cain't hang out here no more. Your momma and me, we're done." "But how come I can't come by?" he asks. "'Cause that's just what happens, son, when a man tangles up with a woman," I say. "Shit gets lost." "What gets lost?" he asks. "Half the time it's things," I tell him, "other times it's people." "What have you lost?" "In my life? To a woman? Too much to count." "Like what, though?" he asks. "Like a two-thousand-dollar ten-gallon hat, for one," I tell him. "Gal's name was Cherie." "What else?" "Three dogs, just about." "Three dogs?" "I also lost my fourteen-karat gold belt buckle I got from the Cowboy Hall of Fame. Lost it to a woman cain't even remember her name." "How did you lose *dogs*?" he wants to know. I reach out and lift him up by the scrawny arms.

"You were her cousin," I tell him, depositing his ass on the first stair, "then I might allow you to hang out down here from time to time, providing you had beer. But she shit in her own nest when she had you, and I cain't stand the smell of it. So go on, get out."

Right after Lawton came over calling her names, she started to clean like with a ball of fire up her butt. Since the last time she cleaned, it had been about six months. She started in the bathroom. She had on her big blue plastic gloves. "I'm sick of throwing away men's combs," she said. "I'm beginning to believe a free comb is about all they have to offer." When she got to the toilet bowl, she said, "Look at this. I'll be happy when it's just your hairs and my hairs again. There's nothing more nasty than a man's hairs." She reached out and turned the water on in the sink. "Can you think of a single man worth all these man hairs?" She showed me the sponge with the hairs on it. "The Cop," I said. "The Cop?" she said. "How do you even remember him? Only thing I remember about him was that he wasn't worth a single one of these man hairs." She ran the sponge under the water. "I liked Lawton." "Lawton? Good lord," she said. "How could you like Lawton?" "He has good arm veins," I said. "And he was a cowboy." She stopped cleaning for a minute and looked at me. "A cowboy? What ever made him a cowboy?" "I've seen his card," I said. "What card is that?" "His Cowboy Hall of Fame card. He keeps it in his wallet." She went back to cleaning. "Bob, you fall for what a man says easy as I do, and with about as little sense. Let me tell you something," she said. She stopped cleaning and took her gloves off. She grabbed my arms. "There's three things that man's done in his life approximating success." She let go of my arms so she could count off on her fingers. "He kicked dope, one. He won a paternity suit. And he switched to low-tar. Those are his three successes. Sure as shit he's no cowboy."

She stood up and went into the living room, even though the bathroom wasn't but half clean. She lifted all the sofa cushions and started collecting things. She pulled out three quarters, a fish stick, and a bottle of baby aspirin. I wanted the quarters for myself. Then she moved around the room, picking up things from the floor and putting it all into a lawn-care trash bag, including some of my stuff. "Mom, those are my tennis shoes." "Can I ask you please why I pay you an allowance?" she asked. "Take a look around, Bob. Does this place look clean to you?" She swooped down and came up with a tube sock and shook it at me. "Can't you at least put your stuff away?" "That's not mine," I said. "I don't have that big a foot." She considered it for a while before putting it in the bag. Then she moved over to Lawton's records. There were three yel-low milk crates full. She took up a whole handful from one of the crates and put them in the lawn-care trash bag. "Mom, you can't throw those away." She heard that and swirled around fast. "Why do you stick up for him?" she asked me. "Why stick up for a man that won't even throw a Frisbee with you at a picnic, on account of the schedule of beer he's trying to keep to?" "You can't throw them away," I said. "Then he shouldn't come by calling people names," she said. She was throwing them all in now. "You heard those names he was calling me." "But Mom, they're his life." She picked up the lawn-care trash bag, and the record corners stretched out the plastic. "If these records are his life," she said, "then there's no better place for them than the dumpster, is there?"

Later on I snuck out and took them out where she put them in the dumpster and all together they were heavy. I put them on my crappy wagon I gotta pull with a string because the handle broke. Each record was about a hundred years old. He must have had a total of like three hundred. I pulled the wagon past the playground that's been about a foot underwater since the end of the hurricanes, over the chicken bones and cigarette butts that were mixed in with the wood chips, and into the forest. It wasn't really a forest, more like a hundred trees. That was where my fort was. It was just some plywood nailed together, but that was where I took everything anybody ever left behind. She'd throw it away and I'd rescue it, all their stuff, like belts, and aftershave, and old pocketknives, and packs and packs of cigarettes. She'd say, "I'm beginning to think a half a pack of cigarettes is about all they have to offer," and then she'd put it in a lawn-care trash bag. I wondered did they know about the cigarettes they'd never finish? Did they think, Yep, this is the pack I'll leave behind in that old trailer? I wondered. Sometimes I'd put on some of their aftershave, and then I'd forget about it and go home, and when she came home from work that night, she'd look around and say, "Somebody stop by today?"

I took Lawton's records off my wagon and set them in the corner of the fort. I could almost smell him on them. The one I picked off the top was called *Ghost Town Choir*, by Bluford Tucker and the Abandon Boys. I bet if I looked long enough I could find one Lawton sang on. I didn't want to go home, I wanted to go over to Lawton's. I didn't care that she didn't want me over there, or him either. Whenever he finished a cigarette, he just opened the oven door and threw it in. He *never* cleaned.

The boy come by holding something behind his back. I cain't go but ten feet in any direction for the size of the trailer, but I try to ignore him best I can. "Believe it or not, boy, I got no time for games," I tell him. Not but three seconds later he jumps up on the second stair holding a record album before himself like it's proof of his existence on earth. "What you got there?" I ask, which he takes to mean as an invitation in. "Yeah, shit. Make yourself at home." Trying to get a little tequila in me before I have to see anyone, most of all him. But when he hands it to me, for what he's got there, I could just about hug his head.

"I got this for you," he says.

"I damn well see that," I say, taking it. *Ghost Town Choir* by Bluford Tucker and them old Abandon Boys. Sure is beautiful. Beat to hell, cover art damn near rubbed off. But a dime to a dollar it still sings pretty. "Where'd you get it?" "Stole it from my mom." "Well you done good, didn't you?" "I tried," he says. "No, no, son, it's good. Shit, man needs his music." I take it with me over to the player. "Man's life depends on his music. Without the one, you might as well give the other six months." And I was happy to see it again, was eager for the sounds that are familiar and reassuring, and didn't even mind that the boy was there — until I take the record out and it becomes clear somebody's been fucking with my slip covers. "Where s the slip cover?" I ask him. He's got on the same distracted look as his mother's, the one that says you're speaking music again Lawton and I don't speak music. "All my records have slip covers, see. Keeps them from getting scratched all to hell. Where's this one's slip cover?" He don't say a damn thing — first time he's ever been silent. "You nervous, boy? You been fucking with my slip covers?" "No." "Must be your mother, then." "No," he says. "Then how do you explain it?" "Maybe you forgot to put it back on, last time you listened to it." "Now that is highly unlikely," I say. Just ignores me.

Next thing you know, he's standing over the player right next to me, breathing ugly. "Not too close, now," I say, backing his ass up with a forearm. But you can't stop him, soon enough he's right there again. "It's really nice," he says. "Is it expensive?" "Now don't tell nobody about it till I get that door on. Last thing I need is them crackheads at the 7-Eleven prowling around." "It looks like it's worth about a thousand dollars," he says. I give that a simple reply: "Does, don't it." I poise that pretty disk over the revolution rod, trying to line it up with the hole. "Can I put it on?" He's got his hands ready. "Hey hey ho," I tell him. "Only two people in this world get to use this machine, and that's myself and I. On occasion, I let me use it. I catch you so much as blowing the dust off, I'll turn your ankles inside out." He watches it fall on the slip mat and go spinning, set in orbit, like all things celestial. That's music, right there. A highlight in an otherwise low life. "Lawton," he says. "What happened between you and my mom?" I proffer the universal sign for shut your mouth now, son. "When you get a little bit of your music back with you," I tell him, "it's time just to listen."

When I got home she was pulling up the kitchen floor. She had on her tool belt, and about a hundred tools were everywhere except for in her tool belt, and her bangs were sticking to her forehead like how they do when she cleans. About half the floor had been peeled away. "Mom, what are you doing?" "What does it look like?" she asked, without looking up. "Okay, but why?" "Because it's brown," she said. I didn't understand. She looked up finally and swept her hand across the trailer. "Just look around you, Bob," she said. "Everything's so fucking brown. Aren't you sick of it?" I didn't know what she meant other than the TV and the lamps. And the fridge was brown. And the carpet. I guess I never noticed before how much brown we had with us in that trailer. "How come you don't like brown?" I asked. Then she pulled up the floor really hard with some kind of gripper tool. Her face was scrunched up from it. That strip tore like saltwater taffy all the way across the floor to the carpet. Then she breathed.

"Brown," she said, leaning back on her knees, "is the color of men." She started to count off on her fingers again. "Brown smiles, because their teeth are brown. Brown mustaches from their tobacco. Brown penises swinging all over the place, standing up to say hi under the brown sheets. I'm sick of those fucking sheets, too," she said. "They're going. We're starting all over again at the Wal-Mart."

I went out to play in my fort, and when I came home, she had painted some of the house. I went in for some bologna, and my hand came back all cold and wet and white. She was at the kitchen sink, cleaning off the paintbrushes. "Oh, Bob," she said. "I just finished with that. Now look what you've done." "Mom," I said. "You painted the fridge?" She took one of the paintbrushes and smoothed out the handle of the fridge where my handprint was. "Why'd you paint the fridge?" I asked. "Weren't you sick of putting your food in a cold turd?" she asked. "Don't you want a fridge that's white, like in the commercials?" I looked at it up close. It looked dirty still because the brown showed through the new paint. "Don't you ever just get sick of your old life?" she asked me. "Don't you ever want change? Even if it's just a color? Just some stupid change?"

"Mom," I said. "The handle's dripping."

He come by the next day with some manner of athletic equipment, what looks to be a basketball, though I'm no such expert. I've given up by now trying to keep him out. He starts in again on his new favorite topic of conversation. "Didn't you like her?" he asks. "Things about her I liked." "Like what?" "Well, let's see," I say, firing a new cigarette off the cherry of the old. "Your momma's a smoker. I like that about a woman. Appreciates a beer now and again. She, uh, hmmm . . . she's handy, on account of being a roofer. I did like that. Liked to see her in that pair of knee pads." "So if you liked her so much, what happened?" "Some things I didn't like about her." "Like what?" "Like what's that ball you got there?" I ask him.

The boy's treatment of his basketball is more like what you'd expect from a rare coin dealer, how he holds it with just his fingertips. "It's signed by Larry Bird," he tells me. "Larry who?" "You don't know Larry Bird? He's a basketball player." "I no longer follow basketball," I tell him. "Haven't followed basketball since old Catfish Hunter left the Majors." "You can see it," he says, "if you be careful." He hands me the ball and I consider giving it a dirty bounce, right on the ink. "Looks like a forgery to me," I tell him. He grabs at it. I make him wrestle for it. "Looks like Henry Turd," I say. "Give it back! A ball's round!" "Where'd you get it?" "My dad gave it to me. Give it back! A ball's round, it isn't easy signing." "How'd your dad ever get Henry Turd to sign you a ball?" "Give it back!" he says. First thing he does when he gets it back is pin it between his arm and body so as to hide the signature. "I want you to tell me something and be honest," he says. "What was it you didn't like about my mom?" "Same thing I don't like about you, boy. All the goddamn questions."

"No, what really?" he says.

"Thing I dislike most about your momma is," I tell him honest, "she's got all my goddamn records."

That night my mom and me watched some TV on the pull-out sofa. That was where I slept. Sometimes she fell asleep there, and I took her bed in the one bedroom. "Mom," I said, "what's for dinner?" "I'm too tired, Bob," she said. "Take my purse and go up to the Citgo." "I'm sick of hot dogs." "They got burritos." "I'm sick of damn burritos." "Hey," she said. "Shhhh. Watch your mouth."

It was too late at night to be cussing, she thought. She thought late at night was when God heard us.

I got up and handed her her purse, so she could give me money for the Citgo. "How come you didn't marry Lawton?" I asked. "Marry Lawton?" She said it like I was crazy. "But how come?" "Marry Lawton," she said, this time like I had said something sad. "I don't know, Bob. Probably because of the astrological charts." "No, really. How come?" "Because I'm a bitch," she said finally.

"And he's a son of a bitch. And that combination never works." "Do you think he's a good singer at least?" I asked. "Bob, I told you," she said. "No more hanging out with Lawton. You hear me? No more going down to his trailer. He don't want you any more than I want him." She rummaged around for awhile, pulling out makeup. "But do you?" I asked. "Do I what?" She put on some of her lipstick. "Think he's a good singer," I said. "That's all he ever did," she said, mushing her lips together, "was sing his one sad song." She put her lipstick back in the purse and set the purse on the ground. She forgot to give me Citgo money. "But did you like it when he sang?" I asked. "It was singing," she said. She picked up the remote. "So you did, then? You did like it?" "It's about the worse voice you ever heard, Bob," she said, turning to look at me. "But it was still singing."

Next day he come by with a handful more records and asks me if I won't play a couple for him. "How come you like music so much?" he asks. I'm over by the player with the new albums he brought me. "How come you like basketball?" I ask him. "There are just some things a man likes. I had some of these albums since I was a boy. Connects me to memories, I guess." "What kind of memories?" "Memories of my momma. Other memories." "Memories of your dad?" "Had a couple reminded me of my dad, till they got burned up in a fire." "How did that happen?" he asks. "I set a match to them." "You didn't like your dad?" "Come over here, boy. Let me give you your first lesson in how to be an American." And for the next hour I tried to teach him what's a fiddler's song and what's a slide guitar and how to close your eyes and give yourself over to it so the voice can sneak up on you at a moment you never imagined, and how it can damn near make you forget the four walls you're in. Most times he sat there looking for what he could pick up and flick or spin or whatever, but he got one-fourth of my talk, I expect. Toward the end, he says, "My mom likes the way you sing." I look over at him. "Is that right?" "Yeah," he says. "She thinks you got a good voice." "Now as far as I could ever tell," I begin, but I stop short of saying his momma does not give a *shit* about this voice or the other. "Well you tell your momma that hillbilly music don't require you to have a good voice. You tell her with hillbilly music, a broken voice does you much better." "Have you ever sang on any record?" he asks. "What do you mean? You mean on a recording?" "I don't know," he says. "What record album do you have in mind?" I ask. "I don't know," he says. Just throws up a shrug and waits for an answer. "On a couple I did," I tell him. "A couple record albums. How else you think I got into the Cowboy Hall of Fame?" "If you love your records so much," he asks, "how come you left them over at our house?" I don't know what to tell the boy. "I forgot about them, momentarily," I say. "But they're your life," he says. And I agree they are. "But I got distracted," I tell him. "My mind was on other things." "Like what?"

Like his momma, for one. I wanted to give her something to listen to, on the occasion we might be sitting around together, enjoying ourselves. But she didn't care all that much for music. That's how you know she ain't gonna last, when a woman don't care about the finer things. "Did you love her?" he asks. "You never let up, do you, son?" "But did you?" That's when I decide hell, what's the point in not telling it straight? "In a way I did," I say. "And for a time. But not anymore." "How come?" "How come? Because she's got my records. And she's fucking with my slip covers." "But I'm bringing them over." "Three at a time don't cut it." "How many do you want?" "Every damn one," I say. "Okay," he says. "I'll bring you every one."

Then she came home in a truck I'd never seen before, with two thin blue stripes and one thick one that went all the way around it. Instead of a gate, there was a bungee cord that was supposed to keep stuff in, I guess. There were some empty boxes in back, and she asked me to help carry them in. "Mom, where's your car?" She went inside without answering. When I went in with her I asked her again. "I sold it," she said. "How come?" "'Cause I was sick of it. Weren't you sick of it?" "I liked it," I said. "It had air-conditioning."

"I thought we'd be more like cowboys," she said, "driving a truck around. I know how much you like cowboys." She opened the cabinets in the kitchen and started packing things away inside the boxes. "Bob, will you ever eat these Spirals & Cheese?" she asked me. "Mom, are we moving again?" "I don't know, don't you want to?" "No," I said. "Don't you ever just want to get out of here?" "I don't want to move, Mom." "Come on," she said. "Won't it be fun? You can't like sleeping on that pull-out, anyway." She said that whenever she sleeps there, she wakes up with a sore back from the metal bar. "When we get to where we're going, I'll buy you a mattress with a box spring," she promised me. "But I don't want to move," I told her. "Why don't you, huh? Why should we stay?" "Because." "Because why?" "My fort," I said. "It's got all my stuff in it." "I'll build you a new one." "But what about how you just painted?" "Look at it," she said, pointing at the fridge. "I botched it. Looks like shit." "How come we always have to move?" I asked. She set the tuna cans down hard on the counter. "Because I hate this goddamn life," she said to me. "Don't you? Don't you hate living in the same place every day?" "But what about Lawton?" I ask. "What about him. Bob? What about Lawton? He's a piece of shit. And I told you I didn't want you hanging out down there." "Don't you want to know what he said about you?" "No more hanging out down there. You understand me?" "He said he loved you."

Just then, that's when Lawton came in swinging the aluminum bat.

I take it up from where it leans on the siding, the boy's bat, I figure, and come in there swinging so as to frighten her into submission. No intention of hurting nobody, none at all. "Where are my records, Sheryl Lynn?" I holler. First thing she does is throw a box of food at me. I manage to block it with what they call in the Majors a bunt. "Now don't throw shit at me or it's going to make me mad, Sheryl Lynn. I just want my goddamn records back." I clobber the floor again and feel the whole thing might just give way. The boy's there, though I can't recall how, exactly, maybe sitting on a stool. I remember those days myself, trying to figure what it is between two grown people and one of them's carrying a bat and the other's throwing food. Real soon he'd stand up for his momma, when he come of a certain age. But on this day he just looks back and forth at the two of us. "Go ahead," she hollers. "Go ahead, break everything. See if I give a *fuck*."

So I start with a big can of paint nearby and a good deal of it goes on the sofa where the boy sleeps. I hadn't given much thought to the prospect such a thing would erupt in all manner of white. Only afterwards did I consider what might have become of my albums had they been anywhere near. She come up and starts hitting on me with her fists. Something I always admired about her, she's feisty. *"Get out! Get the fuck out!"* "Where are my records, Sheryl Lynn?" *"I threw your goddamn bullshit away!"* she hollers, fists trying hard as they can. The boy jumps off the stool. "I have them, Lawton!" he shouts. "I have them!"

I don't remember much of anything after that but heading outside and aiming for the houseplants hanging from the trailer and not stopping till every bit of vase was broke and the soil was on the ground.

Next day he come by carrying the rest of them on a child's wagon down the path of wood chips. He pulls up and straightens them out every couple feet, careful so as not to let them spill off. I can see it from the window. As he comes on I feign a busyness by sitting down on the sofa. He stands there some time, not so much as stepping foot on the first stair, until I got no choice but to say, "Don't just stand in front of a man's castle. Liable to get shot doing that." "I brought the rest of them," he says.

A boy his size has some trial lifting a crate so heavy, but he does it, three times, from the wagon to the trailer.

"Believe it or not," I tell him, "I don't even want them anymore."

He climbs up the cinderblock stairs, grabs ahold of the first crate, and with his body pulls all them records across the linoleum, toward the player. All three crates, pulling them with such carefulness I can't think of what to say, except, "You must of learned your manners from your daddy." It might be that wasn't called for, another jab at his momma. It quick brought yesterday to mind, something I'd rather forget. He goes back and stands in the doorway, like making ready to leave. "You ain't coming in?" I ask him. "I can't stay," he says. "You just come by to drop them off?" He does nothing but stand there. "Imagine your momma don't want you spending too much time down here, is that right?" "How come you said you don't want your records anymore?" he asks.

"'Cause time's past," I tell him.

"What's that mean?"

"It means time's past. There was a time I wanted them, now that time's past. I'm not saying another word more till you come in here from that doorway and have a seat."

Reluctant, he comes sits on the edge of the recliner. "There you go." There's a lighter right there in front of him for him to pick up and flick, but he don't touch it. "So how come you don't want them anymore?" he says. "'Cause when you part from a woman, see," I explain to him, "it's what you do is you play your records. No better time for it. It's your company. But after a while, time passes, and so does the need for them."

"How come?" he asks.

"Because you get over the woman," I say.

It's a brooding look that comes over him on the recliner that I'd never seen before and has me rethinking. That I didn't want them was only a partial half-truth anyhow.

"But I suppose that's not the only time a man listens to them. Truth is you got to have your records around you. What if you get the calling to hear a particular selection? You haven't sung to a song in thirty years when it comes out at you from the church of old dead voices and you don't have much of a choice but to hunt it down and turn it on." "So you're glad you have them?" "I'm glad," I say. "Sure, I'm glad. That's me. Me glad." Not exactly the truth,

try as I might. "How about you? You glad?" "Me glad, too," says
the boy. He gets up off the recliner. It rocks but a single time on
account of the bad springs. He joins me on the sofa, picks up my
wallet, opens it, and points. "Can I have this?" he asks. And I have
never told the boy a truer thing. It's what happens when a man
tangles up with a woman. Shit just gets lost.

When I came home she was waiting for me in the truck. All the
boxes were in back, and they were full up and folded. She was just
sitting in there, waiting, but she didn't have the engine turned
on. "What you got there?" she asked. "Nothing." "I can see it's
something," she said. I showed it to her. "Cowboy Hall of Fame
card," she said. "Huh." She turned away and punched the lighter
in. "I thought I told you not to hang out down there." "I wasn't."
"Where'd you get it then?" "I was giving him his records back,"
I said.

I stood there looking at her till the lighter punched out, but she
didn't even have a cigarette to light. "Are you mad at me for giving
them back?" I asked.

She looked out the front window. "What's a cowboy," she said,
"without theme music."

Something was a little bit different with her hair. I reached
through the window and touched it. "How come you changed
it?" She grabbed for the rearview mirror. "I can't decide if I like it
or not. It's just highlights. Do you like it?" Really, she looked just
about the same to me. "It's pretty," I said. "Where are we going?"
"For a drive," she said. "Where to?" "Why do boys always have
destinations on their minds? Can't we just go for a drive?" "How
come the boxes are packed?" I asked. "Are we leaving?" "Just get
in, Bob."

I walked around. The passenger-side door wouldn't open, so I
knocked on the glass. She unlocked it, then tried to open it from
the inside. "Must be broke," she said. "Come around this side."
She opened the door for me and I crawled over her and slid across
the seat. "Mom, does this have air-conditioning?" She turned the

ignition. "How come it's not starting?" I asked. She kept turning the ignition and turning it, until she gave up. "It's just flooded," she said. "Give it a minute." She punched the cigarette lighter in again. "Think of us like cowboys in our new truck," she said. "Only difference is, we're not going into the sunset. I'm sick of the sunset, aren't you?" "Why don't you like the sunset?" I asked. The cigarette lighter popped out again. We sat there a long time.

––––––––––

Joshua Ferris is the author of the novel *Then We Came to the End*. His short fiction has appeared in *The Iowa Review, Best New American Voices,* and *Prairie Schooner*. He currently lives in Brooklyn.

KELLY CAMPBELL

In 1984, when I was nine years old, my family relocated to Cudjoe Key, Florida, roughly twenty miles east of Key West. On rides into Key West, my mom played a mix tape full of old country songs, numbers by Mel McDaniel and Don Williams and Johnny Paycheck, and we would pass Big Coppitt Key along the way. At the time, Big Coppitt seemed to be nothing but a tumbled-down shack an island wide. My mom let that tape roll over again and again, and there was no hope for us, my siblings and me, all great revilers of country music. But over the years the tape worked an alchemy that has to do with childhood and nostalgia, songs now lost to memory and the magic of mix tapes broken or forever misplaced, so that by the time I moved back to Illinois, to the Chicago suburbs where I attended high school, I was country where and when country was not cool. My mom shares only one quality with any of the characters in "Ghost Town Choir"—a love of country music, which I thank you, Mom, for passing on to me.

Tim Gautreaux

THE SAFE

(from *The Atlantic Monthly*)

When the safe came in, Alva's head was down sideways on his desk. When he heard the junkyard's box-bed truck grind through the main gate, he got up and stepped out of the office door, giving a hand signal for the driver to get up some speed so he could make it onto the scale through the slurry of mud, battery acid, cinders, burned insulation, asbestos, and grease. The tires pinwheeled in the olive-colored slop, and the truck waddled into place, dripping and sizzling. The crane operator swung an electromagnet over the scrap in the truck bed and began picking up dumps of cast-iron fragments, dropping them in a pile next to the yard's wracked fence. Alva checked an invoice and saw that this was another load from the demolished sewing-machine factory, tons of rusted-together treadles, fancy flywheels, ornate stands. The magnet crane finished its work in twenty minutes, and Alva, who owned the junkyard, would have returned to his nap, but he noticed that the truck was still squatting low. He watched the crane operator disconnect the magnet and attach a hook to the end of the cable. Little Dickie, the welder, got up into the truck's box to attach the cable to something. At Little Dickie's signal, the cable jerked taut, and the whole truck rose on its springs. An antique office safe, at least eight feet high and six feet wide, swung up into the sooty air.

The rambling brick sewing-machine factory had been out of business for sixty years, its huge inventory of parts and partially assembled machines rusting in heaps even after most of the buildings were taken over in the late forties by a tire-manufacturing plant. The new management jammed all the left-behind equipment into the owl-haunted foundry building and went about their business until their tire process became obsolete in the 1970s. A millworks took over the hulking factory but soon failed and was replaced by a warehousing firm, which gradually vacated the crumbling plant as roofs fell in and smokestacks tumbled across the storage lot startling only pigeons and rats. Finally, a chicken processor bought the site, and the owners decided to tear the factory down as quickly as possible and sell all the scrap metal to Alva. Hills of sewing-machine components, and the machinery that made them, had been coming in for two weeks. The truckload containing the safe was the last shipment.

Discarded safes showed up at the junkyard a few times a year, but this one was older and larger than most, a symbol of a substantial business, which Alva felt his own enterprise was not. He studied the safe's thick, arched legs that showed off their rusty iron lilies, and he noted the precisely cast rope design rising along the borders of the double doors. He was a man who enjoyed the artful details of things, even of objects he shipped daily to the smelter. The crane operator pulled a lever in his cab and the safe came down, slowly falling back and flattening a Chambers range. Alva walked over as Little Dickie climbed out of the truck box. The crane engine died, and they stood there, listening to the stressed porcelain popping off the range's shell.

Alva climbed up on the safe and tried the dial, which was pitted and green. It rotated with a gritty resistance. The safe looked as though it had been dug up, and it was slimed with a rusty wet clay. Alva hollered to the driver, "This thing hasn't been opened. Who told you to bring it on?"

The driver had only his right eye, so he turned his head severely in the truck window. "The head construction foreman hisself."

Alva stepped back to the ground and bobbed his boot toes in the mud a few times. "Hell, this thing might be full of diamonds."

The driver looked at him. "It was facedown in a pile with the rest of the junk. Foreman said you bought every piece of iron out there, including this thing."

"Well, I better call him."

"It was left behind in a sewing-machine factory. What could be in it?"

"That foreman didn't want to know?"

"He had thirty cement trucks lined up and ready to pour around where the safe was. Soon's I loaded up, he run me off."

"All right, then. Go on to the transmission shop." The truck slithered away toward Perdue Street, and Alva turned to the burner. "Open it up."

Little Dickie grabbed a cutting torch off a nearby tank dolly, then stopped to give the safe a look. "I don't think so."

"What?"

"Remember Larry Bourgeois?"

Alva crossed his arms. Larry had worked for the yard when Alva's father ran it. An old riveted safe came in one day, and when Larry started to cut it apart with a torch, it blew up. Larry and the door came down two blocks away. The safe had belonged to a construction firm and held a box of dynamite. "Ain't you curious?"

Little Dickie pressed the lever on his torch and let out a derisive spit of oxygen. "I'm curious about what's on TV tonight. I'm curious about what Sandra's gonna make for my supper."

Alva walked to his office, a cinder block cube, and pulled open its leprous steel door. The room's interior walls were lined with possibly functioning automobile starters, tractor transmissions, boiler valves, chain saws, bumper jacks, and one twin-floppy computer. Though he made good money, Alva was in no way proud of his business. He had started out working part-time for his father, intending to go on after high school to live in New Orleans — maybe take drafting, or even art lessons, since he loved to draw things — but somehow his hours had gotten longer, and then his father had passed away, leaving him with a business that nobody but Alva knew how to run. He looked out his dusty window at the taken-apart world of his scrap yard, a place where the creative process was reversed, where the nasty burnt-umber insides of everything spilled across his property.

His eyes fell on the safe. He thought about how his yard workers had no curiosity, no imagination, how too many people glanced at the surface of things and ignored what was inside. For the rest of the afternoon he tallied the scale sheets and figured his little payroll, but in the spaces between tasks he daydreamed about the insides of the safe, wondered how many times in its life it had been opened and shut. He closed his eyes and imagined himself inside the safe, some sort of invisible eye that saw the light-flashed face of the sewing-machine-factory employee who opened the door each day to retrieve patent drawings, payroll, gold leaf for the fancy embellishments on the machines' black-lacquered bodies.

That night at supper he sat with his wife, Donna, and his two daughters, René and Carrie. He told them about the safe, and René, a somber child of eight with a narrow head and watery eyes, stopped eating for a moment and said, "Maybe a ghost is inside."

Alva frowned, but was delighted by the way she was thinking. "Couldn't a ghost get out by just passing through the metal?"

René stabbed at her potato salad. "At school Sister Finnbarr says our souls can't get out of our bodies."

Her sister gave her a sharp look. "Oh, be quiet." Carrie was eleven, already pretty, and smarter than all of them, and Alva dreaded her growing up and leaving them behind like bits of her broken shell. "A ghost isn't a soul."

Alva avoided her eyes. "How do you know?"

Carrie made a little huffing noise against the roof of her mouth. "A soul is either inside you or it's in heaven or hell. It sure isn't hiding in some rusty safe sitting in a Louisiana junkyard."

"Then what's a ghost?" Alva asked.

René put up her hands, palms forward alongside her pale face, and began to sway from side to side while speaking in a wavering voice. "It's this smoky thing that drifts around and talks."

"You're crazy," her sister told her. "A ghost is something made up, like in funny books or movies." The girls began to bicker in rising complaints until their mother stopped them.

Donna put a hand on her husband's arm. "When you gonna open that thing up? It might have some money in it."

Alva noticed for the first time since he could remember that her brown eyes were bright, glistening under her sandy bangs. "There's probably nothing in it but drawings of sewing machines and stuff like that."

"Or the last payroll."

"Don't think so." Over the years he'd noticed that his wife's interest in him depended on how much money he brought home. Three years before, when the margin on copper was high, she was his best friend. Last year she'd cooled off a bit. "But there might be something interesting."

She took a swallow of iced tea and banged the glass down. "What's more interesting than money?"

He looked at her, wondering if she had finally defined herself. "I don't know. Maybe I'll find out." He glanced into the darkening backyard, where his yellow dog, Claude, sat placidly with a fore-paw planted on the back of a large toad. Claude was an older dog, vaguely like a golden retriever, but really just a yellow dog, which is what happens when every breed on earth is mixed up in the course of a hundred years. The animal had been a gift from Alva's brother, who worked for a federal agency. Claude had been trained to find bodies, but was never a stellar performer, so he'd been retrained to find drugs at airports, a task at which he excelled only too well. If he found marijuana, he tried to eat it all in a gulp.

The next morning, a yard crew was busy crushing all the old washing machines and dryers that had come in from the burned-out coin laundry at the edge of town. Snyder Problem, a big ex-preacher whose job it was to stand at an anvil and break bronze and copper out of the ferrous scrap, was cracking open rheostats with a maul when Alva walked by. Snyder was an old man, but his arms were still round and firm. The sleeves had been cut off his blue work shirt at the shoulders, and his biceps jumped each time the hammer fell against the anvil. It was a hot day, and sweat rolled off his bald head in beads. Alva couldn't imagine Snyder in a shiny suit addressing his congregation back in the days before his church burned down. "Seal welds," Snyder announced in his big preacher voice.

Alva stopped and looked over his shoulder. "What?"

"Me and Little Dickie was lookin' over that safe, and ever' door seam and joint on it is welded up with thin seal welds. Looks like Heliarc work, too, so that dates it."

"How's that?" Alva walked over and saw that the mud had dried on the doors and someone had swept it off with a broom.

"Heliarc wasn't used till the early forties." Snyder picked up a brass bibcock and broke the iron handle off with a sparking blow of his hammer. "Somebody welded it up about when the sewing folks went out of business. That big ol' thing's tight as a sardine can."

"What for?"

Snyder shook his head slowly and looked Alva in the eye. "It's a mystery, and I don't know if you want to solve it or not." He spat a dart in the safe's direction. "Some men would just get a backhoe and bury the thing."

"It's a safe, not a coffin."

Snyder picked a brass doorknob off the ground and shook the iron shaft out of it. "I *hope* it's a safe," he said.

Alva took a step back. "You're letting your imagination run away."

"I thought that's what a imagination was for. It didn't run away, it'd just be like seeing."

Alva looked at him for a long time. "I didn't think you thought like that."

Snyder waved his hammer toward the safe. "You got to use your imagination. You can make stuff with it, like ideas nobody never had before."

In the cluttered office, Little Dickie draped an arm around the watercooler jug, holding a triangular paper cup in his free hand. Alva pointed at him. "Seal welds, huh? You decided to burn off the hinges yet?"

Little Dickie shook his head, his long bronze-colored hair shining like a schoolgirl's. For a welder, he took uncommonly good care of it, always putting it in a ponytail when he was using a cutting torch. "Taking the hinges off won't help open that type. Big iron rods come out the door and pass into the frame. It's lying on its back, so it'd be easy to drill it and sniff at the hole to see if dynamite's in this one. It has a pretty plain smell."

Alva opened a rusty file cabinet's bottom drawer and pulled out a 5/8-inch tungsten drill bit. "Here. Put a hole in it, then."

By 11:30, by standing on the doors and taking turns with an enormous drill that smoked and spat sparks as it ran, Snyder and Little Dickie had managed to drill two holes in the safe, one in each door. A quarter-inch-thick iron skin covered a deep layer of cement backed by another plate of steel. Dickie's sinuses were smarting and running from all the dust caused by the drill, and he couldn't smell anything, so Snyder got down on all fours and put his big red nose close to one of the holes. Alva walked up behind him and watched.

Little Dickie hawked and spat as he wound up the big drill's cracked cord. He had been a foreman at the wire plant, Alva recalled, but had been let go because he couldn't do enough math. He was supposed to be working in the scrap yard temporarily, but he'd been on the payroll for three years now. Alva looked through the windows of a '78 Volare that Dickie had been cutting up, and thought about how his junkyard employees generally had fallen down the work ladder for one reason or another. The crane operator had been a trained mechanic, and even the old one-eyed truck driver had once made good money, back when he owned his own shrimp boat. Alva had always been what he was, going neither up nor down in fortune. He thought about how he was forty-five and in a small way envious of the men on his payroll because they at least had done something else in their lifetimes. He looked over at the wrecked and rusted chain link forming the west corner of the yard, where a bramble mountain concealed a heap of uncrushed car bodies and refrigerator doors. The thought that he might straighten the place up a bit crossed his mind and kept on going.

Snyder Problem stood up and blew his nose into a red shop cloth. "Just smells like a hundred-year-old safe to me. Dynamite has a sweet smell, maybe with some rubbing alcohol mixed in." He gave Little Dickie a look.

"I don't know," Little Dickie said. "I guess I could grind off those little seal welds to start with, if you want me to."

Alva looked at his wristwatch. "Lunchtime. We'll get on it when I come back at one."

His house was just down the street, and Donna had a hot lunch on the table for him for a change. She walked over from the stove and stood by the table. "How about that old safe? You get it open yet? We rich?"

He swallowed and looked past her out into the yard, where Claude's blond body mounded above a bed of asparagus fern. "If nothing is in it, will you start serving me a cold sandwich again?"

Donna didn't blink. "I might. It's the old hunter-gatherer thing. You bring home an ox, we eat ox. You bring home a little squirrel, that means slim pickings around here."

The analogy pleased him for some reason. "This is good stew."

"Thanks." She sat down across from him and began to eat. "You think I don't think much of you?"

"No," he lied, taking another bite. "But you know, I'm the junk-man."

"You're Alva." She pointed at him with her fork. "And *you're* the one who decided you're the junkman."

He thought about what she might mean. "You're saying I could be something else?"

She began wiping her plate with a pinch of white bread. "Only you can decide what you want to be."

"The junk business is all right, I guess, though sometimes I feel like I'm going about it wrong."

Looking out the window, she said, "I wouldn't worry about it too much. Be like Claude and take a nap."

When he finished eating, Alva stood up. "Where's his leash?"

"Hanging on the coat hook by the door. Why?"

"I'm going to take him down to the yard."

"What on earth for?" Donna put down her fork, alarmed. "You'll drop something on him."

"Naw. I just need his nose for a minute."

Snyder and Little Dickie were already back at work when Alva walked through the big yard gate, pulled along by Claude, who was panting, his long pink tongue dripping beads on the dirt.

"Hey, boy," Snyder said, holding out a thick, blackened hand. Claude put his nose in Snyder's palm, wondering at the paint, silicon, putty, zinc, cupric oxide, lime scale, and graphite he smelled there.

"I figured I'd let him get a sniff of the safe," Alva told the men. "See if he gives a reaction."

Little Dickie looked doubtfully at the dog. Claude sat and returned his steady gaze. "That the dog trained for dead bodies and dope?"

"Sort of."

Little Dickie extended his arm in a sweeping motion. "Well, be my guest."

Alva pulled the dog over to the safe and grabbed his collar, bringing his nose close to the door. At first Claude seemed uninterested, but then he put one nostril to the drilled hole and sniffed in short intakes, as though he were pumping his head full of air. He snuffed loudly, blowing his nose free, then smelled again, putting his forepaws on either side of the hole. He drew back, cocked his head sideways, and rolled his ears forward; then, raising his snout to the gray sky, he howled a long sorrowful note that flew over the fence and haunted the whole neighborhood.

Little Dickie took a step backward into a puddle of dark fluid leaking from a refrigerator compressor. "Damn. That yell could peel paint off a porch." Claude howled again and began scratching at the safe door, drawing scent from one hole and then the other.

Alva had never seen the dog express anything close to excitement, and for the past few years had considered him to be little more than a slow-moving lawn ornament. He was the kind of dog that didn't do tricks, didn't ask to be scratched or to be let in or out. He was a drifter dog, a brassy apparition noticed only when he was discovered on the sofa or found blocking the walkway to the mailbox. But now he was pulling the leash like a caught fish, dancing on the rusty safe's front like someone who's been told a relative is locked inside. He made so much noise and got so upset that Alva towed him over to the office and shut him in.

Snyder Problem rested a hip against his anvil. "Know what I think?"

"What?"

"If you call the chief of police and tell him what that dog did, he might could find someone to unlock the safe. Save you the price of a locksmith."

"What about the seal welds? A safecracker can't get past those."

"They're thin," Little Dickie said, reaching up to put a rubber band in his hair. "I can take them off with a angle grinder before the law gets here."

Alva looked back toward the office and could hear Claude's muffled barking. He didn't like the idea of bringing police into the yard. He lived in secret envy of their clean uniforms, nickel-plated decorations, and shiny boots, the possibility that one of them might be promoted to something. Claude began to howl like a wolf. "Tell the operator to get the crane and stand the thing up, then."

At first, the policeman who answered the phone was not interested, but when Alva explained how the dog had been trained, the receiver went dead for a minute, and then the chief of police came on the line. "What brand of safe is it?"

"It says *Sloss* on the knob. Why?"

"I'll tell that to Houston, the locksmith."

"I thought he was dead. You think he can open it?"

"Is it a real old safe?"

"Yes."

"That's his game."

In an hour the chief's cruiser pulled up, a black, freshly waxed Oldsmobile with an elaborate gold-leaf badge on the door. Alva saw that even the tires were shiny, and he pursed his lips. The chief was a short, balding man, and with him was Jack Houston, who slowly rose out of the passenger side and seemed so pained by a general arthritis that he stayed bent over, almost in a sitting position, as he walked around the hood.

"Hey, junkman," Jack Houston said.

"Mr. Houston." Alva took his soft hand and then the chief's big paw.

"You say your yellow dog smelled something he didn't like?" the chief asked.

"It's unusual for him to get upset."

The chief hitched up his gun belt. "I'll listen to a dog's opinion before that of most people I know."

Jack Houston looked around and seemed surprised at the big safe sitting upright under the yard's crane. "That thing ain't gonna topple over on me, is it?"

"It's stable where it is. The legs have sunk into the ground."

"If it fell on me, that'd be a sad end," he said, moving in his creaky bowlegged stride toward the safe. He pulled out a stetho-scope from his baggy khakis. "You say it's a Sloss?"

"Yessir."

"Is it marked on the door or the knob?"

They had walked up to the safe by then, and Houston was look-ing right at the knob. "Well?"

"It's on the knob there," Alva said, noticing the locksmith's milky eyes.

The old man touched the dial. "I need a spray can of brake-parts cleaner."

"I got some spray lube."

"Is it got the little plastic squirter?"

"Yessir."

"Then fetch it," Houston said, twisting the combination knob back and forth, trying to work the grit from under it. Alva re-turned with the spray. After Houston used all of it blasting behind the knob, he pitched the can and plugged the stethoscope into his hairy ears. He worked the dial for five minutes or so, then his head came up. "Damn it, turn off the crane engine." He looked over at the office. "That air condition, too." After a few minutes he pulled off his earpieces and stuffed the stethoscope into his pocket.

"Give up already?" the chief asked, his tongue fat in his cheek.

Houston chuckled. "Stethoscope's mostly for show. It don't tell much." He cracked his knuckles, clapped his hands, and hung his arms at his sides. "Got to let the blood build up in my finger-tips."

Alva looked around at the other men, who were waiting pa-tiently for something to happen, a treasure or a body to fall out onto the crushed battery casings and muck of the yard. "How'd you learn to crack safes?" For the moment at least, he envied the crippled and near-blind Jack Houston.

"Pressure," the old man said.

"What kind of pressure?"

"The pressure of eating a sandwich every day. Of paying the light bill. Sometimes more than that." He looked down, closed his eyes, and allowed only the very tips of his fingers to touch the dial. "One time a little four-year-old girl got in the Moeller safe down at the dime store, and damned if she didn't pull the door shut on herself. If you don't think that wasn't a scene, with me on my knees in the storeroom in August and her mother crying down my back while I'm trying to feel my way through those tamper-proof Moeller tumblers. It took so long we all knew she was dead, a pretty little girl with black hair and violet eyes. The daddy comes in and starts punching me in the back to hurry me up like I'm a balked mule, the Catholic priest is praying in Latin behind the safe, and here comes my young wife to stand to the side and look at me while I worked. The store manager offered me two hundred extra dollars to hurry me up, like a boxcar full of money would of done any good." He pulled his hand away and brushed his fingertips with a pale thumb.

Little Dickie went into a squat. "Well, what happened?"

"What happened? What you think happened? I got the door open and jerked her body out like a fish and gave her to Doc Prine. She was blue in the face and limp, but after a pretty scary while he brought her around, and when she opened her eyes I went from the stupidest ox in town to some kind of saint. You never heard such noise in your life."

"That was the Delarco girl?" Snyder Problem asked.

"It was. She grew up and is a school principal over in Pine Oil. Had four children and one of 'em's named Houston." He put his right hand on the dial and began to move it slowly.

"How long's this gonna take?" Alva asked.

Jack Houston closed his eyes. "Shut up and we'll see. This big nasty-looking baby was made in the 1800s. It's simple as a box of crackerjack. I'd as soon put my money in a cigar box behind the piano."

The men walked over to the entrance gate and stood in a little circle in the shade of a hackberry growing through a rotted tractor tire. "You know," the chief began, casting a long look around the yard, "I had a call or two about the rats living in this place."

Alva put a foot on an engine block. "You want me to talk to the rats?"

"No. But you could teach them to work a weed whacker."

Snyder guffawed. "Chief, you could loan us a couple prisoners to pull up the brush."

The men went back and forth like this, weaving a meaningless talk just to pass the time. They knew what they were doing, clouding their minds' eyes to the fact of what might be in the safe — some sign of murder, a crumbling body falling to gray ash as the air reached it, or sign of thievery, a stingy payroll never given out to the perhaps-starving laborers at the factory, or the stale air of nothingness, a sixty-year-old breath of fiscal shame and bankruptcy. They talked and tried not to think for an hour, moving with the ball of shade thrown down by the hackberry. At last, Jack Houston's voice came around a hill of tire rims: "I've got it."

They all walked slowly, as if toward a grisly diagnosis. Houston beckoned them with his thin arms. He turned to the safe door and spun the wheel that drew out the deadbolts from the frame. "Someone will have to pull the right door open for me. If there's another thin door inside, I'll have to deal with that one a few minutes."

Snyder stepped up and muscled open the squalling door, an antique and sweet air gliding past his face and on into the universe. He worked a lever and swung wide the other door. He saw no inner barrier, just a system of low metal shelves that stopped halfway up and then what appeared to be a large pile of sacks wedged into the remaining space. Snyder seemed disappointed. He cocked his head and stepped back. "I guess the dog was smelling those hemp sacks."

Little Dickie looked back at the office. "He got a snootful and thought he was in for a big buzz. Thought it was hashish."

Alva walked up and felt around in the sacks, which were whispery as dry hay. He turned to the men. "Something's inside the pile." He and Snyder pulled the sacks away, revealing a maple crate with dovetailed corners. The men slid it off its shelf and carried it into the office, where they placed it on the gray metal desk. The lid was nailed on, and Alva pried it up with a small crowbar. Inside the box he saw a layer of thick burgundy velvet cloth, which he unfolded as the men gathered around.

"Hey," the chief said, "it's made out of thick glass, whatever it is."

Snyder picked up the desk lamp and held it high. "It's a big glass dome with a handle on top. Kind of shaped like a suitcase. What's that in it?"

"Let's see." Alva pulled up on the handle, which was textured and also glass, and he raised something — what, he couldn't tell — out of the enveloping cloth. It was too close to see for a moment, heavy, two feet long and a foot wide. Snyder moved the crate to the floor with a wheeze, and Alva set the object on the desk where the crate had been. He stepped back.

The locksmith adjusted his glasses and leaned in. "Oh my gosh," he said. "Will you look at this."

The men bent down at the waist, hands on knees like school-boys, and studied the oblong cut-glass dome etched with the emblem of the Wiewasser Sewing Machine Company, a logo shaped like a shield, with a waterfall in the middle surrounded by alternating stars and lightning bolts and fine, careful crosshatching. All over the glass beyond the emblem's borders were hand-cut leaves, little women in Grecian dress walking up a mountain path leading to a tunnel formed by the leafy limbs of trees, and on the other side of the dome the etched water of a rock-studded stream ran before a long temple whose fluted pillars framed the figures of goddesses, their hands aloft to a sun crosshatched white. With a forefinger Alva traced the handle, a glass dolphin. On the two long sides, near the bottom, four gold-plated latch hooks swung on golden rivets in the glass. Inside the dome, the men began to comprehend an elegant sewing machine, antique, with a hand crank on the wheel. Alva slid the latches through their bright arcs, lifted off the dome, and placed it in the hollow place under his desk.

Little Dickie whistled. "Man, they coulda sewed a suit for the pope on this thing."

The base of the machine was shaped like a fiddleback, made of intricately cast and clear-lacquered brass. The edges stepped down in a triple ogee to four detailed turtle feet, each cast toenail bearing an amber jewel the size of a small kernel of corn. The feet planted themselves on a dark subbase of burled rosewood, showing a carved border of miniature ocean surf. "I know they didn't make them like this to sell," Alva said.

"Not hardly." The locksmith's face brightened in the machine's glow. "In the old days, there were international machinery expositions. Factories would make up special exhibit versions of their products. They'd go all out trying to best the other makers, no matter what it was they manufactured, even putting together fancy locomotives and giant mill engines, steam gauges that looked like religious items off an altar. This thing's gotta be a hundred years old."

"They used to crank them by hand?" Alva touched the flywheel's bone-white handle. "This an early plastic?"

The locksmith's eyes swam and focused. "Ivory. Do you see a pattern?"

Alva looked closer. "Little shallow fish scales. Helped you grab it, I guess."

Snyder straightened up and laughed. "It's a tree."

"Damned if it ain't," Little Dickie said. The machine's bright gildings placed star points in his eyes. "The whole body of the thing's like a bent-over tree."

Alva was gradually disheartened by the cleverness of the design. The main body of the machine was gold plated, indeed rising like a tree trunk and then leaning into an arch that ended in the machine's head, a flattened mass of bunched metal leaves. The presser foot and needle protruded from the bottom. The bark pattern Alva knew well — water oak, like the big one in his yard — but this metal tree showed sinewy ridges of gold. Out of the machine's leaf pattern stared the embedded garnet eyes of birds, squirrels, and toads hiding in the foliage. The casting and fine engraving showed the handiwork of what must have been the factory's most talented worker. Near the flywheel was the maker badge, a repeat of the design on the glass cover, but here the stars were inlaid with small diamond-cut rubies, and the lightning bolts were coated with alternating layers of gold and silver. The flywheel itself was gold plated and scalloped along the rim, with a serpentine row of hyacinth inlaid with ivory dyed apple green.

Alva felt belittled by the apparatus, as though his life were suddenly small and beside the point. He knew the feeling would pass after a while, but really, who could make this? He hardly understood how to look at it. Every surface was a surprise of coherent innovation. The men pointed and stared for fifteen minutes before the police chief motioned toward a small wishing well protruding from the lower frame of the machine, exclaiming, "The little crank and shaft for the well bucket is the bobbin winder!"

It was a good while before anyone thought about value, which even to the scrap men seemed beside the point. Little Dickie pushed back his hair and straightened up. "What's something like this worth?"

Snyder Problem closed one eye. "Even if someone would bust it up into scrap and jewelry, it'd bring a good bit."

Alva put two fingers on the flywheel handle and turned it around through a cycle. The machine made no sound, and the motion was as smooth as water pouring from a teapot. "Mr. Houston, who could appraise something like this?"

"Oh, everybody knows everything nowadays because of that Internet. Just get your wife to take a picture and e-mail it around to some antique dealers. You'll get a ballpark figure, anyway."

At the end of the day, after everyone had left, Alva sat in his desk chair and toured the sewing machine, touching the inlaid slide plates, the platinum tension adjustment, and, on the fiddleback base, the mosaic peacock inlaid with bars of amethyst. He even examined the machine's innards; the shuttle in the bottom was engraved with boat planks and false oarlocks. The machine's glow was warming, clarifying, and when Alva took his eyes away from it, he saw that the dingy office was subtly changed. He could see it for what it was.

Nearly every day, some of the men would come in during break and look through the glass at the machine where it rested on a low double file cabinet. His wife took photos and sent them to appraisers. She spent a great deal of time with the photography; in fact, she spent a whole afternoon shooting frame after frame, finally just sitting in front of the machine with her mouth open a little, as though exhausted by looking.

He'd walked up behind her and asked what she thought they ought to do with it.

"Well, I can't just sew curtains with this thing, can I?" She closed up her camera case. "But I'd hate to see it go."

Alva discovered that a small number of exhibition machines were in private collections, and those with semiprecious stones were worth upward of $10,000. One dealer responded with a letter, not just an e-mail, admitting that the machine was among the finest he'd seen, and could bring up to $19,000 at auction. Donna told Alva that it was up to him to decide whether or not to sell it, but his daughters wanted to bring it home and put it on the mantel-piece. What Alva did do, after the final appraisal came in, was have a beefed-up security system installed in his office so he could keep the sewing machine there. If the appraisals were right, he couldn't even purchase an average sedan with the proceeds. And what would $19,000 buy him that wouldn't turn to junk in ten years and wind up piled on the oily ground outside his office window.

He moved the dusty spare parts lining the room's walls to a storage shed and then painted the inside of the office antique white. He bought a new desk, chairs, and filing cabinets, as well as a rubber plant and brass lamps. Sometimes his daughters brought their friends to the yard to study the machine, and these were the first visits René and Carrie had ever made to their father's place of business. His wife, who'd always liked to sew, bought an expensive Italian machine and began a small alterations business; in her spare time she embroidered butterflies and name tags embedded in crests on his work shirts and even on Claude's soggy collar. One day she followed him back to work from his lunch break and filed his invoices for the week. Sitting in his padded chair, she looked over at the machine. "If you want, one of these days I could get some new velvet and make a dustcover for it with a little lifting strap on top. Run some embroidery around the bottom with gold thread."

He stepped next to the desk, followed her line of sight, and rubbed his chin. "Yeah. That'll work."

She reached out, put a forefinger through one of his belt loops, and gave it a tug. "I won't charge you hardly nothin'."

Over the next several weeks Alva began to tolerate the bookkeeping of the scrap yard. He paid a crew to pull up all the brush and saplings from the hills of twisted metal that had lain unexplored since his father's death, and he had the exposed junk crushed and shipped out in a railroad gondola. He graveled the yard. He put up silvery new fencing.

Snyder Problem would wipe his feet and come in during hot weather and linger at the watercooler next to the sewing machine, looking down on it where it rested in a cone of light cast by a brass floor lamp. When he was at his anvil he seemed somber and bored, hitting at the scrap as if he were angry with the steam gauges and toilet valves under his hammer. Two months after they had cracked the safe, Snyder began meeting with his old congregation members in the low neighborhood behind the sawmill, and during August he leased the empty Woodmen of the World hall and reopened his church there. Alva was surprised when Snyder told him he was leaving but not as surprised as when a month later Little Dickie departed for an exotic welding school in Dallas.

"What brought this on?" Alva asked Little Dickie, the day he gave notice.

He shrugged. "I don't know. I figure I can do better if I learn some real welding. You know, Heliarc, and some good pipe-joining technique."

"I guess I can give you a raise, if it'll change your mind."

"It's not all money," Little Dickie said, snapping his gate key down on the shiny desk.

"What then? I'm still not used to Snyder not being here."

"I just figure I can do better than burning stuff apart. Time to put some stuff together for a change."

In the next month Alva hired two new workers, mildly handicapped men provided by a federal program. His truck driver and crane operator stayed on, but they hardly ever came into the office. One or two times he saw them look briefly at the sewing machine, but he could tell they didn't understand what it was and that they thought it was some shiny plastic thing he'd bought on vacation in Gatlinburg, Tennessee.

About once a week, right before leaving the office in the evening, he'd lift Donna's sea-blue dustcover, which flowed like an expensive gown. He'd remove the cut-glass cover and turn the machine through a few cycles with its ivory handle. On one of these occasions, five months after he'd opened the safe, he bent down to examine the machine yet again and discovered that even the needle was engraved. The next day, he brought a magnifying glass from home and squinted at the script running along the lightning-silver shaft. It read ART STITCHES ALL.

He sat back in his chair, feeling as though his skull had become transparent, letting in a warm illumination he didn't comprehend any more than an animal standing in a winter's false dawn understands the physics of the sun. He had become satisfied in his business and wasn't sure why.

Alva turned and looked out of the office window at a hill of I beams cut into rust-red chunks, and he wondered for the first time about the steel mill where the pieces would be reborn into plates and coils and rolls. He used his imagination, and a long flowing image, such as on a running length of cloth, showed steel panels night-riding a railroad flatcar under streaking stars all the way across the Great Plains toward a factory where they would be stamped into automotive frames, surgical instruments, brackets for church bells, braces for thick glass shelves holding diamonds and pearls, and he felt that he was now part of this flowing upward toward all the things that people make. He reached down to re-place the dome, and the glass dolphin swam in his palm.

Tim Gautreaux's fourth book, *The Clearing,* is a historical novel set in the cypress swamps of Louisiana. His fiction has appeared in *The Atlantic Monthly, Harper's, Zoetrope, GQ,* and university textbooks. He taught creative writing for over thirty years and retired from Southeastern Louisiana University. He is currently working on a novel, set in the 1920s, about a quest for an abducted child.

I used to have a friend who worked in a junkyard, and I would visit him and we'd talk about all the odd stuff that came in since my last visit. I remember that there were several old safes sunk into the mud along a fence. Some of them came in unopened and stayed that way. While I was writing "The Safe," I realized that there was a mystery in the story that would be solved and that all the tension of the tale would go away when that happened. So I figured out another mystery to put into the safe, something that would keep the reader's imagination going, and that of the characters as well.

Allan Gurganus

FOURTEEN FEET OF WATER IN MY HOUSE

(from *Harper's*)

I.

My hometown flooded. Prediction, as usual, failed us. Come midnight I was the sixty-year-old owner of a river-view colonial, asleep on his second story. By 3:00 AM, the river was my first floor and wanted my second.

I kept an aluminum flatboat in the backyard; hadn't thought of the thing since last bass season. And yet it waked me like some good pet. Its prow kept beating gentle against my upstairs bedroom wall. Spooked, I set my bare white feet . . .

. . . into six inches of cold gritty water. I soon went headfirst out my highest window into a waiting boat. It was all so weird it felt natural.

A 1970 outboard motor, untouched for months, somehow sputtered to life. Starting off I felt fearless as a boy. No streetlamp worked. Just a crescent moon refolding over currents as I chugged between treetops.

"This is real," I told my Evinrude's racket. "Dad's house is ruined. — Boat seems fine though. People probably stranded . . ."

Our neighborhood is called "Riverside." No lie! Three-acre lots, four-car garages, one canoe dock per home. This happened September 15, 1999, a North Carolina hurricane named Floyd. Winds, threatened all afternoon, proved nothing much — the unexpected sneaked in after dark.

Tonight what first seemed silence became a million suckings, bubblings, gurgles. Instead of rain driving down, it was wetness, black, canceling us from underneath. Wind spares *some* things. Water, climbing, testing, claims them all.

At least in mid-September it wasn't too cold. I sounded like my late wife: Jean was always finding the glass half-full. Now everything was.

I motored our Alumi-craft from house to major house. I made all my usual walker's shortcuts but now at roof level.

The Hutchesons, half-dressed, on their third-floor turret, stood behind two barbecue grills blazing as signal pyres. I tied up to their Flemish-bond chimney, calling, "Ride, folks?"

"Well, well, our favorite insurance agent. We covered for 'acts of God'?" Hutch, wearing only polka-dot boxers, sounded amused. "Because just yesterday I paid a man twenty-six thousand for finally painting this doggone barn!" Hutch kept gesturing toward water, hinting with his arms that it should split like the Red Sea. Hutch laughed till he coughed. His wife gave me a look. Their teenage daughter said, "Even tonight, Dad, you talk only about money, Dad. You're sadder even than *this*," and she nodded toward our former neighborhood. We eased Hutch into my boat.

Familiar streets seemed the canals of Venice, and we always had right-of-way. Humidity sogged your clothes then shoes. The darkness smelled of transmission fluid and ginger lilies. There came roarings from the distance.

In a friend's sunken carport, his new Lexus acted mighty shorted-out: under five feet of green sludge, it ran every possible lighting combination, brights to dim to flashers, oddly beautiful, a dead loss. —Which neighbors were home, which home drowned?

We tacked by all three Alston boys paddling boogie boards,

wearing just Hawaiian swim trunks. They told us the mall was still above water, rescue trucks gathering there.

These kids had surfed since age six and now, splashing off no-place, called back to me, "Is this not *awe*some, man?" — For once, the word fit.

I might've shouted: "It's not some mountain stream you're swimming in. Our neighborhood's gone septic tank, kids." But they would all three learn this later. I just let it go. You can't moni-tor everything.

On top of a gazebo, Charlie Hague, four-time winner of our Top Golfer Cup, nursed the flame of his gold lighter. Kneeling in p.j.'s, he stared out of an avocado facial. Tonight Charlie'd actu-ally forgot his Hollywood handsomeness. Face caked green, the guy looked like some Fiji headhunter, especially once in my boat. The Hutchesons helped Charlie and his tough-talking new wife down into our sixteen-footer. The wife rose behind him, pressing one finger across her lips. For her, a flood was worth letting all of Riverside see her ex-Marine CEO primped for usual beauty rest. — Charlie, as my late wife called it, "moisturized."

Moisturize! Our mall lot, overlit by twelve generators, glowed the only brightness for whole square miles of night. Approached by boat, it looked like the shores of Heaven, I swear. I started dropping off my neighbors. Nine drowned bodies were already stretched beyond the dumpsters. Seven had been nonswimmers from the projects.

People said not to worry, refrigerated trucks were on the way.

II.

I just kept boating back for more. Excellent — staying busy. Since Jean died, aside from my golf-and-coffee pals, it'd been mostly me and the leading sports channels. One genius secretary pretty much ran my office. I had perfected Sitting on a Dock with Bourbon-and-Water, had brought that sport to new heights.

Overnight, I'd been shanghaied back to action. Odd, but losing everything made me feel decades younger. That couldn't last. (Adrenaline, always a good idea. The opposite of prediction!)

My neighborhood stood two stories deep in . . . well, in shit. Wasn't this some early practice-form of dying? And yet, at first at least, I felt alive because once more a little useful.

Didn't know quite how this mess had happened. But, some way, I knew exactly what to do.

Bart Tarlton waved a flashlight, signing I should boat on past, just leave them atop their carport roof. "Others will be by, and she's not . . . ready." He shined the beam on Caitlin, squatted, arranging soggy child-photographs across the roof's white gravel.

"Cait's got lots of Saran Wrap up here." Bart sounded sad. "She's busy sealing all of Carolyn's baby pictures. Keeps saying, 'First things first.' — Thanks for stopping, pal, but we've got to get through this part. Hell, where *else* are we going?" He shook his head. "Oh, and Mitch?" he hollered as we passed. "Sure glad your dad didn't live to see this. I know he thought the world of your house."

It amazed me that while his own wife sat playing dollhouse with baby photos, Bart would be imagining my father.

True, this would have re-killed Dad. In 1950 he overpaid for our stone manse, guaranteeing my boyhood social standing. On a street known for its brain surgeons and college presidents, my dad was manager of Milady's FootFair. To make the fierce down payment on our 1939 colonial, he would gladly kneel half a century before Riverside's worst female feet.

Dad's wish? That I run wild with our Episcopal rector's delinquent (if platinum blond) sons. We did shoot hoops; we raced our boats; we took bourbon to a science. Still, neighbors never called Dad anything but "Shoe" Connelly. "Proves I know my stock," the sweet guy smiled.

He titled our house "Shadowlawn"; painted its front door a

shiny tomato red. Pals forgave me. Being scrawny and funny, I knew to never claim much. Always sent these buddies home when Dad, back late from work, three vodkas in, started, "Best in town? I'd say young Diana du Pres has the toes of a Greek goddess. — Joy to see, touch, and serve."

Dawn came pink and gold but with many a wet and sorry sight. Numbers of drowned long-horned cattle — washed into town from where? These stacked up under bridges like something from the Wild West. And on top of a pile of such carcasses out near the underpass? Two live deer, a mother and baby, just stood grooming each other.

I heard, "Mister? Boat! Mister Boat!?" Soon I wrestled onboard two skinny water-treading black kids. They'd Australian-crawled clear from the projects. The weakest swimmer was looped within an inner tube he kept blowing up while kicking forward. Each tried shaking my hand as thanks, even while — with my bad back — I fought to pull them in. Water beaded like mercury across their thick hair. Kids were about fifteen and looked scared to death and we didn't talk much. I had a boat. They were in it now. Happy ending.

With them settled, I figured I'd go rescue a gal my age I've always liked. She'd probably be alone tonight: her dashing husband was two-timing her with his freckled college-boy "executive assistant." Every local knew except maybe my friend.

I sloshed toward her now: our generation's all-time Riverside glamourpuss. The face that launched . . . at least one bass boat. Hers were certainly the feet that kicked off my dad's praise. "White marble," he announced, as Mom and I gave each other steady looks. But Shoe Connelly was right, she was perfect. Unfair advantage in a town this small. I hated loving the very one my dad would want for me, for us. I lacked the looks, height, trust fund. Only had such access as Shoe'd overpaid for. (Dad would love see-

ing me tonight, boat at the ready, an oar in the boat, the beloved
ole coot, so naturalized he's colorless.)

And yet, even now, with me sogged and sixty, I still pictured my
ideal, stranded on her second-story balcony, wearing satin like her
"Juliet" in our school play. Figured I'd go muscular up a vine, then
bring her to my waiting gondola below, her satin frock pressed
damp within these brawny arms, etc., whatever. Pathetic. Still, I
aimed her way. — I *am* a widower now.

Churches, sunken as private homes, somehow looked sadder,
having once claimed more. At least their steeples gave every boater
bearings. As I motored past First Baptist's chromium upright, it
showed a thousand steel rivets, a fuselage of copper flashing. Each
steeple seemed just so much armor. Poking above our waterline,
every denomination insisted on itself.

In our Williamsburgy town, even the synagogue sports a steeple. Churches are often set face-to-face on corners opposite each
other, paired like fighting cocks. Could a Christopher Wren mina-
ret be long in coming? — Ours is a God-fearing community. Afraid
of what? Plagues? Wars? Floods?

Looking clear downtown, I saw just trees and steeples bristling
to the blue distance. And over all this, without form, and void,
news-channel helicopters getting great shots of poor people clawing up their chimneys waving bedsheets.

You didn't need to be a structural engineer to know that most
of our street's fine old homes were done for now. You let a house,
however well-made, stand in twenty feet of water for one week,
that's curtains. The mold alone will kill you ever afterward.

I sputtered past the Epsteins' pink stucco Spanish colonial, the
Murchesons' replica of Andrew Jackson's home, The Hermitage.
In its basement rec room I'd first felt a girl's breast, the left one
only, but enough aplenty to interest me in life. Now I banked
behind my dead wife's girlhood home. The breast in question

had not, I'm afraid, been Jean's. But, here among the camellias of her mother's formal garden, Jean and I married, June 1968. Now around our altar-pergola's Corinthian columns, sewage bobbled.

I chose not to Alumi-craft past *my* house. I recalled overhearing an old dowager say, "Those shanty Irish *would* shoehorn themselves into the biggest home right on the river." Photo albums were most of what I wanted, and my bronzed baby-bootie that Dad made much of. Those, stowed in the attic, might still be safe. But for now I had *peop*le here . . .

The boys sat discussing friends: "You think they got Lottie up on they roof? She say she couldn't be leaving them kids but, still . . . somebody bound to find them, maybe one these choppers? Could be, this here City Man, once he finishes gettin' his folks out, might could go on back, fetch Lottie and her kids . . . ?"

So my passengers saw me as a town employee paid to rescue them! Hmmm. That was okay, I guess, but strange. (Son of "Shoe," after all.) What had I expected, Life-Saving Merit Badge? Did it really change anything — being assumed? Till now hadn't that been pretty much my life's goal hereabouts?

Unlike the boys' pals, most of mine got rescued by first light. Other Riverside boaters, using personal canoes, Sailfishes, and paddle wheels, had hoisted neighbors off their butlers' quarters, SUV roofs, pin oaks, and from the head of at least one life-size bronze St. Francis. My bass boat had retrieved maybe thirty to the mall when we finally sloshed into the yard of the woman I have loved since age thirteen. (In fact, her left breast was my first breast, ever.)

Her Wright-style low-slung home seemed missing in action, but I saw she'd breaststroked toward the only sturdy vertical around. I found our town beauty treed like a wet raccoon.

Prediction so regularly fails me: For fifty years I've believed she was maybe meant as mine. Dad encouraged such faith. He thought our owning in Riverside outranked our lace-curtain Irish-ness, made us Lord Proprietors. Man never really guessed that "Shoe" is a servant's name. (I fought to keep it from him. Of that at least I'm proud.)

She'd been born rich with red hair and green eyes so you didn't know if you were coming or going. Seeing how I and six other boys from the cul-de-sac loved her, she had promoted her plainer sidekick for my attention. She offered me the girl who let her copy homework, who held her coat and laughed at her usual jokes, the gal Friday who personally delivered her sarcastic notebook-paper come-ons to us sad hopeful males. One such note, hand-brought, explained: *Jean here is smarter than I and looks-wise grows on people. She has scads more money than I'll get (even when Dad finally goes). And trust me, she loves you WAY more. Choose Jean, Mitch.* I stared into the fine if simple face of this love-note delivery girl. She could not know how its contents had just shifted her future and mine. "Return answer?" she, innocent, asked. — I smiled at her.

I kept that note for twenty years. A town beauty always makes such matches for her handmaids. And somehow I had done as told. Was Jean also just following orders? Dad, even knowing Jean's net worth to the dollar, still always treated her with fond pity.

And yet our marriage proved fairly lively, forty years. Not a love match, maybe, but . . . practical. We were really just best friends. I guessed at my own face's sketchy net worth. I'd really wanted to head North to college, where my brightness — or goodness, whatever — might get me noticed as more than the byproduct of flatfooted others.

My Jean had proved a wit, a "man's woman" regularly out snag-ging bass with me from this same boat. I had chosen well, at least, in picking the one who picked Jean *for* me.

The treed survivor's hair, this wet, had all but disappeared. Not since our thirteenth year had I ever caught her without benefit of makeup. Now aside from orange-nylon panties, poor thing was damp and bare as God made her. Coiled around a rough-barked pine tree, her white marble was curdled all over.

"Uh-oh. That old lady she butt naked," one kid observed.

"It's okay," I said. "I *know* her."

"Gosh, it's Mitch. And me hoping to be rescued by some handsome Yankee new to town. — But, hell, no secrets 'twixt old friends, hunh?"

"Diana," I nodded, as if greeting her at the club.

I had a tarp in my boat and soon wrapped her with it. Her lips were blue (the nipples also, truth be told). There have been years when I worried I still loved her more than my wry, quiet wife. This lady up the tree should've founded Flirters Anonymous. I'd been too good a loser in the long battle for her hand.

III.

What I remember best is how the flood confused or dignified our animals. Some little neighbor kids I ferried, they would have their Yorkie terriers wound in doll blankets or their tetchy Siamese cats along. I saw how it comforted even four-year-olds to take care of something still smaller than themselves. A dozen water moccasins tried crawling in the boat with us and had to be discouraged, but I couldn't bring myself to crush one with the oar. You'd just redirect them and hope they'd swim against some sturdy log.

A few birds were very noisy, as if sounding the alarm for all us other creatures, but most kept silent. They lined up along lower tree limbs, looking out and down like tourists.

The oddest things floated. A yellow high heel. An oil-painted photo, some bride and groom shown smearing cake across each other's laughing mouths, its wooden frame like a life preserver bobbing them along.

I felt more shocked by each dead drifting dog (a boxer, one beautiful collie), by all the swollen pigs and cows, by those clever living deer swimming here and there in a strange but mild-looking panic.

•••

By 8:30 AM, having found these kids and then Diana, I figured I had my boatful. Could reverse directions.

Doing a last hairpin curve over the former Shady Circle Drive twelve feet under, I thought I heard shouts. The kids stayed quiet if with teeth chattering. Though teenaged boys, they kept their arms around each other for sheer warmth. Diana sat hidden within tarp, silent as royalty, looking out at all the water hiding her old holy stomping ground. She rested, staring in a clear and noiseless sort of way that made me remember why I loved her.

The mall would have its bonfires, media, hot tomato soup. First I'd just swing back by, check if Cait Tarlton and her photo show had been saved.

Odd, it seemed that I, full of tidal surge myself, would *always* run this bass-boat shuttle out of our disaster. I liked the work, this leg-up shoe-clerk service. I felt relaxed in ways that might have been hysteria or gratitude or both. Water seeks its own level.

Without one real possession past my clothes, this motorboat, a wedding ring, I felt lightened, simplified. But also babyish, exposed. The damp fetus somehow sixty, out on good behavior. A nineteen-room house? Dad's idea. Marrying Jean? Some great notion of Diana's then Jean's then all of Riverside who loved us two sweet runts. "Good idea. Who else will they get? I think they're *cute* together."

Surely now I could finally move on.

We heard a terrible yodeling. It sounded pitiful but violent. I glanced back at my boy passengers. I could tell they dreaded what-ever sight such sounds would bring us.

I chugged across Hutcheson property, over Greta's beautiful knot garden spoilt in brown water beneath. At the corner of Carter and Shady Circle, in what was the front yard of some new doctor from Nash General, we came on two young golden retrievers.

Flailing, by now they were barely afloat. Dogs kept paddling in gulping circles, reduced to saving themselves by climbing up onto each other's backs. Nails and teeth of each had slashed the other bloody.

Seeing help, they howled and, spastic, flapping, angled to face us.

But what most struck us in the boat: Though water here easily went down fourteen feet, despite higher ground's being visible close by, these yellow dogs still made themselves swim — whimpering circles — right over their owner's yard. No wall, no street was visible, only drifting firewood and the dark free currents coursing everywhere. And yet both animals stayed put, treading the very water they were bloodying.

On a playground twenty feet away, they could have saved their lives and rested. Instead, as if assigned one jail cell, pets spasmed back and forth, to and fro, floundering in that one brackish narrow.

We called them and, treading half-under, they gladly turned and watched us. But each kept whining in place, wanting help yet scared to come for it. One kid behind me asked, "Why they hanging *there*, Mister?"

I only knew while answering, "It's their 'Invisible Fence.' They think the power's still on. So scared of one little shock, they're drowning right above their yard."

We slapped water, "Here boys!" No go. The dogs' collars were fitted with electrical stunners meant to keep them in the yard. A triggering line lay buried, sunken. Just the idea of a jolt kept them trapped. Electricity citywide had been shut off since 3:00 AM. Their owners were not home to help. I saw one dog had actually shed its red collar. Still the poor creatures stayed. They must have scrambled up the house's sides as water rose, then onto its roof, and finally out to the property's front edge. And here they swam in bloody goldfish circles these hours later.

I tried explaining their security system to the kids. But, dazed, boys didn't quite register the setup. It would've seemed over-elaborate, wasteful, in their neighborhood. Seemed that way here, too.

Diana kept silent. I was now so glad for these youngsters' strength. As I watched drowning dogs go under, gnashing at each other, teeth chewing each other's necks, I started feeling sick. I went half faint myself — from motor fumes? Maybe stress.

Since waking to find my first floor sodden — I'd had a surge superhuman, pure attention mainly for others. Heck, I'd been in this boat for what? six hours straight. Need be, just peeing off the side. But now I understood I hadn't eaten since the night before, and then only a bowl of warmed-over stew.

Could I somehow be a skinny ole guy suddenly sixty? Oh definitely. And, considering another rescue — of dogs so crazed and young and heavy — I felt myself go weak as water. Such gratitude now as four able brown hands (ivory palms) hooked the one poor creature's collar then got another's foreleg while heaving both with damp loud thwunks into the bottom of our rocking boat.

Soon as the gasping dogs were with us and safe on their sides, their tails, almost mechanical, beat three times very hard against aluminum. For a split second they looked over at each other. Just that once, but with such great joint effort. Then both fell dead asleep. This, of all things, shook me.

Of every triggering sight today, this seemed so sad and wonderful, their being saved if bloody, their staring at each other to acknowledge that, then *out*. I could see now: one was male, one female. So, a marriage.

But the way they'd checked on each other before agreeing to lose consciousness, that was a true killer. I cannot describe it well enough. But when I looked at the kids astern, I felt glad they'd gone half wet-eyed, too. Pals sat hugging. Diana barely noticed anybody, gazing out at all our water. Then oh but I wished my best friend were here. People always praised Jean's jokes and smile as "dry" — a holy word today. Shouldn't I have felt more grateful, forty years spent riding alongside someone so forgiving? I'd been the worst sort of snob — mine, a shoe-clerk's snobbery. Now, finally qualified, I wanted my wife back. Now I was *earn*ing her.

One of the boys saw me shaken. Polite, he waited a few minutes before calling, "When you done with this load? if you still on the clock? figure you could maybe take us back to where some *our* folks need hep, too?"

"You bet you."

With final prizes — three people and two live dogs, after all — I could head to higher ground. Our neighborhood smelled of raw pine sap so strong it burned your eyes like Lysol. You got a snootful of hog waste and this strange new scent, almost sweet. It was the smell of just so goddamn much water left all to itself and allowed to rush anywhere, everywhere.

Dust had powdered each twig with a pinkish talcum (dust flying in odd puffs as if fearful of becoming mud). But far under our boat, braiding currents pushed blackness over former golf courses and car lots. We squinted in the smell of what's *wild*. Freedom, chaos, everything let loose at once.

It was something not even my great-grandparents got to sniff: it was the smell of wilderness, doing all it wanted before any of us ever got here.

— Doing all it will do once it has finally shed *us*.

IV.

Well, I just turned sixty-five. "Mitch's Boat People" they call themselves? they threw me a surprise party.

Antoine and Sam and Lottie and her kids were all there. Plus Diana, again looking forty-eight if a day. And the Hutchesons and Charlie Hague (with his skin like a girl's).

Before floodwater dropped quite four feet, I'd already retired from Insurance. If you think that *pay*ing it is hard, imagine the torture of quadruplicate record-keeping. Went out of that office like I'd bailed from my second story. (Insurance had been Dad's idea: "Take advantage of our *con*tacts," Shoe said.)

The flood made me a thinker, made me mad, or smart. Not sure. Was it a breakdown afterward or some overdue insight? Maybe all the above. A flood, after all.

We'd been on our own and somehow briefly managed for each other. There truly *was* no government. No electricity, no property lines. No houses! There was whoever, in swimming distance, needed your little boat.

One thing I know now: It's a privilege to at least *try* saving each other. It's also a full-time job.

Riverside had been our one blue-chip sure thing, the citadel everybody in this part of our state aspired to. Now? it's a huge contaminated park, river view, not one 1939 "colonial" still standing. So much for American history (a series of revivals anyway, I guess).

Six years after our night of high water, the number of people in Falls still seeing shrinks you would not believe.

Me, I have a new lady friend actually. Total charmer, too. Must be doing a little something right. I was spared owning even one stick of furniture worth saving. Blessing in disguise. And Dad's "ancestral home," well insured? So much harum-scarum flagstone way downstream.

These days I occupy a year-old maintenance-free condo, three miles from any river, thanks.

I like it here. White interiors. No floral wallpaper. One table, one bed. I guess I live like a 1950s shoe clerk, strictly within his means. I live like a renter.

Retired, I take three morning papers. From the *Times* to the localest, I read them religiously. Aside from Sports, I'd let the world drift to hell in a handbasket. It sure got worse without my monitoring! Prediction and leadership keep failing us. Is it as bad as it seems or does this just mean I'm sixty-five?

Both. Corrupt as it is, Washington, D.C., must presently smell like Falls did right after the flood.

These days, maybe only the old and semibrave should even *bother* keeping up with current events?

Only those with boats!

•••

Now I sit quiet and dryly puzzle out my whole career: the choosing Insurance, marrying Jean, not waiting for Diana, my old choices. Probably unadventurous to stay put in my hometown. And in that Founding Fathers palace Dad bought for me, one high heel at a time.

"Never let 'Shadowlawn' pass out of family hands," he begged at the end. — Poor old Shoe. He died believing in American permanence. He didn't notice China waiting, humongous, behind us in line. He never guessed how fast we'd squander our foolproof national inheritance.

Finally, I can now live anyplace on earth. Some other locals my age moved en masse to bone-dry Phoenix. But so many folks are still stuck here, still getting over that one night.

We've become good company for each other, way better than before. New kinds of people in my circle. These days, between us, so much can go unsaid. Since that night, I've given lots of Jean's family money away. It never really felt mine.

Now that I can really begin again, I seem to have chosen to be here. It's no longer my father's neighborhhood, not Jean's or Diana's. There's nothing left of Riverside. And, see, that's what makes my staying put a choice. You can come to know your place, even this late in a life.

Six years later, the swimming amimals still agitate my dreams:
I'll walk into a mall, our mall, and it has been sealed then flooded as if to make a skating rink but overfilled with floating scared wild animals, smelling not terrible but more like wet-wool overcoats, these creatures making no sounds except the frantic slaps of paws, the kicks of their hard hooves, splashing then knocking against mall glass, mall stanchions, mall Sheetrock.

I wake, sitting, terrified.

I'm left to guess:

How many fences still hold me to this spot?

I am Mitch, sixty-five.

I have been a loyal dog-paddler here my whole life.

Overly loyal.
To what?

Before our flood, my drink of choice was Jack Daniel's and water.
These days? I take it straight.

––––––––––––

Allan Gurganus has published novels (*Oldest Living Confederate Widow Tells All*), novellas (*The Practical Heart*), and short stories (*White People*). Winner of the Los Angeles Times Book Prize and the National Magazine Award, he is a 2007 Guggenheim fellow. Last year he served as the first guest editor of *New Stories from the South*. He lives in North Carolina and is working on a big fat novel.

ROGER HAILE

When my hometown flooded in 1999, I rushed there. I drove my car and then had to climb aboard a handy passing pleasure boat. I didn't "interview" survivors, just talked to them. I knew them or their cousins. Everything they said, everything I saw, became "Fourteen Feet of Water in My House."

One difference between journalism and fiction is the length of any story's gestation. Newspaper accounts must breed overnight with fruitfly speed; fiction resembles the elephant. Though I'd talked to many locals whose pant cuffs were still soaked, it took me five years postdisaster. Only then did I feel strong and dry enough to wade back in.

That's why I finished this tale six days before Katrina struck New Orleans. Watching that horror, I considered myself the best kind of prophet, one with a good memory. My Harper's *editor congratulated me on so speedy a response; I assured him otherwise. I'd benefited from my local friends' hardest trials: those tests that arise years after the water descends. I'd seen folks' slower surprises: What remains once we are robbed of — or freed from — our very homes. What we truly know — after losing all possessions but our souls themselves.*

HOLLYHOCKS

(from *Five Points*)

Every one of Dudley Fenton's six older brothers is married, and when Dudley is drunk, he can't remember the names of their wives. On nights when Dudley is locked out of the house, his head buzzing, the harder he tries to remember, the more the names elude him. The only sure thing is that eventually he will remember them, and eventually, he'll get back inside the house. As he circles from one door and window to the next, he knows he's safe: Philip the cook will have left a pantry window cracked open for him. Yes, there is the window: he finds it in the moonlight. The window is high off the ground, off the brick patio at the back of the house, facing the Blue Ridge Mountains.

Dudley has to haul a stepladder from the tool shed, climb it, part the hollyhocks that grow so tall beneath that window, all stiff and dead with stalks so spiny they cut his hands, and jimmy the window up. The effort takes all his strength. While he pushes and pries, thoughts of his sisters-in-law run through his mind: the rich one, the shady one, the fussy one, the loud one, the prissy one, and the sweet one, who is his age and a new bride, and whom he loves.

Who locked him out? Why lock the doors of a house so far out in the country, you can't even shout to your neighbors? His own mother did it. It's her comment on his drinking. She waits until he goes outside to check on the dogs or to get a hidden bottle from his car or from the barn. Then she'll lock the windows and the heavy doors, and he has tried them, every one. In the summertime or the fall, he'll climb the ladder, or a tree limb, if necessary, to the second floor, to ease through a French door or an open window. In winter, if it weren't for Philip and the pantry, he'd be out of luck.

The cold's a bear on his back, hanging onto him, blasting its breath down his neck.

When at last the window is up, he launches himself inside, crashing across the cabinet beneath the sill, a space cluttered with glassware and crockery and cake pans, his body unwieldy, knocking all those clattery breakables to the floor. Always he plans to thank Philip for leaving the window unlocked, but they have never spoken of this. Philip understands about Dudley's loneliness and the drinking and probably, Dudley figures, even knows how Dudley feels about Patsy — there, her name comes to him even as he untangles his legs, bumping an iron skillet to the floor — Patsy, the sweet one. The visits to her husband's family, Dudley can tell, are a trial to her. Constantly she twirls strands of her hair or bites her lips. She doesn't have the competitive spirit of the other wives. Her husband, Barrett, Dudley's next-oldest brother, blurts out truths that embarrass her, revealing how she worries about thank-you notes, wondering if hers are all right. Barrett announces these things at the table, and Patsy flushes red. The other wives pick on her or ignore her, except for the shady one, who is sometimes her friend.

This big house, where Dudley and his brothers grew up, contains three floors and twenty-two rooms, not counting the bathrooms. When Dudley's brothers, their wives, and children visit for holidays and vacations, the house easily holds the entire Fenton family. Usually, only Dudley and his seventy-year-old mother live here, and Philip the cook and Edmonia the live-in maid (though Dudley thinks Edmonia declared a half-day off, this being Christmas, and went home to her people), along with Dudley's mother's two spoiled Standard poodles. Those poodles ought to be out with the hunting dogs, in Dudley's opinion, out in the pen in cold fresh air acting the way dogs ought to act, but nobody can say a word to his mother about her dogs or her horses.

It is Christmas, 1953. Dudley leans against the cabinet and catches his breath, and the night air rushing in behind him smells of cedars and woodsmoke. It's 2:00 AM by his watch, so he guesses it's really the day after Christmas. In a moment, he will close the window, but first, he'll rest.

Just before supper, there was a scene. It all comes back to him. The rich wife announced her new necklace was missing. She'd left it on her dresser, she said, and it was gone. She is from New York, and in times of excitement, her voice goes very nasal. Standing on the steps that lead down into the dining room, where everybody was gathering for the meal, she accused the shady one: "I think you took it, Theresa."

"I saw your old necklace, and it's too ugly for me," Theresa shot back.

"And the fur flew," Dudley reports now to his nephew Bobby, son of the rich one, Bobby who appears in the pantry rubbing his eyes, having gone to sleep immediately after the large mid-afternoon lunch and dozing all through the adults' cocktail hour, the drama of the missing necklace, and the argument itself, in which his own mother had starred.

"I heard a little bit about it," Bobby says.

Dudley steps away from the window, and Bobby closes it with some difficulty. Bobby is twelve, and his uncles are beginning to include him in their manly talk and quail-shooting excursions. "I think everybody's still mad," Bobby says.

"Mercy," says Dudley.

They laugh. Dudley wants a drink. He has hidden bottles everywhere, no matter that his mother and Edmonia root them out. Right here in the pantry, behind a row of canning jars, is a bottle of whiskey. He offers some to Bobby, but Bobby shakes his head. He's got a bag of candy in the pocket of his bathrobe, and while Dudley sips the whiskey like a man just come off the desert, Bobby sifts through the sack for the little red flower-shaped sweets that the family calls cranberries, hard enough to break a tooth.

The house is quiet until you listen close, and Dudley, drunk, has ears like a lynx. The Christmas tree shifts in its stand out in the well of the staircase, like a tired, thirsty person who has stood up too long. It is Dudley's job to water the tree, yet he has forgotten; he should apologize to the big shaggy cedar in its tin bucket, the bottom of it swathed in a sheet. He was the one who found the tree in the field, cut it down, and brought it back to the house on a wagon drawn by one of the horses. He should get some water for the tree right now, but the thought wavers out of his mind. He takes another drink.

In the very silence of the house, he hears all those people upstairs, his sleeping family, on the second and third floors, except maybe Philip who sleeps out in the stable, Philip who knows so much about them all. Philip goes for men, not women, and doesn't drink anything stronger than the cocoa he served the boys on winter nights when they were growing up, cocoa made with milk from the farm's own cows. Philip would whip an egg in each cup to make the boys grow up strong.

Bobby is a big boy for twelve, always hungry. He sets down the candy, and he and Dudley make their way to the kitchen, where Bobby opens the refrigerator and takes out a Smithfield ham. He carves the dense, dry meat and eats the slices from his hand. "Last I heard, Mom still didn't find her necklace," he says. "They looked all over. Dad wanted to call the police, but Grandmother wouldn't let him." Bobby's lips shine with ham fat. He carves and eats, picking out the cloves from the fragrant brown-sugar crust and setting them on the platter.

How did Bobby turn out to be such a sensible boy? Dudley will always wonder. Bobby's mother, the rich wife, sometimes puts her hand on Dudley's arm and looks him in the eye in a way not unfriendly. She was elegantly dressed when she announced her necklace was missing, her waist bound in green satin, her breasts displayed in a shiny bodice as if on a shelf.

Flying to her aid was the loud wife, the second-richest one, money being its own greatest ally. Together, then, the rich one, the loud one, the fussy one, and the prissy one shut out shady Theresa and sweet Patsy, so that there, too, an alliance formed, a flimsy trust built on shared ostracism, forbidden laughter between shady and sweet.

Between them, Dudley and Bobby reconstruct all of it: the genesis of the fight and its continuation. Dudley takes a pull on the bottle. Christmas night, 1953. He is twenty-eight years old. He should be Bobby's age, going to prep school.

"So then they all went to bed," Dudley says. There's a satisfaction in that. Everything's clear and in focus. He still has the youngest child's pleasure in being the last to go to bed. "We're smart, Bobby," Dudley says. "We know enough to stay out of trouble."

Bobby laughs, but it's the polite laugh of a child who has stayed up too late. In a flash, Dudley sees Bobby in fifty years: good-natured, his face red, swollen, his voice and gut a boozer's. "Stick with candy, Bobby," Dudley says. He stands up from the kitchen table. Philip will be in this kitchen rolling biscuit dough by six AM.

Dudley wobbles, and Bobby's beside him steadying his arm. "Easy, Uncle Dudley." Bobby's father is the brother Dudley likes least — Vernon, the third brother, four ahead of him. Everybody caters to Vernon. Philip always fixes sweetbreads at Christmas time, because Vernon loves them. Such a mean streak in him, yet he got the rich wife. Real rich, heiress to a grocery store fortune.

"What kind of necklace is it, anyhow?" Dudley asks.

"Kind of a pretty one," Bobby says. "Diamonds and stuff."

"Aw, it's around here somewhere. Could it be in your mother's pocketbook? Maybe she stuck it in there and forgot about it."

"I guess so," Bobby says, bored. Then he blinks. "Hey, Uncle Dudley. Have you ever looked in that dresser in the room where I am?"

Dudley knows the dresser, up on the third floor, part of a set of mahogany furniture that was once in his mother's room. "What's in it?"

"Fur. Tails," Bobby says. "Dead animals."

Dudley laughs. "That's your grandmother's hobby. Fox hunting. Well, used to be, when she was younger. She kept the brushes, the tails. You go on back to bed, young fella."

Bobby heads out into the hallway and up the stairs, and Dudley is alone again. He puts the bottle back in the pantry, resolute as he hides it behind a jar of dried beans. He has the whole house to himself. He wanders into the living room, where the Christmas presents are piled: shirts and cashmere sweaters folded in cardboard boxes, bottles of Arpège perfume and talcum powder, sets of crystal goblets and monogrammed sheets, things people want when they are grown up and married. Deputized, he bought many of these items himself, with his mother's list in his hand and her money in his wallet as he navigated stores in Culpeper and Charlottesville, enlisting the help of clerks.

"For your girlfriend?" a salesgirl asked smiling, as she wrapped bottles of cologne.

"That's right," he answered, thinking of Patsy.

He touches the tissue paper that surrounds a pair of leather gloves. Each son received gloves this year. His mother gives all of her boys the same gift. There are stock certificates, too, and sterling silver spoons. Each son and each son's wife can lay claim to a designated stack of lovely presents in this room: on the mantelpiece, in the armchairs, on the embroidered bench in front of the fireplace. The Christmas tree is dazzling with its ornaments and tinsel. Its lights are still on, bound to be scorching hot by now.

The logical place for that necklace to be is down the rich wife's dress.

Dudley laughs out loud. Did she look there? Thinks she's so smart. Maybe she found it in her brassiere when she took her clothes off and didn't tell anybody. Spiteful, that one, her and Vernon, with all that money. How is it young Bobby has such a level head? But the daughter, Bobby's sister Elizabeth, is another story. She's fifteen, hates her mother, wouldn't come home for Christmas, insisted on going to visit a friend from boarding school. Last summer, when Elizabeth was here, she banged her head against the wall because her parents wouldn't let her go out with a boy too old for her. She's scary, something not quite right about her, and Dudley doesn't like the fact that her mother lets her smoke. Oh, he started smoking when he was younger than Elizabeth, but it's different for boys.

How long has he been sitting in front of the Christmas tree, its lights pulsing in his nearsightedness like glowing fists opening and closing? He reaches up and brushes the cedar branches, the tips so needle-sharp he jerks his hand back. Has he been sleeping, sitting up? His glasses are gone. He might have set them down somewhere or they might have fallen when he was outside. That seems hours ago, when he checked on the dogs and drank in his car.

Just as he remembers that he needs to put the ladder away, the ladder out there in the cold darkness, he hears footsteps on the stairs.

Even without his glasses, he recognizes Patsy, her hand on the bannister, Patsy wrapped in a quilted pink robe, her hair pressed to her head with little pins. She pauses on the steps. He's always surprised by how tall she is, how large her feet are in her pink slippers. Usually, tall women aren't shy, the way Patsy is.

She says, "I was just about to fall asleep, and then I wondered if anybody remembered to unplug the lights."

"Oh!" Dudley cries, as if Patsy has announced a fire burning right in front of him. He crawls beneath the tree and yanks the plug from the socket, which results in total darkness, except for scanty starlight, or moonlight, which glimmers through the long windows of the living room. Awkwardly, Dudley rocks back and sits on his haunches. For a long time, they are quiet, and again Dudley wonders if he has fallen asleep, if he dreamed that Patsy is there.

He has lain on the front lawn, drunk under those stars more

times than he can count, beginning when he was younger than Bobby, out in all seasons, hot summer nights when the Milky Way blurred over the Earth and his ears buzzed with the cries of insects. He has been so drunk, he has fallen down in the snow and would have died if Philip hadn't come looking for him, flashlight in hand, nudging him awake: "Mr. Dudley, lemme help you up," though whether that was last week or ten years ago, Dudley can't say.

Somebody laughs: Patsy. She gives the relaxed chuckle that he loves and says, "Let's plug them back in."

He does, fumbling under the cedar branches, knocking an ornament to the floor with his head, working the prongs into the socket. As the lights come back on, one bulb fizzes and pops. Patsy hurries over beside him and picks up the tiny shards, collecting them in her palm. He thinks it was a red light, but the bits of glass look black.

"Where should I put these?" she says.

As he stands up, his head spins. "Give them to me." As she puts the broken pieces into his hands, her fingers brush his. He takes tissue paper from one of the boxes of gloves and wraps the pieces in it.

"Well," he says, throwing the pieces into a trash can. He wonders what he should say or do next. His mother used to tell him and his brothers that they would learn manners if she had to beat them to death. It's got to come naturally, she said. She did beat them, with hairbrush and riding crop, on the fanny and the hands, though by the time Barrett and Dudley, the last two, came along, she was sick of raising boys. She hardly paid them any mind, was always off on horseback. She had another man, would ride off to see him, even when she was what, forty-something. He pushes that thought away. His father dealt with that situation with such, he searches for the word, dignity.

So it's Christmas night, and he is alone with the woman that he loves, Patsy, here in her robe beside him at the Christmas tree, with a little smile on her face, as if they're children having a party of their own. She says, "Wasn't that awful, about that necklace?"

He laughs, wishing for a drink. "It was right bad."

"I do hope she finds it, though." She reaches out to the tree and touches a hollow glass globe. Santa and his reindeer ride across it, in white glitter. Patsy's red fingernails sparkle.

He has lost his train of thought. They were talking about a necklace. He has to bring in the stepladder. If he forgets, Philip will cover up for him, struggling to fold the ladder and stow it in the toolshed before anybody else is up.

"What are you thinking about?" asks Patsy.

"Nothing much. Don't get cold down here," he says and could kick himself, for now she'll go away.

But she stays where she is, examining the decorations on the tree. "I like the real old ones the best," she says.

He points out a tin star. "This one's mine. Dad gave me that, when I was a child."

"It's beautiful."

"I hated that nickname they used to call me. Dovey. Terrible thing to call a boy."

Many women would laugh, but Patsy doesn't. "You outgrew it, though."

"Sometimes Mother still calls me that."

He knows nothing about women, has dated several but they drop him quickly. He's been to a few whores, white and black. He can't remember the last time he saw Patsy, probably the Fourth of July. She and Barrett live in Roanoke, a long drive away. Oh, not that long. They just don't visit very often. Who could blame Barrett for wanting to keep Patsy to himself?

"You picked out this tree, didn't you?" Patsy asks. "How did you choose it?"

Nobody else would think to ask him that. Before he can answer, Patsy clears her throat and says, "I'm going to have a baby."

"Oh. That's wonderful," he says, too fast. And he feels shocked and breathless, the way he did when he was kicked by a horse, back when he was twelve years old.

•••

He and all of his brothers fought in the war, despite flat feet and bad vision. Vernon is deaf in one ear. Barrett lied about the eye chart: He'd overheard the man in front of him say the letters. Their mother wanted to keep Dudley safe. He was so young. She offered to have a word with the right people, but he stood his ground on that and wouldn't let her. He was in college then, down at Blacksburg. He left college to enlist. He felt so slow in the army, commands always registering late on his ears. He dug the ground in Belgium with a bayonet, pretending he was a child again, digging for arrowheads in the red Virginia clay.

He and the land go a long way back, though he's better at birds and trees than he is at farming. Black walnut trees show the land is good. His mother grows the traditional crops of the Piedmont, corn and wheat and hay, but the overseer, Mr. Ellis, does most everything. Mr. Ellis and his wife practically raised Dudley. He spent so much of his childhood at their house, in their yard. Now that he's grown, he and Mr. Ellis still talk about weather and crops and fishing, but it was better when he was ten years old and could ride the tractor with Mr. Ellis, then go to their cabin up in the field and ask Mrs. Ellis for milk and pie.

Dudley has been telling his mother to let him buy a few cattle, he'd like to try his hand at raising them. She wants him to raise horses, to love them as she does, she who rode daily — sidesaddle, which is harder than riding astride, she likes to emphasize — rode until just recently, when old age and arthritis caught up with her. She scolds her daughters-in-law for their fear of horses. Only the loud one is comfortable in a saddle. Dudley doesn't blame the others for their trepidation. Truth be told, he doesn't much like horses. Falling off and being thrown really hurt, and the animals are dangerous and sly, rewarding their benefactors with nips and bites, developing dozens of ailments that used to keep his mother out in the stable at all hours of the day and night, tending lame legs and sores and all manner of ills, never trusting the stable boy or even the vet to take proper care of her beauties.

Luckily, the horse that kicked Dudley when he was twelve was just a foal, and he was standing close to it. The farther away you are, the worse the kick; the kick gathers power. He finds himself explaining this to Patsy as they sit on hassocks pulled close to the tree.

"That's how I got this scar," he says, pointing to his cheek, "and why my eye looks funny. It broke the socket." Pressing the skin with his fingertips, he feels the craggy bone.

He and Patsy are smoking cigarettes, with square glass ashtrays on their laps. Where did the drink in his hand come from? There's a bottle at his feet. Vaguely he remembers searching in a sideboard, closing his fingers around the bottle, insisting they celebrate. Patsy has a cup of eggnog in her hand, but she won't let him add whiskey to it, because of the baby. He realizes she has never liked to drink, that she's glad for the excuse of the baby. She is the only daughter-in-law who doesn't drink champagne by the tumbler. The others are proud of how much they can hold. That always surprises him, how bold they are about it, how they tease his brothers for not keeping up with them. They do not tease him. He has collapsed in front of everyone, has fallen off the porch, has disgraced himself so many times. His drinking has ceased to be a joke. His brothers have had hard talks with him, prompted, he knows, by their mother, though all of his brothers except Barrett keep six-packs of beer in their cars even for short drives. And his brother Gordon, the only one who used to drink even more than Dudley and gambled, too, a high roller, Gordon ran over a man at a railroad crossing but never went to jail for it. During those talks, Dudley is Dovey again, meek and sickly, the youngest, nodding while a brother lectures. When the talks are over, he always goes out to his car in the garage and has a drink.

"I can't imagine," Patsy is saying, "what it would be like to grow up in such a big family. It must have been fun, growing up with all those brothers."

"A lot of the time, it was fun," he says. "Not always, though."

"Boys can be mean. Children can be so mean to each other, even in a family," Patsy says and nods, as if she's the only person ever to realize this. She is the most innocent person he has ever known. He would die before he told her how his brothers used to shove him down the stairs; how it was Gordon's fault that the foal kicked Dudley in the face, because Gordon was hitting the little horse with a stick.

Dudley and Barrett were at the mercy of the older boys. Vernon and Gordon were the worst. One time, Vernon held Barrett's head underwater until Barrett almost drowned, right outside in the pond, frozen now with rough ice, his mother's fantail goldfish sleeping numbly in its depths, descendants of the fish that lived there while Vernon pushed Barrett's head under the water and laughed as Barrett thrashed, until Dudley and some of the others, he thinks it was John or Alex, the two oldest, pulled Vernon away. For the first time, he wonders if Vernon is crazy, if the cruel streak in him and Gordon is more than just meanness.

"Barrett has told me the others heckled him right bad. You didn't, though," Patsy adds, with a smile in her voice. "I thank you for that."

"Barrett and me, we stuck together, being the youngest ones," he says and drains his glass.

"You and Barrett got the blue eyes in the family. Your father's eyes. I've seen pictures of him. I wish I could have met him. That was a lot of children, wasn't it?" Patsy says, as if she's getting sleepy, as if she's looking through a window far back on his life or Barrett's life or maybe her own. After a pause, she says, "It took me a while to learn all the names of your brothers. Barrett used to get me to say them out loud before we'd come here, to practice. Seven boys! John, Alex, Vernon, Gordon, Miles, then Barrett of course, and you. Gordon and Vernon, used to get those two mixed up."

"You do just fine," Dudley says.

She is here beside him, her slippered feet tucked beneath her on the hassock, putting out her cigarette.

Then her eyes open wide. "Listen. What's that sound?"

Dudley cocks his head. "It's Philip. He's in the kitchen to start breakfast."

"You mean it's morning?" Patsy is incredulous. That is what he'll remember best about her: her amazement, what the other wives call naiveté. He'd never heard the word before they hissed it, bandying it about like a code: naive. It is not a compliment. The other wives are much more experienced, even the prissy one, who finds opportunities to remind everybody that she has a head for business, why, she kept the books at the airplane hangar where she met John and was mighty good at it, too. All but Patsy are experienced in this wide world, meeting it with fashionable faces and proud bosoms and maybe a cussword and a hangover thrown in for good measure, some of them Yankees like his mother, and others, like the loud one, Miles's wife, Southern debutantes, and one — the shady one — a Westerner, from Colorado or Nevada or some such place, with sun-strained eyes and a smile like barbed wire. Patsy has more class than any of them, and now she doesn't have to worry about this family any more. Her life will be her children, a life of hiding behind the youngsters as a way of avoiding these family gatherings, or when she must come, she will mother her little flock every moment, hovering away from the grownups until even Barrett chides her.

Dudley knows that his feelings for her will never change. She is his age, and she will put on weight with each child, and her hair will go gray early. Unlike the other wives, she'll never color it, will stop wearing makeup and lipstick, and will wear shorts bought at a discount store and socks that fall down around her ankles, but to him, she'll always be breathtaking.

"It's morning, all right," Dudley says. Already he smells the wood burning in the stove. There's a new electric stove in the kitchen, but Philip prefers the old one. Soon, there will be bacon and eggs and biscuits, and oranges sliced in half, and small glasses of pineapple juice.

"I've never stayed up all night in my life," Patsy marvels. "My sisters and I, when we were little, we used to try, but we always fell asleep." She sets down her empty eggnog cup and rises from the hassock. "Nobody knows yet," she says, "about the baby. Not even Barrett. I'll tell him soon. Don't say anything."

Dudley stands up too, swaying a little. An ache started some time ago, a slight drilling behind the eye with the socket broken so long ago by the foal. "I won't tell anybody," he says. He decides to stop drinking. Yes. Today. He'll have a drink before breakfast, and that will be the last one. For good. Yet as the pain sharpens to a beam behind his eye, he knows he won't stop, not yet.

When at last he does, in forty years, he will do so by attending meetings three nights a week in many different counties, at country churches and VFW halls all over central Virginia, tiny buildings whose lights look orange as pumpkins in the cold dark. He will stop drinking, successfully and forever.

To his surprise, smoking will prove easier to quit. At seventy-five, he will attend a single session of hypnosis — he, who on this day after Christmas in 1953, would scoff at the idea of hypnosis. The hypnotist will announce to a hundred smokers in a Holiday Inn conference room: "Ladies and gentlemen, after I clap my hands, you won't ever want another cigarette."

In his sobriety, Dudley will realize the hollyhocks died back so completely each winter that they disappeared. He must never have contended with them when he crawled through the pantry window, yet the memory of those weedy stalks lives on in his hands. He will marry twice, both times in his old age, but those women are not Patsy, who will die long before he does.

"Time to give the lights a rest," Patsy says and maneuvers carefully beneath the Christmas tree, as if she's already months along in her pregnancy, to unplug the lights. The time he has spent with her was far too short. He has never known a night to pass so fast, a morning to come so soon. But before the house wakes up, before all the others wander downstairs and the hubbub of breakfast begins, he'll answer the question she asked about how he chose this Christmas tree, how he couldn't decide on one tree among the thousands of cedars and pines on his mother's land, and then snow started falling, and all of a sudden, there it was: this one.

Patsy announces, "The tree needs water. The bucket's almost empty. I can tend to that."

"Just stay here and rest," he says. "I'll do it." He'll get water for the tree, speak to Philip, and maybe take a drink to knock back the ache in his head, a hurt that cups his eye now as if the socket is one big bruise. He'll have one drink, and then he'll tell Patsy how he found the tree. "Want anything from the kitchen?" he asks her.

"Oh, let me think a minute," says Patsy, as if there are a thousand pleasant things she might desire.

It's so early that the house is still charmed and secretive. In the northeast room where Bobby sleeps, the fox brushes are gathered in close, dark places. When Christmas is over, when all the others have departed, Dudley will go to that room with its sleigh bed and looming dresser and take out the pieces of fur which once belonged to living animals, killed by his mother during hunts in the days when she rode. It has been years since he thought of those brushes, all soft and a lovely shade of red, with something of their wildness still there. Alone in that room, in the still silence of winter sunlight, he can hold up the brushes and admire them.

"A cup of coffee would be nice," Patsy says, stretching her arms above her head, "with lots of cream and sugar."

"Patsy," he says, and the words come out as if he's dreaming, "I love you." He's clear, mind and body, as if it's been weeks since he drank, clear and steady. "I might as well say it."

Patsy looks at him for a long time. She touches her hair, still tightly pinned, and smiles up at him. "I know," she says. "I've always known. It's okay."

But by the time he comes back from the kitchen, Patsy is gone.

Cary Holladay's newest collection of stories is *The Quick Change Artist*. She is the author of two previous story collections, *The Palace of Wasted Footsteps* and *The People Down South*, as well as a novel, *Mercury*. Her work appears in recent issues of *Glimmer Train*, *The Georgia Review*, *The Idaho*

JOHN BENSKO

Review, and *Five Points.* Her awards include an NEA fellowship and an O. Henry Prize.

A native of Virginia, Cary is married to the writer John Bensko. They teach in the creative writing program at the University of Memphis.

*H*ollyhocks" started in my mind as a direct result of the way those flow-ers grow to great heights and produce blossoms that hummingbirds love and then die back in wintertime so that they virtually disappear. I imagined a man locked out of his house, crawling through the dense foliage to open a window and get back inside.

This work is part of a collection in progress. The stories all take place in Orange County and Culpeper Country in the Piedmont section of Virginia. Together, the stories span two centuries, from frontier days to modern times. Several, such as "Hollyhocks," concern the Fenton family, a large and compli-cated clan born in imagination and seasoned with observations about people I love.

Toni Jensen

AT THE POWWOW HOTEL

(from *Nimrod*)

When the cornfield arrived, I was standing in our hotel's kitchen, starting Lester's birthday cake. It was raining outside, foggy, too, for the sixth day in a row, and there was flour all over my blue jeans. I was trying to figure out what the book meant by *sift*. Lester had been outside by the canyon all morning, inspecting bugs or digging holes or looking into the sky. But then he was in the kitchen, looking up at me, saying, Dad, it's here, his hand on the dish towel I'd tied around my waist. Lester had only spoken about ten words since his mother died last month, so I put down the flour and followed.

We live in West Texas on a three-hundred-acre cotton farm at the edge of Blanco Canyon. We own the Blanco Canyon Hotel, all twelve rooms, though everybody in town calls it the Powwow Hotel on account of Lester and me being Indians, Blackfoot, more specifically. My wife, Charlene, she was Indian, too, Comanche, from around here. There had never been a powwow out here to any of our knowledge, but that's just how people are in West Texas — what they know about Indians involves the Texas Rangers, powwows, or pictures of Quanah Parker they've seen in bars and restaurants, way in the back by the bathrooms. We were never sure whether to ignore the joke or to capitalize on it, to change our name and market ourselves that way. We talked about it, Charlene and me, laughed over it.

But there hadn't been much laughing lately, with it being just Lester and me, with Lester not talking and getting picked on at school for it. This kid had said, Hey, Lester, I hear your mom died. I thought all you Indians were extinct already? And then, according to his teacher, most of the other boys in the class laughed. She said the kid who said it was a bully, that the other kids were afraid. But I said when I was in school, fourth grade was when kids started to get mean, that I couldn't imagine things now being too much different.

It was late fall, just before Thanksgiving, and most everybody had their cotton in, except for a few late fools who now were having to wait out the rain. Out here, where we live, it's four miles to the nearest neighbor and nine miles in to Crosbyton, the nearest town. It was a record rain year according to the papers and the blonde girls with big smiles on the TV. Lester followed the weather on the Internet, had been writing in his journal about the rain — how we were over five inches for the month, how the conditions might be right.

Lester was supposed to be using the journal to write down how he felt, what with his mother being gone and his not talking much. But mostly he wrote about the weather here in Texas, and north of here, all the way up to Canada. It worried me, this obsession, because the only jobs I knew of where you got paid to think about weather were on the TV, and they involved being smiley and blonde and a girl.

Lester still had a hold of the dish towel, was pulling me toward the western side of the property to the grassy area in between the canyon and the biggest cotton field. He stopped about twenty feet shy of the grass, his face turned up to mine, his eyes the size of silver dollars. At first, I thought the grass had gone crazy, what with all the rain. But then, through the thick fog, I saw something waving above my head, something tall and green but not like grass. I stepped forward, kept stepping forward though my heart stuttered and my throat went dry. I kept stepping forward until I was in the middle of it, touching its rough edges, stalks towering over me, next to me, short ones, too, some only knee-high. I was standing in the middle of it, breathing in the new smell — green and raw and still like dirt, somehow — when I felt his hand, on my arm this time.

Dad, Lester said, they're going to be here soon.

And he led me back out of the corn to the hotel, and we started to prepare.

The first carload of Indians arrived two hours after the cornfield. Lester and I had spent the time making beds and sweeping floors, clearing the dust off everything as best we could. November was never a busy tourist month, not like May or June, and we hadn't had any guests since Charlene died, since the rain started turning the caliche road into wet cement. The whole time Lester talked about the cornfield — how it had started showing up in Canada, on the reserve north of Selkirk last spring, how it had been traveling south ever since, how along the way, Indians had been following.

How come I haven't heard about this? I said.

Lester rolled his eyes, which were still large, almost all dark pupil, and he shook his head at me. His dark brown hair fell into his face, and he pushed it behind his ears, all business. Dad, he said, you only read the Lubbock paper. He snickered. And you watch the local news.

We went into his room then, and looked at his computer for a while, and he showed me the places where people were talking about the corn.

The meteorologists, the scientists, the ones who believe it exists, say it's global warming, Lester said. That it's all the rain bringing it.

I nodded like I understood.

But a lot of scientists say it's just an Indian trick, Lester said.

I nodded again. This I understood. And what are the Indians saying? I said.

A car honked out in the lane. We looked out the window, found an old Buick, its tires caked with the cementlike caliche, its side splattered. Five people were pulling themselves from the car, stretching and laughing and moving toward the corn.

Lester was already at the door when he turned to me.

Dad, he said, you can ask them yourself.

The first family, the Jenkins, were from Alberta, from the Blood Reserve, and they had been following the corn since the beginning. Melvin, Sr., knew my uncle Jack, who I was named after, and we shook hands out in the muck of the caliche lane, grinning at each other, then looking down at our feet, then back up at the corn.

It's something, Melvin said. He hitched his pants back up to the middle of his belly and rubbed the top of his head. He wore a buzz cut, ex-military, maybe, and his nose looked like it had been broken at least three times. He was well over six feet, a half foot taller than me, but standing next to him didn't make me feel short. It made me feel like I should stretch a little, should try to be taller.

Yes, I said, it's something.

I wished Charlene was here. She was the one who knew how to talk to people.

Lester and me were a little pitiful that way, although today Lester seemed to be doing better than I was. He was over in the corn with Melvin, Jr., and even through the rain, the next car pulling up, honking, I could hear them laughing.

After the Jenkins, the cars came one behind another and pickup trucks, too, and then the news crews, of course, and the anthropologists. The last anthropologist's old truck bogged down in the caliche half a mile in, and carloads of Indians drove by, honking and waving, leaning out their windows to take pictures, yelling, Don't worry, we'll document it for you. But somebody picked the guy up, eventually. He was here in time for dinner, for the extra place we'd set at the picnic table.

By dinnertime, the rain had finally calmed down to a drizzle. Later, it would stop altogether. Almost everybody had brought their own food, and those who hadn't were fed by Lester and me or by someone else who'd brought enough. Some Lakota named Artichoker flipped hot dogs and hamburgers on the grills, which had been set up under the tallest sycamore. The Jenkins helped pass out paper plates, and a group of middle-aged and old women had taken over the kitchen inside. Someone had finished Lester's cake, and a big group gathered around, singing, and Lester blew out all ten candles in one try, which seemed like good luck.

Our neighbor Tom Miller drove the four miles over from his place and brought an extra picnic table. He worked in town at the school, but he also worked part time for the *Crosby County News and Chronicle*. He brought along a notebook, but his camera was broken.

Shit, he said. He ran his hand through his gray-blond hair and stared. I didn't know there were this many Indians.

He was so busy looking at all of us that I wasn't sure the cornfield ever registered, not really. He went around interviewing people, asking just a few questions at a time, mostly where were they from and what did they think of Crosby County, of our fair state?

I was busy running around with a garbage bag, picking up Coke cans and paper plates, when I saw Tom trying to back his truck down the lane through all the chaos. He rolled down his window when I came over.

I suppose your competition will be here soon, I said.

Doubt it, Tom said.

Oh?

I called it in, Tom said, tried to stir up some interest, but the Lubbock editor said he didn't think their readers were much interested in Indians. Indians or corn.

Oh, I said. Well.

Good for business, though, Tom said, gesturing at the crowd.

Yeah, I said, good for business.

He thumped the side of the truck with his hand, gave a little wave, and weaved his way down the lane.

The stars came out thick, with the canyon underneath, and those who were going to be sleeping outside joked they had the better lodging, the room with a view. The twelve rooms inside were taken up by the Jenkins and the Artichokers, another Lakota family called Blackbonnet, some Anishinaabe named Bairnd, a Pima woman named Smith, a Laguna Pueblo called LaLee, some Navajo named Richardson, a Cherokee family called Jones, two Hualapai newlyweds named Whatonome, a Choctaw named Byrd, and the anthropologist, Becker, who'd called ahead from his broken-down truck and snagged the last room.

On the back porch, a Navajo and a Laguna Pueblo were talking about why the corn had skipped them, had set its course east of their tribes.

We're from corn tribes, right? the Navajo said.

I know, said the Laguna Pueblo, shaking her head. Maybe it'll change course, come our way next.

This was the favorite conversation, of course, predicting where the corn would go next or guessing how long it might stay. According to the Jenkins, its average stay in one place was only forty-eight hours. Just like the average hotel visitor. Just like the time between Charlene's diagnosis and her death.

Melvin, Sr., and I took over the porch after the women from Arizona went inside, and we sat on opposite sides of the porch swing, letting it move a little but not too much, looking out at the people setting up their tents in front of the corn, the canyon. I couldn't see the corn that well, but I could hear people moving through it, the rustling of them against the stalks like candy wrappers being opened, a good sound, full of expectations.

There were even some people with bedrolls and sleeping bags who liked to sleep in the cornfield itself, right there with the itchy stalks and that bright green smell.

I'd been thinking about what Melvin had said — only forty-eight hours — thinking about Lester, who was in his room playing with Melvin, Jr. I'd been wondering if there was any way to prepare for it leaving.

Melvin, I said, is there any way to know? To know when it'll be gone?

Nobody ever sees it, he said. People have tried, but it always goes at night, comes to the new place before dawn.

Angela, Melvin's wife, came out of the kitchen, bringing the smells of coffee and baking bread with her.

Those boys are going to want to sleep in the corn, she said. That all right with you?

She was asking me, but she was smiling at Melvin, her arm moving up and down his back. I looked away. Over in the cornfield, flashlights blinked and flickered. The scientists were examining its root system, Melvin had said, trying to figure out how it attached and detached.

Sure, I said, that's fine. I'll go tell them.

When I walked through the kitchen, the women were cleaning up. They got quiet for a moment, the hum dying down, and all I could hear was the whir and hiss of the big coffee pots. The smells of coffee and soup and baking bread were making my mouth and eyes water, even though I was full. It hadn't smelled like that in our house in a long time.

Charlene had only been gone a month, but she hadn't been herself, hadn't been cooking for a long time before the doctors said it out loud, cancer, before the last quick days and the long quiet after. I realized I was just standing there staring, that I was making the women nervous, so I passed through, and they started up their talking again, and everything sounded right.

Lester and Melvin, Jr., were in Lester's room, studying the computer, their heads together, talking soft.

Lester, I said, it'll be time for bed soon.

He turned around fast, startled, but he still smiled at me. He and Melvin exchanged a look, and Melvin grinned.

Okay, Dad, Lester said. That's fine.

He and Melvin were laughing when I backed out of the door-way, and I had the feeling they were laughing at me, something I'd done or said that I didn't know about, but that was fine with me. Any kind of laughing was fine with me.

The next morning rose bright and clear, and by the time I was up, the women had taken over the kitchen again, or maybe they'd never left. Either way, they were fixing cereal bowls for the boys when I came downstairs, and I carried the bowls out to the corn-field, calling Lester's name as I went. He and Melvin, Jr., were lying face down in between rows of corn, examining the roots with a magnifying glass. When they rose, they looked serious.

What do you think? Lester asked.

I opened my mouth, but then I could see he was talking to Melvin, Jr., so I shut it again.

You might be right, Melvin said.

No, Lester said. No, no, no, no, no.

And he was off, running past me and the cereal bowls, the corn fronds opening for him, then closing behind.

I found him in his room, clicking away on the computer, his eyes narrow and tight, his mouth a line there'd be no arguing with.

Hey, I said. I set down his cereal bowl. It's going to get all mushy.

He ignored me like I figured he would, and for the thousandth time, I wished for his mother. Charlene knew how to joke him out of his moods, knew when to back off or step forward. I had retreated to a space halfway between Lester and the door.

Lester, I said, What's —

Go, he said. Just go.

After breakfast was served and the sheets put in the washer, I cornered Melvin, Jr., who was bouncing a Super Ball off the side of the house.

They've moved a sixteenth of an inch, Melvin said.

What? I said.

The roots, he said, they're starting to move.

Lester spent the day in his room on the computer, tracking the weather patterns, praying for rain. The sun here was so bright the paler Indians were applying sunscreen, the blondes in particular. A group of teenagers played Hacky Sack, another tossed around a Frisbee, and a large group of Choctaws started a game of softball that went on past lunchtime and only ended after dinner when the sun started setting, sinking red and orange and yellow into the canyon.

I was on my way into Lester's room with a plate of hot dogs when I saw Angela in the doorway. I stepped around the corner, leaned into the wall, trying to hear, but I couldn't. It wasn't long, though, before the two of them came out, Lester looking less angry, holding a hot dog in one hand, his magnifying glass in the other. And it was then that I heard it: drums starting up low, voices rising alongside the drums.

By the time I weaved through the women in the kitchen and got back outside, the dancing had started. No one was in costume — no spare room in the cars, I guess — but everyone was moving anyway. Old women stepped forward in time with the music, their hands clutched to their chests, though few held fans or shawls, and some had their hands hanging down, keeping the rhythm at their sides. Teenage boys and girls were leaping and falling in blue jeans and T-shirts, the drummers speeding up or slowing down, trying to make the showoffs miss a step.

Melvin nodded to me, and I went over to the edge of the circle, stood next to him.

Say *hi* to Uncle Jack for me, I said.

Sure, he said. Anything else?

Tell him he missed it, I said. Tell him he missed a hell of a show.

Lester was across the circle from us with Melvin, Jr., and beyond them, some people were packing up already, anticipating the morning. Angela finished up in the kitchen and made her way over to us. Some teenagers at the edge of the circle were drinking from liters of Mountain Dew, sliding little pills into the sides of their mouths like no one could see if they did it that way.

They're trying to stay up, Angela said. Trying to stay up to catch it moving.

I leaned forward and turned my head a little, listening for the corn, but there were only the sounds of the drums and the laughing and the feet pounding. I leaned forward further, squinting, but it was too dark, and I couldn't make out where our yard stopped and the cornfield began. I could still smell it, though, even if it was a smaller smell now, less green, less bright.

What did you say? I asked Angela. What did you tell Lester?

She sighed and looked out over the crowd. I told him this is it, she said. I told him he could wait in his room all he wanted, but that his mother wouldn't want him to miss this. So much has been taken, but I told him to look — to look at what we have.

I nodded.

And I brought a hot dog, she said. That helped.

We laughed, and Melvin joined in. Across the circle, a tall, skinny girl took Lester by the hand, and a shorter, plump one grabbed Melvin, Jr.

Hey, Melvin said, look at that.

Melvin, Jr., and the short girl were swept up right away, into the counterclockwise stepping, both of them keeping good time. Lester held back at first, pulling away so hard the skinny girl's arm looked like a rubber band that might snap. She started to walk away, and I held my breath. Go, I wanted to shout, go on, Lester. She was three steps away, headed toward a large boy to her left, when Lester started to move. It was slow at first, like he was having to tell his legs to go, but soon he caught up to her, was tapping her on her bony shoulder, and she was turning.

I breathed out, and I thought I heard Angela and Melvin doing the same.

Angela took Melvin's hand and pulled him a step toward the circle. Come on, she said, dance with your wife.

Lester was keeping rhythm better than I would have guessed, was matching up with the skinny girl's long strides. They moved past me, and the skinny girl leaned down to say something in Lester's ear, and Lester laughed and said something back.

In the morning, the sun would still be shining. I knew that. In the morning, a quiet was going to descend that could expand, could make that other quiet grow in a way that would bring on even more sadness. I knew that, too. But tonight, there was the sound of feet, moving counterclockwise, the smell of the coffee and bread and the raw greenness of the field. And tonight, there were my legs, too, stiff at first, but surprising me by doing anything at all, and then there I was, part of it, moving.

———————

Toni Jensen is Métis and is from the Midwest. She teaches creative writing in the MFA program at Chatham College, where she edits *The Fourth River*. She has published fiction in *Fiction International*, *Passages North*, *The Tusculum Review*, and *The Dos Passos Review*, among others. Her short story "At the Powwow Hotel" won the 2006 Katherine Anne Porter Prize for fiction from *Nimrod International Literary Journal*. She earned a PhD in creative writing from Texas Tech University in 2006.

JACQUELINE BECKER

*A*t the Powwow Hotel" came about when I had what I thought were two ideas, which turned out to be stronger, better, if linked and made into one story. The first idea involved a moving cornfield. I grew up in Iowa and spent summers detasseling corn — the only job I've ever liked much, other than writing and teaching. I liked the rhythm of pulling the tassels from the corn, the quiet of the cornfield. There were not many other American Indians in our part of Iowa, but there were some, and though my story is not based on any old, traditional corn story, it's an effort on my part to bring Indians into this place where they hadn't been acknowledged — an effort to say, "We're here, too."

At the time I wrote the story, I was living at the edge of Blanco Canyon in West Texas, and like Lester and Jack in the story, probably, I felt a little isolated from other Indians, from any larger sense of community, so the second idea for my story grew out of those feelings. There's a historical marker on the only road to the canyon and the house where I lived that tells about the Texas Rangers "eradicating the Indian menace" in the region. Every time I'd drive by it, I'd think, "not quite." The story, then, comes from the impulse to bring Indians into landscapes deemed "non-Indian," to create a present where healing comes from community, where there is hope at the end, not tragedy, not eradication.

Holly Goddard Jones

LIFE EXPECTANCY

(from *The Kenyon Review*)

Coach Theo Burke was standing outside his classroom during break when he noticed Josie across the hall, pinned up against a locker. One of the varsity basketball players, Jatarius, was doing the pinning — his near seven feet making Josie seem almost short in comparison, big hands straddling her shoulders, too-handsome black face leaned in to kissing distance. The worst thing — the thing that felt like a punch in the gut was the look on Josie's face, a look Theo knew. Her head was tilted, and she was smiling, but just a little: that smart smile, that sexy half smile with the bottom lip barely caught under her front teeth, an expression that Theo recognized as the smallest bit calculated but mostly genuine. Mostly the only way Josie knew how to be.

He strode over, hands shoved so deep in his khakis that his watch got caught on one side. He cleared his throat.

"Jatarius," Theo said.

"Yeah." A slow breath, dusky, directed on Josie and not at him.

"Move it along."

Jatarius pulled to a slow stand, languid, his skin gleaming as if oiled. "Just talking, Coach," he said, and Josie giggled. Theo turned to her, and she looked away.

"You're supposed to be swapping books now, not talking," he

said, realizing as he said it how ridiculous — how *old* — he sounded. Josie was losing interest in him, and all he had to cling to was his authority as her teacher and her coach. Her better. And how false that felt, watching her, knowing what her breasts looked like beneath that T-shirt and hooded sweatshirt: small, spread apart — a tall girl's breasts.

Jatarius pulled his bookbag up over his shoulder. "See ya," he told Josie, and she fluttered her fingers at him as he sauntered off.

"What are you doing?" Theo whispered, looking around to make sure nobody was watching them.

She tried to laugh again, but her voice caught a little, and she stopped. Her eyes were overbright, her shoulders stiff, but she smiled — for him, for the group of girls crossing behind him. "I'm pregnant, Coach," she said. She opened her mouth, then closed it again. She shrugged.

The bell rang, and Theo turned to his classroom, to twenty-six sophomores waiting to learn about the Fertile Crescent, the first bloom of civilization.

Abortion, she told him. Soon, now, so I don't have to miss any game time. Right away. Yesterday.

"All right," Theo said, fanning the air with his palms, that implied *calm down* that he gave students when they freaked out about a bad test score or got into fights. He and Josie were in his coach's office. He'd let practice out early that day, after only an hour. Josie had seemed normal — made her warm-up sprints at top speed, missed only a single basket as they ran figure-eights — but he could barely concentrate enough to follow the action or to guide the girls to the next drill. They looked the same out there in their practice jerseys and white high-tops: lanky girls with brown ponytails and acne. Only Josie stood out, her gold hair alight under the gym's fluorescents. Only Josie seemed real. "All right, slow down. Give me a minute."

She looked at her hands, as if she were counting off the seconds.

"Antibiotics," she said finally. "I was sick over Christmas break. That's what did it."

Theo was thinking: *baby*. He had a baby, and a wife. His baby was eleven months old, and they called her Sissy, short for Cecily. Five months ago they found out that her breathing problems were caused by cystic fibrosis, which turned the name — their affection — into a lousy pun, a cruel joke. "Wait," he said. "What? Did what?"

"The antibiotics affected the pill," she said. "I looked it up on the Internet. At least I'll know better from now on."

"From now on?"

"Jesus," she said. "I'm eighteen. I'm not going to stop having sex."

"I'm just saying," Theo said. He wondered, despite himself, if she would want to have sex with him again.

She pulled a package of gum out of her purse and unwrapped a piece. "I'm just ready to get this over with," she said, now chewing. "I've got a lot to worry about. School and all."

"Of course," Theo said. She was going to WKU in the fall, a full ride. He had helped her get it. He had posed with her, her mother, and Western's basketball coach three months ago when they signed the letter of intent, and the photo ran in the *News Leader*. "Cute girl," his wife had said when she saw it. And Theo — who was already meeting Josie for fast screws in his office and his car and a few times at her house, when her mother was pulling seconds at the sewing factory — only nodded.

Now Josie sat in the chair opposite Theo's, the desk between them, and played with the end of her thick, yellow braid, wanting, he saw, to put it into her mouth. He'd done his best to tease her out of that habit, seeing it as the one solid piece of evidence between them — other than the obvious facts of their positions as teacher and student — that being together was scuzzy and wrong, an embarrassment to them both. Because in so many other ways, it hardly seemed like a problem at all. She'd turned eighteen in December, and she was about to graduate. She was mature. She had a good future ahead of her. There was the infidelity, but Theo tried, with some success, to keep his home life and school life separate, and it seemed to him that he was OK — getting by, at least — as long as he was able to do what had to be done in both lives. He was an average teacher, but better than most coaches: he liked his World Civ sections, tolerated Kentucky Studies, and at least he wasn't just popping a movie in the VCR every day like Mathias, the boys' basketball coach, who famously screened *Quigley Down Under* for his freshman geography students during their Australia unit. He thought that he was a better than average father, at least most of the time. He'd hoped for a son, sure — pictured a boy all those years he and Mia were trying and failing to conceive, a boy to play basketball with and to fish with, all of the clichés. But he'd been happy with his girl, and if her delicacy dismayed him a little — how could it not? — in so many ways, it only made him love her more.

Some days, driving home from work, he thought, *I have a house,* and was instantly filled with pride. House, yes — he was a man, all right. *I have a wife, I have a child.* Before coming in the front door, he could picture all three, house, wife, daughter, as they ought to be: clean, happy, healthy. *This is my life,* he'd think, and then he'd open the door.

"My mom probably wouldn't be too upset if she knew," Josie said. "She likes you. She doesn't get hung up on stuff like you being a teacher. She'd take care of it if she had the money to, but she doesn't."

"How much?" Theo asked.

Josie shook her head. "I don't know yet. I'm not sure what to do."

"I'm not either," Theo said. How much was an abortion? Two hundred dollars? A thousand? He tried to imagine withdrawing that much money from the checking account without Mia noticing. Mia was in her own world a lot of the time these days, but she could surprise him with her sudden sharpness, awareness.

"But you'll take care of this, right?" Josie said. She was going to cry, he was sure. *Put the braid in your mouth,* he thought. *Do it if that'll shut you up.* "Right?" Josie said.

No less than five hundred, he bet. But he could scrounge it up. Mathias might loan it to him out of his pot fund. He could pay it back slowly that way, twenty this week, fifty the next. There wasn't any question, though; it had to be done. His job paid for shit — and he'd have to work tobacco this summer, probably, just to make ends meet — but it was all he had, and the insurance was good. He couldn't lose that. Not with Sissy to worry about.

"OK," Theo told her. "You get the information and set it up, and I'll pay for it."

"And drive me," Josie said. "I can't ask Mama to do that."

"I'll drive you, too," Theo said.

She pulled the rubber band off the end of her braid and raked her fingers through the thick weave of her hair, setting it loose. It ran over her shoulders, halfway down her back, wavy and almost iridescent. Rapunzel hair, he'd always thought. Her nose and cheeks were freckled, and she had that balance between strength and delicacy that most of his girl athletes lacked. Miraculous.

"We could have sex," she said, almost with resignation.

He nodded.

When Sissy's cystic fibrosis was confirmed, the doctors threw a lot of numbers at Theo and Mia, too many to make sense of. Life expectancy. Percentage of cases in the U.S. Chances of this, chances of that. But the fact that stayed with Theo — the data that confirmed for him everything wrong with his marriage and his life — was this: a child could only get the disease if both parents carried a defective gene. *Defective,* the doctor's word. Dr. Travis — the first of several — told them this in his wood-paneled office with the dark green carpeting, and Theo could remember thinking he, Mia, and Sissy, who was too small at six months but still porcelain-pretty, were lost in the woods together. He and Mia, two unknowing defectives, had somehow found each other, beaten the odds, and brought forth a child who was drowning in her own chest because the two of them should never have been together in the first place.

When he came home that night, Mia was in the old recliner, Sissy in her lap, and they were rocking, watching TV. Mia's bare foot bobbed above the floor, keeping time. The house was filthy, and Theo was nauseous at the smells that assaulted him as soon as he walked in the door: soured food stuck to the dishes that were piled up on the kitchen countertops; the heavy metallic tang of piss, where the toilet hadn't been flushed; and shit, too, he was sure of it. Maybe the baby's, but probably the dog's. Mia took care of Sissy to the point of obsession, but she seemed to forget that they had a dog — a Beagle mix they'd gotten for free from an unplanned litter — though bringing him home was her idea. She'd read in some magazine that dog owners had longer life expectancies, and cancer patients with dogs more often went into remission or had spontaneous recoveries. He didn't ask her how the cancer thing was supposed to apply to their daughter.

"Smells like crap in here," Theo told her, setting his briefcase and duffel bag down by the front door.

"I hadn't noticed," Mia said. "Baby-Girl's clean." As if in support, Sissy erupted into one of her chants: *ma ma ma ma ma MAAAA!* Theo picked Sissy up and kissed her clean neck, trying to fill his nose with her scent. She hooked her small hand and paper-thin fingernails into his ear and twisted. "Ma," she said again.

"I hear you," Theo told her.

"Might be the dog," Mia said. She kept watching TV, and Theo knew what she was thinking just as clearly as if she'd spoken out loud: *You'll take care of this, right?*

Theo put Sissy down, his stomach already starting to churn. "I'd say that's the most likely option." He whistled and walked around, trying to find the source of the smell. "Joe!" he yelled, whistling again. The odor, thick, sickly, seemed to be everywhere at first; then he rounded a corner, and it hit him like an arrow, coming from the bedroom. He got down on his knees and looked under the bed.

"Christ," he said. "Fuck."

Joe was in the corner, far from the bed as he could get, and Theo could see the fast rise and fall of the dog's stomach. "Hey, boy." The dog cowered at first — his eyes, so eerily human, rolled up at him warily — then let Theo lift him. He packed Joe into the living room like a baby.

"Dog's sick," he told Mia.

She nodded.

"Did he get into something?"

"I don't know. He was out back for a few hours. Maybe he got into the garbage." She was watching the TV around him. "Poor boy," she said without interest. "Should we take him to the vet?"

"Probably just needs to finish his business," Theo said, and he put the dog out. In the low light, he could see Joe make a slow circle in the backyard, then lie down. He went back inside and tried his best to clean up the mess, using every chemical he could find under the kitchen sink, moving the bed and pulling up the corner of the carpet so he could get to the pad and subfloor, too. The smell lingered, and he opened a window.

In the living room, Mia hadn't moved. He sat on the couch and watched what she was watching: a cooking show. Not a regular show, though, like his own mom had watched on PBS when he was in high school — *The Frugal Gourmet* or that one with the old Cajun guy, Justin Wilson — the shows where somebody stood behind a counter and cooked the food regular-style. This show had a fattish woman with brown hair, and she looked to be in her own house, because the sunlight seemed real and not put on. The camera zoomed in as she dropped an egg into a mixing bowl, which you didn't see happen on Justin Wilson.

"What is this?" he asked her.

"My favorite show," Mia said. Her voice was dreamy. "This woman owns a restaurant in New England. She cooks very simple foods. She doesn't use margarine, only butter."

"Margarine's better for you," Theo said.

"Not true," Mia told him. They watched as the woman dipped a fancy silver measuring cup into a bowl of sugar. *This dish is fragrant and delicious,* the woman was saying.

"Margarine is a trans fat, which doesn't break down in your system. Natural foods are better," Mia said.

"Why do you like this so much?" Theo asked. The woman was grating lemon peel.

Mia stroked Sissy's arm as she talked. "Her hands. She has such clean hands and fingernails. And her sugar, it doesn't just look like sugar."

Her medication. She'd been a mess since Sissy's birth — postpartum depression, her doctor had said — and she had just started to come back, to be herself again, when Sissy was diagnosed. Her meds were a square dance at this point: Prozac helped for a while, then made her worse than ever. Paxil worked, but they couldn't get the dosage regulated, and the doctor warned them that taking her off it early would result in a major crash. They'd gone on a date a few weeks ago — left Sissy with Mia's mother, tried to dress up and make a night of it — and at the movie, *Million Dollar Baby,* Mia had stared, emotionless, through all the parts that would have had her sobbing a few years before. Theo had asked her what she thought of it on their drive home, and she seemed confused by her own answer — or not even confused, exactly. Perplexed. Like the changes in her were a cause for a scientific kind of curiosity and nothing else. *I don't know what I thought of it,* she'd said. *I could see that it was sad. but I didn't feel sad. It was intellectual. Is this what being a man is like?*

"Looks like sugar to me," Theo said now.

"Figures."

"You could try making that," Theo told her. "Doesn't look hard. I bet it's real good."

Mia kept rocking. "No, I couldn't do it," she said.

Theo left her and went to the kitchen, unbuttoning his shirt cuffs and rolling up the sleeves to his elbows. He started organizing the dishes and cleaning the counters, pitching empty Lean Cuisine boxes and a Tropicana carton and Ramen noodle bags into a Hefty sack. He couldn't get Josie out of his head, not even for a second. Too easy to think of her, to feel her warm hips between his hands even as he plunged his hands into scalding dishwater. He pictured her in the hallway that morning, with Jatarius, and tried to remember the exact look on her face. *You'll take care of this, right?*

He noticed the wet circle in the driveway as he was taking out the trash, but the detail didn't click into place until he was closing the lid of the garbage can, and he realized that Joe wasn't there to meet him. It occurred to him that there *wasn't* any strewn garbage out back, any sign of disturbance at all, and he remembered the wet spot then — not oil, not water, but antifreeze, leaked out while his car was warming up that morning. He peered into the dark shadows of the far corner of the yard, where the security light didn't hit. "Joe," he said. "Joe, old boy."

There was a tire propped up against the toolshed — Theo had been meaning to take it to the rubber yard for months now — and he found Joe curled up in the space between it and the concrete wall, the thin scrim of green foam on his jowls barely visible in a sliver of moonlight. "Joe," Theo said. He looked at the still body. "Joe," he said again.

The first time he kissed Josie was in August, two weeks before Sissy's diagnosis. Someday, he might be able to blame the whole affair on his difficult home life, on the fear of losing his baby girl before she could have a home and family of her own. Someday, he might be able to forget that those two weeks existed.

When it happened, though, he wasn't thinking of Sissy, or of Mia. He'd known Josie for four years by then, pulling her from jayvee when she was still in eighth grade — she was that talented — and letting her start power forward on her first game as a high school student. He had recognized in her that quality which would later attract him: the blend of rawness and refinement, power and grace. In the beginning, though, she'd only seemed a grand kind of experiment. What could he turn her into?

The girls came in for mandatory weightlifting in the summer and through September, before real practice started, and the kiss came after one of these late-afternoon sessions. She was telling him about her father — how he left her mother in June to move to Nashville with his new girlfriend, a thirty-year-old wannabe country singer. How her mother had been struggling since then to make ends meet. She wasn't crying, but Theo could tell she wanted to, and the desire he felt for her — until this moment hypothetical and even harmless, like a childhood crush — was overwhelming. So he kissed her. He did it because she looked like she needed it. He did it because he knew he could get away with it.

Now, two days after the dog's death, Theo was determined to make it through a full practice without stopping early or fading out mid-speech, which had been his habit since Josie dropped her news. Some of the girls were beginning to look at him strangely, though he actually wondered more about the ones who weren't. He wondered if Josie had told a friend about them, and if that friend had told a friend. She had always promised him complete secrecy, but he'd worked with young girls long enough to understand how unlikely that was, especially among teammates. Before the news of her pregnancy, he and Josie had fallen into a strange sort of complacency with one another, an ease that he was now terrified to remember. How careless they had been — with the sex, of course, but also with too-long looks, knowing smiles, risky, ridiculous moments between classes when they passed in the hall and let their fingers brush. They should have been caught already, he knew. They would get caught.

On the court, the girls were running a pass drill. Josie caught the ball, made it around Lisa in three easy strides, and pistoned upward, sinking a two-pointer. She landed hard, and Theo felt his heart wallop. "Josie?" he said.

Her expression was bewildered. "What?"

"Are you OK?"

"Yes," she said testily, already dribbling again.

He'd buried Joe in the backyard, not far from the spot where he died. Mia cried, which was more emotion than Theo could remember seeing from her in a while. He'd dug the grave; then, still sweaty and dirt-streaked, he'd hosed the greasy patch in the driveway, watching the liquid blur, blend, then run off into the grass, indistinguishable from a light rain. *I couldn't have known he'd gotten into that,* Mia had said, and Theo had only stripped off his old UK sweatshirt and blue jeans, wadding them into a ball and throwing them in the hamper. His muscles, once so long and powerful, ached now. *Sissy was coughing again, and I had my hands full. You know how it is.* He'd nodded and started the shower running. *It was your car, for fuck's sake.*

The girls thundered down the court, mechanized, rehearsing a series of dribbles and passes: Sasha to Rebecca, Rebecca to Carrie, Carrie to Josie. Josie was in top form, her gold braid snapping behind her with each lunge and jump. Her breasts quivered under her jersey and spandex sports bra, and each time she landed — each time the ball connected with her hands, rattling her — Theo felt his chest tighten. If he and Mia ever had another child — as if they'd want another child together — there was a twenty-five percent chance that it would have CF, like Sissy. *Chance, chances.* A gamble. Josie was a gamble, too, or maybe just a stupid risk, but she was carrying their child, and Theo felt — no, he *knew* — that their baby wouldn't be sick. Their baby would be OK.

Josie caught the ball and Lisa slid into her, knocking them both out of bounds. Theo ran over, and Josie quickly jumped to a stand. "I'm OK," she said. She still had the ball.

"I think you should take a break," he told her. The gym was suddenly very quiet.

"I'm fine," she said, tapping a nervous rhythm on the orange skin. She started to dribble and put a hand out to block Lisa. "Come on, babe. Let's do this."

Theo leaned forward and knocked the ball out of the way, mid-bounce. "I told you to take a break," he said. The ball rolled across the floor, and he imagined that every eye in the gym was following its path. "So take one, unless you'd rather be running laps."

Josie stared at him, face bright with sweat, then bounced on her toes. "All right," she said. She started to jog, and the rest of the girls looked at each other, then Theo, and he knew he had to go on with practice or lose them all completely. He clapped his hands two times. "Back to the court," he said. He pointed to Amanda, who was on the bench. "Take her spot."

The girls resumed their drill, and Josie ran laps. Theo lifted his eyes every time she rounded the corner and passed in front of him, and her speed actually seemed to be increasing instead of slowing. Her braid trailed behind her.

"Pace yourself, Jo," Theo yelled.

She didn't look at him.

They started a new drill, and while he tried to focus as the players ran layups, he watched for Josie in the periphery of his vision, sure that she would lose steam and stop at any moment. But she kept going. Thirty minutes passed this way, and though the practice shouldn't have been over yet — they had a big home game coming up against Franklin-Simpson — he called it to a halt. The girls, who normally would've been happy to have a long evening ahead of them, hovered mid-court, looking at him. "Hit the showers," he told them.

"I'd like to get a little more time in, Coach," Carrie said. "I don't feel ready for Saturday yet."

"Practice at home," he said, and pointed to the locker room. "Go on, now."

The girls jogged off court, and Josie continued to run. Her face was dripping, her hair dark now with sweat, and her pace was finally beginning to flag. Her big leg muscles trembled with every jolt against the polished wood floors.

"Stop now," Theo yelled to her. "Practice is over."

She shook her head.

"Do it, goddammit!" he said. "Unless you want to ride the bench Saturday."

That did it, as he knew it would. She lunged off a final three or four steps, then hunched over, grasping her knees. She coughed, the sound seeming to rise from the bottom of her stomach, scraping her insides raw. Theo ran over and put a hand on her neck.

"Get the fuck off me," she gasped, knocking his hand away. Her freckled face was scarlet across the nose and cheeks, ivory on her forehead and chin. Her neck was red-streaked, too, welts that could have been made by a claw.

"You happy now?" Theo asked. He could hear a couple of the girls sneak out of the locker room behind him, could feel their eyes on his back, on Josie, who had lain on her side and was pulling her knees to her chest.

"You're going to kill that baby," Theo said, keeping his voice low and steady, more steady than he felt. "You're going to bleed him out right here on this gym floor you love so much, if you aren't careful."

"Good." Her eyes darted to his and away, childlike.

"You stupid bitch," he said, thinking, absurdly, of Joe. He hadn't wanted a dog — hadn't seen the sense in committing to another responsibility — but Mia had insisted, and he'd gone along. And the dog was all right. Not man's best friend, exactly, but good enough. Joe didn't get walked much, but when the walking got done, Theo did it. Joe was always full-steam-ahead, too. Didn't matter where they were going, or coming, he wanted to dig into the ground with his toenails and drag, mush, himself forward. Joe didn't care about the destination, so long as he was moving. "Maybe you don't know what's good for you," he told Josie.

She looked up at him, her face now bleached, the freckles like tiny bullet holes in her fair skin. "What do you mean?"

"Have you made an appointment yet?" he whispered.

She stood up and brushed off her shorts. "I was going to tell you after practice."

"Come to my office," he said.

He could still hear showers running in the locker room, so he closed and locked the door behind them, hoping anyone remaining would assume he and Josie had both gone home. Unlikely, given the public nature of their weird argument, but he couldn't think about that right now. "What did you find out?" he asked her.

"It'll be four hundred," she said.

He nodded, relieved but detached. This wasn't as bad as it could be.

"I found out about this clinic in Louisville online," Josie said. "So I called them, and they told me I'd have to come in for counseling, then wait twenty-four hours, because of some law. The closest day I could get was next Friday for the counseling, then Saturday for the other."

"Saturday's the Todd County game," Theo said.

"We'll just have to miss it."

He rubbed his forehead and laughed. "You can miss it, maybe. But I can't, hon. What would people think, both of us gone? It wouldn't look right."

She was very still. "It would look a lot worse if I started to show."

She was right, of course. But part of him was picturing his future, *their* future, and how quickly a thing like this — her one remaining semester of high school, the fifteen years between them — would blow over in this town. People would probably be more upset if they found out about Mathias's little stash in the head coach's lounge, the nicer office near the boys' locker room, with the windows. People in this town would understand that there's a difference between taking drugs, being purposefully incompetent, and falling in love with the wrong person. Because he *did* love Josie, he was sure of it. He wanted to do right by her, and he wanted to hold on to her. People here would understand that, too. And if they didn't, so what? There was always Bowling Green or Lexington or somewhere else.

"I don't know, Josie," he said.

Her face crumpled — that was the only word for it — but she still didn't understand him, still didn't realize what he was proposing. She drew an invisible line on his desk with her finger, trembling, and then the action turned loopy, and her face drew into her old sexy look that Theo knew so well, and he was fascinated by how he could follow her thought process with that one nervous finger, like she was a planchette, divining messages from a supernatural power.

"We could make a whole weekend out of it," she said. "We could go early, you know? Maybe go to Kentucky Kingdom — "

"They'll be closed," Theo said. "For winter."

"Aw, that doesn't matter. Not there, then. We'll have dinner somewhere nice. And I can wear something for you. Real special."

"What would you wear?" Theo asked. He sensed his cruelty, but he was also following her, imagining with her. Honeymoon: the word seemed silly, ridiculous, even, but he thought it anyway.

She tilted her head. "You know," blushing, "like a nightie or something. The night before won't matter. We can really live, right? It'll be the best time."

"I hear you," Theo said.

She stopped tracing with her finger. "You're screwing with me, aren't you?"

"No way," he said.

"You're not going to take care of this."

"I'm going to take care of you," he told her. "I just don't know that this is the way to do it."

She started to cry, the first time he had ever seen her do it. "You bastard. You selfish asshole. I'll tell. I'll tell the principal."

"Tell her," Theo said. She wouldn't, he felt sure. She had as much at stake as he did. He thought about Sissy, his insurance. *I don't care,* he told himself. *None of that has to matter anymore.* There were other schools, other jobs — positions at factories, right in this very county, that paid better than teaching did.

Josie picked his cup of pencils up off his desk and threw them against the wall, but the sound was small, lightweight, and Theo could tell that the gesture embarrassed her. "I'll tell my mom!" she yelled.

"Calm down," he said, waving his hands at her, open palms patting air.

"My scholarship," she whispered.

"Honey," he said, "you can still use it. We could do this."

She ran out of his office. He didn't follow her, but he felt certain she would come around. He wasn't being reasonable, exactly, but this was the right thing to do. His adrenaline was high — he hadn't felt this way since college, when his own feet pounded the court, matching his heartbeat.

When he came home from that night's practice, Mia was in the kitchen, scrubbing the counters, and Sissy was in a bassinet across the room. Much as he'd been disgusted by the state of the house for the last several months — and the dog, the dog had been the most senseless, irresponsible kind of loss — it hurt him to see her like this: so ardently domestic, so desperately sorry. She raised a finger to her lips when he walked into the kitchen, and he wondered if he were supposed to play a part in this scenic little moment: tiptoe across the linoleum in his sneakers, silently plant a kiss on her forehead, then her mouth. She had an apron on, for Christ's sake; should he untie the neat bow, unbutton her clean blouse? He remembered her as she'd been before the burden of Sissy's birth and disease had landed so heavily on them both: not his soul mate, maybe, but a woman to feel proud of. A woman to feel good about coming home to. Mathias had called her "eleven different kinds of fine" just after Theo came to RHS, and that was maybe the best compliment he'd ever been paid. She'd been dark-haired and lively and lovely. She'd been a thing worth beholding.

Her eyes now, though, were just as empty to him as they'd been the night Joe died. She smiled and turned back to the counter, yellow rubber gloves brushing the bends of her elbows as she scrubbed hard water stains out of the grooves around the faucet,

SOS pad rasping against the stainless steel. Maddeningly single-minded. He went to the bassinet, leaned over his daughter, and brushed his lips against the satiny skin of her temple. She was gorgeous, tiny, doll-like. Mia took good care of her. Theo worried for them both — and already, the thrill of deciding to be with Josie and raising their child was ebbing, becoming entangled and complex. Sissy sighed in her sleep: a luxurious sound that made Theo ache. He wished he could have done better by her. He'd spent the first few months of her life resenting her, despite himself; he'd expected hard work and lost sleep, but he hadn't been prepared for the sudden changes in Mia, who cried so often that her face always shined and who told Theo one night, with a calm that chilled him, that she was thinking about swallowing a bottle of pills. He understood that what he and Mia had was fine in the good times, when they could rent movies and eat out and shop for a new car together. Hard times were another matter. Then Sissy started getting sick, and he realized at some point that he wasn't thinking of her as a child anymore, or his daughter: she was a hypothetical, a baby who may or may not live to see thirty, and if he expected too much, or loved her too much, he'd be disappointed. Her weakness dismayed him, but he was weaker. "Night, baby," he whispered, and Sissy sighed again. He went to bed.

Mia slipped in beside him an hour later, skin still faintly redolent of Windex and Lysol. "I do the best I can," she whispered against his back, and the sensation stirred him, surprised him. She ran her fingers lightly across his ribs, tickling.

"I know you do," Theo said. He rolled over and kissed her, slipped his hand into the open neck of her gown, touching the familiar slope of her breast — the first time in a long time, and maybe the last. He traced the line of her collarbone, making a chart in his head, two-columned: *Mia, Josie.* One bigger in the chest, one taller. One with lines at the corner of her eyes, one with acne clustered around her temples. He thought about songs they liked — songs he thought they liked — and the way they wanted to be touched. One of them liked him to flick his tongue lightly across the nape of her neck, where her real hair turned into the fuzzy, baby-down of soft skin. One liked him to breathe into the cup of her ear, not words, just heat. He couldn't remember which was which. Sissy slept, and as he pushed the gown up around his wife's hips, raking his boxers down at the same time with his knees and then his feet, he imagined the wet gurgle of her chest as she drew in air, mobile of stars suspended above her, the moon a smiling crescent in neon.

They won the game against Franklin-Simpson. He and Josie had never been so in synch. If he thought an instruction, seemed like, Josie reacted: cut quickly to the left, passed the ball to Lisa, who was open, took the chance at the three-pointer and made it, sealing the victory. At some point in the game, he looked up at the bleachers, and in a throng of black and gold sweatshirts and flags, he thought he saw Mia. She used to come to his games, unannounced, before Sissy was bom, when she was still teaching special ed at Stevenson. She'd sit closer down, though, just behind his row of benched players, and it seemed to him now that some of the best moments in their marriage had been unspoken, when the Panthers would score, the crowd would erupt, and the band would kick into "Land of a Thousand Dances," all the sounds punctuated by the occasional slide-whoop of one of those noisemakers the Band Boosters were always selling in the lobby. Amid all of this — his favorite kind of chaos — he'd turn around, savoring his moment, and see Mia just a few paces away; they'd smile at each other, and he'd know that she understood him. That she was feeling the same way he was.

This woman he thought was Mia, though, was up pretty high, just short of the second tier of bleachers that only got full at the boys' games, and she didn't smile or wave when she saw him, and why would Mia be at the game anyway? She'd no sooner bring Sissy than she'd don sequins and dance to "Tricky" with the cheerleaders at halftime. He turned away from the woman in time to see the other team score, and when he looked back, she wasn't there anymore. A guilt hallucination, he was sure. He wasn't made of stone, after all.

The game ended, and Theo felt someone sidle up beside him, shoulder hitting his shoulder.

"Theo, man," Mathias said.

Theo glanced at him, then back at the court. The girls were filing out, and Josie was already gone. He scanned the crowd for her.

Mathias stuck his hand out and Theo shook it, hesitantly. Mathias wasn't in the habit of coming to girls' games, even when his boys played the occasional Friday night game and the schedules didn't conflict. Theo had always been sore about that, but now he wanted Mathias to leave — to hightail it back to his bachelor's pad and his dope and his easy life.

"Good game," Mathias said.

"Yeah." Theo looked over his shoulder, where the Mia look-alike had been. "Yeah, the girls did good."

Mathias crossed his arms. He was almost a foot taller than Theo, broad through the chest, and he had a presence — as a player so many years back, now as a coach — that Theo deeply envied: the reason, he knew, that Mathias was coaching boys, though they'd joked a few times together that the boys' team didn't have Josie-style perks. Uncomfortable joking.

"You're out, friend," Mathias said. He didn't lower his voice at all, but parents and teenagers were a churning mass around them, and the words felt muted, unreal. But Theo understood them.

"Out," he repeated.

Mathias looked at the court. "I guess things got around. You know — some parent, then a teacher got involved. Then Rita Beasley."

"Well, don't draw it out, for Christ's sake," Theo said. "What's going on?"

"They're having an emergency school board meeting tonight, and I expect that you'll get a call by tomorrow. That's what Noel Price told me." He sighed, and Theo could smell Listerine. "They'll let you resign. They won't want a big stir."

Sissy. Theo couldn't breathe.

"You OK?" Mathias said.

Theo laughed out loud. "She's pregnant, Matt."

"Mia?"

Theo shook his head.

"Goddamn," Mathias said.

"She's going to leave me," Theo said — out loud, but to himself. Saying it, he realized that she probably already had: *Things got around*. Mia had been in the bleachers, watching him, and now she was gone: to her mother's, with Sissy. He would come home tonight to an empty house, to the lingering smells of Joe's sickness and Sissy's baby lotion, and the rest of his life would begin. He didn't know what kind of life that could be.

"I'm sorry," Mathias told him.

Theo went to the locker room, where the girls were gathered for his wrap-up talk — Josie, nowhere to be seen — and he said the nonsense things he always said — "Good game, good teamwork, let's focus on defense at practice this week" — watching the girls' faces, wondering who among them knew. All of them, of course, but they made their expressions innocent and blank, and he appreciated them for it. He said a prayer with the girls and called it a night, and he could hear, leaving, their talk shift from *amens* to discussions of parties — Chad's house or Tresten's? — prom dates, and *man, we were so fucked up!* It occurred to him that Josie had a second life, too. On game nights, when Theo went home to Mia, changed a token diaper, and made himself watch Sissy sleep for thirty minutes, she was over at some kid's house, nursing a bottle of Boone's Farm that somebody's older brother had charged her eight bucks for. She studied for tests, asked her mother for money. In another month or two she'd start shopping for prom dresses, and whatever she'd find would look awkward and hopeful, and on prom night she'd stand out in the middle of this very gymnasium wearing too much eyeshadow and lipstick, unsure for once, graceless.

He saw her as he was walking to his car, the February night air like novocaine to his bare arms. She was with Jatarius in the parking lot and the light from a security lamp fell over them softly, the scene picturesque, staged. She was still in her jersey — she'd never showered — and Jatarius was working his big hands up and down her bare arms, warming them, and in a moment Theo knew that they would kiss, that Josie was just waiting for him to see it. He could get in his car and follow them — she'd let him, she'd make sure Jatarius slowed down, using any excuse that came to mind: and he'd do it, do whatever she asked, spurred on by the promise of her. He'd do it, because Josie was a girl — a woman — who would, Theo was understanding, have her way: with his help, without it. Now, no more than thirty feet away, she lifted her chin, and Jatarius lowered his, and they were a single dark shadow outlined in a hazy yellow nimbus. She was gone already and he had been a fool to think otherwise.

Later, he could turn off on whatever country road they turned off on, drive a little past the thick of trees where they'd park, and pull his own vehicle over to the shoulder, quieting the engine, shutting off the headlights. His overcoat was in the passenger seat. He'd put it on, creep back down the road, take a spot behind the trunk of a leafless water maple. And they'd watch each other through the rear windshield of Jatarius's car: Josie's slow undress, her mount, her gentle rocking, baby between them.

Holly Goddard Jones's stories have appeared or are forthcoming in *The Kenyon Review, The Southern Review, Epoch, The Gettysburg Review,* and elsewhere. A graduate of the MFA program in creative writing at Ohio State University, she is now back in her home state of Kentucky, having joined the creative writing faculty at Murray State University.

BRANDON JONES

I sometimes like challenging myself with despicable characters, and a man who would exploit the teacher-student power dynamic is, on the surface, pretty despicable. That said, I'm not usually very successful when I try to write stories that hinge purely on concept or formal curiosity, and this one would have fallen apart if Josie hadn't surprised me. Sometimes that happens: you think you've figured out all of your characters, and then you find yourself writing down a line of dialogue or an action and wondering, where did that come from? When Josie told Theo she'd "know better from now on," I started to suspect that she was a more formidable opponent than Theo would realize. Later in the story, when she began her marathon of laps, I knew. My initial desire had been to make the reader understand what factors might drive a man like Theo to sleep with a student, but Josie made me realize that the real challenge would be to make a reader give a damn about such a man's broken heart. As the writer I learned to care, but I also got a bitter thrill out of Josie's final and probably reckless act of rebellion.

Agustín Maes

BEAUTY AND VIRTUE

(from *Ontario Review*)

Rivers of waters run down mine eyes, because they keep not thy law.
— Psalm 119:136

He drove fast on the unlit, narrow road, unafraid of the sharp curves that cut through thick brush and elm and moss-covered oak whirring by in the darkness outside. He'd driven the car up on Interstate 55 from Memphis and by now knew its quirks and idiosyncrasies and capabilities, how it could take turns a hundred times faster and cleaner than the fifteen-year-old Impala he'd driven into the lot at Texas Microware each day, pinging noises that could be heard even after it was parked on the heat-softened blacktop. Good to be away from all that, he thought, craning his neck toward the windshield to spot the Mississippi he knew was ahead. The moon wasn't quite full but enough light shone through the trees so that when Vaughn rounded the last wide curve he could see the river in the near distance.

He parked near the tree line and doused the headlights, getting out to walk across the soft earthen beach to the river where it looped here at the Bootheel of Missouri, moonlight reflecting off the slow-moving Mississippi and dark branches that drifted half submerged in the ancient water like giant bones. He crouched down on his haunches, ran a finger around in the damp soil of these swampy bottoms. The distant shore was the most westerly part of Kentucky, a five-mile anomaly of geography between Missouri and the Tennessee border. He and Harvey had rafted across one morning when they were teenagers, hidden the rubber dinghy in some bushes with the intention of hiking to Tennessee, hoping to accomplish the feat of being in three states in one day. When they got back they told their parents they'd gotten lost, looking at one another nervously, drunk and sweaty and addled. Their stepmother had made them pick every last briar and weed and dried mud clump from their clothes before she would allow them to be placed in the hamper, scolding them about being out on the river where they could've drowned.

Vaughn stood up and headed back to the car, kicking the tips of his old cowboy boots into the dirt as he walked. Pin oaks and cottonwoods still lush and green stood juxtaposed alongside those with leaves that had begun to turn and fall away, the bottomland hardwoods settling in to autumn. In Dallas it had been mostly asphalt, highways and wide boulevards and malls; his sterile white oversuit and shower cap and the soft synthetic booties that covered his feet to prevent contamination at an assembly line where he stood fiddling with software for a computer he didn't own or understand the purpose of.

He opened the driver's side door and leaned down and pulled the lever that popped the trunk and walked around to the back of the low-slung sports car. He lifted the small lid all the way up, the light attached to its underside switching on. The girl had shifted a little during the trip and Vaughn had to use both hands to scoot her away so he could pull out the Igloo Playmate he had transferred from the trunk of the Impala and stocked with ice and two six-packs of Busch. "C'mon . . ." he grunted, tugging at the army surplus blanket he'd wrapped her in. He pulled at the cooler and it came out with a hard yank, Vaughn stepping back quickly to keep from falling over.

He set the cooler down and opened it and took out a beer, cracking open the can and sipping foam from the top while closing the trunk with his free hand. He leaned against the side of the car and lit a cigarette, looking out over the river, recalling the summer he'd accidentally caught a snapping turtle, a number ten Eagle Claw hook set so deep in the creature's angry mouth he'd simply cut the line, tossing the reptile back with the hook still embedded in its beaked maw. Better to keep a finger than to lose it out of mercy, he figured.

An owl made its call in the distance with a quick series of low, short hoots. The air was chilly. He was tired and still had his brother and sister-in-law to deal with before he could get any sleep. And the retard, he thought, running around mumbling nonsense like a toddler. Harvey wouldn't be expecting him. But Vaughn had come to Lilbourn unannounced before, whenever he had vacation time and felt like getting back to the river. His fishing pole was in its hard plastic case but he worried the girl might have rolled in the small trunk and bent it. It should be okay, he reassured himself. Vaughn figured they could do the work tomorrow. The plates would have to come off, too.

A rotten elm branch swayed tentatively in the light breeze, the only thing preventing its fall from the trunk a conglomeration of vines hugging themselves around it. Vaughn flicked his cigarette away and set his beer on the top of the sports car and groped around for his Swiss army knife, pulling it out of his jeans pocket. He stood on his tiptoes and cut the branch down and turned the fragile piece of wood around in his hand. Maybe Harvey might want to go fishing if he had any time to spare, he thought, evening around sunset when bass swam up near the warm surface to feed on what remained of the late summer insects.

Vaughn pulled off the road and traveled slowly down the long gravel driveway. The lights of the screened-in front porch were on and he could hear the yipping of his sister-in-law's little dog coming from inside it. He parked next to Harvey's van, the words DEXTER'S TV & RADIO painted on its dirty white exterior in faded red letters. Vaughn killed the ignition and sat, waiting for his little brother to come out. The dog went on barking over the steady song of crickets. A nightbird called from a perch somewhere nearby. He watched the screen door, thinking maybe they were out at one of those lodge dances, that maybe they'd all gone to some family night and left the lights on purposely. But it was a weekday and too late.

Vaughn got out of the car and walked slowly to the house and up the wooden steps. He knocked on the screen door. There was no answer. The dog continued to bark from someplace at the far end of the porch. He pushed through the door and made one step before jumping at the feel of something being poked hard into his back.

"You put up your hands or I'll shoot you right now."

"It's me, Harvey, Vaughn. Vaughn."

"Lord Jesus."

Vaughn turned around slowly, his hands out at his sides. "Going blind already?" he said.

"Well fuck me . . . How'm I supposed to know it's you? All I seen is a fancy little car coming into my yard. Jesus, Jesus. I was having a beer on the porch when you come on the property. Got my gun and squirreled out the door on my stomach. Had my sights on you from before you even shut her off."

"Guess you don't get too many visitors this time of night."

"Jesus Christ," Harvey said. He leaned his shotgun against the doorframe. "What're you doing back up this way? You was just here about a couple or three months ago. Didn't figure you'd come back around till next spring."

"Quit my job," Vaughn said.

"Well . . ." Harvey put a hand to his chin and rubbed it and then lifted his head. "Shut up!" he yelled toward an aluminum-frame lawn chair at the far end of the porch. The barking stopped. "Let's go inside so I can tell Rosie it's just you. Poor woman's probably wide awake by now. Carolyn, too."

They walked inside and Harvey told Vaughn to have a seat at the

kitchen table while he went to his wife. Vaughn looked around.
The place seemed to be in better shape than it was when he'd come
in mid-July. A new kitchen window, he guessed. A new refrigerator, too. Crayoned drawings were hung from it with magnets:
scrawls and scribbles made by a twelve-year-old. He switched on
the tiny black-and-white television that sat on the counter and sat
down and lit a cigarette. The end of *David Letterman* was on and
he sat smoking and watching until his brother came in through
the doorway.

"She's pissed, boy," Harvey said.

"I reckon I would be, too," Vaughn said. "I reckon I'd tell me to
get the hell out." He watched his younger sibling walk over and sit
down across from him and put his elbows on the table.

"She likes you, Vaughn. Why you got to go making her mad?"

"Didn't mean to come so late. I drove straight up I-30 from
Dallas to Little Rock and stopped for gas and kept right on going
up 40. Time I got to Memphis I had a few drinks and got tired.
Took a rest maybe a little too long, I guess."

"Well . . . You know you're welcome here," Harvey said.

"I know," Vaughn said. "I'll just get out of you all's hair." He
stubbed his cigarette out in the ashtray on the table and got up and
headed for the front door.

Harvey put up a hand and grabbed his brother by the arm,
"Quit playing around. You sleep on the fold-out."

"Damn, you're strong. How'd you get a grip like that fixing
teevees?"

Harvey snickered. "How'd you get to be such a pain-in-the-ass
night prowler?" he said. "Besides, I ain't fixing shit these days.
No money in it. People just go out and buy a new one when their
teevee breaks. Cheaper to buy a new one these days, boy."

"How'd you manage that icebox, then?" Vaughn said, motion-
ing to the refrigerator. He sat back down.

"Dexter's Video," Harvey leaned back and ran his hands through
his hair. "Changed the store into a rental place. Sold what I could
of the old stuff and now me and Rosie are renting movies. And

some other stuff like chips and soda pop. And candy. Just little things. We got a big old slide-door cooler for the pop."

"Videos," Vaughn mumbled almost inaudibly, squashing the insides of his cheeks in his teeth. "Must be making some good money on that I guess."

"Not all that much more than before. There's a place in New Madrid gets most of the business, neon lights and more than twice the rentals we got. And they rent video games. There's a place over in Dexter, too," Harvey chuckled and shook his head. "Dexter Video it's called. Rosie says I ought to change the name on the sign out front of the store."

"Why don't you?" Vaughn asked.

Harvey's expression darkened. "Now that's a stupid question, Vaughn."

Vaughn caught himself. "I didn't mean nothing by it."

"Daddy left you the place, Vaughn. Ought to be yours except for all that running around you done. You know he was ready to let you back. After JoAnn disappeared he told me right to my face how . . ."

"I don't know about teevees or repairs," Vaughn interrupted. "I spent lord knows how much on my car at the auto shops. Easy-to-fix stuff most likely. If I knew how to do it." He pursed his lips and pulled another cigarette from his shirt pocket, turned it around in his fingers.

"Where *is* that car of yours?" Harvey said. "I'm not sure I want to know about the speed mobile you got parked out front."

"You probably don't." Vaughn pulled the pack of cigarettes from his pocket and slid the one he held back into it. "You probably don't want to know I got a little favor to ask you, either."

Harvey stared at his brother, his eyebrows lifting quickly. "I can't goddamn believe it . . ." He put the fingers of a hand to his temple, "You go on out and move that thing around back. Right now."

Vaughn sat still, his shoulders hunched. "No money down," a commercial announced, "only three forty-nine a month."

Harvey rubbed his forehead and got up and walked to the kitchen doorway looking down past his feet to the linoleum floor. He lifted his head, "Vaughn . . ." Harvey raised his hands and opened his mouth again as if to say something more but then closed it, hanging his head and shaking it slowly with his gaze once again toward the floor. "I'll see you in the morning. Early."

Vaughn listened to the sound of his brother's bare footsteps going down the hall, the sound of the bedroom door being opened and a few hasty, impatient words whispered too softly to be understood. He turned off the television and got up and walked into the dark living room and switched on the lamp on the end table next to the couch. He pulled up the cushions and tried to ease out the fold-out mattress as quietly as he could. The stiff hinges creaked and groaned. Vaughn didn't know what he would do for a pillow or blanket. He thought for a moment about using the blanket in the trunk and quickly put that thought out of his mind, figured he ought to get out and move the car like his brother told him to.

He went to go out through the porch and stopped, looking at a little oval frame on the wall beside the door: their parents years younger than either of them were now, a handsome couple not barely into their twenties, childless yet, baring their teeth for the photographer, their mother's neck long and graceful. A much larger frame hung below it, a certificate from the Lilbourn Chamber of Commerce that bore their father's name in large black calligraphy. DEXTER OTIS. It had yellowed faintly at the edges, the two pieces of red ribbon hanging from the raised gold seal in a corner curled and faded. Vaughn studied it for a while, touched the frame lightly with an index finger.

Vaughn stepped across the porch and through the screen door. Crickets sang as he walked down the steps, a gentle breeze ruffling the just turning leaves on the tall maple that stood to the side of the house. He stopped at the bottom of the steps and breathed the air, standing quiet and tilting his head upward. The moon waxed brightly, the sky similar to how it was when he opened his eyes to the bedroom window before anyone in the house had wakened, the darkness almost the same as the pre-dawn morning he and Harvey had stood out in the barn where their father showed them how to milk a cow. "Like wrapping your fingers," he had said while sitting on the short milking stool, demonstrating while the sun came up outside the huge open doors, "like wrapping your fingers while you pull." Their father had worked the udders expertly, thin streams of milk resonating flatly against the bottom of a white plastic bucket, warm and sweet when he let them drink handfuls before breakfast. And he'd let them drink the dregs of his beer when they were in his worn aluminum motorboat on the river later that day, cleaning the tiny sunfish he and Harvey had been so proud to have caught but that were worthless as far as meat. Runts that should have been thrown back to grow bigger instead of meeting their end on the garden compost heap for yellow jackets to feed on.

Vaughn crunched across the gravel to the car and got in and started it. He backed out a little and pulled forward and drove slowly around to the back of the house, parking next to the old walnut tree that used to stand in front of the barn before their father had it torn down. When they were in grade school he and Harvey and their friends used to climb the ladder to the hayloft, jumping from wire-tied bundles onto the long rafters, hanging by the tips of their fingers before dropping down to land hard on their feet. After-school contests. He gazed through the passenger window at the now empty space where cows were once milked, where he once stood at the base of the ladder in the musky, dusty air, looking upward where pencil-sized shafts of afternoon light rained down through knotholes and chinks in the barn roof.

He hoped the car was back far enough, away from the road and out of sight.

Vaughn turned the key back in the ignition so that the battery switched on and pressed the button that reclined the seat and turned on the heat and grabbed his light jacket from the backseat, spreading it across him as a meager blanket. Sleep didn't come, only thoughts and the wind hissing through dying leaves. Daddy had wished him good luck, shook his hand and repeated what a shame it was he was throwing away everything he had before him, said he might as well not come around again if he wasn't going to live up to the business. Vaughn closed his eyes and beheld his father's pained face, his shakily pronounced words, his stepmother standing at the top of the steps in the days before the porch had been screened in, waving after him with a smile like stale candy. How he wished her dead as he drove out of the driveway, looking in the rearview mirror to see his father standing there, JoAnn holding the door open, waiting for her husband to come inside.

The engine was cold and no warmth came through the vents. Vaughn leaned forward to turn the key so the battery wouldn't run out, curled into a sideways position. He tried to sleep.

They drove in silence. Vaughn's neck hurt from sleeping in the car but he didn't complain to his brother who sat rigid in the passenger seat next to him, Harvey's mouth a tight straight line above his stubbled chin. A thin layer of morning haze gave way to the first fingers of dawn as they approached the river. But it was still dark, occasional low-hanging branches and the painted dashes on the county road the only things illuminated by the headlights. Vaughn reached for the glowing knob that would switch on the radio and then thought better of it, retracting his hand and placing it back on the steering wheel. The sports car's engine and the faint hum of the tires on the narrow, dewy road were the only sounds. It was quiet.

A white-tailed deer shot out in front of the car, a wild flash in the headlights. Vaughn pumped the brakes, swerving toward trees lined along the shoulder to avoid the animal's athletic leap into the woods. He swung the car back toward the divider and sped up, looking over at his brother. But Harvey's eyes stayed fixed straight ahead as though he hadn't noticed anything, stiff, hands folded in his lap.

Vaughn parked the car far off the road near a wide grove of ash trees. The Mississippi was visible through spaces in the trees, glittering under the brightening sunlight in thin scintillating slivers of gold and silver. He killed the motor, pressed the button that opened the sunroof. The woods were still but for morning bird-songs chattering and chirping. Neither of them spoke.

"You forgot to turn off the kitchen light," Harvey said finally, unmoving. "Lamp in the living room, too." His eyes were focused somewhere out the windshield far ahead.

"Sorry," Vaughn said. He rubbed his palms nervously against the steering wheel, not knowing what to say, waiting for his brother to speak.

"River's a bad idea," Harvey mumbled. "I brung a spade in my fishing bag."

"Okay," Vaughn said.

"I ain't going to dig, Vaughn. I ain't going to do nothing but help you get it out of the trunk once you're done and then I'm going to sit here and take a nap and then maybe do some fishing like I told Rosie we were out to do."

"Okay," Vaughn said again, reaching behind him to the back seat and lifting Harvey's green nylon fishing bag that sat next to the cooler he'd placed there the night before. He unzipped it and set his brother's tackle box on the driver's seat as he got out.

Vaughn stood still for a moment and then started into the woods, fending off branches and brush, nostalgic for its smells and textures. He thought of Santa Cruz, where he wound up when he was just near twenty, the hills and the beaches and the university there, the way the sun set so spectacularly behind the Pacific, fog and redwoods and huge ferns with their wide green blades splayed out like serrated fingers; the red-haired college girl he'd been with in the cramped backseat of a Volkswagen Bug, pulling off his pants and boxers so that all he wore was a T-shirt when he was inside her mouth, her head pumping up and down, drunk on beer and lust, straddling him, bringing him inside her. How different it had felt to see the way her eyes lost their wide, panicked shine when he brought his hands from her throat. So much more true than that first time out on the little slice of Kentucky across the river when they were too young to know what to do once the excitement was over, to keep from being scared witless after they'd frenzied themselves sinking their heavy sin into the water with stones, panting, looking at one another like strangers.

Going to need more than this, he thought when he stopped and unzipped the bag and pulled out the small military-issue shovel folded up at the hinge between the handle and the scoop. Vaughn set the bag on a rotted stump where a tree had once fallen, examined the dark ground at his feet. He hacked at the undergrowth with the spade for a minute before admitting to himself that he'd have to get to the earth with his hands. He wished he at least had work gloves, wished he didn't have this same problem all over again. And he wondered why it was this thing happened from time to time, why God let him live this way and for what reason.

Vaughn saw Harvey casting from the shore when he emerged from the woods. He walked across the beach toward where his brother stood, his hands scraped and bloody and dirt covering his jeans from the knees down. The sun was much higher in the sky. A row of empty cans stood in the silty earth next to the plastic red and white cooler, the better part of a six-pack gone.

"What you using?" Vaughn asked. He bent his knees and eased himself down to sit.

Harvey stayed facing the river. "Red Devil plug."

"How're they biting?"

"They're not." Harvey reeled in and put the pole over his shoulder and flicked it forward again, sending the line back out. "Not one hit."

Vaughn sat and watched his brother cast and reel for a while, not wanting to tell him it was time to go back to the trunk of the car and begin the long, heavy walk into the woods. He took a beer from the cooler. The air was warm. Near seventy, he estimated, looking across the wide river to the opposite shore, its thick greenery in the distance. Madeline her name was. Or was it Marlene? He couldn't remember. The girl was with her parents who were someplace upriver in their motor home, people vacationing from somewhere in Illinois. She wore only a one-piece bathing suit and sneakers and was crying, had gotten lost while hiking. Older than them by a year or two. Pretty. They said they'd raft her back to her campground, given her some of the Jim Beam they'd lifted from the cabinet in the back room of their father's shop and had been drinking since driving from town. She'd laughed at their jokes, told them they talked funny, sat down under a tree and got drunk with them. Must have been over a hundred that day, Vaughn thought.

"You need some help now, don't you," Harvey said. He cast his line out again, reeling in slowly and jerking the pole up at intervals until the line came back out of the river. He picked up his tackle box and walked the few paces to where Vaughn sat and jabbed the butt end of the pole into the earth so it stood upright and sat down on the ground next to his brother. He reached and got a beer and cracked it.

They sat watching the river, sipping at their beers.

"You got to know that I'm sorry, Harv," Vaughn said softly. "You know it's been a long time."

Harvey sighed through his nose. "Two years ain't so long at all," he said. "The Good Lord knows how I been counting the days till you come around with another 'little favor.' And you always come with one."

Vaughn took a long drink from his beer and stayed silent for a moment. "I already told you I quit that damn job of mine," he said lamely. "Figure maybe I'll head up to Saint Louis. Maybe even Chicago. I saved up a little."

"Where's your car?" Harvey asked curtly. He leaned forward to adjust the tongue of his work boot. "You can't go driving the one you got." He hushed his voice. "Not hers is it?"

"Hell no. I ain't that stupid. Got it in Memphis and I can change the plates. I plan to. That old Chevy I had is nobody's business now."

Harvey crooked his elbows across his knees and hung his head between them. "Changing the plates ain't going to do shit," he said. "I can't believe you still out running around without the law on your ass. Can't believe it." He lifted his head and looked at Vaughn and jabbed a thumb into his chest, raised his voice. "I got a kid, Vaughn. I got a kid and a wife and a business. You get caught doing something around here and that's all there is to it."

"I know," Vaughn said, his eyes down at his boots, working their pointed tips into the soft earth, burying them.

"I just want to keep things regular," Harvey said, "like when you come the other month." He picked up a flat rock and winged it out across the river. It skipped four or five times, slow concentric ripples easing away from the places it had sliced the surface of the water. "I can't take this, can't take you showing up and getting me to help . . ." He stopped short and puckered his mouth, working his lips around.

"I try, Harv. I know that's no excuse, but I try. Things get into me and I just don't know what happens."

"Why you got to come around here with this shit? What's a matter with some other place where I don't got to be involved?"

"I don't know," Vaughn mumbled. "I just get coming here or maybe it happens someplace along the way and I just don't know. You remember what Mama said about habits. Before she . . ."

"Let's go," Harvey interrupted. He got up and brushed dirt from the seat of his pants and grabbed his pole and tackle box. "Rosie's at the shop waiting for the Frito-Lay distributor. The Pepsi guy's coming, too. I want to get there before she gets any madder than she already is. Told her I'd be back before lunchtime to open up."

Vaughn closed the cooler and stood up with it, downing the last of his beer and tossing the empty can toward the shore. They lingered for a second, avoiding each other's eyes, started walking back to the car. Vaughn thought he ought not to open his mouth unless he had to, stepping up his pace to walk alongside Harvey whose face was set rigid, the bones of his jaw moving visibly when he clenched his teeth.

Vaughn opened the driver's side door and tossed the cooler in the backseat and popped the trunk. He went around to the back of the car where Harvey was, lifting the lid and grabbing the blanket where the girl's shoulders were. He jerked his chin up in silent direction for Harvey to lift the other end. His brother stared at the dirty blanket, eyes wide, the corners of his mouth turned down. Harvey stumbled back and then ran toward the woods, knocking over his still-rigged fishing pole that had been leaning against the car, vomited at the base of a skinny sycamore.

Vaughn eased his end back down in the trunk, closing his eyes to the gags and chokes. He wondered what their parents would think looking down on all this, envisioning the hell he was destined for and hoping his little brother wouldn't be there with him.

The rusty thermometer nailed to the doorframe said it was seventy-seven degrees. Vaughn lay flat on a rough wooden bench at the bottom of the porch steps, eyes closed to the late morning sun that shone on his face, one of his legs over the edge to keep him steady on the narrow plank. The little dog sniffed at his boot and Vaughn scooted it away. Harvey had made him park the car behind the house, told him to stay put in a hoarse, whispery voice, nervous and pale-faced when he went inside to take a quick shower and change clothes before going to the shop. Still "the shop," Vaughn thought, patting his hair that was damp from the shower. No shop if it's just videos. No business like it was.

The dog trotted back, snooting up the cuff of the clean jeans Vaughn had put on. He was irritated enough to get up and kick the little mutt hard in its ribs when it turned its attention to the road, barking. Vaughn lifted his head and saw the van come turning into the driveway. He swung his other leg over the edge of the bench and sat up.

The old vehicle rolled in across the gravel and stopped just in front of where he sat. Vaughn could see through the windshield that Rosie was behind the wheel, her daughter in the seat next to her. She shut off the motor and got out, smiling and shaking her finger at him. He smiled back, knowing by her good humor that she'd forgiven him for showing up so late the night before. The dog was at Rosie's feet, jumping and pawing at her shins. She scooped it up and held it in her arms, squinting her eyes while it licked her face. Carolyn lumbered out the passenger door and slammed it shut and ran toward him with her arms outstretched. Vaughn stood up and braced himself for the graceless hug she bestowed on him.

"Vanny!" she screeched, "Vanny Van like the van! Like the van!" She released him and stood hopping in place, pointing to the van and then back at him.

"You leave your uncle Vanny alone and go on inside," Rosie called to her daughter while she stooped to set the dog back down. "Go on inside with Zip-Zip."

Carolyn smiled openmouthed at her uncle and then jogged up the steps and went through the screen door, the dog following at her heels, wagging its stubby tail.

Rosie looked at her brother-in-law. "Hi there, night owl," she said. She walked over to hug him. "What brings you around here so soon?"

"Quit my job."

"What for?" she asked, grinning and stepping back and placing her hands on her hips in mock chastisement.

Vaughn took in her stance, the way the black jeans she wore hugged her thighs, the round curves of her hips.

"You are one tasty looking woman," he said.

She fluttered her eyes jokingly. "I'm your brother's wife."

"Let's get rid of him," Vaughn said in a low voice, growling and moving toward her with his arms outstretched.

She laughed, slapping his hands away. "You're a little dirty bird is what you are," she said, "just a dirty little I don't know what."

Their time at the drive-in in Sikeston flooded his mind, that time just before he'd graduated and left town and before she and Harvey had started going out. They'd looked over at one another, not paying too much attention to the movie, their eyes meeting occasionally. Rosie Willard still wearing her black and gold cheer-leader uniform from the Saturday game, a sophomore, not stopping him when he put his hand on her thigh and crept it down and in and not stopping him when he reached the place where her panties were and letting him slide his fingers under the elastic waistband to her wiry pubic hairs until they left halfway through *Jaws* to drive off to a place more private. They lay among the thick trees that lined a creek bed behind a supermarket, groping under each other's clothes. Vaughn had had to fight himself then.

"You look good enough to eat with a knife and fork," he said.

"You look like you done something to your hands," Rosie said. She pulled at the shoulders of the light green cotton top she wore. The clingy ribbing stretched and her brassiere showed in relief for a moment.

Vaughn stared at her chest, looked up quickly. "I scraped them up trying to fix that old car of mine before it give out on me," he said.

"You got a new car?"

Vaughn hesitated. "I saved up a little," he said.

"Pretty good for a man without a job," Rosie said, leaning inside the open driver's side door of the van to get her purse and her daughter's backpack. She stood upright and swung the door shut with an elbow. "You look like you need a shave."

"What I need is a nap. Harv gets religion when it comes to fishing. Too damn early if you ask me. And what we got to show for it?"

"You're the one gets crazy about fishing. Harvey looked like a ragamuffin when he come in to the shop. Don't know why you were so hot to fish when you been driving all night. How you two get so tired just settin there with your poles in the water?"

"Just what happens, I guess," Vaughn said. "Ain't so easy as you think."

"Well, you go on in and take a nap and I'll fix you something for when you get up. I got to get Carolyn some lunch and drive her back to the tutor and go bring Harvey his lunch."

"She getting any better?" Vaughn asked.

"What do you mean *better*?" Rosie frowned. "She's mentally retarded, Vaughn."

"I didn't mean . . ."

"Let's go inside," Rosie crooked her head and shook it once, hitching the backpack up on her shoulder. "You can sleep in our bedroom."

They walked up the steps and through the porch into the house. Carolyn lay on the floor on her stomach watching television, the dog curled up next to her. Rosie told her to get up and go in the kitchen and told Vaughn to get some rest.

He walked down the hallway to the bedroom and sat on the edge of the bed and pulled his boots off, looking around at the dresser and the drawn curtains with the late morning light showing softly through them. The wallpaper was different but he remembered this room as it had once been, the same one he'd slept in as a child, nestled between his parents when thunderstorms or nightmares drove him to their bed. Harvey had never been afraid of storms but sometimes he would sleep there, too. When their father married JoAnn she had made him put a lock on the door so that there wasn't a knob on the outside, just a brass plate and keyhole. After that the door was always closed and locked. "Off limits," she'd told them, thunderstorms or not.

Vaughn shifted himself and lay flat on the bed. He closed his eyes and dozed off for a little while, wakened by the sound of the van on the gravel outside. He lay staring at the ceiling, listening to the vehicle turn onto the road, knowing it was going to be hard to get any real rest while he was here, all the things that came into his mind at the smallest details in this house, in Lilbourn and the river and countless other places. He turned his head, looking at one of the curtain's heavy green tassels hanging at the end of a braided rope, thinking how much it resembled the knotted head and frayed dress of an old-fashioned corn-husk doll, watching it though it didn't move.

Vaughn got up and put his boots back on and walked down the hallway to the kitchen. A plate with three sandwiches wrapped in cellophane sat on the counter with a note written on a piece of brown paper torn from a shopping bag: *Tuna Vanny Love XX Carolyn* scribbled with a felt-tip pen in large, irregular letters. There was still some coffee in the pot. Lukewarm. He poured a cup and put it in the microwave to heat. A copy of the *Missourian-News* lay on the table and he got his coffee when the machine beeped, blowing on it as he sat down. The county was being audited by the state government up in Jefferson City, the Portageville Bulldogs beat Gideon 60-54, a seventh-grader found a frog with an extra hind leg, center-cut pork chops were on sale at the R&R Food Fare for $2.49 a pound. Vaughn folded the paper and put it down and looked up at dust motes floating about in the shaft of sunlight coming through the new windowpane above the sink. No news, he thought, just little tidbits of nothing, the reason he left to go west in the first place.

And now he was back once again, same as ever, no great news to relate about his own life except that he quit a lousy job at a software company and was just going to go off to another place and probably do the same thing or something much like it. "No great news to speak of," he said aloud. The dog trotted in at his voice, its nails clicking against the linoleum. It stood next to Vaughn's chair, looking up at him, tail wagging. He cupped a palm under its shaggy jowls and bent down and looked into its face, "No news worth nothing, doggie. Just a nothing little shit like you."

The license plates looked wrong. Vaughn dangled the glove compartment screwdriver from his hand and stood back away from the car to examine his work. Missouri plates would have been best, he thought, Arkansas or Oklahoma would have been fine, too. These were green with white letters and numbers, rusted in spots with faded registration stickers over ten years old. Colorado. He grumbled at the way the new sports car looked with its weathered plates, wondering how the overgrown husk of a truck he'd got them from could have originated from a place so far from the place it finally came to be abandoned. But they'd have to do for now.

He crouched down and turned his head to look at the truck in the near distance. The hood was completely gone. And the engine. Only one front driver's side tire remained, flat and rotted. Tall weeds grew up through the space where the windshield once was, up through the other missing windows and through the empty engine well. Vaughn picked up a stone and threw it, listening to the way it bounced off the corroded body with a dull, hollow tone. He felt sorry for the decrepit thing, feeling as though he should know what circumstances must have been for it to come to the pitiful end it did.

He spat between his feet and stood up and tossed the screwdriver and the Tennessee plates in through the car's open passenger side window, turning and moving past the truck while he unzipped his fly. He held his dick and swiveled his hips, pissing in a wide arc on patches of weeds and foxtails, the stream broken by tree trunks and bushes. She'd made them pick the briars and stickweeds from their jeans and shirts when they came back from the river, told them they could have drowned. Told them they stunk of liquor. Vaughn had drunkenly burst out about the time their real mother had had to suck water moccasin venom from her own mother's big toe, that she didn't know a damn thing about the river or anything else but being a sorry whore, would have let her own filthy mother die. He put the fingers of a hand to his lips, feeling in his memory the sting of her palm slapping him so hard across the mouth his lip bloodied.

She was around here somewhere. Maybe a mile back. Two miles, maybe. He hadn't marked the place, just patted the earth down and covered it with brush and fallen branches before heading west on 60. She'd cost him a whole day of waiting until he was sure Daddy was at the shop and Harvey at school before he could go back to the house, making certain nothing was out of place when he was done. A whole day before he could get out and be done with everything, see the ocean so many hundreds of miles away.

Vaughn shook himself and zipped up and walked back to the car. He got in and started it, low hanging branches slapping the windshield when he brought it up the slight grade to the road. The traffic was spare. Harvey would reprimand him about taking the car out when he got back from the shop. But not in front of Rosie, he knew.

He drove fast, away from the late afternoon sun that shone behind him, descending into the west. He slowed as he came into town limits behind a school bus that lumbered ahead. The screwdriver and the plates he'd taken off the car were on the passenger seat. They made him nervous and he sent them to the floor with a swipe of his hand. The bus moved too slow but there was no way to pass it, its large red taillights flashing on and off as it came to a stop at Fourth and Dawson. Vaughn stopped behind the bus as he was obliged to, watching anxiously while a few kids with backpacks disembarked in front of the First Baptist Church.

The graveyard stood beside the church but Vaughn only glanced at it and looked away again. He hadn't gone to visit her more than once since the funeral when he was eight or nine, didn't remember exactly where his mother's stone was among the many rows. BEAUTY AND VIRTUE was what his father had had inscribed below MARY ESTHER OTIS and below that the dates of her birth and death. Unfamiliar relatives from Kansas and far-off counties around Jefferson City had come, cousins and uncles and aunts he'd never met until the reception. Vaughn chewed his bottom lip and waited for the bus to go, keeping his eyes on the children that filed into the open church door for what reason he didn't know. Some kind of evening Bible class, maybe.

Darrell Medlock was the pastor there when Vaughn was a boy, had been the minister at his mother's funeral. And his father's though Vaughn hadn't been there. He wondered if the sonofabitch was still preaching, still giving lessons to Sunday schoolers. The Catholics and Jews were going to hell Pastor Medlock had said, gently touching the heads of the boys he preached over, talking about the love of Jesus and the sins of everyone alive on earth.

Vaughn pursed his lips, curling them into a downward smile. Medlock had taken a few quiet words with him after he'd caught the pastor in the woods near the river one night with his pants down, a weird-looking college kid Vaughn had seen once in Cape Girardeau kneeling shirtless on the ground before him. The pastor and the college boy got their clothes back on and had driven off in a hurry. Vaughn had kept his mouth shut, had a good five hundred dollars saved by the time he left a few months later. Enough to get away from Lilbourn and go west and see the Pacific.

The bus pulled away from the curb, thick black exhaust exhaling from its tailpipe. Vaughn kept his foot on the clutch, idling in neutral. He waited until the school bus was a good distance away before shifting into first. He drove slower now, trying not to look too long at the familiar sights of a place he hadn't lived in since he was eighteen. Things had changed, but only in the bright green of an old store's new awning or a gas station's tall sign now replaced with the name of a different oil company, nearby attendants shifting their shabby weight from foot to foot, whittling time away. The Dairy Queen was still a Dairy Queen, standing where it always had, now flat roofed and without its tall plastic dome styled like soft serve curled from the machine into beige, flat-bottomed cones that children begged their parents for like he and Harvey once had, barefoot and innocent.

The shop came into view and Vaughn considered stopping in for a minute. The van was parked out front. He thought Rosie might be there. Harvey usually closed up at six but Vaughn didn't know what his hours were now that the business had changed. The clock on the dashboard read 6:29 in bright blue digits. Videos, he thought.

A portable electric sign stood on the street side of the small parking lot, red plastic letters like those on a movie theater marquee clipped to the center: 2 FOR 1 MON & TUES. Vaughn slowed almost to a stop and then pulled into the lot and drove around to the back of the shop where the Dumpster was. He sat with the car idling for a few minutes, worried that Harvey might get unreasonable at the fact that he'd taken the car out. But nobody'd been around. And there weren't more than two cars parked in front.

He shut off the engine and got out and walked the few paces to the back door. The door itself was open, only the slightly torn screen door closed, evening moths flitting jerkily about the yellow light fixture as the sun dwindled, butting themselves against the screen and against peeling green aluminum shingles Harvey had been so proud to armor the exterior of the shop with some years ago. A dead opossum lay half under the Dumpster, ants and flies feeding off it, its thick pink tail curled up like an inverted question mark.

Vaughn didn't bother to knock, only opened the creaky screen door and stepped inside. Fluorescent lights illuminated tall shelves on which sat rows of videotapes in black plastic casings, ordered by numbers handwritten on stickers affixed to them. Remnants of the old business lay out in places: naked, dusty television screens with their funneled insides trailing like limp spinal cords, dials and knobs and spools of colored wire left scattered alongside rubber-handled tools on worktables Vaughn remembered from his childhood. He and Harvey had played under them while their father labored over the mysterious innards of televisions and radios, fooling with toads and toy cars, earthworms still wriggling when they were cut in half, the perfect, delicate husks cicadas left grasped to tree trunks after they'd molted, like tiny ghosts frozen brittle. Vaughn ran his fingers over the scars in the grayed wood of one table, looking at a calendar that hung on the wall with a picture of some snow-capped, faraway mountain, years out of date and faded to dull blue-green shades, half the days of an August long past X-ed out with a black marker.

He jumped when his brother pushed through the thick maroon curtain that covered the doorway to the front of the shop.

Harvey stopped short, one of his hands raised. "What you doing here?"

"Christ! You scared the love out of me, Harv," Vaughn said. He took a deep breath and calmed, blowing out with his cheeks puffed.

Harvey took a step forward. "You ain't been driving that little sports car to get here I hope."

Vaughn hesitated. He pulled a cigarette from his breast pocket and lit it, thinking that if he acted casual his brother might not get more upset than Vaughn knew he was going to. "Nobody around," he said. "Nobody noticed."

Vaughn watched his brother's expression harden into a tight frown. And he knew he shouldn't have even thought about stopping by.

Harvey pushed past him, looking quickly at a slip of paper he carried and yanking three videotapes off the shelves. He went to go back through the curtain and stopped. "You stay right here," he said in a low, serious voice.

Vaughn stood where he was, his muscles tensed. He smoked and listened to the beeps of the cash register and a few words exchanged and the jingle of the tiny bells on the shop's front door and then the sounds of the door's lock being secured and the old-fashioned blinds drawn down with a hasty rapid flapping. When Harvey came back through the curtain Vaughn dropped the butt of his cigarette and ground it out with the heel of his boot. He'd smoked it down to the filter.

Harvey looked squarely at his brother. "I can't have you come around no more," he said flatly. "Can't have you coming to Lilbourn no more."

Vaughn examined his brother's face and knew Harvey meant it. He looked toward the floor, staring at a tiny shred of electrical wire and wishing again that he hadn't come stopping by and not knowing what to say. A headache began to squeeze around his head like an iron band. He'd felt it before.

"I got this business to take care of and Rosie and Carolyn," Harvey said. "I can't have you around, Vaughn. Been weak as a newborn since this morning with what you brought. I can't be in this no more."

"I know . . ." Vaughn whispered. He looked up. "You can't just throw me out, though."

"Goddamnit, Vaughn!" Harvey shouted, thrusting himself forward. "Why can't you understand what you're doing when you come around with shit like this? What we done will send us both to hell but I got to live while I can. What you think would happen to me and Rosie if you got in with the law?"

"I wouldn't say nothing," Vaughn said.

"Don't you think they could figure things out anyway? How can you be so fucking stupid, Vaughn?"

Vaughn felt the band tightening around his head and wished it would stop. He clenched his teeth, willing it to go away. "They never figured anything out before," he said.

Harvey paled. He puckered his mouth. "I'm closing up early, got a Lodge meeting tonight," he said tersely, his voice low. He hung his head and shook it slightly. "I want you to get in that damn car and get it to the house and park it out back. And I want you gone up to Saint Louis or wherever you're going before sunup tomorrow."

"You just throwing me away, ain't you?"

Harvey clenched his fists and put them to his cheeks, squeezing his eyes shut. "I can't have you around no more, Vaughn. Jesus Christ, you got to understand." He rubbed his temples, looked at his brother. "I got responsibilities," he said, "God Almighty . . ."

Vaughn stood silent, looking at his younger brother and hoping for a sign that he'd said what he'd said rashly, out of anger and frustration. But there wasn't one. His head felt as though a snake were flexing around it. "You rent dirty videos here?" he asked.

"What?"

"Pornos. You rent out those porno videos?"

"I got a few. Vaughn . . ."

"You get a lot of customers for them?"

"Who in the fuck cares? I got to do the receipts and get to the meeting. You remember what I said. I want you gone in the morning." Harvey turned and pushed aside the curtain.

"You know what I done to JoAnn, don't you," Vaughn blurted.

Harvey stopped, his back to his brother. "I knowed a lot of things for a long time," he said without turning around. "I don't want to see that little car of yours in the morning. Can't have you around here no more."

Vaughn watched the curtain's cheap polyester pleats sway stiffly when Harvey went through it. He watched it until it hung still. Then he turned and pushed through the screen door, fending off moths that were in greater numbers now, one flitting against his lips as though it wanted to fly into his mouth toward some bright light inside him. He slapped it away and got into the car, sitting with his hands on the wheel. The sun had set.

A few raccoons loped around the base of the Dumpster, rummaging, sniffing at the dead opossum. He switched on the headlights and watched them for a while, their black-ringed eyes reflecting an eerie, luminous green. His head hurt. The house wasn't far.

She didn't cringe at his touch, only looked at her uncle with an expression of bewilderment while he led her into the bedroom and began undressing her, as though she were only being readied for bed by a relative whose hard, callused fingers and palms she was unfamiliar with. Rosie was secure where she was: thrashing at the corner of the bed, strapped by her wrists to the headboard by wide strips torn from the sheets, half-clothed and pantiless, muffled and wide-eyed at what her little girl didn't realize was happening to her. What was going to happen.

"Vanny?" Carolyn said.

"Vanny Van," Vaughn said softly.

He unclothed his niece gently, speaking in low, reassuring tones whenever he saw her dull expression heading from mere befuddlement toward concern, telling her about sex, about how happy her mother was that she was grown up enough to do it, that that was the reason she kicked her legs the way she did, that she liked being tied up because some grown-ups liked that and maybe she might like it too one day. "Like Baby Jesus in the manger," he said in a whisper, "how you were made by your daddy and your mommy over there." He pointed to Rosie, watched Carolyn's dull eyes follow his arm. She looked toward her mother and looked back at Vaughn. And the panicked expression on her face was something he recognized. He put one large hand over her mouth and shoved her to the carpeted floor with the other. Harvey wouldn't be home for another few hours Rosie had told him when he arrived and sat at the table with them for a beef roast she'd made. A Moose Lodge meeting in New Madrid, he wouldn't be back until after midnight with the poker and the drinking, she'd said.

All that bullshit lodge talk, Vaughn thought, keeping Carolyn on the floor with one arm while he undid his belt, business and politics and who put up this or that fence on some property or the price of the latest John Deere. And Harvey was probably talking about his own business and how it was doing, half of those sitting around drinking beer and laughing at stupid jokes his customers. All the filthy pornography he rented and sold for a living like a pimp, trying to pretend everything away like he was something better, like he'd forgotten what he was. What he'd done.

Vaughn pulled his niece's skirt off, vaguely disappointed at how easy she made it. The girl from Illinois and the one from Texas and the ones from who knew where had put up a greater thrash than this. But none of it was anything now. Too old, he thought, pinning his niece to the carpet with his own weight, too old and full of the sin even Pastor Medlock could lecture righteously on.

He entered her, pressing his hand harder against her face so that only her wide, rolling eyes spoke out in protest. He could hear his sister-in-law banging against the headboard, faint horror audible from the cloth he'd stuffed into her mouth, his niece losing herself to something he was familiar with when he let up his hand, knowing that even a retard would not scream, knowing she had come to the point other girls had come to, surrendered and resigned to a place he could only guess at, bleeding and quiet as though they were in some distant, faraway locale. And Carolyn was bleeding. And done with herself. And then Vaughn was done, listening calmly to Rosie's frantic flailing on the bed like it was some natural background noise: wind or crickets or the occasional lowing of cattle on a peaceful evening.

•••

He stood at the shore looking at a moonlit streak in the water where a branch had snagged, smoking, wondering how anyone could be fooled into forgetting its power, how it could have its way with any boat or barge navigating with or against the current. But it seemed gentle, what debris the nearly full moon showed flowing down along the hundreds of miles to the Gulf of Mexico like devout pilgrims on a voyage toward some holy place. He blew out a stream of smoke and squinted toward the Kentucky shore, the place where he and his brother had been that summer, young and scared, Harvey bedridden for two weeks afterward, sick more by conscience than fever. Now his brother lay still and wrapped in bedsheets like his wife and child, tiny waves licking up the beach and against the heels of their feet.

A wide raft lay next to them, skinny cottonwood logs hacked from the woods with an axe Vaughn had brought from the house and lashed together with a large spool of thick nylon twine from Harvey's fishing bag. It had taken him a long time to build. He wondered how long the rickety thing would last and if it did last what might capsize it or if it would lodge on a towhead somewhere downriver. But he knew it would all come to the same thing regardless.

He flicked his cigarette into the water and went to drag his brother onto the raft, grunting and sweating, trying not to look as he pulled backward with his head turned to one side, his hands sticky by the blood on the flower print sheet, pebbles stuck to the sides of his palms. An old hunting rifle kept in the toolshed had made all that blood, not the shotgun he couldn't bring himself to use. He'd stood motionless afterward, not wanting to see Harvey on the gravel of the driveway next to his van, not wanting to see his own brother and what had come of mercy: crosshairs meant for the white patch on a deer's chest on a man's, Vaughn anchored in place with an eye still to the scope even after Harvey had fallen, only the shadows of trees that had been behind him visible through it. He had cried for a long time then, lurching over to sit crookedly on the driveway with his face buried in his brother's wet, warm stomach in the dark while the moon rose, sorry he had had to spare him the agony of life without his family. But he didn't cry now, only dragged his niece and sister-in-law onto the raft and positioned them alongside Harvey's body.

Vaughn closed his eyes and hung his head and mumbled a fragmented jumble of what he remembered of the Twenty-third Psalm. He swallowed and stooped almost level with the ground, leaning into the edge of the raft to get it into the water, pushing it before him until he'd waded in up to his chest and it caught the current and drifted on its own. It didn't float completely but sunk a little below the waterline when he let go. Vaughn thought they might drift off the raft. But they didn't. And he stood where he was in the cold river, watching the shining figures ferry away until the moonlight failed and darkness swallowed them out of sight.

The dog barked when Vaughn parked the van and walked in through the porch screen door. He went to the front door and opened it and leaned inside to flip the switch that turned on the porch lights. Zip-Zip went on yipping from underneath an aluminum-frame lawn chair. Vaughn stared absently at the doorframe, then over at the dog whose hair poked through the worn nylon strips of the seat. He walked over and lifted the lightweight chair, setting it away and scooping the small mutt up in his arms, telling it to shush. He noticed a few feathers on its snout, feathers scattered on the boards of the porch. The remains of a brown wren lay at the place where the lawn chair had been, on its back with its beaked head crooked to one side, the thin pointed toes of its tiny feet curled up, a torn-off wing lying a few inches beside it. Vaughn gripped the dog by its jaw, looked into its face. "You think you a cat, dog?" he said. He batted it lightly on the nose. "You a dog. A stupid little shit-ass dog." He was shivering, his bottom half soaked through.

Vaughn set Zip-Zip back down and went inside. He went into the bathroom and got his duffel bag and changed quickly in the living room, shoving his wet clothes into the bag's large pocket, glancing back toward the hallway for a moment at the open bedroom door, a wide shaft of light from inside the room across the hallway floor. He zipped the bag closed and hastened back out onto the porch. The dog sat with its front legs flat in front of it, its head tilted sideways, pulling at the breast of the dismembered bird with its teeth. It yelped when Vaughn grabbed it by the scruff of its neck. He carried the dog out the porch door and down the stairs and around to the back of the house where the sports car was. He opened the door and flung the dog inside and got in and put the keys in the ignition and started it, letting it idle. Then he shut it off.

Vaughn sat staring through the windshield. The barn was gone. And the cows. The long clothesline sagged from a metal hoop screwed into the back of the house, the other end tied around the scarred trunk of an old apple tree. He watched the line move in the late night breeze, swaying gently the way it would when their mother strung the wash on Thursday mornings, clothespinning wet sheets and pants and shirts. Weighing the rope down until it hung still.

He looked over at the dog on the seat next to him, watched it chomp at a hindquarter. He grabbed its collar, lifted it up with his arm outstretched so that the dog dangled in midair. It whimpered. "You a cat or a dog?" he breathed quietly. "Bark, motherfucker."

Agustín Maes was born in Albuquerque, New Mexico, and grew up thirty miles north of San Francisco in Novato, California. His fiction has appeared in *Blue Mesa Review* and *The Gallatin Review* and in *Ontario Review* as a finalist for the Carter V. Cooper Memorial Prize in Short Fiction. He holds an MFA from the New School writing program and an MA in theology from the University of San Francisco. He writes in Oakland, California, where he is at work on a novel.

JENNI KELLER

*T*his story began with a map. While looking through an atlas, I was drawn to an extreme bend in the Mississippi River at the southeastern corner of Missouri, curved sharper than a fishhook and inexplicably sinister. It seemed a place possessed of terrible things. Though I've never been to Missouri's Bootheel region, the river's great oxbow and the strange exclave of Kentucky trapped inside it stirred up the notion of a man at the moonlit shore, bound to the watery land by the sins he had committed there. That man became Vaughn Otis, a character I grew to care deeply for, despite his evil acts.

Stephen Marion

DOGS WITH HUMAN FACES

(from *Epoch*)

You can tell so much about a man by how he kills something. The boy from the jail tried to pass it off as work. Now I'll work, he said the first morning they brought him in. You'll see how I'll work. But I seen that coming. He was a boy, and a boy of a certain age, no matter how mean he is, is looking for his way into the work of the world, long before he even knows what that work is. I ought to know by three brothers.

It was cold enough to see the breath of the dogs when they barked, and they were all barking. But the boy had the sleeves of his orange jumpsuit rolled up to his shoulders, one of which had a crude little tattoo of a dagger. He was real slicked down with about the suggestion of a beard, and he was one of those boys that is too light in the hips, as if his pelvis isn't made out of bone but maybe aluminum. I had him spraying out the dog runs. That gets everybody excited. The dogs were leaping and pouncing at the little rope of water and the boy was liking that. He was grinning with one side of his mouth and there was something hopeful about him. The barking was all around us like a smell. Sometimes I can't remember when it ever was quiet. Of a morning early when I pull up it is, but soon as I get out and unlatch the gate at the bottom of the driveway they know the sound of the chain. A big one set them off this morning with a big voice soft and wet as a mop, and then every kind of barking, little, sharp, deep, every kind there is, so much it rang the metal of the air.

Come back here, I hollered.

The boy stared at me. He had been doing a lot of staring at me. They all do, but the stares are different. Half of them are crazy. So far his was just what I call the beady-eyed look of good fortune. They all have that. The beady-eyed look of good fortune comes from being in jail and being put to work at the animal shelter and then finding out that you will have a live woman to look at all day long for free. Not just any woman either, but a voluptuous goddess. That was what the last prisoner said about me. He was a fruit cocktail. He'd stand there and talk to himself while you were looking straight at him. A voluptuous goddess, he said when he first seen me. At first I thought it wasn't me because I used to be a chunky little girl. I was chunky right up to age twenty-five before I decided to starve myself and go to aerobics. The instructor looked at me the first day like you fat thing you will quit. But now I teach it. Three times a week. And what do I get but a fruit cocktail prisoner describing me under his breath. Long red hair, he whispered. Or pretty green eyes. Or my name, kind of singing it. Starla. Staaaarla Coffey. Staaaaarla pretty name. Bending over to kiss the puppies. Please kiss the black puppy first, please. Oh god look it.

Hey, I finally told him, I can hear what you're saying.

He looked at me funny. Then he said, She can hear what you're saying.

I was almost glad to have the boy. He didn't seem crazy yet. He was looking at me like he hated to quit spraying the hose. Spraying a hose among dancing dogs was a good thing to do for a boy who was in jail to pass the time. I could tell he liked spraying all the dog mess down the drain. It was better than picking it up. He liked the fresh air smell of the water cutting into the smell of the shelter.

But he had stopped spraying.

What? he said.

I was standing there with the little ammunition box. I thought it was funny they kept the materials in an ammunition box. Pick you some out, I said.

Pick some what out?

You know what. What do you think what?

The boy looked around at the dogs looking at him from the dog runs. I knew they looked different to him then.

I can't pick them out, he said.

Yes you can.

I can't pick them out. You pick them out. You're the boss.

But you work here.

But I aint got no authority.

I got authority, I said. And I said to pick you some out.

He sprayed a little short thinking spray.

I thought you said you'd work, I said.

After a minute he said, How many?

A dozen.

A dozen? He made a little exasperated sound and kind of stomped one foot. I can't pick out no dozen.

At least a dozen, I said.

I opened one run a crack and kneeled down and lifted the metal box lid. I had some eye medicine in it. The dog with the bad eye backed up at first, but he backed up happy like he wanted to come forward.

My baby with the bad eye, I said. Come on over here, baby. I got something to help you out. Come over here, baby.

He started coming a little at a time. His tail was going.

Come on, baby, I said.

I could feel the boy still looking at me.

But I'm in jail, he said.

Come on, baby. I didn't turn around. Exactly, I said. That is exactly where you are.

I got my baby's head in my hands and started rubbing his ears and he licked me between all my fingers.

Lick me, baby, I said. I love you. Do you know that? Do you know I love you?

He looked at me as if he did. Some people like dogs, my Grand-daddy Dooley used to say. But I love dogs. Granddaddy Dooley was as gentle as my brothers were mean. He bred squirrel feists, up to two dozen. He let me name them all. Sometimes I was nam-ing as soon as they came out. If one died I saved that name and gave it to another one and that way nobody ever died for long. Granddaddy Dooley was so gentle he wouldn't even let me watch him clean fish. He'd let me, but he would act like I wasn't there. I remember he would whistle. About dustdark he would come off the lake and he smelled like the lake and like fish and beer and sweat. It was a sweet smell. I loved to watch him take each fish and scale her and then saw off the heads and while he sawed them off the fish would open her mouth a little like she was surprised, but not too much. While he was cleaning his fish he would clean them as if I were not there, but when he was done and the clean white meat of their bodies was piled up next to the bloody newspaper he would look up and say, Well, hello, Doll, because that was what he called me. I aint Doll, I said, and he said, Well, then who are you? You know who I am, I said, and he said, Who? I said, Starla, and he said, Starla who? You know who, I said. Starla Coffey. Then he always said, Starla Coffey who? And that made me laugh.

I heard the hose sprayer hit the concrete, and the boy went up toward the front. When I dusted the yellow medicine on the dog's eye, he looked at me as if he resented that but he guessed it was necessary. Dogs are nothing but love. How they die tells you a lot. In a cat the wild comes out. Something rips through them like a nerve when the needle goes in, and they go back wild. But not dogs. The soul of the dogs aint wild no more. They let their lives be taken, licking our fingers with their final breath. I have had so many lay their heads down on my arm, or if they are big enough, my shoulder, my neck.

The ironic thing, the president of the Alexander County Humane

Society told me once, is that we love the animals, and yet we are the ones that have to kill them.

Aint it though, I said.

A short-haired woman, she looked at me with sympathy. Believe me, she said, I know what you go through. I don't know how you have stayed with us as long as you have. I've had others, she said, who couldn't stand one day.

It's been worse, I said. And it has. Back when I was a kid they used to euthanize with a little doghouse they hooked the truck exhaust to. I've been through tick infestations where it seems like they're coming out of the walls, and I've seen parvo, which smells so bad it makes you pray for the regular smell of the shelter, kill everything in here. But she don't know the secret, I have been here four years and never put one animal to sleep. I have not killed a single one.

K9 was doing it when I come. He's got a name, but everybody calls him what they call him on the two-way radio. K9 loves animals too, but with him wild animals are just about a sickness he loves them so much. If a deer gets hit on the highway he'll go down there and sit with it and pet on it, and he gets so excited hives break out all over him. He has some medicine he has to carry in case of a deer. K9 showed me how to do it, how to euthanize, but when he turned the shelter over to me I seen what I could do. The prisoners don't know no better. I think of it as their pet therapy. They don't know this aint part of their punishment. Or, there are other ways. The older ones will do it because I'm a woman and some others will go ahead to show they aint afraid. For a while I told myself I'd start pretty soon. If a prisoner come along who was cruel or couldn't do it I would start. But you know how things in your life get to be like a record. The funny thing is, I never have got a prisoner that liked it. You'd think you would, them coming out of the jail, with the things they have done. But I never have.

After I got the eye doctored, I stood up.

Are you picking? I hollered.

He didn't answer. I could tell it was bothering him. Sometimes when I get a new one like the boy I hate to turn him to this. But I aint going to stay here forever. I've got plans of going to the Knoxville Zoological Park. This woman that come in with puppies give me the idea. She said how good I was with animals and how obvious it was that I loved them and that I would be working for the zoo one day. I never had thought of that. I really didn't have no goals in life. I never even liked the zoo, because they had the animals all caged up and stinking. But the more I thought about it the more I liked the idea. The cages were a lot bigger now and they had natural habitats. None of the animals ever died, I figured, except of old age or some rare disease, and some animals, like rhinos and certain tropical birds and even the bigger snakes, lived for a long long time. Maybe at the zoo, I thought, death was something else. Maybe it wasn't so usual.

After a minute he called out, I got four.

I laughed. A dozen is twelve, I said. I thought you said you would work.

I can't get no twelve.

His voice came from different places, like he was casting around. I knew what he was doing. How do you pick? Do you take the oldest or the poorest or the sickest? Or do you go the other way with mercy and take the fittest and the youngest? You can tell a lot by how they pick.

He came back in. If I get twelve, will you come Sunday morning?

I aint coming Sunday morning, I said. I done told you that.

He had been after me the whole week to come see him baptized. There was a preacher that came to the jail and baptized the inmates. I knew when I first seen this boy that he was waiting to tell me something. He didn't wait long. He told me the first morning.

What are you doing Sunday morning? he said.

It aint none of your business what I'm doing Sunday morning, I said.

I was just going to invite you.

Invite me.

To the baptizing.

What baptizing?

Me and another boy is going to get saved Sunday morning.

Is that right? I said. Saved from what?

From sin.

You mean saved from sitting in the jail all morning.

Huhuh, he said.

You don't know what sin is.

I broke into some cars, he said.

I laughed. That aint sin, I said.

Then I'd like to know what it is, he said.

I know you would.

You're going clubbing Saturday night, aint you? You can't get up on Sunday.

It don't matter to you where I am going.

You got you a man, don't you?

You shut up, I said, but I seen right away that I said it too loud. I was sorry I ever said anything to him about clubbing. That had perked him up and you don't perk them up like that. It wasn't what he thought, anyway. It was different, or at least I was waiting to see if it was. Two weeks ago at the Saddle Rack I had this man start to following me around. I'd had them follow me around before but not in the way he did. I went on to the Wagon Wheel and he was in there too. He kept looking at me like he wanted to say something but he didn't know what it was. Finally I got bored and let him talk to me and he was awful good to talk to. We talked all night long, just about everything. Now he won't hardly let me out of his sight, because of what I told him. I told him something I never have told anybody, but sometimes it is easier, too easy, to tell something to somebody you don't even know.

What I told Mickey was that I had thought about killing myself. It just come out. I don't think I even knew it before then, not in the part of my mind where you know things, so maybe it was a lie. It's not like you think. Everybody thinks somebody who wants to kill herself is the most miserable creature on earth, but it aint necessarily that way. Maybe you are miserable, but it aint the misery that you feel. It's more like an idea you had that keeps on drawing you on and won't go away, like it's the only sure way there is to get ahold. I think it went all the way back to Granddaddy Dooley and me watching him clean the fish and seeing the peace they died in and this idea just come open the way a seed does. It opened up and it started to grow and I just let it, and whenever I need something I take it out and I look at it. I look at it and the roots are all wrapped around like a plant in a pot, but I can unfold them if I want to.

A lot of men would just say something like how you are too pretty to do that and so on, but Mickey was different. He's a lot older than I am. Mickey said he was like that too. He said his plant grew until it was stronger than he was and he tried to do it. I wanted to know how but he wouldn't tell me at first. But he said he saw it. At first I was happy that he did. He saw that I was like that from across the room at the Saddle Rack and that was how come he hung around me like he did. He won't hardly let me out of his sight. He said he's my guardian angel. If I stay in the bathroom too long he is knocking on the door. I don't even sleep with him. We have kissed a couple of times but it felt funny so I stopped. He reminds me too much of my middle brother, but he only looks like him and he aint like him in any other way. Mickey works midnights. Sometimes he waits until I fall asleep to leave. Or if he's off he will stay all night on the couch. I wake up in the morning and he will be there, already dressed, and I think I could have forgotten it longer without him. I could have forgotten it until lunch at least.

I bet you are the queen of that shelter, he said one time.

I got the leash. The boy had gone around picking like it made him mad. Sometimes that is good. He knew what to do. He did it by turning down the little card on the front of the cage. I know the dogs know what that means when they see it. They all do. And the one that is picked just looks at you when you pick him, like well if that's the way it has to be, and the others on the other sides bark and go on like a protest, but the protest is not too loud, because it aint personal.

I opened the run on the first one and he went down in front and put his head nearly to the ground and looked up at me licking out his tongue. He was short-haired, part hound, the color of clay mud. His tail was just going. I talked to him nice and he let me put the collar around his neck and on the way to the euth room he even got a little swagger the way a dog will when he is about to get something the other ones are not. I love you, I told him, and he said he loved me back. A lot of them this is the best they ever get treated the minute before they die.

The boy was standing there watching me like something was my fault, but I just looked back like he was the one whose fault it was.

Get in there, I told him.

Get in where?

In here.

The boy walked into the euth room. He had a broom now, like he had other work to do.

Put down the broom, I said.

He did.

Help me weigh him.

The boy reached under the hound and lifted him up and the dog got that being lifted up look and then he set him down on the scales.

Thirty-two pounds, I said.

You put one cc for every ten pounds, I said. I took a needle and drew up the Fatal Plus. Fatal Plus is blue as the October sky.

Now put him on the table.

When we lifted him up the dog looked at us both as if he sure did appreciate all this. It was the biggest morning of his life to have two people with different smells touching him and lifting him up to a place where he could see. He was so excited he started to piss.

He's pissing, said the boy.

Shut up, I said. It's all right, aint it? I said, talking to the dog. It's all right. I got paper towels.

The boy tried to laugh, but it was too loud. See, that was the boy in him. I tied the leash around the metal arm on the table. The whole shelter had gotten real quiet the way it always does when the souls of the dogs start shifting around.

Take that, I told the boy. I nodded to the table where I had laid out the syringe on a paper towel. Take what, he said.

Take that and I'll show you what to do.

No, he said. I aint doing that.

Yes you are.

The boy had backed away from the table. Our dog was looking at him as if he sure was sorry we weren't getting along.

I picked, but I aint doing that.

I thought you said you would work. I said it in his tone of voice. What do you think you're here for?

I don't know what to do.

Now I'll work, I said. I sure will work.

I can't do that.

Then we'll call and get you on back to the jail.

I don't care.

Where you can do straight time.

Straight time.

They aint no more good time when I call and have you sent back.

No more good time, he said.

All the prisoners love good time. Good time means you're working and not causing trouble and serving two days for the price of one.

He got an idea. I can do it, he said. If you come see me on Sunday morning.

There aint no deals, I said. I aint nowhere on Sunday morning. Nowhere but my own bed.

He smiled. That seemed to pacify him. I could tell he was

thinking about my bed. That was why I had said it. He stood there as if he had had another idea, this one the best of all.

I aint afraid to do it, he said.

Good, I said. I'm right here to help you.

I looked at him real sweet. If you keep on with them, it finally comes out. You just have to find the right way. I could tell with the boy I already had. He picked up the syringe but his hand was shaking.

Take his paw, I said sweetly, and put the needle in above the joint, and then be slow.

He frowned.

I had turned our dog around to him. Sometimes they lift a paw, as if to shake. But our dog hadn't ever had nobody say, Shake, buddy, shake. He was ignorant of that. He just looked at the boy and looked at me and I reassured him that it was all right.

I put my finger on the spot of the vein. Don't you stick my finger, I said. I'll kill you if you stick my finger. Put it all in there. If you don't get it at all in there it won't work.

I watched him. He put the needle in and started moving the little plunger down with his thumb, just like he was supposed to do. It's odd. It's like they know how to do it. It takes very little instruction. Almost immediately, our dog went limp. One second his eyes were looking at me, and then they were staring at nothing. His soul gave up from his body and lifted to the ceiling. Pretty soon the air up there would be full of the souls of dogs. I was sorry. I had meant to stroke his muzzle like I usually do and tell him I loved him, but now he was in the air above us and I couldn't reach him because I had been too busy watching the boy. The boy looked surprised at the ease of it.

It's all right, honey, I said. I started to say, I love you, anyhow, but we both knew the dog was dead and I was afraid the boy would think I was talking to him. He was standing there, kind of shocked, with the empty syringe in his hand, like he had been about to dance. The needle had a drop on the end of it.

Is that all they is? he said.

I held out the garbage bag and the boy slipped him in and then laid him down in the corner. I could tell from the way the boy walked that the dog was heavier. He was suddenly very heavy. It's the soul that keeps the body light. I looked at the shape of him in the white bag. We couldn't put him in the freezer because it was full. We'd have to take them up to the landfill after we got finished. Before I went to get another one I saw the boy standing and looking at me. He looked like a boy who had just done his first job of work. He was torn up, but he was a little proud too. The little proud is what strikes me. It strikes me every single time.

Don't you put it under the skin, I said about the needle. You have to put it in the vein. Watch out, because the vein will roll around. You don't know how much can go wrong.

We did five. He did good. The boy was the best one I had ever had. He had a feel for what to do and it was pitiful that he was excited and scared at the same time. I started to like him. I always like them while they're doing it, but I have to be careful. I usually just talk to the dogs but I started talking to the boy too.

You won't go to church, I told him, when you get out.

I said it a little easier than I had said the other things.

Because you'll be too busy, I said.

Too busy doing what.

You know what.

What.

You know what, I said.

The boy didn't come alive like most of them would. He just lifted the next one up, a great big shorthair. It looked around as if it were on top of the world.

We didn't do any puppies. I don't let them do puppies the first time. We don't do cats early on either. Cats are ugly, like I said. But when he brought the seventh one in I know he seen I was surprised.

What's the matter, he said.

Nothing, I said.

What?

I looked at the dog. It was that old one. I had been seeing him for a week. He was a strange low to the ground bleached out. He was old. He had white hair all over his face.

How come you picked him? I asked.

The boy looked odd.

I don't know, he said. He was old.

I didn't say anything.

I didn't have to pick him, he said. It was a mistake.

No, I said, you picked him.

No I didn't, he said. It was a mistake.

I had to stop. The strange low to the ground bleached out dog was looking at me with his brown eyes and wagging his tail. His tail was old and bleached out too. Even his eyes were old. You don't get attached to a dog here and I never had. Something just hit me. I had never cried in here. The boy could tell I was about to, though, and he was getting more excited.

I didn't pick him, he said. I didn't.

Just shut up, I said. Help me lift him.

I didn't, he said.

But we lifted him up and the low to the ground bleached dog was so happy like they all are. That was when the boy took the syringe and stuck it in his own arm, fairly deep.

I must have took a breath in, but he looked more surprised than I did. His thick eyebrows had gone up and for the first time I noticed his eyes, which were big and blue and full of white.

You dumbass, I said. I didn't know what else to say.

I wanted you to come see me this Sunday, he said. He said it like he was about to cry too.

Take that out.

I aint taking it out, he said. His hand was trembling. Not until you say you'll come see me.

He started to feed a little into his arm. He was good at it. I could see some of the blue bleed out under his skin.

You bastard, I said. Take that out.

The long low bleachie was watching us as if of course this was happening.

I don't care if I die, he said. I done killed all them poor old dogs down yonder.

I'll come on Sunday, I said. Take that out.

You aint coming, he said. You're just saying that.

He gave the plunger a good push and it did something because his eyes changed. I saw that he had planned this out because he had drawn up a big full blue syringe. Take it out, I said. I started toward him but he backed up and raised his foot as if he would kick me. He looked funny.

You care more about them dogs than you do me, he said.

I said I'm coming.

Swear you're coming.

I felt the souls of the dogs in the air over my head. I wished I could set them on him. I swear, I said.

He stopped squeezing it in. You swore, he said. You remember that. You swore.

He pulled the needle out, but he was stupid pulling it out like his arm was a stick of wood, and he tore a place in the flesh. It started off bleeding. He handed me the syringe and I stood there looking at him.

You dumbass, I said.

You swore.

Dumbass.

You aint supposed to be doing this. If you tell what I done I'll tell what you done. He waved his arms a little as if he were real excited about that.

I don't care what you tell, I said. I aint got no help here. I don't know what they expect. Goddamn you. You just messed up.

He shrugged.

I knew I had five more. I wondered if I could quit. There was no way. We had to have the cages. The answer came to me. It always does. I could say we ran out of Fatal Plus. Then tomorrow I would find it. I'd have to find it because I have to record the amounts. But I didn't listen to myself. I still don't know why. Long low bleachie looked at me and I took his paw and put the needle in and killed him. I looked at the boy the whole time the dog sank down, licking. I didn't even look up when the soul came out. It came out like a bug from its skin, because the skin was so old and the soul was so new. It went up with the others and they looked down at us. The boy watched it happen. Then he carried him over to the corner just like he had done the others.

You didn't have to do him, he said.

I just looked at him. It hadn't felt like I thought it would. It just felt like time had swollen up inside a balloon and I realized that about the last word long low bleachie had heard was Goddamn. I felt tricked, but it wasn't just the boy who had tricked me, but something bigger and way trickier. I hadn't felt this way since I was a little girl and my brothers tricked me some awful way, but I didn't cry. I did four more. The boy helped me like the most helpful helpmate a person could have. I hated him. The reason I hated him was I wondered if that was what I had looked like. I wondered if I had looked like the most helpful helpmate. I was afraid that was what I was.

When K9 came back his truck was full. I tried not to show anything. His whole truck was barking and screeching. It was like the dogs we killed had just run around to the front of the shelter and jumped in. I told the boy to go help him unload.

You know where the empty cages are, I said. You picked them out.

I went outside and K9 was getting out of the truck. He looked at me like he could tell something was different.

Smokebreak, he said.

I said all right. K9 knows I don't smoke but one day he said I ought to get a break just like all the ones that do. I knew he was watching out for me. I think he knows. I think that is why he leaves.

I got a dog back there I want you to see, he said. I aint never seen nothing like her before.

He said it like he knew I needed something like that.

Okay, I said.

K9 is always finding something unusual. He sees unusual even in the usual. He believes in all kinds of things. He thinks there are bigfoots and so on. If it is unusual, K9 is interested in it.

There is a little path back through the woods that I always use. The woods are pretty. The trees are so big and tall the limbs don't start until way up, but it was awful cold and windy. I was afraid of what the wind would do to the souls of the dogs. The wind was combing through those limbs and blowing over my face like ice. I had on my thick coat. The little path comes out on a bluff over the landfill. It's not a natural bluff but a man-made one where they dug out for the landfill. All of a sudden the woods open and this big red clay bluff is there. It's just open. The landfill was all spread out with a big white whirl of seagulls over it. They wheeled around, squeaking all over like a thousand rusty wheels. I stood and watched them. K9 knows why I come up here every morning. He knows it's to cry. Crying to me is like feeding. You know the way dogs eat, so hungry, is the way I cry. I tell myself that I have to cry for the souls of all them dogs and if I do the souls go into new dogs. They blow away and go into new ones.

But this time I couldn't do it. I couldn't feed. At first I thought I couldn't because I felt nasty. I felt nastier than if I had cleaned out the whole shelter on my hands and knees. It was like I had to be clean to cry the way I had to take a bath before I went to bed at night. Not being able to cry was like not being able to sleep too. It got later and later and earlier and earlier and I thought about all kinds of things. I thought about the winter. They said the winter of 1985 was the worst of the century. The landfill dozer backed up and spun and went ahead. It vibrated deep into the ground with a sound as if it were saying. Fool. Fooool. Fool. I thought about just leaving for the day and telling them I was sick, but I couldn't. I had the zoo to think about, and I was afraid Mickey would be there when I got home. I didn't want to see

Mickey. I never wanted to see him anymore. I went back down the path to the shelter.

When I got there, everything was the same, even though I hadn't cried. I still had the souls. K9 and the boy had loaded up the truck. It was loaded with frozen dogs and cats. K9 had left it running, so the cab was warm. That was just another thing he does for me, but today I felt like I didn't deserve it. K9 was letting the boy sit on the front step.

He says he's sick, said K9. His face was real wide with a lot of concern in it. Do you think he's telling the truth?

I looked at the boy. His eyes were half closed. He had been crying.

No, I said.

She said you aint sick, said K9.

The boy didn't look up. I can work, he said.

But he said it real slow.

I took the truck by myself. I pulled it up on the scales and rolled down the window. Snow was starting to fall. It was that dry snow of cold weather, the kind that comes even in the sun. It wasn't going to amount to anything. Granddaddy Dooley used to call it blue snow.

There she is, said the guy in the scalehouse. Where you been, honey?

I shrugged and drove on through.

Tiny operates the dozer. He was way up on a hill rolling the frozen dirt over when he saw me, but he stopped immediately and hopped off. I had already backed it up. I was under the seagulls now. They went way up, squeaking and turning. It was like my crying, the crying I couldn't get, was somewhere up on top of the gulls. I did roll the window down and look out and smile at Tiny and he smiled back.

You're lucky it's you, he said. I wouldn't do this for no other human being.

He unloaded the truck for me. He has done this since the first day. Being as big and fat as he is, Tiny knows he wouldn't have a chance with me. But something about that just makes us closer. It makes us more able to talk. In pretty weather I get out and stand and look around and let him look at me. I know he's doing it but I don't care. Today I tried not to look in the rearview mirror, but there was nowhere else much to look so I watched everything. The frozen ones landed stiffly, but there were some that did not. They were the ones from this morning. Some of them were mine, I knew. A few of the white gulls had landed in the frozen clay in front of the truck. Tiny just waved me off. He didn't even stop to talk. It was cold, I guessed. I rode back over the frozen mud and he was headed back to his dozer. He was taking little steps. I wondered why Tiny did this for me, even if I did nothing but wave at him. He didn't even seem disappointed, the way the scale guy did.

Four hundred and twenty-nine, said the scale guy.

This time my window was right up against his and he was looking in the truck like I didn't have pants on.

I wrote that down. Four hundred and twenty-nine pounds.

That's one big old cur, said the scale guy.

I didn't say anything. You don't say anything to the scale guy.

K9 had let the boy lie down inside the shelter office. He was on his side on the floor. He was curled up a little.

K9 whispered to me, I think he's drunk, but I can't smell no alcohol.

I shook my head.

Do you think he's been smoking something?

K9 showed me the dog he had wanted me to see. It was a great big wolf-looking dog. K9 said he thought it was part wolf. He said you could tell by the eyes and the paws and something about the ears. This, said K9, was what dogs was before they was dogs. He was always thinking something like that. One time he got called to a crazy woman's house out in Gobbler Knob and she told him there were dogs running around with human faces and that really got his attention. He talked all day about those dogs with human faces. The more he talked about it, I thought he halfway believed it himself.

The boy went to sleep. He slept in a funny way for a boy because he was snoring. It wasn't really a snore but a kind of whine that moved his whole body. He was doing it regular as a machine. Finally up in the afternoon he got up and sat against the wall and kind of looked at us. A woman brought in a box of kittens. They were wild. They opened their throats and hissed at me. She wanted me to tell her they would all be adopted.

I wanted to say, Do you see anybody standing here waiting on them? But I didn't. I am very nice to the public. I can't guarantee that, I said, and she looked at me as if she wanted me to know how sorry she was about that. I looked back to let her know I had run out of sympathy just before she arrived. This was usually when I asked for a donation, but I had to wait for the dog to quit hollering. He had been hollering so loud, more a howl than a bark, that it had been hard for us to talk. The woman turned to look at the boy, still leaning against the wall, as if maybe he would comfort her, but he didn't even smile.

What's the matter with him? the woman said.

I realized the dog was howling out front instead of in back. I had figured it was one of the new ones K9 had brought in, but it wasn't. He was bringing it in the front. K9 had his heavy gloves on and he came carrying it through the front door. It was so loud the woman covered her ears. I stood up. Even the boy was looking.

Where'd you get that? I asked.

He was out front, said K9. He just come up.

The dog was a yellow, but it was covered with red mud. It was a harsh slick red mud and it was all over him. The mud was sticking to K9's coveralls too. He ran it in back and opened a pen.

I asked the woman for a donation and she started looking in her purse. While she was taking out tissue I saw another dog go across the front porch. They're getting loose, is the first thing I thought. The boy left a run open. But I knew the dog. I know all of them. I got up and went out and there was another around the woman's car. It was pissing on her left rear tire. It wasn't dirty as the first one, but it had mud in odd places, in the ears and on the knobs of the backbone. It did what I call digging a wheel, with his back legs, and ran around the corner of the shelter the way dogs let loose will run with totally jaunty freedom.

The thought came to me then. I started to run toward them, but I went back inside first. The woman had come up to the front door and was watching me, but I went past her to the boy. He was curled back up on the floor on his blanket. I got down and kissed him in his suggestion of a beard.

You fool, I said. You blessed fool. You must have missed the vein. You weren't as good as I thought.

When I stood up the woman had a big look of excitement as if she had brought in a box of lintball kittens and gotten so much more in return, but I ignored her and went on outside and up the path through the woods. I was just in time. Two, five more were coming up through the frozen mud of the landfill beneath the wheels of seagulls at a run. There would be no frozen ones, I knew. There would only be the boy's, unless I had messed up too. Another one was popping up out of the red clay. I saw it. I saw the head come out, pointing straight up at the sky and wiggling around and around like a worm, and then the legs were out, and it was kind of humping the dirt and then it was out. It was out and shaking off and running a little ways and shaking off some more. The others were coming too. I laughed. It was the most I had laughed in a long time, but then I ran back down the path to the shelter, and by the time I got there the first ones were coming through the woods.

Go back, I said. Go back.

I had felt so happy running through the woods. It was like when I used to run toward Granddaddy Dooley when he would come home off the lake. Go back, I hollered, and they stopped and looked at me as if I were the funniest thing they had ever seen. Go back! I hollered. But they could tell I wanted them. I wanted them to come on because I hoped not all of them would be the boy's. I hoped one of them, maybe just one, would be mine.

Stephen Marion is a newspaper reporter and photographer who lives in East Tennessee. His novel *Hollow Ground* was published in 2002, and he is the recipient of a National Endowment for the Arts fellowship in fiction.

JEFF DANIEL MARION

I used to stop by the local animal shelter every week to photograph the dogs and cats available for adoption for the newspaper, and I ended up writing a series of feature stories about the place. The animal control officer told me a story of dogs and cats coming back to life one afternoon because the euthanasia drug wasn't effective. I wasn't able to forget it. Why don't you go over to your local animal shelter and see if someone is waiting for you?

Philipp Meyer

ONE DAY THIS
WILL ALL BE YOURS

(from *McSweeney's*)

My father grew up in a mining town in West Virginia; baths outside in a coal-fired tub, missing strikers found buried in the slag piles, the vein giving out and the whole town with it. His father and twelve others died in a shaft collapse.

I went to see him after my mother left, ten years after the rest of us. My brother and sister still wouldn't talk to him. My sister got pregnant in college and married a banker; she must have played up the family saga because he treated her like a rescued bird, though she'd gotten off easiest of the three of us. I'd visited her in the Keys and she was nervous, and then the banker scolded her in front of my face for leaving the children alone with me. I headed back to Georgia that night, but my appetite was ruined and my face went gray for weeks and I told everyone I had a virus. I'm a big man. I could have wrecked that banker's jaw with one swipe.

My brother lived in Canada; he and I were on good terms. We spoke often and he asked me to visit and I wondered what he'd told his new family about me. I decided it was better if I never found out.

As for my father, he'd been alone a week before I called him. I had to work up to it. None of the others would even consider it.

"Nice to hear from you," he said. "I mean your timing."

"I was wondering how you were holding up."

"Been working on the house all week."

"Maybe you should be around people."

"Thank you," he told me.

"I was just saying."

"Did you know about this?"

"I didn't know anything," I said.

"You two didn't talk much, I know that."

"She and Melanie talked, mostly."

Melanie was my sister.

"Melanie probably knew."

"It doesn't matter," I told him.

"Things don't get easier. I thought they would, but I was wrong. In fact, they go downhill, generally speaking."

"This is just a rough spot," I said. "You'll get over this."

"My loyal son."

"Maybe we can just pretend to be nice people."

"There are things about us," he said. "There are things I've learned and you're not going to know them until it's too late."

"Come off it," I told him.

"I named Bud Mitchell executor."

"Pop."

"I'm just telling you."

"You don't even talk to him anymore."

"I called him last week. Everything is straightened out."

"Are you sick?" I said. "Tell me. Mom didn't say anything."

"I don't want your mother to find me. At first I thought I did."

We were quiet. I could hear him breathing.

"I'm calling the cops," I finally said.

"That would be best. I don't want your mother to be the one."

I had trouble staying between the lines on the road and finally I pulled over. My skin was cold and I was damp everywhere and my hands were tingling, and in my ears I could hear my blood.

When I was a kid I shot a groundhog with a deer rifle from ten feet. I thought about that and how my father would look. Then I was sick.

Afterward I lay on the hood and took off my shirt to dry. The sun felt close and bright and the hood burned my back but I was shivering. I touched the padding on my gut — the softest it had ever been. Trucks went by and the air shook but I didn't hear anything.

I called my father to tell him I was on the way.

"You're not coming," he said. "I knew it before you called."

"I just had to pull over a minute."

"Sure."

"Are you outside? It sounds like you're outside."

"The neighbors are all looking at me. These people are afraid of everything."

"Wait for me," I told him. "I'll be there in ten minutes."

When I was younger I would hold broken glass in my hand and squeeze it until I couldn't think about anything else. Even now I can spin a carving knife into the air and catch it by the handle. In college I went to a palm reader, and she took one look and refused to say anything.

I pulled back onto the highway and called my brother and sister but they didn't pick up. *I know you're there,* I said into their machines. I thought about calling my mother and decided against it. She would go back if she knew. She was the only one of us who deserved better.

Their house was a rancher. All the windows were closed and it was stale inside. I started sweating and the blood came back to my ears. There were unwashed dishes in the kitchen, which my mother would not have allowed. In the living room, there was a sheet on the couch and a pillow, empty beer bottles on the side table, a dirty magazine, unopened and still wrapped in plastic. The dining-room table was bare except for a piece of paper with my address and phone number in careful print. *Son,* it said. My father was outside, at the edge of the pond with a skeet gun across his lap.

He didn't look up when I walked out.

"Pop?"

There were dozens of new homes. I could see faces of the people inside. Their fences ran to our lawn. Long rectangles of orange dirt lay where the sod in their yards had died, and the sky beyond our house looked immense and empty where it had once been blocked with trees.

"Sorry about the lawn," he said.

I looked around for a sign that the gun might be unloaded, but there was a box of shells on its side in the grass, half scattered.

"You mind if I hold that," I said.

"I lent the mower to the woman down the street and she drove it off a curb. It's at the shop."

"Have you called Tim or Melanie?"

"You can't trust women with complex machinery," he said. "Their brains get all haywired."

"A riding mower isn't really a complex machine," I told him.

"All you're doing is agreeing with me."

"I'm not trying to fight."

"You didn't have to come over. You haven't come over for nine years and all of a sudden here you are."

"Let me hold the shotgun," I said.

He didn't let go of it, but he didn't tighten his grip, either.

"Notice anything different about the yard," he said. "Other than the woods are gone."

"No."

"Look carefully."

I thought I could wrestle the gun from him. I looked around the yard. It was the nicest part of the house, an acre with the pond at the center, a white pergola running up one side, dogwoods and apple trees. There were tulip beds around the pond. When my father was a kid, he'd seen something like it in a magazine. We pulled the weeds by hand, cut the grass around the flowers with scissors, watered sunup and sundown. There were gophers, and the poison killed our dog. When my brother left for college he filled his truck with rock salt and was going to dump it everywhere. My sister and I stopped him.

But, standing there with my father, I noticed something new. There was a sandbox, as if for children.

"Where'd that come from?"

"You guys all seem to be spawning. I thought it might come in handy."

My sister's four children, the oldest nearly twelve, had never met him. My brother and his wife had their third on the way but they'd insisted he not know.

"You need to talk to someone. I'm worried about you."

"You bought a house yet?"

"No. I put in for a transfer to Denver."

"Shack up the road just went for two hundred thousand. Believe that?"

"You'd probably get half a mil with all the land. Move someplace smaller."

"The house would be full enough if it weren't for your mother."

"Don't."

"She doesn't know how stupid she looks," he said. "Running around at her age."

"Let's not do this."

"Be glad you never married."

"I'm thirty-two."

"Your grandfather passed when he was thirty-four."

"That's a nice thing to tell someone."

"I keep thinking about that Cadillac I bought her. She drove it right out of here."

"She could have taken more," I said.

"I'd kill her before I let her have this house."

I didn't say anything.

"She's a whore. I'm not afraid to say it."

"I'm going home now."

"Come on. I've got steaks in the freezer."

"You are fucking impossible."

"I'm just lonely, Scotty. I worked so hard to make her happy."

"You don't really think that."

"I gave her that car last year. And a goddamn plumber. It burns me up, that guy riding around in my Caddy."

"Actually," I said, "he's a steamfitter."

"What?"

"Not a plumber."

"What the hell," he said.

"I want to stop this," I said. "I'm sorry."

"You know I took baths in an outdoor tub that we heated over a coal burner? That's how much we had."

"I know you had it rough, Pop."

"You had everything you asked for."

"Pop," I said.

"Your grandfather could do a hundred pushups. He'd cuff me and my ears would ring all morning."

I didn't say anything.

"It's in the blood."

"That doesn't mean anything," I told him.

We watched football for two hours without speaking. My father correctly predicted the final score. I'd been a guard at Michigan for a season, then quit to spite him.

As for the shotgun, I'd unloaded it and pocketed the shells.

"Plenty more where they came from," he said about the shells.

"Clemson is on fire this year," is what he said about football.

"They seem fine," I said.

"They're a lot better than fine."

"You need someone to talk to. Other than the guys at the trap range."

"Let me ask you a question, Scott."

"Probably not."

"Are you mad at your mother?"

"Dad."

"Well. Are you?"

"Off-limits," I said.

"Do me the favor," he said. "For ten years of not seeing you."

"That's not on me," I said. "That's on all of us."

"Just answer it. I want to hear you say it."

Of course I was mad at her. At eighteen you can look at your father and know you'll never be anything like him. At thirty it's a different story. All three of us blamed her for not seeing it when she married him, but in the end we'd paid her back. We'd escaped to colleges in different states, stayed away summers and holidays. I was the youngest and the last to leave and my mother couldn't look at me when she dropped me at the airport. *I guess I won't be seeing you much,* she said. *I guess not,* I told her. Then I disappeared like my brother and sister. I've always known it was the worst thing I've ever done.

"I'm not mad at Mom," I told him.

"Sweet Jesus Christ," said my father. "Now I've heard it all."

He picked up the remote to turn the TV back on, but I stopped him before he could.

"I used to think you did everything on purpose," I said.

"Everything what?"

"But now I'm not sure. I think it comes from someplace you don't understand."

He didn't say anything.

"I liked it better when it was on purpose."

His fists balled up like the old days and his face got dark.

I left him on the couch and got a case of beer from the kitchen.

"I'm going outside," I told him.

The sun was going down when my father came onto the patio. I don't know if he saw all the neighbors. I watched him load his gun. Then I looked away.

Where the people stood with their children and fences I imagined everything as it had been before, land unbroken all the way to the river, pigeon hawks hunting the clearings, foxes and deer, owls at night. When we were kids we would camp in those hills, my father and brother and I, and I thought about the feeling of the cold air on my face and the warmness inside the sleeping bag and the sound of my father's soft breathing as he slept.

I threw my beer into the pond. I could feel him watching me. I threw the rest of the bottles one by one. They skittered across the grass, cracked on the slate path. I expected to hear a shot. When the case of beers was empty I went into the garage and dragged back a trash can full of bottles. I aimed them against the rocks in the pond, against the pergola and the flagstone in the yard.

The neighbors stood at their fences and watched.

"Do you want us to call the police," one of them said.

My father didn't answer. I kept throwing. The sun was getting lower and the glass on the lawn was glowing like embers from a wreckage.

"You can stop now," he said.

I barely heard him.

"Scotty," he said.

Then there was a noise, a gunshot, and a bottle cracked apart in the air. Something cut me on the face. The neighbors started away from their fences. My father had the gun shouldered and the pieces of the bottle were spinning and falling over the yard and I touched my check and it was sticky hot. We're even, I thought quickly, but then I knew we weren't and that we couldn't be. I watched him and he couldn't hold my eyes, and I saw the thinness in his arms and legs, the slouch in his back.

"That's enough," he said, but it was a whisper. It was so quiet I could barely hear it. I didn't know what it meant, or what he wanted me to do.

Then he was leaning and I caught him and held him up. I was lifting him from under his elbows and he was sagging back against me.

He doesn't want me to see him like this, I thought, but after that we didn't move. The sun was in our faces. I could hear the sound of his breathing, soft like I'd remembered it, and the light was spread across the hills and trees as if the land had been set on fire.

<hr />

Philipp Meyer's stories have appeared in *McSweeney's* and *The Iowa Review* and his nonfiction has appeared in *Salon, The Austin Chronicle,* and *Baltimore Times.* Among other things, he's worked as an ambulance driver, a carpenter, a derivatives trader, and a bicycle mechanic. When Hurricane Katrina hit New Orleans, he was one of the first emergency medical technicians to arrive in the city. He's currently a fellow at the Michener Center for Writers in Austin, Texas, where he's finishing a novel.

Most of the time, the feeling or image that inspires me to sit down and write a story is only vaguely related to the final creation. In this case, a friend and I were sitting in his backyard drinking beer one afternoon when we were struck with a brilliant idea — instead of throwing our empty beer bottles away, we should throw them into the air and shoot them with a shotgun. As it turned out, the broken glass falling through the sunlight was quite beautiful, and from that image came a story about the moment a father and son begin to forgive each other.

Jason Ockert

JAKOB LOOMIS

(from *The Oxford American*)

Therm is in the woodshed rubbing gasoline on his blood-stained sneakers when he sees a handcuffed man break from the woods and amble toward the house. Hefting an axe, Therm calls out, and the man, surprised, arms defeated behind his back, freezes.

The men consider each other over the short distance of semi-mowed backyard lawn in the cool pre-rain breeze. The mower hunkers to the bloodied ground between the woodshed and the house. For a moment the men feel the weight of their guilt, and then the moment breaks.

What the Hell are you doing? Therm asks, stepping forward with the axe.

Hoping I could get a little water, the handcuffed man says, nodding to a green hose heaped next to the house.

Therm is a big man with broad shoulders and a measurable gut. He isn't a fighter, but he can defend himself if he has to. Especially with an axe. And if his potential opponent is handcuffed. There is nothing threatening about the restrained man; he is a foot shorter than Therm and has wiry hair, sun-browned skin, and a long chin. What makes Therm uncomfortable are the man's eyes. There is something off about them — not crossed exactly, just crooked.

Looks like you've gotten yourself into some trouble, Therm says, squaring himself against the other man.

The man raises his eyebrows, cocks his head back, and gazes down his chin at the bloodied patch of lawn. You too, he responds.

What, that? That was an accident. I hit a snake, Therm says.

A lot of blood for a snake.

A nest of them, I guess.

Therm was new to his house, just out of a wasted marriage to a woman who cheated on him with several of the felines in a low-budget theater troupe who performed an interpretation of *Cats* in town for a season. Therm discovered a long whisker on the stairs and thought nothing of it because of Molly and Digger, both big, nervous cats. Then whiskers started turning up everywhere. Whiskers on the love seat, in the hamper, next to the lava lamp, in the trunk of their Suburban: brown, blond, green. Green, of course, made Therm suspicious. Then, because his wife considered herself an amateur actress, and because he wanted to make an effort to understand her passions more, Therm bought two tickets to the show. He was shocked by the performance; the unitard-clad men with unrealistic bulges in their crotches meowing and fawning across the stage didn't impress him. When the green cat came out, Therm's wife had emitted a low purr of sorts, and that was that. Therm didn't make a fuss. She kept the property, he was rewarded a significant check her family could afford if the reason for the divorce stayed discreet. Molly and Digger remained with the wife.

Therm moved south and into the country where he wouldn't be bothered. He was a contract cartographer and worked at the drafting table he erected in the family room. The missing boy, though he wasn't missing yet, let his pet parrot free. The bird flew to Therm's property, landed in a tree infested with gnats, and started squawking. Therm went outside to look at the pretty bird thinking that maybe parrots were native to this neck of the woods. He tried talking to it. He said, *Hi birdie, birdie, hi, birdie, birdie,* and so on. The parrot squawked and sometimes bobbed its head. Therm retired back inside for work on the rivers of the Middle

East. The parrot kept at its racket. Therm tried to ignore the bird. He put cotton in his ears. Music didn't help. Outside, he talked reason; *Okay, bird, enough. Shoo or shut-up, birdie, birdie.* The parrot preened its feathers and continued screeching. Gnats were abundant. Therm tossed rocks. When he called Animal Control they said that a noisy bird wasn't an animal they considered a nuisance. He had been put on hold for a minute. When the operator came back, he said to Therm, We'll send a rescue squad over immediately, you're in grave danger, whatever you do, don't let it hit you on the head with its lethal crap. You wouldn't believe how many people die from parrot dookie every year. There was laughter in the background. Therm hung up.

All that night the parrot made its noise. The next day, more of the same. Therm couldn't concentrate on the complicated tributaries of the Euphrates River. He took a long hike and disrupted a fox chasing a rabbit. The fox hid behind a slash pine and angrily glared at Therm as the rabbit dashed away.

A half mile from home, Therm heard the parrot. When he listened hard, Therm detected a squawking pattern that he imitated for a while for fun. Then the pattern broke.

In bed that night, trying to ignore the bird, Therm thought of Madeline, his ex-wife. They had been an attractive couple in college, lost their virginity together, wrote their own marriage vows, enjoyed the mall on late afternoons. Damn her for throwing that all away, he thought.

In the morning, Therm started drawing irrational parallels between the parrot and Madeline and frequently yelled for Maddy to *pipe down* or *put a sock in it*. This made him feel a little better.

The bird kept calling and eating gnats and staring at Therm with sidelong eyes as Therm stood below it with the old rifle his grandfather had left him in the will. Therm figured he'd scare the damned thing by firing near its head. But the parrot didn't budge, just twittered uncomfortably and changed to a higher pitch. A couple shots later, Therm knew he wasn't trying to warn the bird anymore. Still, he couldn't get a bead on the multicolored beast as it hopped from branch to branch.

At Food 4 U, Therm bought fruit he knew his ex-wife enjoyed; grapes, strawberries, and bananas. On the front door of the store was a black-and-white picture of the missing boy, smiling, that the clerk had just posted. Therm paid for his food. At home, he diced the fruit and laced it with rat poison from a bottle he kept under the sink. He placed the concoction on a paper plate and set it on a stump beneath the trees. He hid himself in the shed with the door cracked and waited all afternoon for something to happen. The bird squawked. A squirrel nosed the fruit but left it alone. Finally, just before the sun set, the parrot glided down to the fruit and investigated. It ate a grape and spit it out. It overturned the paper plate and shat. Therm rushed out of the shed with the axe, but the parrot was too quick and settled itself back in the tree.

Therm couldn't get Madeline out of his head as he smudged the Tigris River. She had really whipped him good. She never let him eat spicy foods and complained when he walked around the living room naked. She wore wool socks to bed and rubbed her feet over his legs at night. Some mornings, he'd wake up with a rash. Then she sleeps with a clowder of cat-men? She didn't even like sex, he thought. She had a bevy of excuses when he was in the mood; *I'm tired, I've got cramps, Molly's in heat, I just washed these sheets,* and so on. Supposedly, one of the actors had a SAG connection and Madeline was going to be an extra in some romantic comedy coming out next fall. She screws me, Therm thought, finds success doing something she loves, and I'm here with the loudest parrot in the world.

Therm decided to call Madeline's house and let the parrot bark its brains out over the answering machine.

In the morning, Therm went to Widgit's Hardware and asked a Widgit employee for the most powerful nozzle they had. Next to the register was the black-and-white picture of the missing boy, smiling.

Are we talking fifty feet? the Widgit employee asked.

A hundred and fifty, Therm replied.

That's a specialty item, it'll cost you.

Charge it.

Therm attached the high-powered nozzle to the hose and tested it against the side of the house. It chipped the paint. Satisfied, Therm unwound the hose and stalked up next to the parrot-tree. The parrot quieted and watched suspiciously. Therm let it rip. The parrot was caught off-guard and fell from the tree. It started to fly, but Therm kept the water steady and knocked it from the sky onto his lawn where it lay stunned.

Therm stood over the bird and sprayed it again for good measure. He bent down to flick the parrot's head and it snipped his hand. Blood welled up around his knuckles. There was a rag in the shed. Also in the shed, the axe. By the time the bleeding stopped, he had convinced himself to chop the bird to pieces. He raised the axe. The parrot blinked a few times and made a feeble chirp. It kind of pouted like he'd seen his ex-wife pout. Therm couldn't follow through. He went back into the shed, noticed that his hand was bleeding again, and fired up the lawn mower. The bird raised its voice. Therm set the mower on course, closed his eyes, told himself, *This won't hurt a bit,* and pushed the machine forward.

Jakob Loomis was told to be home before dinner. That gave him plenty of time, he figured. He was meeting Tommy Tucker at the baseball diamond and the two of them were going to take Tommy's pellet gun to the pond and shoot tadpoles. When Jakob got to the baseball field, Tommy was already there, waiting in the dugout. He had a worried look on his face.

Can't do it today, man, Tommy said.

Why not? Jakob asked.

Mrs. Pratt called my mom and told her I cheated on our math test.

Dumb Mrs. Fat, Jakob said.

My mom grounded me. I told her I had to meet you and get the homework assignment, but I have to get back now. I brought the pellet gun if you want it.

Sure. Jakob took the gun.

See you in school tomorrow, Tommy said, and ran away.

The pond was located between two mounds of sand that Jakob had to walk over to get to the bank. The water was green and full of cattails and lily pads. Jakob spotted a tadpole, took aim, but decided not to fire. He couldn't figure out why he should. When Tommy had the pellet gun, he took careful aim, his tongue lolling out of his mouth, and fired. Nine out of ten times, the tadpole floated to the surface. This was impressive. But Jakob thought differently. There was no need to kill baby frogs, or any animal. He even set his pet parrot free because it seemed to complain about being caged all the time.

Your hand's bleeding, the handcuffed man says. Snakebite?

No. I must have cut it on the axe.

Therm lets his hand hang loosely and bleed. A thin rain begins to slant down over the men. The handcuffed man tilts his head back and lets the water cool his face. Droplets of moisture linger on his eyelashes and a fine layer of precipitation forms on his forehead and chin.

Therm glances down at his stained sneakers. When he tried to clean them with the hose, the blood had merely smeared. Therm had washed the pulpy remains of the parrot from the mower down to the fringe of the woods. A cloud of gnats hangs over the remains. In a wicked moment, Therm tries to imagine Madeline's face opening a package with the dead bird in it. Her jaw would drop and she'd cover her mouth with her ring-less hand. She'd probably shriek something dramatic like, *Oh, Christ, No!* and ask her cat-boyfriends what to do. They'd say call the police. Therm would send the package anonymously, of course, and he'd use gloves so that fingerprints weren't an issue. But there was a problem, Therm remembered. When the police asked Maddy about anything suspicious lately, she'd recall the odd message on her answering machine. The police would replay the tape with the recorded squawking and use a forensics team to determine that the pulpy mess had been a parrot and that the cawing on the tape had been a parrot. They'd trace the call somehow, arrest Therm, and he'd spend time in the slammer, humiliated. Better let the bird decompose in the rain and not make a big deal out of it.

If you're not going to give me a drink of water, I think I'm going to move on, the handcuffed man says.

You can't drink from that hose. There's a high-powered nozzle that'd shake your teeth. The rain should be enough.

The handcuffed man licks his lips.

As far as letting you just walk off, Therm says, give me one good reason why I shouldn't call the police?

The handcuffed man tries to look as relaxed as possible in handcuffs. He says, Sometimes the police shouldn't be involved.

Maybe so, but that doesn't explain the handcuffs.

I'd rather not say.

Then I better call the police.

If you'll feel better about it, call them. But the reason for these cuffs has got nothing to do with them. It's more domestic.

I'm listening.

Cole's Daddy was a snake handler and a preacher of the Gospel and of Jesus Christ the Savior, Our Lord. His Daddy told Cole he was born from a Godblessed serpent. Cole shared his crib with snakes, he learned to walk with snakes, and the first word out of his mouth was *hiss*. These things made Cole's Daddy proud. He took his son all over Texas to preach the faith and demonstrate with serpents that the Good Lord watched over the faithful. In a trance with a viper, Cole's Daddy got bit in the mouth. His lips and tongue turned rotten and made speaking nearly impossible. He tried to preach with just his hands, but nobody listened. So he turned to drinking. And he turned to his boy.

Cole really did like snakes. They were mostly quiet and friendly, and if there was any evil in them, he couldn't find it. After his

Daddy got bit, Cole tried his best to keep the faith. He learned some sign language and tried to teach it to his father. His father just shook his fists and Cole got the message.

When the money ran out, Cole's Daddy figured he could use his son's natural snake abilities to earn them a living. He believed God owed him that, at least. There were a lot of tourists and non-believers who would be impressed if they saw his boy crawl out of a sleeping bag filled with rattlers and moccasins and such. With the little money he had saved, Cole's Daddy made flyers that said: SEE THE SNAKECHILD ESCAPE FROM A SLEEPING BAG FULL OF POISON SNAKES! The performance didn't draw a big crowd, but it brought in enough money to travel and to get Cole's Daddy cross-eyed drunk.

Cole found it tricky to crawl out of the sleeping bag filled with snakes because the snakes were packed so tightly together that they became irritated. He had to wait until they calmed down and then very carefully pull himself out to the crowd of anxious people and the applause. Each time he had to move a different way to keep from rolling over a snake's head. Once, after years of crawling out of the sleeping bag, during a Snake Roundup, just as Cole had pulled his head and shoulders out of the bag, a drunk said, Bullshit, those snakes aren't poisonous, and he threw his bottle. It wasn't a good throw and when it shattered in front of Cole a thin shard of glass struck the boy in the eye. The snakes hissed and snapped at one another as the crowd tried to decide what to do. The drunk thought he might have made a mistake. Everybody waited. Cole breathed lightly as his eye bled and the snakes settled. Finally, he crawled the rest of the way out.

The hospital couldn't save Cole's eye so they made him a glass one. Police went around arresting people for disorderly conduct and child neglect. Cole was sent to a foster home and Cole's Daddy found refuge in the church, where he tried his best to apologize through cheap religious cards on which he wrote, *Son, I'm so sorry, I'm really proud of you, God loves you and I do, too!* in sloppy cursive.

Cole finished growing up quietly. He made few friends and had trouble looking people in the eye. His closest relationship was with God. After Cole understood that he wasn't born from a serpent, he tried to figure out who his mother was. Through hospital records, and with reluctant help from his Daddy, Cole learned his mother lived in Florida and worked for a theme park there. Cole turned eighteen, took a bus to Central Florida, and paid for a ticket. Information directed him to the *Hop Along Trail!* His mother was a costumed, pink-furred rabbit who sang a happy song and hopped from foot to foot. Cole watched her in the thin crowd and munched on a candy apple. She was good at her job, a group of children clapped and danced to the song. The tune was catchy. Cole hummed along with the children. Nearby, a tall, young couple with a video camera glanced over disapprovingly. Cole realized he was out of place, all grown-up with candy apple on his mouth trying to have a moment with his mother in a sea of children. He blew a kiss and left.

An ad in the paper mentioned big bucks for capturing venomous snakes and selling them to pharmacies in order to make anti-venom. Cole became a hunter and aged. On good days, he'd gather a dozen serpents. Once in a while the law gave him trouble for trespassing while he was wrangling snakes in private property. He bought a trailer out in the country and tried to mind his own business. He had girlfriends here and there. He attended a Methodist church. His Daddy passed away Godless and broken. On the television, Cole learned about the missing boy and made a mental note to keep an eye out for him.

Out of the corner of his eye, Jakob caught sight of a frog at the waterline. It was a white frog. Jakob couldn't believe it. He had never seen a white frog and as far as he knew, they didn't exist. But here one was. Setting the gun aside, Jakob crept closer to the frog and dove for it. He missed, slid half into the water, getting his pant leg soaked, and leaned against the mound to wait for the frog to reappear. It popped up on the other side. Jakob stalked it more carefully and when he got close enough, he wiggled one hand out as a distraction and plunged his other hand in after the frog. This time Jakob was successful. He pulled it from the water by a long white leg and clutched it to his body. His heart pounded and he tried to catch his breath. A white frog. Tommy wasn't going to believe this. Jakob had to keep the frog to show Tommy tomorrow after school. The frog was slippery and he nearly dropped it as he climbed over the mounds and away from the pond. He'd leave the pellet gun there for now, find an old soda can or something to put it in, and show it off tomorrow. Then he'd set it free. It wasn't dinnertime yet, the sun still had some life in it. All he had to do was find a container.

I've been seeing this woman named Samantha for a while, and the other day she says she wants to spice up our lovemaking, Cole says to Therm after a considerable pause in their conversation.

The rain turns to a wet mist. Cole leans his shoulder against the side of the house. Therm sets the axe between his legs.

Of course, I don't know what this means, Cole continues. She says the ways we've been doing it is how she's always done it and she wants to try bondage.

Bondage? Therm asks.

That's what I said. I don't know about you, but I'm not exactly the most experienced rooster in the coop.

Therm nods. Maddy never mentioned bondage.

So, I go over to her place around noon to see what she has in mind.

She had handcuffs planned, huh?

Yes, and a blindfold. She cuffed me and called me a filthy bastard. I thought she meant it, but she explained this was role-playing and told me to wait in the dungeon while she freshened up. The dungeon was the bedroom, but I was supposed to use my imagination. I waited a long damned time sitting there on her bed. When you can't see and you don't know what's coming to you your mind starts thinking awful things.

It does, Therm says, it sure does.

I tried to get out of the handcuffs but couldn't. I wondered where she got the handcuffs and where she put the key. Hell, I even started thinking that she was going to chop me up like you read about in papers. Lovers get chopped up for one reason or another.

True, Therm agrees.

Then I heard some shouting out in the front yard. There was another man's voice. This made me nervous, as you can imagine. I didn't know if she was going to bring some guy into this bondage experience or what.

So what did you do?

I put my face into the bed and rubbed that blindfold off. Out the front window I saw Samantha arguing with this big guy, bigger than you, about something. Come to find out, it's her husband.

She's married? Therm asks.

Cole blows a low whistle.

That's awful.

I thought so, too. I looked for the handcuff key, but it wasn't in the bedroom. About the time that big boy comes busting in the front door, I manage to get out the back door and run for my life. I had to leave my car there. I imagine he had it impounded.

Therm rubs his fingers on the axe handle. After a moment he says, You shouldn't have run.

He probably would have given me a good whupping.

Maybe you deserved it.

Not in handcuffs.

How long have you been cheating with her?

Oh, I don't know, a month.

And you never thought to ask her if she was married?

It never came up.

Couldn't you tell a man lived with her? Men's shaving cream in the bathroom, shoes under the bed, trophies? Therm shifts the axe from hand to hand.

Most of the time she came to my place. She didn't wear a ring.

Of course she wouldn't wear her ring. Cheaters know better than that, Therm says.

Well, whatever. I just hate being caught up in this mess. I'd like to go back and sort it out with this guy. He's probably rational enough. I'll apologize. Is that what you think I should do?

It won't be enough, but it will be a start. The major damage is done. Don't even think about seeing her again, though. How would you feel if your wife was bonding with some other man?

I've never been married.

Yeah, well.

But I didn't know she was married.

Now you do.

I'll talk to him.

Therm sucks on his teeth.

I'll go right now. I just wish I didn't have these damned handcuffs on.

At approximately 3:15 PM, officer Ferris noted, a man in a blue Chevy Nova, 1986 or so, drove by with a busted taillight. Ferris had been instructed to stop any vehicles that drew suspicion and might possibly be carrying the missing boy. A busted taillight suggests a struggle; the boy could be in the trunk, tied down and helpless. Ferris flipped his lights on and pursued the blue Chevy Nova.

The afternoon was calm with heavy, low clouds above harboring rain. Since the boy disappeared, the weather had been somber. Ferris had tried to stay objective about the disappearance, he didn't want to rule out all the possibilities. The boy could have run off or fallen into a sinkhole or just gotten himself really lost. But Ferris had dismissed these considerations after combing the woods with the boy's mother a few nights ago. Ferris had been assigned to survey the woods with the mother while other officers worked deeper in the woods and the surrounding neighborhoods. After nightfall, the mother and Ferris followed their erratic flashlights around the soft sounds of crickets and distant shufflings. The first time the mother cried her son's name, Ferris had flinched. The immediate loudness of her pain-filled voice frightened him. The more she called out, the more serious the situation seemed. Ferris eventually yelled for the boy, too, as much to hear his own voice responding to hers as to hope for a feeble reply from the woods. By sunrise, Ferris was spent and hoarse and convinced the boy had been nabbed. The mother's doomsday worry had seeped into Ferris throughout the night. A mother knows, she said, and Ferris knew better than to disagree.

The team of officers uncovered a pellet gun by the pond, and a dead frog in a paper bag near the old elementary school. Footprints were either trampled by the team or erased by the drizzle and mist. Now, though, with the weather keeping the ground soft, if the kidnapper made a move, there was a good chance they would find prints or tire tracks or something that spelled foul play.

The blue Chevy Nova signaled and pulled to the shoulder of the road. 3:18 PM, Officer Ferris noted, and it's showtime. He exited his squad car, adjusted his belt, keeping his hand near his sidepiece, and approached the car. The perpetrator rolled his window down, stuck his head out, and said, Is there a problem, officer?

The perpetrator had stringy hair, sun-darkened skin, and a long chin. His eyes, Ferris determined, were shifty and cold.

License and registration, Ferris demanded, keeping his eyes on the perpetrator's hands.

The man dug into his glove compartment. A Bible fell out, which seemed odd to Ferris. Why would a man keep one in his glove box? It didn't make sense. You a man of the cloth? Ferris questioned.

No, sir, I'm not. There are some passages I like to read before I go to work.

The man handed Ferris the documents. The perpetrator's name was Cole Bateman, born on December 16, 1979. He had vision impairment and lived in a remote trailer park just over the county line. This Cole Bateman fit the profile of a child molester, Ferris knew: late twenties, white, scrawny, a loner, overly religious, dirt under the fingernails; all typical. As Ferris returned the license, he heard a faint thud in the trunk.

Out of the car, Ferris said, withdrawing his gun and pointing it in Cole's face.

What? Cole asked, recoiling.

Out, now. Ferris flung the door open and Cole cautiously stepped onto the road.

Hands on the hood.

Cole put his hands on the hood. Ferris yanked the perpetrator's arms behind his back and cuffed him.

Stay put, Ferris said.

What did I do?

Ferris glared at the handcuffed man. I'm going to find out just what you did.

It took Ferris a few moments to locate the trunk-release latch and his adrenaline made his hands fumble and his heart jump. He heard movement in the trunk again, no mistake about it. The trunk popped.

The perpetrator said, I caught those on public property, and Ferris raised his gun again. He told Cole to shut up, pervert.

In the trunk was a large potato sack thrashing from side to side. Ferris holstered his gun and pulled the sack to the edge of the trunk. It was lighter than a boy should be. He was probably starving, poor thing. Ferris loosened the knot at the neck of the sack and opened it. A cottonmouth struck his wrist, released its fangs, and struck his hand in an instant. A pygmy rattler attached itself to a finger on his other hand. Ferris flung the sack back into the trunk and shook the pygmy rattler from his finger. He screamed some oaths, drew his gun, and shot at the sack of snakes.

Cole ran.

Ferris lifted his gun and fired at the retreating perpetrator. His shot missed badly. The man scurried off into the forest. There was only a moment of hesitation, and then Ferris was in pursuit. A copperhead escaped, slid across the asphalt, and buried itself in a pile of woody pulp.

Jakob wandered around the woods looking for litter. He found a battered trash bag and broken glass, but nothing he could keep the frog in. His old elementary school was not far from here, maybe a half mile. The school had burned down after a fire started in the boiler room. The police said nobody was hurt, but the students believed the janitor had been trapped down in the basement and died. Tommy Tucker said that the teachers and parents didn't want the kids to know because the janitor's corpse had been burnt so badly it would give everyone nightmares to think about. Everyone thought about it anyway.

In a trash can on the playground Jakob found a paper bag that could hold the white frog. The school was nothing more than a pile of rubble with a few scorched half walls tugging out of the ground. Firefighters had cleaned up the site and there were plans to reconstruct it in a few years.

The playground was undamaged. Jakob poked a few holes in the bag for the frog to breathe, set it near the jungle gym, and ran over to the merry-go-round. Jakob couldn't resist the merry-go-round. He grabbed the rusty green bars and grunted as he pushed it around, kicking up dirt. The merry-go-round squealed in protest, but as Jakob persisted and it gathered momentum, the noise stopped and with a final shove, he leapt up on it.

Jakob stood in the middle and tried to keep his balance without holding onto the bars. He loved the sensation of being dizzy; it was as if he were in a different world when he was spinning, a slower, dreamy world. He went around and around. Overhead, the high afternoon sky threw his shadow to the graveled ground. Jakob watched the image in front of him grow from kid-size to adult-size to giant-size. At its peak, Jakob raised his arms so that the shadow's fingers stretched nearly to the woods. And in an instant, as the merry-go-round rotated and he turned to face the sun, his shadow diminished to regular size and smaller until it disappeared altogether.

Blinded, Jakob could not see the shadow that had been pacing him rise up and out of the ruins of the school.

●●●

I'd help you, but I'm no good at picking locks, Therm says, considering the handcuffs. Besides, if you go to the husband restrained, you'll score sympathy points.

Yeah, or he'll see what Samantha had in mind. He'll be forced to think of she and me getting it on in bondage. Cole thrusts his hips. Probably won't paint a pretty picture.

Good point, Therm agrees.

No, I think it would be best if I went to him with open arms. Also, if you free me, I can look at that wound on your hand. If a snake bit you, we should do something about it.

I told you it wasn't a snake, and I told you I don't pick locks.

Well, I don't either. Do you know any locksmiths?

No, I'm new around here.

Maybe we could clip it with something from your woodshed?

I use that for the lawn mower and not much else.

What about the axe?

Therm lifts the axe and raises his eyebrows.

I'll bet you could bust the chains in three swings, big boy like yourself.

What if I miss?

I don't know, try not to. Take good aim. I'd do just about anything to have these off. You ever been handcuffed?

When they were children Therm and his brother used to play Cowboys and Indians. Therm always ended up the restrained Indian, but he didn't mind. Those were toy handcuffs made from plastic and when Therm pulled hard they'd open enough to slide free. When Therm tried to run away, his brother shot him up with cap guns.

Sure, Therm says to Cole, I've been cuffed before.

You know, then, the Good Lord never intended to keep a man locked like this, Cole says, shaking his arms. How am I supposed to pray with my arms behind my back?

Therm doesn't pray, but he thinks about it sometimes.

I've learned my lesson, Cole says. My wrists feel like they've been rubbed over with sandpaper.

They're red.

I'll go kneel by that stump, stretch the chain back as far as it will go, and let you have a whack at it. Then I'll go apologize and take myself out of Samantha and her husband's relationship for good. Maybe they can get counseling and patch things up.

Counseling could work if they're both willing to try, Therm agrees. It isn't a bad idea.

3:53 PM, Ferris notes, and he is in trouble. The snakebite at his wrist has quickly pumped poison into his bloodstream. According to the police handbook, which Ferris knows by memory, you aren't supposed to try and suck the poison out of a snakebite, but he tries anyway. With a piece of his shirt, he makes a tourniquet around his arm. He fears this is too late. He has gotten himself lost in the woods and regrets his hasty decision to pursue the perpetrator. The handbook never mentioned chasing a suspected child molester into the woods after you've been bit repeatedly by deadly snakes. The handbook mentioned backup. So, Ferris rationalizes, I've made a mistake. His right hand looks like an eggplant and the damaged finger on his left hand is paralyzed and swollen. Breathing is difficult. It had rained around 3:45 PM and then it stopped; now there is mist. Ferris is pretty sure he has passed that pepper tree three times.

In a small clearing, Ferris notices footprints that are smaller than his own. They lead around a bramble bush and farther into the forest. Unsteadily, Ferris follows.

4:10 PM, and Ferris is on his hands and knees, gasping for breath and crawling from one footprint to the next. He can no longer feel the right side of his body and his vision has blurred. Still, he struggles forward, not yet ready to die.

The footprints stop. Ferris props himself on his elbows where the woods end and the grass of someone's backyard begins. In the yard, a man lifts an axe and hesitates. Ferris only sees the back of a small person kneeling, arms behind him, before the executioner. He thinks of the missing boy. With his left hand, Ferris draws his gun, a last surge of energy carries his shaking arm up, and he fires. The axe falls.

Therm feels a burning in his chest as he heaves forward and drives the axe hard into the handcuffed man's wrist. He falls to his knees beside Cole and tries to find some explanation in the man's face.

The bite of steel in Cole's wrist doesn't hurt at first. He can't believe the idiot missed. He was so close to freedom. But the pain comes when he tries to move his hand and feels that it is mostly detached from his arm. The warm flow of his blood down his backside drains him quicker than he thinks it should, and Cole finds he cannot stand up or stop the bleeding.

Ferris congratulates himself for doing the right thing. The police handbook clearly says, in Chapter Three: At all costs protect the victim. He rests his face in the grass. He thinks he should check his watch to note the time of rescue. He doesn't have the energy to lift his poisoned arm.

Therm fingers the hole in his chest and recalls Cowboys and Indians. The wound is perfectly circular and seems fake peeking out from his torn shirt. He figures he'll play dead for a while as he falls forward and hides his face in the lawn.

Cole collapses, chin first. He tugs at the handcuffs weakly, but his hand won't snap off. There's still enough bone to keep him locked.

The men take in the scent of the earth. Each locates a memory from when he was a child playing in the freshly cut grass, invincible and alive. They remember how easy it was to be a boy.

Jason Ockert has won several national fiction awards and is the author of the short story collection *Rabbit Punches.* His stories have appeared in many journals, including *The Oxford American, Black Warrior Review, Indiana Review, Alaska Quarterly Review,* and *McSweeney's.* He teaches at Coastal Carolina University.

D. WINTERS

*I*t seems to me that there is a propensity for the wayward to seek direction from the blueprint of their youth: to plumb a time when once maybe something had been good. Childhood, seen as uncomplicated and innocent, often becomes the vessel in which we take emotional refuge. I think, though, that it is impossible to get around the fact that childhood is uncomplicated and innocent only in our selective adult renderings of it. With Jakob I wanted to capture a sense of loss and menace.

(When we were kids, my brother claimed he spied a white frog along the bank of a creek we frequented. Most people he told thought he was making this up — a white frog? — but I believed him then and believe him still.)

George Singleton

WHICH ROCKS WE CHOOSE

(from *The Georgia Review*)

Luckily for everyone in the furthest branches of the family tree, the mule spoke English to my grandfather. Up until this seminal point in the development of what became Carolina Rocks, a few generations of Loopers had tried to farm worthless land that sloped from the mountainside down to all tributaries of the Saluda River. From what I understood, my great-great-grandfather and then his son barely grew enough corn to feed their families, much less take to market. Our land stood so desolate back then that no Looper joined the troops in the 1860s; no Looper even understood that the country underwent some type of a conflict. What I'm saying is, our stretch of sterile soil kept Loopers from needing slaves, which pretty much caused locals to label them everything from uppity to unpatriotic, from hex-ridden to slow-witted. Until the mule spoke English to my grandfather, our family crest might've portrayed a chipped plow blade, wilted sprigs, and a man with a giant question mark above his head.

"Don't drown the rocks," the harnessed mule said, according to legend. The mule turned its head around to my teenaged grandfather, looked him in the eye just like any of the famous solid-hoofed talking equines of Hollywood. "Do not throw rocks in the river. Keep them in a pile. They shall be bought in time by those concerned with decorative landscaping, for walls and paths and flower beds."

That's what my grandfather came back from the field to tell everybody. Maybe they grew enough corn for moonshine, I don't know. My own father told me this story when I complained mightily from the age of seven on about having to work for Carolina Rocks, whether lugging, sorting, piling, or later using the backhoe. The mule's name wasn't Sisyphus, I doubt, but that's what I came to call it when I thought it necessary to explain the situation to my common-law wife, Abby. I said, "If it weren't for Sisyphus, you and I would still be trying to find a crop that likes plenty of rain but no real soil to take root. We'd be experimenting every year with tobacco, rice, coffee, and cranberry farming."

Abby stared at me a good minute. She said, "What? I wasn't listening. Did you say we can't have children?"

I said, "A good mule told my grandfather to quit trying to farm and to sell off both river rocks and fieldstone. That's how come we do what we do. Or at least why my grandfather and dad did what they did." This little speech occurred on the day I turned thirty-three, the day I became the same age as Jesus, the day I finally decided to go back to college. Up until this point Abby and I had lived in the Looper family house. My dad had been dead eleven years, my mom twenty. I said, "Anyway, I think the Caterpillar down on the banks is rusted up enough now for both of us to admit we're not going to continue with the business once we sell off the remaining stock."

When I took over Carolina Rocks we had already stockpiled about two hundred tons of beautiful black one- to three-inch skippers dug out of the river. I probably scooped out another few hundred tons over the next eight years. But with land developers razing both sides of the border for gated mountain golf course communities, in need of something other than mulch, there was no way I could keep up. A ton of rocks isn't the size of half a French car. Sooner or later, too, I predicted, the geniuses at the EPA would figure out that haphazardly digging out riverbeds and shorelines wouldn't be beneficial downstream. Off in other corners of our land we had giant piles of round rocks, pebbles, chunks, flagstones, and chips used for walkways, driveways, walls, and artificial springhouses. Until my thirty-third birthday, when I would make that final decision to enroll in a low-residency master's program, I would sell off what rocks we had quarried, graded, and — according to my mood — divided into color or shape or size.

I had decided on Southern Culture Studies, and the department chair of the one particular low-residency program I looked into wrote that I should mention the degree with purpose, as if capitalized, no matter what. Maybe I should've taken his advice as an omen.

Anyway, I never really felt that the Loopers' ways of going about the river rock and fieldstone business incorporated what our competitors might've known in regard to supply and demand, or using time wisely.

"Hey, Stet, can we go back to trying our chosen field?" Abby asked. She wore a pair of gray sweatpants and a MoonPie T-shirt. Both of us wore paper birthday cones on our heads. "Please say that we can send out our résumés to TV stations around the country. Hell, I'd give the news in Mississippi, if it got my foot in the door."

She pronounced it "Mishishippi." She wasn't drunk. One of our professors should've taken her aside right about Journalism 101 and told her to find a new field of study or concentrate in print media. I didn't have it in me, either, to tell Abby that my grandfather's mule enunciated better than she did. When she wasn't helping out with the Carolina Rocks bookkeeping chores, she drove down to Greenville and led aerobics classes. I never saw her conducting a class in person, but I imagined her saying, *"Shtep, shtep, shtep."*

"It's funny that you should mention Mississippi," I said. I thought of the term *segue,* from when I underwent communications studies classes as an undergraduate, usually seated right next to Abby. "I'm going to go ahead and enroll in that Southern

Culture Studies program. It'll all be done by e-mail and telephone, pretty much, and then I have to go to Mississippi for ten days in the summer and winter. Then, in a couple years, maybe I can go teach college somewhere. We can sell off this land and move to an actual city. It'll be easier for you to maybe find a job that you're interested in."

I loved my wife more than I loved finding and digging up a truckload of schist. Abby got up from the table, smiled, walked into the den, and picked up a gift-wrapped box. She said, "You cannot believe how afraid I was you'd change your mind. Open it up."

I kind of hoped it was a big bottle of bourbon so we could celebrate there at the kitchen table as the sun rose. I shook it. I said, "It's as heavy as a prize-winning geode," for I compared everything to rocks. When hail fell, those ice crystals hitting the ground were either pea gravel or riprap, never golf balls like the meteorologists said.

"I'm hoping this will help you in the future. In *our* future." Abby leaned over backward and put her palms on the floor like some kind of contortionist. "I don't mind teaching aerobics, but I can't do that when I'm sixty. I can still report the news when I'm sixty."

Sixschtee.

I opened the box to uncover volumes one, two, and three of *The South: What Happened, How, When, and Why.* Abby said, "I don't know what else you're going to learn in a graduate course that's not already in here, but maybe it'll give you ideas."

I might've actually felt tears well up. I opened the first chapter of the third volume to find the heading "BBQ, Ticks, Cottonmouths, and Moonshine." I said, "Man. You might be right. What's left to learn?"

I'm not sure how other low-residency programs in Southern Culture Studies work, but immediately after I sent off the online application — which only included names of references, not actual letters of recommendation — I got accepted. An hour later I paid for the first half year with a credit card. I e-mailed the "registrar" asking if I needed to send copies of my undergraduate transcripts, et cetera, and she said that they were a trusting lot at the University of Mississippi – Taylor. She wrote back that she and the professors all believed in a person's word being his bond, and so on, and that the program probably wouldn't work out for me if I was the sort who needed everything in writing.

I called the phone number at the bottom of the pseudo-letterhead but hung up when someone answered, "Taylor Grocery and Catfish." I had only wanted to say that I, too, ran my river rock and fieldstone business on promised payments, that my father and grandfather operated thusly even though the mule had warned to trust nothing on two legs. And I didn't want to admit to myself or Abby that perhaps my degree would be on par with something like that art institute that accepts boys and girls who can draw fake pirates and cartoon deer.

A day later I received my first assignment from my lead mentor, one Dr. Theron Crowther. He asked that I buy one of his books, read the chapter on "Revising History," then set about finding people who might've remembered things differently as opposed to how the media reported the incident. He said to stick to Southern themes: the assassination of Dr. Martin Luther King, for example; the sit-in at Woolworth's in Greensboro; unsuccessful and fatal attempts at unionizing cotton mills; Ole Miss's upset of Alabama. I said to Abby, "I might should stick to pulling rocks out of the river and selling them to people who like to make puzzles out of their yard. I have no clue what this guy means for me to do."

Abby looked over the e-mail. I was to write a ten-page paper and send it back within two weeks. "First off, read that chapter. It should give you some clues. That's what happened to me when I wasn't sure about a paper I once wrote on 'How to Interview the Criminally Insane' back in college. You remember that paper? You pussied out and wrote one on 'How to Interview the Deaf.'"

I'd gotten an A on that one: I merely wrote, "To interview a deaf person, find a sign language interpreter." That was it.

Abby said, "There's this scrapbooking place next door to Feline Fitness. Come on in to work with me, and I'll take you over there. Those people will have some stories to tell, I bet. Every time I go past it, these women are sitting around talking."

We sat on our front porch, overlooking the last three tons of river rock I'd scooped out, piled neatly as washer-dryer combos, if it matters. Below the rocks, the river surged onward, rising from thunderstorms up near Asheville. I said, "What are you talking?" I'd not heard of the new sport of scrapbooking.

"These people get together just like a quilting club, I guess. They go in the store and buy new scrapbooks, then sit there and shove pictures and mementos between the plastic pages. And they brag, from what I understand. The reason I know so much about it is, I got a couple women in my noon class who showed up early one day and went over to check out the scrapbook place. They came back saying there was a Junior Leaguer ex–Miss South Carolina in there with flipbooks of her child growing up, you know. She took a picture of her kid two or three times a day, so you can flip the pictures and see the girl grow up in about five minutes."

I got up, walked off the porch, crawled beneath the house a few feet, and pulled out a bottle of bourbon I kept hidden away there for times when I needed to think — which wasn't often in the river rock business. When I rejoined my wife she'd already gotten two jelly jars out of the cupboard. "There's a whole damn business in scrapbooks? Who thought that up? America," I said. "Forget the South being fucked up. America."

"You can buy cloth-covered ones and puffy-covered ones and ones with your favorite team's mascot on the cover. There are black ones for funeral pictures and white ones for weddings. There are ones that are shaped like Santa Claus, the Easter Bunny, dogs, cats, cars, and Jesus. They've even got scented scrapbooks." Abby slugged down a good shot of Jim Beam and tilted her glass my way for more. "Not that I've been in Scraphappy! very often, but they've got one that looks like skin with tattoos and everything, shaped like an hourglass, little tiny blond hairs coming off of it. It's for guys to put their bachelor party pictures inside."

I said, "I wonder if they have any bullet-riddled gray flannel scrapbooks for pictures of dead Confederate relatives." I tried to imagine other scrapbooks but couldn't think of any. "Okay. What the hell. When's your next class?"

We drove down the mountain the next morning, a Wednesday, so Abby could lead a beginner aerobics class. Wednesdays might as well be called "little Sunday" on a southern calendar, for small-town banks and businesses close at noon for employees to ready themselves for Wednesday night church services. My common-law wife took me into Scraphappy!, looked at a wall of stickers, then said, "I'll be back a little after noon, unless someone needs personal training." She didn't kiss me on the cheek. She looked over at the six women sitting in a circle, all of whom I estimated to be in their mid- to late thirties.

"Could I help you with anything?" the owner asked me. She wore a name tag that read Knox — the last name of one of the richer families in the area. In kind of a patronizing voice she said, "Did you forget to pack up your snapshots this morning?"

The other women kept turning cellophane-covered pages. One of them said out loud, "Pretty soon I'll have to get a scrapbook dedicated to every room in the house. What a complete freak-up."

I had kind of turned my head toward the stickers displayed on the wall — blue smiling babies, pink smiling babies, a slew of elephants. Raggedy Anns and Andys, mobiles, choo-choo trains, ponies, teddy bears, prom dresses, the president's face staring vacantly — but jerked my neck back around at hearing "freak-up." I thought to myself, Remember that you're here to gather revisionist history. I thought, You want to impress your professor at Ole Miss–Taylor.

But then I started daydreaming about Frances Bavier, the actress who played Aunt Bee on *The Andy Griffith Show*. I said, "Oh. Oh, I didn't come here to play scrapbook. My name's Stet Looper, and I'm enrolled in a Southern Culture Studies graduate program, and I came here to see if y'all wouldn't mind answering some questions about historical events that happened around here. Or around any- where." I cleared my throat. The women in the circle looked at me as if I had walked in wearing a seersucker suit after Labor Day.

The Knox woman said, "Southern studies? My husband has this ne'er-do-well cousin who has a daughter going to one of those all-girls schools up north. Hollins, I believe. She's majoring in women's studies." In a lower voice she said, "She appears not to like men, if you know what I mean — she snubbed us all by not coming out this last season at the Poinsett Club. Anyway, she's studying for that degree with an emphasis in women's economics, and I told her daddy that it usually didn't take four years learning how to make a proper grocery list."

I was glad I didn't say that. I'd've been shot, I figured. The same woman who almost-cursed earlier held up a photograph to her colleagues and said, "Look at that one. He said he knew how to paint the baseboard."

I said, "Anyway, I have a deadline, and I was wondering if I could ask if y'all could tell me about an event that occurred during your lifetime, something that made you view the world differently than how you had understood it before. Kind of like the Cuban missile crisis, but more local."

One of the women said, "Hey, Knox, could you hand me one them calligraphy stick-ons says 'I Told You So'? I guess I need to find me a stamp that says 'Loser.'" To me she said, "My husband always accuses me of being a germaphobe." She held up her opened scrapbook for me to see. It looked as though she'd wiped her butt on the pages. "This is my collection of used moist towelettes. I put them in here to remember the nice restaurants we've gone to, and sometimes if the waitress gave me extras I put the new one in there, too. But even better, he and I one time went on a camping trip that I didn't want to go on, and as it ended up we got lost. Luckily for

Wells, we only had to follow my trail of Wet Naps back to the parking lot. I don't mind bragging that that trip was all it took for him to buy us a vacation home down on Pawleys Island."

I wished that I'd've thought to bring a tape recorder. I said, "That's a great story," even though I didn't ever see it being a chapter in some kind of Southern Culture Studies textbook. I said, "Okay. Do any of y'all do aerobics? My wife's next door teaching aerobics, if y'all are interested. From what I understand, she's tough, but not too tough." I heard my inner voice going, Okay, none of these women is interested in aerobics classes, so shut up and get out of here before you say something more stupid and somehow get yourself in trouble.

I stood there like a fool for a few seconds. The woman who complained about her baseboard started flipping through pages, saying, "Look at them. Every one of them." Then she went on to explain to a woman who must not've been a regular, "I keep a scrapbook of every time my husband messes up. This scrapbook's the bad home repair one — he tries to fix something, then it costs us double to get a professional in to do the job. I got another book filled with bad checks that got sent back, and newspaper clippings for when he got arrested and published in the police blotter. I even got ahold of some of his mug shots."

I felt like I was standing next to a whipping post. I said, "Okay, I'm sorry to take up any of your time." The place should've been called *Strap*happy, I thought.

As I opened the door, though, I heard a different voice, a woman who'd only concentrated on her own book of humiliation up until this point. She said, "Do you mean like if you know somebody got lynched, but it all got hush-hushed even though everyone around knew the truth?"

Everyone went quiet. You could've heard an opened ink pad evaporate.

I pulled up one of those half-stepladder/half-stool things. I said, "Say that all again, slower."

Her name was Gayle Ann Gunter. Her daddy owned a car lot, and her grandfather owned it before him, and the great-grandfather had started the entire operation back when selling horseshoes and tack still made up half of his business. She was working on a scrapbook that involved one-by-two-inch pictures that gradeschoolers hand over to one another, and she had them under headings like "Uglier than Me," "Poorer than Me," "Dumber than Me," — as God is my witness. She said, "We're having our twentieth high school reunion in a few months, and I want to make sure I have the names right. It's important in this world to greet old acquaintances properly."

I said, "I'm no genius, but it should be 'Dumber than I.' It's a long, convoluted grammar lesson I learned back in college the first time."

The other women laughed. They said, "Ha ha ha ha ha" in unison and in a weird, seemingly practiced cadence. Knox said, "One of the things that keeps me in business is people messing up their scrapbooks and having to start over. I had one woman who misspelled her new daughter-in-law's name throughout, the first time. She got it right when her son got a divorce, though."

"This was up in Travelers Rest," Gayle Ann said. She kept her scrapbook atop her lap and spoke as if addressing the air conditioning vent. "I couldn't have been more than eight, nine years old. These two black brothers went missing, but no one made a federal case out of it, you know. This was about 1970. They hadn't integrated the schools just yet, I don't believe. I don't even know if it made the paper, and I haven't ever seen the episode on one of those shows about long-since missing people. Willie and Archie Lagroon. No one thought about it much because, first off, a lot of teenage boys ran away back then. Maybe 'cause of Vietnam, I guess. And then again, they wasn't white."

I took notes in a professional-looking memo pad. I didn't even look up, and I didn't offer another grammar lesson involving subjects and verbs. For some reason one of the women in the circle said, "My name's Shaw Haynesworth. Gayle Ann, I thought you were *born* in 1970. My name's Shaw Haynesworth, if you need to have footnotes and a bibliogeography."

I wrote that down, too. Gayle Ann Gunter didn't respond. She said, "I haven't thought about this in years. It's sad. About four years after those boys went missing, a hunter found a bunch of bones right there about twenty feet off of Old Dacusville Road. My daddy told me all about it. They found all these rib bones kind of strewn around, and more than likely it was those two boys. This was all before DNA, of course. The coroner — or someone working for the state — finally said that they were beef and pork ribs people had thrown out their car windows. They said that people went to the Dacusville Smokehouse and couldn't make it all the way back home before tearing into a rack of ribs, and that they threw them out the window, and somehow all those ribs landed in one big pile over the years." She made a motorboat noise with her mouth. "I'm no expert when it comes to probability or beyond a reasonable doubt, but looking back on it now, I smell lynching. Is that the kind of story you're looking for?"

Abby walked in sweating, hair pulled back, wearing an outfit that made her look like she just finished the Tour de France. She said, "Hey, Stet, I might be another hour. Phyllis wants me to fill in for her. Are you okay?"

The women scrapbookers looked up at my wife as if she had zoomed in from cable television. I said, "We have a winner!" for some reason.

"You can come over and sit in the lobby if you finish up early." To the women she said, "We're having a special next door if y'all want to join an aerobics class. Twenty dollars a month." I turned to see the women all look down at their scrapbooks.

Knox said, "I believe I can say for sure that we burn up enough calories running around all day for our kids. Speaking of which, I brought some doughnuts in!"

I looked at Abby. I nodded. She kind of made a what're-you-up-to? face and backed out. I said, "Okay. Yes, Gayle Ann, that's exactly the kind of story I'm looking for — about something that happened, but that people saw differently. How sure are you that those bones were the skeletal remains of the two boys?"

A woman working on a giant scrapbook of her two Pomeranians said, "They do have good barbecue at Dacusville Smokehouse. I know I've not been able to make it home without breaking into the Styrofoam boxes. Hey, do any of y'all know why it's not good to give a dog pork bones? Is that an old wives' tale, or what? I keep forgetting to ask my vet."

And then they were off talking about everything else. I felt it necessary to purchase something from Knox, so I picked out a rubber stamp that read "Unbelievable!"

I'm not ashamed to admit that, while walking between Scraphappy! and Feline Fitness, I envisioned not only a big A on my first Southern Culture Studies low-residency graduate-level class at Ole Miss – Taylor, but a consultant's fee when this rib-bone story got picked up by one of those TV programs specializing in wrongdoing mysteries, cold cases, and voices from the dead.

Since I wouldn't meet Dr. Theron Crowther until the entire graduate class got together for ten days in December, I didn't know if he was a liar or prankster. I'd dealt with both types before, of course, in the river rock business. Pranksters came back and said that my stones crumbled up during winter's first freeze, and liars sent checks for half tons, saying I used cheating scales, et cetera. After talking to the women of Scraphappy!, I sent Dr. Crowther an e-mail detailing the revisionist history I'd gathered. He wrote back to me, "You fool! Haven't you ever encountered a little something called 'rural legend'? Let me say right now that you will not make it in the mean world of Southern Culture Studies if you fall for every made-up tale that rumbles down the trace. Now go out there and show me how regular people view things differently than how they probably really happened."

First off, I thought that I'd done that. I was never the kind of student who whined and complained when a professor didn't cotton to my way of thinking. Back when I was forced to undergo a required course called Broadcast Station Management I wrote a comparison–contrast paper about the management styles of WKRP in Cincinnati and WJM in Minneapolis. The professor said that it wasn't a good idea to write about fictitious radio- and television-based situation comedies. Personally, I figured the management philosophies must've been spectacular, seeing as both programs consistently won Nielsen battles, then went on into syndication. The professor — who ended up, from what I understand, having to resign his position after getting caught filming himself having sex with a freshman boy on the made-up set for an elective course in Local Morning Shows, using a fake potted plant and microphone as props — said I needed to forget about television programs when dealing with television programs, which made no sense to me at the time. I never understood what he meant until, after graduation, running my family's business ineffectively and on a reading jag, I sat down by the river and read *The Art of War* by Sun Tzu and *Being and Nothingness* by Sartre.

I said to Abby, "My mentor at Ole Miss – Taylor says that's a made-up story about black kids and rib bones. He says it's like that urban legend about those vacation photos down in Jamaica with the toothbrush, or the big dog that chases a ball out the window of a high-rise in New York."

Abby came out from beneath our front porch, the half bottle of bourbon in her grasp. She said, "Of course he says that. Now he's going to come down here and interview about a thousand people so he can publish the book himself. That's what those guys do, Stet. Hey, I got an idea — why don't you write about how you fell off a turnip truck. How you got some kind of medical problem that makes you wet behind the ears always."

I stared down at the river and tried to imagine how rocks still languished there below the roiling surface. "I guess I can run over to that barbecue shack and ask them what they know about it."

"I guess you can invest in carbon paper and slide rulers in case this computer technology phase proves to be a fad."

•••

All good barbecue stands only open on the weekend, Thursday through Saturday at most. I got out a regional telephone directory, found the address, got directions from MapQuest, then drove around uselessly for a few hours, circling, until I happened to see a white plume of smoke different than most of the black ones caused by people burning tires in front of their trailers. I walked in — this time with a hand-held tape recorder I'd gotten for opening a new CD down at the bank, I guess so people can record their last words before committing suicide, something like "Two fucking percent interest?" — and dealt with all the locals turning around, staring, wondering aloud who my kin might be. I said, loudly, "Hey, how y'all doing this fine evening?" like I owned the place. Everyone turned back to their piled paper plates of minced pork and coleslaw.

At the counter a short man with pointy sideburns and a curled-up felt cowboy hat said, "We out of sweet potato casserole." A fly buzzed around his cash register.

"I'll take two," I looked up at the menu board behind him, "Hog-o-Mighty sandwiches."

"Here or to go?"

"And a sweet tea. You don't serve beer by any chance, do you?"

"No sir. Family-orientated," he said. He wore an apron that read COOK.

I said, "I understand. I'm Stet Looper, up from around north of here."

An eavesdropper behind me said, "I tode you."

"By north of here I mean just near the state line. I'll eat them here. Anyway, my wife introduced me to a woman who told me a wild story about two young boys being missing some thirty-odd years back, with something about a pile of bones the state investigators said came from here. Do you know this story?" I mentioned Abby because any single male strangers are, in the sloppy dialect of the locals, "quiz."

"My name's Cook," the cook said. "Raymus Cook. Y'all hear that? Fellow wants to know if I heard about them missing boys back then. Can you believe that?" To me he said, "You the second person today to ask. Some fellow from down Mississippi called earlier asking if it was some kind of made-up story."

I thought, Goddamn parasite Theron Crowther. "I'll be dog-gone," I said. "What'd you tell him?"

"That'll be five and a quarter, counting tax." Raymus Cook handed over two sandwiches on a paper plate and took my money. "I told him my daddy'd be the one to talk to, but Daddy's been dead eight years. I told him what I believed — that somebody paid somebody and that those boys' families will never rest in peace."

People from two tables got up from the seats, shot Raymus Cook mean looks, and left the premises. One of them said, "We been through this enough. I'mo take my bidness to Ola's now on."

Raymus Cook held his head back somewhat and called out, "This ain't the world it used to be. You just can't go decide to secede every other minute, things don't turn out like you want them." At this precise moment I knew that, later in life, I would regale friends and colleagues alike about how I "stumbled upon" something. Raymus Cook turned his head halfway to the open kitchen and said, "Ain't that right, Ms. Hattie?"

A black woman stuck her face my way and said, "Datboutright, huh-huh," just like that, fast, as if she'd waited to say her lines all night long.

"You can't cook barbecue correct without the touch of a black woman's hands," Raymus said to me in not much more than a whisper. "All these chains got white people smoking out back. Won't work, I'll be the first to admit."

I thought, Fuck, this is going to turn out to be just another one of those stories that's bloated the South for 150 years. I didn't want that to happen. I said, "I'm starting a master's degree in Southern Culture Studies, and I need to write a paper on something that happened a while back that maybe ain't right. You got any stories you could help me out with?"

I sat down at the first table and unwrapped a sandwich. I got up and poured my own tea. Raymus Cook smiled. He picked up a flyswatter and nailed his prey. "Southern culture?" He laughed. "I don't know that much about Southern culture, even though I got raised right here." To a family off in the corner he yelled, "Y'all want any sweet potato casserole?" Back to me he said, "That's one big piece of flypaper hanging, Southern culture. It might be best to accidentally graze a wing to it every once in a while, but mostly buzz around."

I said, of course, "Man. That's a nice analogy." I tried to think up one to match him, something about river rocks. I couldn't.

"Wait a minute," Raymus Cook said. "I might be thinking about Southern literature. Like Faulkner. Is that what you're talking about?"

I thought, This guy's going to help me get through my thesis one day. I said, "Hey, can I get a large rack of ribs to go? I'll get a large rack and a small rack." I looked up at the menu board. I said, "Can I get a 'Willie' and an 'Archie'?"

I thought, Uh-oh, though it took me a minute to remember those two poor black kids' names. I thought, This isn't funny, and took off out of there as soon as Raymus Cook turned around to tell Miss Hattie what he needed. I remembered that I'd forgotten to turn on the tape recorder.

On my drive back home I wondered if there were any low-residency writing programs where I could learn how to finish a detective novel.

I told my sort-of wife the entire event and handed her half a Hog-o-Mighty sandwich. She didn't gape her mouth or shake her head. "You want to get into Southern Culture Studies, you better prepare yourself for such. There are going to be worse stories."

Wershtoreesh. I said, "I don't want to collect war stories."

"You know what I said. And I don't know why you don't ask *me*. Here's a true story about a true story gone false: This woman in my advanced cardio class — this involves spinning, Pilates, steps, and treadmill inside a sauna — once weighed 220 pounds. She's five-two. Now she weighs a hundred, maybe one-o-five at the most. She's twenty-eight years old and just started college at one of the tech schools. She wants to be a dental hygienist."

We sat on the porch, looking down at the river. Our bottle was empty. On the railing I had *The South: What Happened, How, When, and Why* opened to a chapter on a sect of people in eastern Tennessee called "Slopeheads," which might've been politically incorrect.

I said, "She should be a dietician. They got culinary courses there now. She should become an elementary school chef, you know, to teach kids how to quit eating pizza and pimento-cheese burgers."

"Listen. Do you know what happened to her? Do you know how and why and when she lost all that weight?"

I said, of course, "She saw one of those before-and-after programs on afternoon TV. She sat there with a bowl of potato chips on her belly watching Oprah, and God spoke to her." I said, "Anorexia and bulimia, which come before and after 'arson' in some books."

"Her daddy died." Abby got up and closed my textbook for no apparent reason. "Figure it out, Stet. Her daddy died. She *said* she got so depressed that she quit eating. But in reality, she had made herself obese so he'd quit creeping into her bedroom between the ages of twelve and twenty-two. Her mother had left the household long before, and there she was. So she fattened up and slept on her stomach. When her father died she didn't tell anyone what had been going on. But when all the neighbors met after the funeral to eat, she didn't touch one dish. Not even the macaroni and cheese."

I said, "I don't want to know about these kinds of things." I got up and walked down toward the river. Abby followed behind me. I said, "Those my-daddy-loved-me stories are the ones I'm trying to stay away from. It's what people expect out of this area."

When we got to the backhoe she climbed up and reached beneath the seat. She pulled out an unopened bottle of rum I had either forgotten or didn't know about. "There were pirates. You could write about pirates and their influences on the South. How pirates stole things that weren't theirs."

I picked up a nice skipper and flung it out toward an unnatural sandbar. Then I walked into the water up to my knees, reached down, and pulled two more out. I thought, pirates, sheriffs, and local politicians. I thought, the heads of Southern Culture Studies low-residency programs. I reached in the river and pulled out rock after rock. I threw back the smaller ones, as if they needed to be released in order to grow more. I flung up perfect stones to the bank. An hour later, I had enough rocks piled up to cover two graves, but I would need a mule to dredge up enough for the appropriate roadside memorials.

George Singleton has published four collections of stories and one novel. His fiction has appeared in *The Atlantic Monthly, Harper's, Playboy, Zoetrope, The Georgia Review, Shenandoah,* and elsewhere. This is his eighth appearance in *New Stories from the South.* His new novel, *Work Shirts for Madmen,* will be published in fall 2007. He lives in Dacusville, South Carolina.

GLENDA GUION

I wanted to write a passel of stories about a guy getting his master's degree in Southern culture studies at a low-residency program. I wanted to name him Stet just so later on it would be a headache for editors when I wrote stet in the margin. If a character were to write about the South for his thesis, I believed, then he would be able to meet up with a squadron of ne'er-do-wells, rogues, misfits, scam artists, freaks, and so on during his picaresque little journey.

It's a pathetic gimmick, I understand.

My first thoughts ran toward Old South subjects butting heads with the New South. But then two things occurred to me: First off, enough has been written about the Old South (the Civil War, tobacco worms, how the *downfall of civilization can be traced back to diminishing indigo supplies and the omnipresence of Rit and Putnam dyes) by superior minds. Likewise, everybody and his sister has delved headfirst into New South territory since Flannery O'Connor.*

It occurred to me that maybe I needed to write about a New New South. For any scholars out there, it's okay by me if you later call it the NuNu South.

I live near Greenville, South Carolina, a fine small city where, in the span of a few blocks, I can visit a Confederate museum (Old South), a New York Style Wigs (New South), and forty-seven Starbucks (New New South). I can pass by an old antebellum mansion that holds monthly meetings for women in the Daughters of Men Who Hated Commercial Dyes (Old South), a working cotton mill (New South), and a former cotton mill that's now a set of condos going for upwards of four hundred grand each (New New South). I got people who buy guns at the flea market (Old South, New South, New New South). There's a bicycle shop that sells two-wheelers that cost more than most cars (New New South) and an art school where the myopic administrators think there's nothing more beautiful than portraits of men wearing gray suits accompanied by fife and drum music (Old South, New New South).

So, since I adhere to the a-story-must-have-conflict-immediately theory of writing, I assume that "Which Rocks We Choose" emanated from the daily time-travels I experience, not so subtly.

R. T. Smith

STORY

(from *Prairie Schooner*)

Orin was sitting on the porch reading an unremarkable magazine story, while the carpenter bees provided convenient distraction, zinging around the cedar soffit they were excavating or studying him, suspended hummingbird-like at eye level. The end of April, eve of the ancient May Day revels, he thought. May Day had long ago suggested something amorous to him: "May I?" "You may." Birds chirruped in the tree line. A sweet breeze swept the last buds off the Judas tree and onto the warping boards like wet confetti. Beyond the drive, he could see the first bangle of blossoms on the empress tree, violet, slightly darker than the sparse wisteria on its struggling vine. He took it all in with a glance, feeling the breeze under his red summer robe with the small polo player stitched over the heart. His wife had presented it as a birthday gift and said it made him look "dapper." That was a word Orin did not much care for: "dapper," like some kind of housepainter's assistant. He kept a steady rhythm with his cedar rocker and felt a current of sadness wash through him. The ardor had long been drained from May Day, but for the moment, it seemed the fault of the story.

In a dispassionate but soigné manner, the author was delving into the fantasies of an upscale Manhattan barber who leered at all the women he saw and wanted vengeance against all the men.

It was winter in the fiction, and ice glittered from the sidewalks. Pausing with his bright scissors over a customer's thinning hair, staring into the mirror across the room, the barber felt neither guilt nor ambivalence, but entitlement. He was convinced he had every right to his appetites. This was meant to signal the temper of the times. Orin dragged his thumb across the glossy page, smearing the ink, obscuring two lines of the story, which made him smile. He could hear a passenger jet in the western sky; "western heavens," he thought, mocking the story's voice, but the tulip poplar's new leaves and dingy flowers blocked out much of the sky, the morning sun, any clouds left over from last night's rain.

The sun was high enough, however, to carve the shadows sharply — leaves and porch rail on the decking timbers, his hands poised above the magazine on his lap. Lifting his cup, he found the last coffee gone tepid and glanced through the patio's glass doors, toward the coffeepot, which would, no doubt, be equally cold. That was when he saw the movement, the dark trousers and white shirt flashing at the far edge of the living room. At first, he thought it was a trick of light, his own reflection blurred by the rocker's motion, hut no, the figure was beyond the sofa, outlined against the wall Mina had insisted they paint leaf-green. "The accent wall," she called it.

This couldn't, he thought, be possible. He and Mina lived in their isolated house alone, absorbed in their books and cribbage and videos, nursing their truce. No children or pets, infrequent guests; deliveries and service people were equally rare. Mina was in Italy this month with her art class. Orvieto, a famous chapel in the cathedral, a monograph she wanted to write while her students drew, or as she said, "sketched the hell out of the place." Even her language made it clear that the torpor in their life was not her doing.

He found he was beginning to scroll mentally through the list of all the visitors who had been in the house during their years of occupancy, but now, certain he had seen a person and not an apparition, Orin rose and, with the *New Yorker* rolled into a blunt instrument, he stepped to the door and slid it open.

The man facing him held a long kitchen knife Orin recognized as part of the Sheffield set Mina's mother had left her.

"Who are you?"

"Mickey. Shut up and sit down."

As the man took a step toward him, Orin couldn't see any other options, though he quickly calculated whether he could reach the stairs and rush up for the empty handgun under the mattress. He had been swift enough when he was young, athletic even at forty, but the chemo and radiation had left him diminished and timid. Fifteen push-ups were a strain. A mile walk left him winded. The intruder was lean, raw-boned, poised.

Mickey was looking at the TV, the DVD player, the white Bose on the breakfast table.

"Cheap stuff," he said. "Where's the valuable stuff?"

"That Bose is about the nicest thing we own. We're teachers."

"I don't like you spying on me while I work. Turn around. Look out the window."

With his back to the intruder, Orin could tell by the squeaking plywood under the carpet where the man was stepping. The hallway. Mina's study. He was suddenly conscious of being naked under the brisk cotton and tightened the square knot in his sash. He listened to his own breathing. The bees outside darted by the pane, and Orin started mouthing the words of the Lord's Prayer.

"Any of this art worth much?"

"It's just prints, posters. We get them matted and framed to look more like the real thing, but they're just copies of museum pieces." Why was he saying this? It was no time for instruction. He noticed he was not shaking or sweating at all.

"Spruce up the place, that the idea?"

"Yes."

"So where'd all the money go?"

"We've always been state salaried. We even have to work part of the summer at Battlefield Park so we can go to Europe in August. We don't save much. I'm retired now. I've been sick." Partly true, but the trips were mostly hers, his gift to her, his penance for the one indiscretion a decade back. The old, unforgivable story, a weekend workshop, too many Glenlivets, the music smoky and then the dance floor, the elevator, the green light winking as she inserted the key card. Ellen? Eileen. He knew even before he got home that he would not be able to keep it from Mina. When he blurted it out a month later, she took a minute to compose herself and then said that they would get past it, that they would not speak of it again. Before closing the dressing room door, she said she would get over it and move on.

She had not.

"Got any liquor?" The board at the threshold of the open kitchen squeaked. It was not quite noon, Orin noticed on the face of the Bose.

"Under the sink."

If he had the cell phone in his pocket, he could make for the woods, get a good head start, dial 911. He could get down the hill to the Tildens, the house with "In-the-woods" in glittery letters on the sign. Or the car keys. In the car, he could lock the doors and then drive off. If the man had needed to pick up a knife, he probably didn't have a gun. His voice wasn't rough. He wasn't very big, really, but Orin decided it was ten years too late for that option. Even Mina would have advised against it. "Thy will be done."

"What's your favorite?" Clink of bottles, scrape of things being pulled across a shelf.

"I like the Jack Daniel's best, or sometimes the vodka. It's Czarina with citron flavor. He was lying. The single malt scotches were his personal extravagance — Aberlour, Talisker, Glenmorangie, a swash of smoky Laphroig at the bottom of its glazed holiday bottle. Every night he drank two shots in a Belgian crystal glass over three half moons of ice. Before the surgeries, he had always taken the whiskey straight and let it linger on the tongue, inhaling through his mouth as he had seen connoisseurs do, savoring the finish, but the membrane scarring was too deep now, and he had learned to experience many of his pleasures in diluted form.

"Yeah, always trust a bourbon man." The cap scraped, and he could hear the swig and exaggerated exhalation.

"Now I've got to get something real out of all this, Pop, some reward. Suppose you tell me where your billfold is and what else is important here, what might bring me some money. What do you and Mrs. Pop own that's expensive?"

Orin was beginning to get a fix on the accent. Not exactly the rich old Virginia cider with its diphthongs and hollow vowels, its murmuring trail-off of word endings, but more the lazy intonation of piedmont poverty, the furniture or textile mills from the Carolinas or Southside. Danville, maybe. He was trying to picture the man but could conjure only a lean, fox-whiskered face and ball cap. Against his deep tan, the shirt was white as moonlight in the shadows of the living room. Orin was frightened but, he decided, calm. He might be able to identify the man in a lineup. He would probably recognize the voice. He took a deep breath. The worst part was having his back turned. Or having on nothing but the flimsy robe.

"My wallet's right there in the cubby on that counter. It's got about forty dollars and my Visa. The only really valuable item I own is my laptop. You'll find that on the den desk, the room to the left. The printer is junk, but the computer is a Dell we've had just over a year."

Why that lie? It was a five-year-old Dell Latitude, slow, idiosyncratic, but he wanted the man, Mickey, to think he had a bird in the hand. He thought of Mina leafing through renovation plans and scrolled documents in a high-ceilinged library with angels on the walls, or in a piazza café sampling white wine from a local vineyard. Pigeons swirled, their shadows elegant on the slate. Half a world away, she was safe.

"Yeah, this billfold's pretty slim pickings. What about jewelry. There's always jewelry. Classy woman that likes art? Always. Where is it?"

He was thinking about the gun again, and it made his pulse race, his voice crack a little.

"My wife has some things in a box in the other room. It looks like a dollhouse church, St. Paul's, but it's hollow. The roof comes off, and it has a few rings and necklaces from her family. Her father owned a trucking company, but he's dead now. He used to give her jewelry. She doesn't much care for anything but her watch."

"And the solitaire engagement ring," he thought, but she never removed it.

"No need for you to get nervous, Pop. Just keep looking out that window while I step in here and snag it."

He could hear the boards' telltale sound like a small bird's mating signal, and he could hear the wind shuffling through leaves that had not existed a month ago. Oak and hickory, of course, the two Bradford pears, wisteria twined into the deck rails, the Judas tree's perfect green hearts. The scanty Rome apple tree annually, unspectacularly, failed to render edible fruit but would not give up the ghost. Its petals were already giving way to green. He always worried about the honey locusts, too, which Mina called "trash trees." Volunteers that appeared right after they built the house, sweet-smelling locusts were the last to leaf, the first to suffer from the beetles that infested the whole Blue Ridge, summoned, the experts said, by acid rain and then the drought. He tried to keep his mind on the trees, their history, the dangers to them, but he kept seeing Mina's green eyes and the graying cascade of ash blonde hair she refused to color. At least she was safe from this. She was in Italy for two more weeks. As he stared at the waving leaves outside the window, the words filled him like a mantra: "Safe, Italy, safe, Italy."

Then he heard the miniature church clunk on the table and pictured its intricate painted surface, the delicate windows and cornices, everything exactly to scale. A Christmas gift from him right before he was diagnosed. He didn't think she liked it very much, but she used it, went through the motions. Mina was an expert at the motions, the insulation of ritual.

"Hide the goodies in a church. I like that. Falwell, you know, that asshole." Mickey laughed, surprisingly, with a musical lilt, highly pitched, a sound milky and generous, oddly estranged from the rasp of his speaking voice.

Now Orin could hear the jewelry scatter across the cherry table-top. Delicate metal on a polished surface, something spinning, then wobbling to a halt. Before he retired, Orin had taught stories to thousands of high school students. All the good ones included details like that, and Hemingway was his favorite. The crisp sentences, the shaped silence, always contained and shadowed by the way desperate people talked, or people on the edge of desperation. The precise, understated verbs.

Now he wanted this scene to be over, to finish with a terse sentence, a rhetorical question. He wanted to return to the neurotic barber and the irritating *New Yorker* writer's fashionable ennui. He would like to will Mickey into the ink, onto the page, into the barber's wintry world. People in their dens, in yard swings or commuter trains or the leatherette sofas in some doctor's waiting room all over the country could be watching the man in the white shirt rifle the tabletop cathedral. Orin didn't care what they thought about it, the church or the jewelry or his betrayal and the scars it had left on the marriage. He wanted to feel safe and whole again, to look into the double-glazed sliding door and see only his own middle-aged reflection — out of condition, thoroughly gray and pale-skinned, but normal, purged of the renegade cells. A cancer patient just a year away from being promoted from "remission" to "survival." But even safer than that. He wanted to turn the clock back to a better time.

That was when he realized he couldn't swallow. No surprise there, but he suddenly needed to. The radiation had destroyed his salivary functions, and not even the doctors could grasp the discomfort. He could no longer afford to be more than ten feet from something liquid and had learned to accept the foolishly trendy ubiquity of that plastic bottle of expensive water. Evian, Breeze, Freshet. The old reliable Perrier didn't come in plastic, and besides, the carbonation didn't provide as much relief, though he'd settle for it now. He had left his glass outside, along with the NPR coffee mug, but now that he was breathing heavier, now that he was registering everything in minute detail, he needed it, and the urge to swallow began to consume him. He knew it was best not to attempt it without lubrication, for that would only amplify the urge and make his throat lining contract, dry membrane on dry membrane, guaranteed to irritate and probably to cause pain. He saw that he had squeezed the magazine in his hand until his knuckles whitened, but he could not feel it. The numbness in his extremities was still further collateral damage from the chemo.

"Mickey, I need your help."

"Tough."

"No, really. I, I've had throat cancer, and I have to moisten my throat constantly. You can tell by the way my voice is changing. I left my coffee outside, and I need some water. Could you run me some from the tap?"

Mickey laughed again. "What about a shot of this Black Jack? Put hair on your ass. Maybe even heal your throat."

"No, really, I just need water." He was breathing hard through his nose now and feeling the first stirrings of panic. If he proved troublesome, he might get the knife, feel the shock of its force between his shoulders before he knew what was happening. Would the man be strong enough or accurate enough to make quick work of it? It might take experience or training. Or maybe Mickey would pull the blade across his throat with an assassin's ease and he'd feel the rip and the warm wetness rilling down his shirt. That would be the end, and it might be best, in some respects. But what about Mina? Would she come home and find him gnawed by animals, the carpet soaked with blood? His body could lie there for days. Their isolation was that complete. Even her return to a house festooned in yellow CRIME SCENE tape was too much to imagine. The thought of her having to sit with polite dignity through the various ceremonies of death troubled him. All the pretense that he had been an honorable and constant husband, that he had faced disease with courage and had not failed her through any fault of his own. But this was all melodrama.

Normally, he did not spend much energy on remorse; what was done was done. Now, however, he felt a surprising need for clarity, for forgiveness and release.

"You a smoker then, sport?"

Was there a taunt in that? Strangers always assumed tobacco was the culprit, and since the treatments, he'd displayed the lassitude and sallowness of someone who'd smoked longer than his constitution could bear.

"Never."

"So what happened?" The barely audible rattle said that Mickey was putting the rings and other trinkets into his pocket. The ruby flanked by glittering emeralds. The black cameo. Ten Chinese pearls, satiny as magnolia petals, which he still loved to see across Mina's throat. A handsome woman. Even young men said that. And the diamond earrings he called "the star danglers." The rest was thin white gold in braids, an onyx ring, an opal broach no one under seventy would actually wear. And these the man could have, for there was nothing that mattered he could really take from them. Everything important had been spent in carelessness and enmity. Denial, too, always the eroding denial. Distraction, with the facts still smoldering deep under the cold ash.

"Here."

He hadn't even heard Mickey open the tap or move across the carpet, but he saw the glass on the end table, the disk of wavering light the sun projected onto the dark woodgrain. Orin let the magazine drop to the floor and lifted the glass, drank deeply, like someone just in from garden work. "Now I reckon you'll have to reach your hands behind you, Pop."

In two minutes Mickey had wrapped Orin's wrists and ankles in duct tape. Orin had watched the shadow on the floor before him, the knife raised, then the wide circle of tape, like the symbolic paraphernalia of some ritual. The sound of ripping tape again.

"Shut your mouth now, tight."

He was bound and gagged on his armchair, immobile but still unharmed, his glasses gently placed on the table beside him.

"I'm going upstairs and have a look-see, then I'll come back and check on you before I call it a day. Don't mess around. Don't try to get loose. Just sit still and take it. This'll all be behind you before you know it. It'll be just like a little dream."

But the man did not go upstairs. Orin could hear the entryway floorboards, then the front doorknob twisting. He heard the suction as the gasketing released and the warped door opened, the steps on the treated boards, and that was it. The man was not upstairs but out of the house. Orin realized that Mickey hadn't planned to search any further, once he got his hands on the jewelry. He had no interest in the computer, either. He just wanted to arrest Orin further with misinformation while he made his escape.

The tape over his mouth was the worst part, and it exaggerated his dryness, the Velcro closure of his tongue against his palate when he had no water. He hated this feeling of adhesion, of skin abrading where it was meant to touch smoothly, eased by saliva.

This was the reason he seldom kissed Mina, his punishment from the treatments that had saved his life. He would wait a few minutes, then hobble over to the kitchen, where the scissors would not be hard to reach. Then he would be free in a jiffy, but first, just in case, it was better to wait.

Outside the window, the fresh boughs were waving, and he could see the pendants of blossoms at the peak of the empress tree. Orin wondered how he would begin to tell Mina this story, the invasion and theft, his helplessness, his foxhole surge of religion, without seeming even less a man than before. However he told it, he hoped he could summon the nerve to embrace her, to caress her hair and face while saying how grateful he was that she was safe, that she was back home. Such words didn't come easily, but he knew he had to manage, that he could. Then he would take a long drink of spring water from its cool cylinder of blue plastic, and he would tell her he loved her and had loved her from the time he saw her smiling radiantly in the college cafeteria. And he would kiss her, lingering the old way, trying to become whatever they both needed him to be, whatever was next, something vernal and remarkable, he hoped, something healed.

He began to walk the chair toward the counter. "May Day," he thought. "Mayday."

––––––––––

R. T. Smith's stories have appeared in *The Best American Short Stories, The Pushcart Prize, The Best American Mystery Stories,* and three previous volumes of *New Stories from the South.* His new fiction collection *Uke Rivers Delivers* was published in 2006, and *Outlaw Style: Poems* was published in 2007. Smith lives in Rockbridge County, Virginia, and edits *Shenandoah* for Washington and Lee University.

Most of my stories are set in the historical or rural South, and they're often outrageous or satiric monologues, but in "Story" I wanted to do something different, to look at some denizens of the middle-class New South, but without either my standard elaborate furnishings or the "fashionable ennui" of the New Yorker *story Orin's been reading. My narrative also features two elements I can't seem to shake: the focal character is both vulnerable and culpable; the action revolves around a crime. Given these preoccupations and always mindful of Twain's trust in the mysterious stranger strategy, it's not too surprising that I'd turn one morning from reading an unsatisfying magazine story to composing one with a guilt-ridden protagonist and an intruder who's more catalyst than cause. I'll also confess that I've long been fascinated by that "May Day" pun, as the phrase can signal either a desperate situation or the season of renewal, or both.*

Angela Threatt

BELA LUGOSI'S DEAD

(from *Gargoyle*)

1

I used to dream. When I was eight, I listened to Earth, Wind & Fire's "Fantasy" and dreamed of riding a horse through the desert, strong winds blowing through my flowing robes. I was fierce, free. When I was twelve, we moved to the projects. For Christmas that year, I finally got the pink and white canopy bed I'd wanted for so long, but I didn't have the dreams I thought I would have in it. Instead, I entered the mouths of dark caves, accompanied by the sounds of Bauhaus: the dark monotony of the two or three chords in "Bela Lugosi's Dead," Peter Murphy's voice deep as the sea.

2

We arrived in December, a few weeks before Christmas. Ma had come out to look at the apartment a few times before, and when I was much older, she told me that she'd practically spent the night once, on the bare concrete floor, drinking beer and listening to the silence bounce off the walls. It was her first place on her own.

I'd never seen any place like this. The streets were wide enough for comfortable driving, but all the houses looked the same, some a dull shade of mint green, some pale yellow, some beige. No matter which way you turned your head, there were flat, squat buildings. Pastel on concrete. They looked unlike any houses or apartments

I'd ever seen. Once we turned onto the main street of the complex, it was as though we'd entered another world; everything outside of that maze of streets had ceased to exist.

We arrived in a caravan, with uncles and aunts to move and unload us. We didn't need a U-Haul, but there was a new blue couch and love seat in Uncle Joe's truck, and a new bed for me, not yet assembled. The houses were flat, the ground was flat, there were no porches for people to sit on, but across the street from where we would live, there was a rather heavyset woman making the most of her one step. She made it a porch by the fact that she sat there, in a white plastic chair. There were two children playing nearby. One had a red ball. The woman in the white plastic chair looked at us but did not speak. The children paid us no attention. The one with the red ball was bouncing it, and it bounced from the narrow sidewalk to the dirt mixed with scattered pieces of grass on either side of it. I frowned. Where were the yards?

In Newport News, we'd had a small yard around our house. The front yard was fenced in by a white picket fence that sometimes had all its pickets, sometimes not. On the east side, an alley separated the house from a small brick church. Sometimes we could hear drunks passing by in the night. On the west side, there was a much taller and broader white brick wall, one side of a building that housed a beauty parlor and one or two other ever-changing businesses. The grass grew out of control, and every summer my grandmother paid my Uncle Buster to cut it on the weekends my cousin Ralph was unable to do it. Not only did the grass grow like crazy, but there were bunches of clover with tiny violets that grew out of them. When I was small and the grass was overgrown, my feet would sink into them up to the ankle. There was a tree in the front yard that grew blackberries. Every summer we'd pick them in bunches, and I was given a little bowl to collect berries in. The first berry of summer was shocking to the taste buds, an explosion of sweet, tangy, dark purple. After that, we couldn't stop until our mouth and hands were stained purple. In winter, the only time the grass lay dormant, our yard became the manufacturing grounds for the stuff that snow cones were made of. Why did the grass here struggle to survive? I'd never seen grass that didn't flourish naturally, and its absence startled me.

The adults parked the cars in the loosely graveled parking spaces in front of our new apartment. I watched my uncles unload the soft blue sofa and love seat, where I would sit two years later, watching *General Hospital* after school. I hadn't yet graduated to watching soap operas, I hated them all and couldn't understand why my grandmother and aunts watched them so avidly.

I am ten years old, I live at my grandmother's house, ride my bike, run in the woods. My mother is the smartest woman in the world. Everyone in the world lives in a house or an apartment on a clean street. They have neighbors who are all black, all white, or of both races. These are the only distinctions. There are no homeless people or projects. I only bleed when I am hurt.

3

I'd have to go to a new school here, even though it was December and there was only half of the year left until junior high. I wasn't happy about it. It was December, but here, in the southeast, on the coast, we were having an Indian summer day, a sixty-eight-degree day. There was still time to enjoy the beach, but how would I get to the beach from here?

At my grandmother's house, the one we had moved to when we left my other grandmother with my father, the blackberry tree, and the picket fence, I used to walk or ride my bike to the beach with my cousins or my friends in the neighborhood. It took less than five minutes on my bike. Sometimes I'd go by myself, picking up shells and bringing them home, where I kept them in shoeboxes or in clear bottles with sand. I had a favorite shell, and I'd brought it with me, along with my other possessions: several pairs of shirts and pants, a few dresses and a winter coat, a good-sized stack of books, my roller skates, my bike, and a set of black Barbies, one named Diana Ross. My roller skates were white, brand-new size six, with new orange pom-pom tassels.

From Grandma's house we could also walk to the roller-skating rink. One time I was holding hands with my friend's older sister so I could go faster. When she let go of my hand, I panicked, forgot about brakes, slammed into the wall, and ended up passed out on my back with a rink full of kids and the owner breathing over me. Even with a lump on my forehead in the twilight, we walked home. I was too embarrassed to call home for a ride, and besides, it was 1979; no one had been shot outside of this rink yet.

Roooooooock Skate *Roooooooool* Bounce

I wondered where I could walk to from here. Even though I had seen their end and their beginning, it seemed as though the flat concrete houses grew out of each other, like they went on for-ever. Already I felt trapped. Nothing beckoned. No thick grove of trees like behind both of my grandmothers' houses; even though in Newport News I wasn't allowed into the grove because of the drunks and the broken glass, it had been there, lush and full of mystery. Looking around, I couldn't imagine that there were se-cret paths here, paths that might lead me to a lonely log in a clear-ing, or a thin, rutted path just right for bumpy, exhilarating bike rides. Here, everything was out in the open: there wasn't even enough grass to hide the bits of glass and paper on the ground, and I worried about maneuvering my skates on the uneven side-walks. The project had a main street which led to an exit at each end. At one end there were a few small, nondescript houses. In ten years, I would never once meet the people who inhabited them.

The woman on her porch across the street was studiously avoid-ing our eyes. I'd seen my aunt catch herself when she got out of the car, about to speak. Inside the apartment, the blue sofa, love seat, and chair convened. I walked inside quickly, anxious to claim the place. The concrete floors hurt my feet, even through my shoes. The rugs hadn't been laid yet. They wouldn't help. Soon, I would start to walk a little more softly.

4

In the spring I took my white roller skates with the orange pom-poms out for the first time. I tried my best to skate along the sidewalks, but they were so cracked I kept tripping. I didn't go out much that first summer.

Before Reagan finished his first term I had breasts.

Seventh grade was the first year we had classes separated by levels: basic, average, and college prep. It was in college prep classes that I began to hear regularly about Nixon and what he had done before my memory became solid. I did not watch the news. It seemed surreal. The white boys on the debate team were enamored with history and its symbols. I was still enamored with some of those boys, even as it became clearer that we cared about different things. I wondered what my old sixth grade boyfriend was doing, if he had any new freckles. I wondered if he'd joined a debate team.

The breasts were quite unwieldy, but they came with junior high. According to the measuring tape that my mother had wrapped around my body since I could remember, *OK, I got your chest, waist, and hips, now hold still, let me measure for the hem,* my chest now measured a solid thirty-two inches. I would have to get a bra. We got a nice lacy beige one from Kmart, a size 32A. I liked it a lot, but I couldn't believe I'd have to wear it or the white one every day. Luckily the breasts were not big enough to be very noticeable. Nobody had to know about the beige lace but me.

I had made a good choice indeed, to come here instead of to the fundamental junior high I had been recommended for. What sense did it make to call a school for the gifted a "fundamental" school? I shuddered to think of what boring days the nerds were having there, while I raced up and down the halls in my designer jeans. Here I was a success. I had made it through most of my first year without the so-called thug girls cutting off my hair, as I had been told they would do to any first-year black girl with shoulder-length or longer hair. I got along with the project kids, the middle-class kids, and kids in classes from basic to college prep. I had new friends from other neighborhoods. My teachers were challenging and my classes stimulating. I was making four As and two Bs on each report card by alternating which two classes I would slack off in. And I was having fun.

I was still a bit of a tomboy, but my new friends and I liked the new designer jeans that the older girls were wearing: Oscar de la Renta, Calvin Klein, Gloria Vanderbilt, and Jordache. Somehow I got a pair of each. The Calvin Kleins were my favorite. They were a size ten and tight, and for the first time, the boys noticed that I had a behind. This was not a good thing. Boys in the seventh grade in 1982 didn't know how to use lines or even wolf whistle. They grabbed. Luckily I could still run, and I had good friends who could fight.

One day between classes, a girl from my class, Michelle, and I were at our lockers. Michelle was wearing her Jordache jeans. When she turned to head to her next class, a boy came up behind her and grabbed her. She tried to push him away, but the boy grabbed her bony arms, slamming her into the wall, and began to grind his pelvis against her. Michelle's hands flew up into the air and then to his shoulders, still trying to push the boy away as he pushed her legs apart and ground his way between them, then slid her body up the wall with his strong arms and simulated sex with her, there in the middle of the hallway. I don't remember how it ended, if teachers or other students saw, what they said, who stopped it. I remember time stopped. The same thing happened to Michelle in math class when Mr. Avondale was out and the substitute had gone to the bathroom, only that time Mark did it. He ground her against the chalkboard while some boys cheered him on. I don't remember what the other kids did. I think time stopped again. At some point I must have wondered if this was happening at the fundamental school. At another point I must have stopped caring. I could still run.

When spring came, we spent our first gym period of the season outdoors. After class was over, Mr. Johnson told us all to grab a bag of balls or cones from the blacktop and head back to the building. The grassy field between the blacktop and the school building was covered in green grass and yellow dandelions. We were giddy with pollen, breeze, and the change in time. The early afternoon sunlight blinded us, and we just couldn't go back to class, my best friend Sandy and I. We lingered behind, the whole class forgot about us, we fell to the ground and watched the world swirl in blue, white, gold, and green around us. We twirled dandelions and chewed their stems, we lay on our backs, crossed our legs at the knees and laughed. She heard the boys first and jerked her head from the grass like a frightened deer. She moved first and I followed; we had to make it back to the building before they caught up to us. The field was empty and quiet. We had to make it back. There were no words between us, just air whistling. I marveled that her strong, thick legs and butt that was bigger than mine carried her faster, always a step or two ahead of me. I was losing my speed, and the thought so disappointed and frustrated me that I almost stopped. She was beating me, losing me. But somehow I knew that she wouldn't make it back without me. Our unspoken fears and the air we breathed linked us. We arrived at the gym door breathless and heaving. Sandy looked at me and grinned, her hands on her knees. Still no words. The boys arrived breathless a few seconds later. There were no words exchanged: no taunting from them, no congratulations between us. The moment was gone, over, already dissolving. I swallowed what was left of my fear and wiped the sweat from my forehead.

5

They say Reagan might win again. I don't care. Nothing changes in this world that I can see. It is my fourteenth summer. I am finished with junior high school, ninth grade, and algebra. Algebra was easy, the study of symbols and how you can add and subtract things that don't exist. If you put the symbol there, you can make the number appear by figuring out the value of the symbol. X. Y. A fun exercise, but pointless.

It is summer. Hot. Weather changes, but nothing else. Who cares. There is no water here. No way I'm riding my bike all the way to Gramma's to go to the beach.

We found out a few days ago that my grandmother's sister in Georgia died. They're talking about a family trip to Hazlehurst for her funeral. When Ma told me, I didn't say anything. Who wants to travel for twelve hours to meet death? Who wants to go to the country where Ma says the nights are darker than any black I've ever seen? Next year, when I start high school, we get to go on an annual day trip to D.C. I'm looking forward to it, looking forward to getting away from here.

I've dyed my hair green with Kool-Aid again. Band practice started yesterday. I was riding my bike back home and I was going pretty fast, but some of the kids still saw my hair and started pointing. I can use band practice as my excuse not to go to the country. I don't want to go to a funeral. This sister is no one I know. I've never even met her. I've never met any of Gramma's sisters. They are not even pictures to me. They don't exist. Besides, the annual summer carnival is coming up.

6

We went to the carnival. Sandy's mother took us, came right to my house and picked me up. She doesn't mind that I live in the projects. She knows I am a nice girl. She dropped us off and said we could stay for two hours, by ourselves. We are fourteen and old enough. But she won't let Sandy stay at my house with me, while my mother is gone. You're welcome to come and stay with us, she says.

We get to the carnival and it's swirling lights like always, rides spinning and people walking, cotton candy, and we're closer to grown than we've ever been. I see my cousin Pete, who is the same age as me and didn't go to Georgia either. We're too old for that; we have our own lives. I am thrilled to see him, but sad, because a year or two ago, we might have been piled into a car together to stay at some relative or friend of a friend's house. This means we're getting old. I don't even know how he got here, who he's with. We ride one ride together. He is still skinny; my wide size-ten hips knock him repeatedly against the side of the car. I am sorry for this and try to tell him so, but my teeth are chattering in my head. We hop off the ride and grin at each other in the summer breeze.

C'mon! Sandy grabs my arm and I wave bye to my cousin and his friends as the day turns to dusk. Sandy holds tight to my arm until she sees a boy she likes and they go off to ride a ride. The boy looks older than us and has a friend. The friend asks me if I like cotton candy and buys me some. He asks me which ride I like best and I say the black widow. He asks if I like the haunted house. I say I haven't been. Oh, you're scared, he says. No, I just haven't been. You're scared. Whatever you say, I say. I like scary movies the best, and my favorite author is Stephen King. I want to be a writer like him one day or a ballet dancer, I say. You're smart, aren't you, he says. I stare at this boy who is almost a man. Get good grades, right? He looks into my eyes and still I don't answer. Says come on then, if you're not scared.

In the haunted house there is nothing scary. It makes me laugh. Something jumps out of a dark corner and I jump, stumble against the boy, giggle. He grabs my hand and it is the first time I have held a boy's hand and nothing like I thought it would be. Maybe because I waited until I was fourteen and the boy is older than me and almost a man and his hand is strong and I can feel bones and veins and muscles that go up to his arm and shoulder and chest. My hand enveloped in his startles me, and I stop laughing. The way the fingers link like they are part of the same hand, the way this happens so quickly and I don't even know him. I am not scared of anything but his hand squeezing mine reassures me anyway, tells me not to worry, I'll be alright. Then we are against the wall of the haunted house, my back against the fake Styrofoam cave wall and the boy pressing against me, and he is firm but not insistent, confident but not forceful and he tells me I will be alright with his hands on my waist and his muscled leg slipping easily between mine, and I am feeling something I haven't before. His lips are soft against mine and it is the first time I have kissed a boy but this boy is almost a man and his legs are strong and his hips move against me, not forcefully but confident, his lips are soft and his kiss is hard but not too hard, and how can something be soft and hard at the same time and oh this is why people do this it's a miracle, this is what lips feel like against lips, he puts his tongue in my mouth his lips are all over me and his thigh between my legs and I am standing but not standing, my legs have turned to liquid.

As we step into the dark light of the carnival night, I see Sandy and the boy's friend and the two boys go off together. When they are gone she says you kissed him didn't you? About time.

7

My mother knew the dead woman, had fond memories of how "mean" she was, in the summer when they used to go down and visit. They said Ma was just like her, and this secretly amused my mother. I did not want to go. I did not want to go to a dead woman's funeral. As far as Gramma's sisters went, the only thing I knew was that she had three. One in Detroit, two in Georgia, now one. I found this amazing, since I had never seen them. Each sister had a separate life in a separate state. While their children, who were cousins, might have known each other from family visits in the fifties and sixties, apparently no one considered any of us born after 1967 important enough to introduce. I had seen a picture once, in Gramma's room, of a light-skinned solemn girl, about six or seven, wearing a pale dress with a blue sash and white stockings. I thought she was pretty. By the date on the picture she looked to have been two or three years older than me, born in the late sixties. Who is this, Gramma? That is my sister's grandchild, she answered. I often thought about the girl in the picture. Why was she so light-skinned?

Most of my cousins were lighter than me, but not as light as this little girl. What did her parents look like? Was she biracial? Was she as solemn as me? Did she like school? In what part of Georgia did they live? Why didn't they visit?

I will meet the girl in the blue dress two years later, when I am sixteen, and her family moves to Virginia Beach. But the time between fourteen and sixteen is not measured by months. By the time I meet her, I will have grown old, and she will seem to me ancient. She will wear glasses and attend college. She will prove to be solemn. Even though I have seen the picture, I won't be able to remember her without breasts any more than I can remember myself without them.

8

When Ma got back from Georgia, she looked tired but rested. She told me she was proud of me and that I was really growing up. She said she knew she could trust me and that I was very mature for my age, even though I sometimes got on her nerves. We laughed. She hugged me tight for the first time in a long time.

I used to sit on her lap even when I was nine; it was my chair, even though my legs were almost as long as hers by then.

I didn't ask her anything about the funeral and she didn't tell me. She said the nights in the country were as black as ever.

9

It is fall. There's a new girl in my biology class. Our names are similar. She's Asian, but I think one of her parents is white. We like the same music. We both hate history, government, and biology. We like English, words. I like band, music. She likes music, but she doesn't want to play it, only dance. She gave me a tape with a David Bowie song on it, "Ashes to Ashes." I hadn't heard it before. I really like it. We both like Bauhaus. I think she might be my first goth friend. I probably can't really be goth because I'm not white, and my skin's not even a pale enough brown or beige to lighten it with makeup to get a gothy kind of look, like paper bag brown Lucinda does. Lucinda lightens her skin with makeup, but she doesn't want to be goth, she just wants to match her white boy-friend and her white friends. We all think it's quite a feat, though some people don't like her. I just want to be goth. But it's okay that I have brown skin. I have green hair, sometimes red, sometimes blue. And I have a new friend. I still have some money left over from my birthday money and I think it's about time to spend it. We decide to go to the concert.

You going?

Yeah, wouldn't miss it!

I can get my dad to come pick you up.

I don't answer; I know that she has not told her parents where I live. She's new in town and has never even seen it, doesn't have any idea where Carver Village is. Perhaps she thinks it's like Riverdale Woods or Aberdeen Farms, middle- or working-class subdivisions where a lot of kids from school live. She's probably gotten some hints in conversations around school, but she's never actually been there, so she can't really know. I try to figure out how I can get out of having her dad pick me up, though every-body knows Carver is on the way to the Coliseum, practically in its backyard. It doesn't make sense for me to say my mom will take me; if we're going together, we should go together. It doesn't make sense to say I'll walk. We're fourteen years old; we don't go out alone after dark. The thought of the things we've already assumed about each other startles me. I look at her across the lab table, her round, pudgy face, slanted eyes staring back at me expectantly.

OK?

OK.

The night of the concert I am wearing all the black I own, black skirt with black leggings and a black jean jacket over a black T-shirt. She grins when she sees me. Her father is looking slightly startled in the car. I am not sure if it is where I live or how I look; he only knows me from the phone, probably only knows of this part of Virginia from relocation books and maps, what the Navy tells him. He is in the Navy; they have just come from Hawaii. He looks like an enlisted man, not haughty like an officer. He is thin, white, brown haired, unassuming. Slightly startled. He drops us off at the concert in his blue Toyota with the old paint. Goes home to talk to his wife. Angelina and I are wearing black and swaying to "Bela Lugosi's Dead." For two hours, we are the undead. Sweaty and alive.

We return to class and smile about the concert. A quiet develops. We don't go to any more concerts. Her father doesn't bring her back to my house. I don't remember how I lose her, but when her father is transferred, she gives me a number but doesn't call.

10

I still hate history. If there is any such thing, I am outside of it. I am in AP history this year, but I don't know why. It's all about wars and men. This has nothing to do with my life. Is life aside from war not a part of hisory? There are kids in my class who have their own cars and wear clothes from the Limited. Black kids too. Their parents know each other. They are the owners of history. To them I am a project kid who, for all anybody knows, was born in the projects, spawned from the blacktop out of the scrawny bushes and scrub grass, left by a project stork, a half person with no history, no past worth claiming. They know nothing about me except what I tell them. I tell them nothing.

Gramma used to bury sweet potatoes in the backyard and pull them up steaming. I haven't learned this yet. My mother is too tired to tell me. I get on her nerves and she works all day. It doesn't matter because I wouldn't want that counted in my history any more than I wanted to see a dead woman in the country that no one ever bothered to introduce me to. History is tall towers in a big city. Biscuits and sausage for breakfast at Gramma's and fried fish and toast for breakfast at Gam's with a little bit of coffee and a lot of sugar and milk in a mug for me with my legs swinging under the table is not history. Sweet potatoes under the ground are not history. My life holds no history. As far as I can see, I don't exist.

My mother is eighteen years older than me, and we have separate beds in separate rooms in the projects. I have no history, no past. I am my present. I would never travel four hundred miles to memorialize a country woman's death. One day I will live in the city. I will travel, and make new history. They will write books about me. I will invent something new, myself.

Angela Threatt's fiction and creative nonfiction have appeared or will appear in *The Truth About the Fact: A Journal of Literary Nonfiction; Gargoyle;* and Stanford University's *Black Arts Quarterly*. She was a 1998 Hurston/Wright College Award finalist and a 2005 Virginia Commission for the Arts fellowship finalist. She has an MFA from the University of Maryland at College Park.

*W*ith the kiss, the narrator's reality shifts; the freakish history of the carnival, with its intimation of hedonism, of blurred and shifting realities, is a vehicle for the death of the narrator's innocence and the birth of her will and her sexual self. In this autobiographical work of fiction, the challenge was to weave together and re-create several moments that did not take place concurrently. The Cyndi Lauper concert was reimagined. The concert needed a darker undertone to fit with the rest of the piece; goth was a better fit. I'd always loved goth culture, and though I didn't know much of the music, I knew Bauhaus was the most important group of the time. At some point I rediscovered "Bela Lugosi's Dead," a seminal early goth piece. I included the lyrics "undead undead undead" in an effort to translate the mood of the song onto the page. Although I worried about whether or not the piece would hold up thematically without the lyrics, I eventually deleted them. All that remains of Bela is the story's title.

Daniel Wallace

A TERRIBLE THING

(from *The Georgia Review*)

Before I met the woman who would become my wife, I went out with women who were in some way disfigured, girls to whom terrible things had happened — things apparent to anyone who looked at them. Not all of them were like that, but a lot of them were — many — maybe even most. One of the women I went out with was missing a hand. Another had been badly burned in a fire. Celia had a birthmark planted on one whole side of her face like an immense, permanent red welt.

There were others like that. I was drawn to these women in a way I could never put words to then. I guess I was some kind of freak myself, though I didn't think so at the time, and I don't think the girls (none of whom knew about the others) thought that either. You might assume, because these days it's natural to assume, that it was a sexual thing, that somehow I got off on the scars and missing pieces. But (though we did have sex sometimes, the same as anyone) this wasn't true. Or that I took pity on these women who if it weren't for me might never have been with another man in their entire lives. But I don't think it was this either. I think it was simply their *observable difference* that was intriguing to me and the degree to which they were able to live a happy and normal life with it. Not that all of us don't harbor some sort of distinction, that thing that makes *us* rather than somebody else, but with these women it was obvious, and clear, exactly what it was.

Anyway, that was then. The woman I married, oddly enough, is practically flawless. She's just plain beautiful: were an alien from some distant galaxy to come to earth, it would know at first glance that my wife was a specimen of amazing beauty. Her name is Andrea — though she likes to be called Andy. Calling her Andy only serves to underscore the fact that she is not an Andy, that she is anything but an Andy, that she could never be an Andy, and this somehow makes Andy the best name for her of all. She's tall, and her brown hair curls in the rain, and her eyes are green and shaped like almonds, and her face is the face of some ancient Egyptian goddess. She doesn't have that faraway perfection you see in pictures of models, though, women who know how they look. Andy doesn't seem to know, and that makes her even more beautiful, to me. Her laugh is goofy. I love her.

One night we went to Charlie's, a Chinese restaurant down the street from our house. It's cheap and good and when you ask for no MSG you get no MSG. We're there once a week; still, people stare. When we walk in they glance up, expecting to see just another couple, but Andy captures their glance and holds it, almost against their will. And it is Andy. It's certainly not me they're looking at. I always feel invisible when I'm with her — the way I've felt with most of the women I've been with. I'm plain, physically unobjectionable, not even outstandingly average. I can pass in front of a mirror without inspiring the appearance of my own reflection.

"The usual?" she said that night, without even opening her menu.

"The usual," I said. The usual was the moo shu pork, steamed dumplings, and the orange chicken — their specialty.

Andy had brought the newspaper with her, and she opened it, read for a moment, and sighed.

"Let's move to New Zealand," she said. I read the upside-down headline: we were going to war. Every time America did something wrong, Andy wanted to break up with it. Now more than ever.

"New Zealand," I said. "That's a long way away. I'd have to think about that."

I thought about it. "Okay. Let's do it." And I winked.

When the waitress came she brought us some water and we ordered the usual.

Andy leaned over and whispered, as though her lack of patriotism was being overheard. "Everybody thinks America is so great. You know? And there are a lot of nice things about it. But I can think of about seven other countries I would much rather live in, if I could take all my friends and family with me."

"Except your mother."

"Except her. Right." She looked around us at the families and other couples eating at the tables and booths. "People talk about freedom. It's not that big a deal anymore, though. It's like those motels you pass on little country roads that advertise 'air conditioning in every room.' Freedom is in lots of places now. We need to stop bragging about it."

She looked up and then suddenly turned to me wide eyed and looked at me with an almost comic urgency.

"There's a woman coming toward us," she whispered, *"and one of her hands is missing!"*

I caught my breath: it was Sybil, it had to be, I knew without looking. Then I heard her voice.

"David?"

I looked up, feigning surprise. "Sybil?"

I stood up and hugged her. Andy watched with the expression of pleasant discomfort every woman has watching her husband embrace another woman. Maybe more so in this case.

"Sybil, Andrea," I said. "My wife."

"Your *wife*? You got married? I didn't — that's so great!"

Sybil was genuinely happy. She smiled, and I could see her teeth, how one tooth folded over the one next to it, something I'd always thought was charming.

She looked at Andy. "Wow. You're a lucky one," she said.

"I know."

"And he is too. Obviously. You're gorgeous. I would have liked him to marry me," she said, joking — she was never that serious — "but where would he have put the ring?"

She laughed and we laughed and then we all looked at the end of her arm. Then Andy stopped laughing.

Sybil kissed me on the cheek. "I have to go. But it's so good to see you — and to meet you, Andrea. Congratulations."

I sat down and waited for what came next. In the long silence that followed I could almost hear Andy thinking, attempting to understand what had happened. But I couldn't catch her eyes. For a while there she was very far away from me, and when she came back she had a question.

"You *dated* her?"

What could I say? I shrugged and nodded.

"I feel like such a . . . bad person," she said, "to say this, to think it. But, I mean, she doesn't have a hand."

"You noticed."

"Ha-ha," she said. "David, she doesn't — did she have it when you were — "

I shook my head.

"Oh my God," she said. "But what — that — what was that like?"

"We didn't play a lot of catch, obviously," I said.

"That is *so mean*," Andy said.

" — but other than that, nothing was very different than, well — "

"Than me?"

"In the hand department? Big difference. Otherwise — "

This hurt her feelings a little, and when I reached for her hand she moved it away.

"But, why didn't you tell me?"

This was a tough one. I hadn't told her about Sybil. I hadn't told her about any of those women. At least not the details. Not the I-dated-a-woman-without-a-hand details. And it was to her credit that she didn't pry or insist on knowing — but then why would she? Andy and I were so in love that the relationships in our past were like those roadside hotels — the old ones Andy mentioned, the ones you drive by and marvel at for their unsuitability. But she knew nearly nothing about the women I used to date.

Walking home, Andy was quiet for a while. Finally she spoke up.

"I just think that, when you date a woman with one hand, it's something that over the course of a couple of years might come up. As a topic of conversation at least."

"I guess."

"It feels like a betrayal."

"But it isn't."

"I *know*," she said. "But it feels like one." She thought some more. "I told you about Roger."

"Roger?"

"The guy with the hairy back I went out with for a year."

"Oh. Yeah. I remember."

"He was like a monkey."

"That's how I picture all your old boyfriends."

"He was actually very nice. And forthcoming."

We stopped at the corner and waited for the light to change. I hugged her, but she didn't hug back.

"Andy. I've never lied to you. Never. But I guess — I know — I haven't told you everything, about everyone who — you know. Other women. We have the rest of our lives together. Maybe I just want to save something for later."

"Nice save," she said. "But still: she doesn't have a hand."

Finally, Andy took mine. She squeezed it, and I squeezed back.

"No," I said. "She doesn't. But with Sybil or anyone else, the differences — even the big ones — they weren't a barrier to having what was otherwise a normal relationship. I promise."

She let go of my hand and looked at me.

"What do you mean, 'anyone else'?"

She kept looking and looking, intense and knowing. And she got her answer.

"There were others," she said. "Like her."

The light changed, and we walked.

This was a long night for Andy and me, a long night and good part of the next morning. It was the sort of thing that happens to men when they get caught cheating and to save their relationship come clean: I had to enumerate and describe every woman I had ever kissed.

But there were only certain details she cared to know.

"Next," she said.

"Jeena."

"Jeena who?"

"I don't remember her last name. We only went out for a couple of months a long time ago."

"Okay. Jeena Doe." She had made herself some hot tea. She blew on it, sipped it, scalding her lips. "Tell me about Jeena."

I thought about her, tried to see her as I spoke. "She had a long brown scar — a big one — down the left side of her face, from her eye to her chin. She'd fallen through a glass door when she was younger, and the doctor who fixed her up had done a really bad job."

"That's terrible," she said. "So she had this scar." She nodded, half to herself, thinking. "Did you ever touch it?"

"Sure," I said. My goal was to keep this as light as possible, but I was having some trouble achieving it.

"So you would . . . what? Draw your finger down the scar, from top to bottom, with your own face right there, close to hers, you would draw your finger across the scar like you were tracing the path on a road map or something like that?"

"I don't know, Andy," I said. "I guess."

"You guess."

"You make it sound so — "

" — what?"

"So intimate. And weird."

"And you're saying it's *not* weird, David?" She was shaking a little bit now. "Tell me this is not weird. But you can't because the fact that you never even mentioned it — these details, this *pattern* — is proof that you think it's weird too."

"No. What's weird is describing these things that took place *years and years ago,* before I ever knew you, when I was alone in a room with a woman, doing something, whatever it was, that was not supposed to leave that room, ever, and here I am talking about it now and, yes, that's weird. It's crazy."

"Did you touch the place where Sybil's hand used to be?"

"Did you go down on Roger?"

"So it's a sexual thing."

"No. It's a *private* thing."

"'Fuck. You. Just really, really. Fuck you."

Andy started crying. We were sitting cross-legged across from each other on the bed, and she fell forward, into my lap. She gasped for air between her heaving sobs and held onto me, her arms around my waist, and mine around her shoulders, and her cup of tea spilled across the middle of the bed.

"I'm your wife," she said, when she was finally able to speak. "I'm your *wife.*"

Marriage for the most part appears to be a series of mostly comfortable silences punctuated by joy, despair, and sudden dialogues that serve to calibrate the relationship, bring it up to speed, reassure and inform, after which we lapse back into our own quiet worlds.

Some of the silences are the bruised kind, though, where things are too sensitive to touch or even to talk about. This was the kind of silence we shared now.

The next few days were no different from the days preceding them, but now it felt as though our lives had been assigned to us, that they were not the lives we had chosen to live at all. Sometimes she looked at me as though she were surprised to see me here. Still.

It didn't help that, three days after seeing Sybil, we ran into

another old girlfriend in the coffee aisle at Food Lion. Candice
Martin. *Where were they all coming from?* I thought. I'd told Andy
about Candice — thank God — and it was she in fact who pointed
her out to me.

"Look," she said, without inflection. "The one-legged girl."

Candice — curly red hair, broad shoulders, and, of course, the
silver crutch tucked under her arm — was investigating the pasta
section. She moved smoothly down the aisle, almost as though
she were floating; she appeared to have assimilated the crutch so
deeply into her body that there was no longer any real distinction
between the two. She had even named it, I remembered: Frank.

Candice hadn't seen me yet, so I moved behind the coffee
stand.

"What are you doing?" Andy asked me.

"What does it look like I'm doing?" I was trying to become
invisible.

Andy almost laughed. "Say hello to her, David."

"I don't want to say hello. I've said hello to enough old girlfriends this week. This month. This year."

"That's so rude, I think."

She looked at me, at Candice, at the coffee. Disappointed.

I sighed and moved back into the middle of the aisle.

"Candice!" I called out.

She turned, happy and surprised to see me, and quicker than
anyone could have imagined she made her way over to us.

"David!" she said.

I hugged her, my arms beneath her arms, lifting her slightly,
temporarily holding her almost in the air, so she could feel what it
felt like to be supported by something other than a crutch.

"I want you to meet my wife," I said.

On our way home, grocery bags like children sitting in the backseat. Early yet, but it had suddenly become fall, and already it was
dark outside.

"How did she lose her leg again?"

"Some kind of circulatory thing. No — diabetes."

"She's also got *diabetes*? Wow. A two-fer." I looked at her: she was smiling so I smiled back. "Well," she said. "She was really nice."

The light changed, but Andy didn't move. She was absorbed, twisted around her own thoughts. A car horn honked behind us, and again, and only then did she pull out into the street.

You imagine a life of idyllic sweetness when you find the love of your life, a Caribbean island of the soul, where you and she rest together, drinking in the sun, the air, the deep blue water. But it isn't like that, not for anybody. Things happen, and when they do they either break you into pieces or bring you closer together, because the island you're on is really a deserted one, and neither of you is going to survive without the other.

Nothing happened to speak of that night; in fact, we didn't speak at all. I thought she might want to talk more about Candice or why all of a sudden these old girlfriends were hobbling out of the woodwork. But she didn't. I watched television; she read a magazine and made a list of things-to-do. When we went to bed around 11:00, I thought the day was over. It wasn't.

A few hours later the jaundiced bathroom light fell across my eyes and woke me. Weird, how eerie it all looked. Andy wasn't in the bed. The to-do list she had been making was on her pillow, and I picked it up and read it.

Sybil — no hand
Candice — no leg
Jenna — scar
Susan — face burned in fire
Arielle — hideous birthmark
Maddy — glass eye
Andy —

I waited for a moment, and listened, but heard nothing. It was so deathly quiet I was overcome with my darkest imaginations, and I couldn't stop the awful, gory pictures from flashing like a horrible slide show in front of my eyes. She wouldn't have. She couldn't. But then I thought, maybe there are things I don't know about her as well.

I got out of bed, moved slowly to the bathroom, and gently pushed the door open.

I saw her before she saw me. She was standing, completely naked, in front of the bathroom mirror, staring hard at her face, her shoulders, her breasts. It was as if she didn't realize the mirror showed her a reflection and thought it was another identical person instead. And she was amazed.

"Andy," I said. But she didn't stop looking. I had to say her name again before she heard me and snapped out of it.

"I had a dream."

She paused, recalling it. "I guess it was inevitable. I was in a room with all of your old girlfriends, all of them, all of those women. And they were terrible — terrible to look at, I mean. Their faces, their arms and legs. We were in this room together, and they were coming toward me, like, you know, zombies, and I wanted to run but of course I couldn't, I was frozen to the spot. And they kept moving toward me. *What are they going to do to me?* I wondered. *How are they going to hurt me?* I couldn't breathe. I couldn't move even a finger. And I tried. All I could do was wait and witness my own disfigurement.

"But when they finally got to me and had me surrounded, they all fell to the floor, and they looked up at me. And their eyes — the ones that had eyes — they were full of fear and respect and . . . *affection.* Even love."

She turned so I could look at her straight on.

"I was their queen." She smiled. "I was their queen, because I had succeeded where all of them had failed, having become your wife. But I was still one of them. I was just the best of them."

"Andy," I said. "It was just a dream."

I wanted to move then too but felt frozen to the spot by Andy's gaze. And her face, those lips, those eyes.

"What's wrong with me, David?"

"There's nothing wrong with you, Andy," I said, shaking my head. "Nothing. You're perfect."

"I've been in here for a while, looking," she said softly. "Trying to see what it is. *But I can't find it.* I can't see it."

"I love you," I said.

"You loved them too."

"But not like this. Not like you."

"I know," she said. She turned back to the mirror. She took a deep breath. "I know you love me. I just want to know why." I could see her eyes moving across her cheeks, her chin, her shoulders. She ran a finger along her collarbone. "What is it?" she said.

"Andrea," I said. I took her by the shoulders and turned her to me gently. "You could not be any more beautiful, more wonderful, than you already are. You *know* that."

"Goddamn it," she said, almost too soft to hear, and laughed hopelessly. "That's what I was afraid of." She closed her eyes, and when she opened them again it was like watching a butterfly open its wings. *"It's inside,"* she whispered, "isn't it? It's something I can't see but that you can. That's why you're with me, because I've got — I don't know — this *place,* this awful part, not diseased really but deeper than that, this thing who I am, that I don't know about, but you do. That's why you love me. Because of that."

I saw in her reflection the first tears silently slipping down her cheek.

"So, what is it, David?"

I looked away. "I don't know," I said.

"Look at me," she said. *"Look at me."*

I looked at her — at the *her* in the mirror. Her eyes, locked on mine, gave me time to take her in. She had given up.

"There is . . . something," she said softly. "Isn't there?"

"No," I said. "There's nothing at all."

"But isn't there always something?" she said. "With anybody, everybody?"

She waited for my answer, but I didn't have one for her.

"Don't do this, Andy. Please don't do this."

But it had been done. Finally she turned away from the mirror and came to me, and held me tighter than she almost ever had, almost tighter than I have ever been held in my life, and I held her back the same. She stopped crying, but her breathing came fast and labored, as if she'd just come back from a run.

"I don't want this to come up again," she said.

"It won't."

"I shouldn't have — I wish I hadn't said anything to begin with."

"We won't talk about it again, ever."

"Promise?" she said, and I promised.

Then she looked at me. "So stop," she said.

"Stop what?"

"Thinking it," she said. "Thinking about what it is. Just please stop."

"I don't know what you're talking about," I said, but even as the words were leaving my mouth I knew what she was talking about and that she had known before I could even know it myself: I was thinking of what it was, or what it could be, the terrible thing, and of how it would look when she showed it to me and what would happen when she did. I could not stop thinking of what it was, and she knew it. And yet she held me anyway.

"I want to go away," she said softly.

"Okay," I said. "Okay . . ."

"*Far* away," she said.

And her clutch came even tighter, and she burrowed her cheek into my chest as if she were looking for a hole, another way to crawl into my heart.

"New Zealand?" I asked her.

New Zealand — now it seemed like a good idea.

But Andy shook her head no.

"Farther," she said. And then she looked at me, and then she didn't. "Farther."

Daniel Wallace is the author of four novels, most recently *Mr. Sebastian and the Negro Magician*. He lives in Chapel Hill, North Carolina.

YORK WILSON

A Terrible Thing" *was a fun story to write. I'm sure it came from somewhere, but I don't know where that place is.*

I've never been as attracted to disabled and disfigured women as the narrator in this story is, though I have always had a soft spot in my heart for crazy ones.

Stephanie Powell Watts

UNASSIGNED TERRITORY

(from *The Oxford American*)

Leslie Pawlowski parks her blue Horizon on the shoulder of the dirt road — the best shade we can find. July is always a killer in North Carolina. It's always hot as blazes, hot enough to fry eggs, and on and on. We are in the thick of it, midmorning, our dresses clinging to our backs, way far in the middle of nowhere, preaching door to door, working in our congregation's "unassigned territory." This is the kind of dirt road, *Hee Haw*, overalls, straw-in-the-teeth place even we Southerners make fun of. Did you hear the one about the country girl who went to a town doctor? The doctor says to her mother, "Ma'am, has this girl had intercourse?" and the mother, wringing her hands, says, "I don't rightly know, Doctor, but if she needs it, you make sure you give it to her."

The passenger-side window sticks in the middle of going up or down. Piece of junk car. And on the way to every house, we shed bits of polyfoam from the car's cracked upholstery. But Leslie has a great attitude about her poverty: "Halcyon, salad days," she will say with a withering chuckle when her future kids complain of their own first cars.

We've visited too many houses without updating our field-service records so we stop before we forget the details. We need to keep records. Records for ourselves, for the congregation file on the territory, and for the official log at the Kingdom Hall.

"What was that woman's name at the blue trailer, Steph?"

I shuffle through my notebook knowing I won't find any useful information. You are supposed to write things like: *Ruth Boaz, 123 Main Street, blue trailer, lived in town all her life, no husband in the house, four kids — one still at home. Took the July 1989 brochure,* Making the Most of Your Youth. *Expressed an interest in tarot. Bring brochure* Why Godly People Shun Spiritism.

My records are, to say the least, incomplete. I wrote: *Trailer is a nightmare. Looks like the time my brother and I played drug czar with an old suitcase and Monopoly money. Ryan threw my clothes and shoes out of the dresser and closet screaming, "Where's the real stash! Where's the real stash!"*

I'm praying that Leslie won't ask to see what I've written. I've been at this long enough that I don't need any guidance from my field-service partner. Sometimes Leslie will say things like, "You're writing a book over there, aren't you?" but she never pries.

"Shoot. I hate to leave her name off. She was nice, too," Leslie sighs.

"Nice" to Leslie means that she didn't cuss us, that she didn't shoo us away or hide behind her curtains, her hand over the mouth of her child like a kidnapper. "But Mama," the kid would manage through her fingers, "there's some girls on the porch."

"Shh," I imagine her saying, "Do you want to be saved? Is that what you want?"

This lady had stood sullen and quiet on her rickety porch, her eyes never leaving my brown face. Leslie, even with her Minnesota accent, was apparently okay. Brown woman on the porch trumps Yankee invader any day. To be fair, they don't get too many black Jehovah's Witnesses out here. There are only two black Jehovah's Witness families in town, for a total of six people. And though our congregation gets to every door in the city limit at least three times a year, the unassigned territory, this deliverance of woods, creeks, and black snakes, gets worked only once a year if we are lucky. More likely, these people won't see any of us for eighteen to twenty-four months. Imagine the odds of seeing a black Jehovah's Witness in the territory. That's Lotto odds.

Besides the absence of black people there are four things to remember about the unassigned territory:

1) You are as remote as you can get in this new world — way out in the boonies, mostly white Southerners who've been holed up here for generations, living on winding dirt roads that lead to more winding dirt roads, with houses, the occasional mansion, trailers, and shacks out of sight from each other. They like it that way.

2) Everybody and his dog has a dog — at least one loose, ugly mutt with cockleburs in his unloved fur and filled with the kind of hatred that only comes from at last finding a body more miserable than yourself.

3) Apparently, the trauma of a visit from Jehovah's Witnesses is so great that just the glimpse of your *Watchtower* will act as a Proustian mnemonic causing the householder to wax nostalgic about your last visit. Never mind that someone from your or any congregation left a tract in the door two years ago. You will hear over and over, "Some of y'all was just here."

4) There is nothing good about the unassigned territory.

Leslie explained the "Offer of the Month," trying to regain the householder's attention. "This is our new booklet, *Enjoy Life Forever on a Paradise Earth.*" Leslie dangled the bright red cover at the woman. Even the color pictures of laughing children and fluffy sheep nuzzling up to male lions (dubiously, I thought) didn't move the woman's eyes. She only had eyes for me.

Does the missus want I should jig, a little tap dance fuh yo pleasure? I wanted to ask, but instead put on my best yes-I'm-black-but-doggonit-not-*that*-black face.

"You got that same Bible?" the woman said to me.

"Yes, ma'am," I held out my paperback *New World Translation* for her to see. When I got baptized, I'd get a leather one.

"That's plenty," she said, folding her arms across her chest. "I know the Bible when I see it."

Leslie gave the woman an older *Watchtower* magazine because she wouldn't have to request a donation for it. Good move, Leslie. She can *get* the literature into the house and not risk rejection. Who knows? This woman might even read it. She might change her life and be side-by-side with us in this very territory next year. You never know. That's why Leslie is a pro. She thinks about these kinds of things. I've seen her talk to grief-stricken and depressed people, whip out the Bible she seems to know by heart, and without a blink tell them that God is a fortress, a rock, a high place, a God of comfort, love, and forgiveness. And for a few seconds, I think she really lightens those people. It is no small thing to give a person even a moment of hope. Of course, when we go back the next week to follow up, those same people, looking like they could kill us — order us away. "Don't you tell me God loves me. Don't you dare — and slam their doors.

Leslie is grooming me, though she doesn't think that I know. I have a big decision to make next year. To serve Jehovah during my youth (which *Making the Most of Your Youth* recommends) or to go to college. I know that my congregation elders have urged Leslie to help me do the right thing.

On the way past the car, past the tired, old dog, through the patchy yard, I can't be sure, but I think I heard the woman say "wetback." I don't know, it could have been the heat or bigoted cicadas, but I think she called me that. I wanted to put my finger in her crumpled face, her skin like the film from Krazy Glue, and say something wise and cutting like, "Get your racial epithets right, Ms. Einstein." But fighting in the field service is looked down upon. Truth be told, at ninety-seven degrees and counting, Unnamed Householder had the virtue of being accurate in a literal sense. Not nice, but accurate. Apparently, the Mexicans who are coming into the county taking all the glory jobs (like picking apples for fourteen hours a day at less than minimum wage) and preaching door to door in glamorous locales like Millers Creek will make anybody sick with envy. I wanted to tell Leslie, but she was the sort of white person who refused to acknowledge racism. Just deny it and it won't exist. She'd say, "Well, I'm sure she didn't mean anything. Maybe she was concerned about the heat."

"What about the man on the tractor? Where did he say he lived?" Leslie asks. "I knew we should have stopped right then."

"Oh yeah," shuffle, shuffle. I want to ask Martin Luther King: Is this the dream you meant? Me and this sweet girl from Minnesota in a steaming car? Dr. King, I am hot today, but I'm trying to remember you at 1400 High Rock Road.

"1400 High Rock Road," I say.

"Okay, you are good for something," Leslie grins, acting like a mother. She's only six years older than I am, but preaching is her career. Her family moved to North Carolina only three years ago to serve "where the need was greater," but Leslie is easily one of the most popular people in town. She's a good girl, with a sweet disposition, and she has committed herself to the fieldwork. Leslie is a pioneer — out in service at least sixty hours a month every month. Sixty hours of door-slammings; "I have my own religions"; "I was just on my way outs"; and lonely old women who will even talk about Jehovah to hear another voice in the room.

"Okay," Leslie says, handing me a Shasta from her cooler; she always gets the cheap sodas. "Let's do two more houses. One if it's too far, okay?"

Thank God, thank God. Thank you. Thank you, Dr. King, thank you. "Are you sure? I'm up for another hour or so," I say, willing the bouncing thing of hope in my chest to stay still for a few minutes; she might change her mind. "I mean, if you need the time. I'm up for it," I manage to say.

"I'll just have to make it up next week," Leslie says breezily. But I know that this month will be especially hard for her. She has all those hours to complete in these backwoods. Think about it. You can't just come any old time. You have to arrive at decent hours, after nine in the morning and before eight at night but not during the dinner hour. You can only count the time you actually preach. That means the forty-five minute drive out there — gratis. The ride in between these houses in the territory — it is more than ten minutes, you eat it. The fifteen-minute lunch break is on your time, sister-friend. Jehovah's Witnesses need a union.

Leslie dribbles soda all over the bodice of her dress. No loss, as far as I'm concerned. Leslie shops at Granny's Rejects or Let's Repel Men or some store like that. I can't believe the kinds of things this young woman puts on her body: shifts (really!), baggy sweaters, long full skirts, gaudy prints. A style my daddy dubbed, "To' up from the flo' up."

Leslie has mostly given up on men. I know that the secret wish of her heart is that Bruce Springsteen comes to the Truth, but she was only hoping in her heart, not in her head. Lately, I've noticed her saying strange things like, "when I was young," or "if I were your age," or "that's for the kids." She is twenty-four. To be honest, she *is* getting a bit too old to be a Jehovah's Witness bride. The faithful marry young rather than burn with desire (according to 1 Corinthians 7:9), and they marry fast to get the pick of the litter of endangered young male believers. The congregation has already picked out my husband for me. A nice-looking white boy with a flounce of blond hair, unswiveling hips, and clunky, clod-buster shoes. Bobby Ratliff. I like Bobby, don't misunderstand me, but only twelve-year-old virgins look at a dopey sixteen-year-old and think, "What great marriage material!" Lord knows that by rejecting Bobby I am dooming myself to Lesliedom. There is precious little else to choose, few kids my age to even compare and contrast.

Jim, another teenager in the congregation, is a possibility, but he and his sister, Lisa, are bad — really bad. Once they brought a dirty magazine on the school bus, passed it around like candy to the other kids. I noticed when it came to Bobby's seat, he wouldn't even look at the filthy cover, wouldn't even touch it. The worst, the absolute limit, was when Jim and Lisa brought a Prince song for us to listen to. When Prince said "controversy" (and he said it often), Jim and Lisa led the bus in a rollicking, racy mispronunciation at the tops of their heathen lungs. Bobby and I didn't tell on Jim and Lisa, though we were tempted. We did explain to the other kids (at every opportunity) that though Jim and Lisa attend the Kingdom Hall, they aren't really of our sort. We insist that we are the real Jehovah's Witnesses. Sure, Jim and Lisa are clever and cool and fun, but salvation? I don't think so.

Lingering in a parked car in someone's driveway is a definite no-no, an unwritten rule; you can't look like you're casing the joint. But we are in slow-motion today, staring ahead at the gravel road, the high weeds and bushes covered with a thick layer of red dust. It hasn't rained for days. We can't see the house that the record indicates is directly in front of us. Somehow this seems important to me. If I had the words, I would say to Leslie, Isn't it funny that we can't see the next house? Doesn't that mean something? I want to tell her that, to take her deeper into my head. I want her to understand me. Leslie wouldn't get it. She would coax me to pray for guidance and direction and she'd be right. I know she'd be right. What is the alternative, really? The house record warns us of one place at the edge of the territory to avoid: "NOT INTERESTED. GUN." I can't help but think that the gun fact should come first. We'll have to come back when we're sure that Jim Caudle — gunman — has moved or is dead. Today we won't even check.

"Your door," Leslie says. "You can have the last door of the day."

The house is small, with a red tin roof. Someone must love the sound of the rain. Hippies probably. This gravel driveway looks fairly new and, sure enough, there is no record of the house in our files.

Another rule: Wait for the dog. Some come on strong, yelping and moaning like they've been stranded on Jupiter with a host of unheralded moons. Others give a quick impotent yap when you least expect it, their only surprise attack.

But this time: nothing. Just the pleasant walkway of paving stones, dotted without any discernable pattern, with terra-cotta pots full of red geraniums. I like this place. I like the porch and bentwood furniture, the chunky table in the center with a photo of a toddler on the potty. An instance when pervs and parents have the same taste in art. But nothing is pervy about this place. Just solid and permanent.

"Hello," I say to the outline of the woman's face behind the screen door.

"Yes?" she asks. Her accent is Yankee.

"Good morning," I say. "We are sharing a word from the Bible with our neighbors this morning."

"Your neighbors?" the woman moves onto the porch.

"Yes, ma'am." I smile. Stupid. Stupid. Leslie would never have used a canned line like that.

"You've got a generous idea of neighbors," the woman grins.

"We've been going for a few hours now," I say, not sure of what I'm getting at.

"You must be hot, then. Let me get you some drinks." The woman starts back into her house. When my mother was a teenager she ironed clothes for Mrs. Rowe, an old white woman in town. When the black man who tended the yard needed a drink of water, Mrs. Rowe would grab the glass from under the sink, bring the water or tea out to him herself. When he was done, she'd rinse the glass out with Clorox water; store it back in its place. Something told me that this woman will not scurry to her kitchen for the Colored glass. Something tells me she is for real.

"Oh no, ma'am," I begin. "We are ready to go home. You are actually our last stop today." Why did I say that?

"You are Jehovah's Witnesses, then?"

She got the name right. The number of people who just can't manage the name is astounding. We are the Jehovahs or simply

Jehovah or, worse, the jokes: Are you a Jehovah's Witness? they ask. No kidding, well, where's the accident?

"I knew some Witnesses a few years back. I worked with one. Nice people. I admire the work you do."

"Thank you," I say.

"I've studied a number of faiths — as a lay person, I mean. The spiritual life is important."

I was right. She is a hippie.

"Well, we want everyone to hear the good news," Leslie chimes in. I'm blowing this call. She is saving me. "We are always happy to find people of faith in these times. You know that the perilous conditions we live in have been predicted in Scripture," Leslie pulls out her Bible. Some householders recoil, as if you've just pulled out a gun. Okay, okay, put the Bible down. You don't want to do anything crazy.

"Well, I'm not much for organized religion, but I do try to keep an open mind. I'm glad that God is available to everyone. Are you sure you don't want a drink? It's brutal out there."

"No," I say too vehemently. "But I'm Stephanie. Nice to meet you."

"Well, take this then." The woman pulls out a couple of bills from her jeans pocket. "I'm Phyllis. I'd like to give you a donation for your work."

"Thank you." Leslie hands the woman some new magazines, taking only one of the dollars from her open hand.

"Okay, so that was Phyllis, new magazines," Leslie says, writing in her record. "I'm giving you credit for placing those. We'll come back to see her next week." Leslie pretends she doesn't know quite what to write, but, of course, she is pondering the best way to make this last call a teaching moment. "Listen, Steph, don't worry if you forget your sermon. I've done it. We all have. As hot as it is, I can hardly remember my name. Anyways, you got a magazine placement. That's the important thing. I don't see much working out with Phyllis." Leslie screws her face into a conclusion. "She's fine, nice really, but we're not going anywhere with her." Leslie pauses, trying to find the most encouraging angle. "Of course, Jehovah is the judge, but she seemed to me too comfortable. I don't think we're going anywhere. If you don't stand for something, you'll fall for anything, right?"

But I am hardly listening. All I can think about is that I am in love with Phyllis. It is too easy to point to her middle-class manners, the slick magazines with no celebrities on the covers, the coasters on the willow furniture, her kindness at the end of a long, hot day. I want her. Wouldn't it be great to walk up to someone's house and just say, I am here and I want to be your friend? Kids do it all the time. No misunderstandings. None of that rooting around for larger meaning. Like with God. He has the key, right? He holds the keys to happiness and to life. Why can't we just show up at the door, just ask for them? I'd open a door, any door, and He'd be on the other side with a whole host of Phyllises saying, "Here you go. Enjoy."

Before being a Jehovah's Witness, I'd been a member of my grandmother's African Methodist Episcopal church. Another world of dogged believers. Mama Ruby preached on lonely dirt roads, black neighborhoods, none of this white man's religion. Black places like Warrior, Freedman, and Dulatown. "Do you need to make water?" she'd admonish before the services, because once we commenced, there was no stopping. Remember: no hairfooling, no gum, no candy, no giggling, no turning to look at the opening door, no smiling, no eye-darting, no talking, no tapping of feet or fingers — clapping at up-tempo songs only, but not too vigorously, like I've had no home-training, no syncopation with the claps (leave that to the elders). No staring at anyone, even the spirit-filled or pitiable. And these are the easy rules, the ones for the very young. No problem. No problem, I say with nods. And if you are very good, do it all to your utmost like Noah, so you too will be rewarded with belief. Oh Phyllis, to believe anyway. What are you made of? I start my house-to-house record:

•••

To poet Philip Larkin: I have felt your breath on my heart today. Phyllis said she likes to keep an open mind and I fear this is the beginning. I will not go down the long slide with you, but stay safe, a dirtroader myself. It is safe here. The copse of pines, poplars, and weeds choking everything but light. Don't you see that? If you can't, I can't love you. Doesn't Scripture say to stay away from bad associates? Friends who will see you dead, all in the name of opening your mind? What about knowing every single thing for sure? What about that?

"A good day. A really good day," Leslie says. "How did you like your first visit to the territory? Different, huh?"

I nod.

Leslie starts the engine. "You seem preoccupied. Are you thinking about a certain young man?" She grins at my surprise, which she takes as proof of her suspicion. My body cringes at the thought. I'll see Bobby at the Kingdom Hall when Leslie drops me off. I'll see him tomorrow morning at the Sunday service and the day after that on the bus. But the thought of his thick fingers any place on my body, his short-sleeved dress shirts with the sweaty armpit stains that never seem to come out completely, the idea of spending one day of life forever with him makes me angry. Though I love him in God's way, I want to stomp him. I will say none of it to Leslie. I don't even want to.

"Maybe," I say.

"I knew it." Leslie wags her finger at me. "Don't wait," she says, "don't wait."

Stephanie Powell Watts is an assistant professor of English and creative writing at Lehigh University. She earned her MA and PhD degrees from the University of Missouri, where she was a Gus T. Ridgel fellow. Her stories, essays, and poems have appeared or are forthcoming in several journals, including *Obsidian III, African*

BOB WATTS

American Review, and *The Oxford American.* She has received honors
and awards for her work from *The Atlantic Monthly* and the Associated
Writing Programs. She is currently working on a novel set in a place
much like her hometown of Lenoir, North Carolina.

*E*arly one summer morning in Prague, Czech Republic, I met two
Jehovah's Witnesses handing out back issues of The Watchtower *and*
Awake *magazine at the entrance to the subway. Neither man spoke English,
and my Czech is at best limited, but I could understand their desire to
communicate, to tell the truth but to tell it unslanted in a way that a hearer
of the word could believe. I was impressed by their faith and recalled a time
when I felt that same kind of desperate reaching in my own experience. I
began this story on the subway train and wrote most of the rest of the day and
night until the first draft was complete.*

APPENDIX

A list of the magazines currently consulted for *New Stories from the South: The Year's Best, 2007,* with addresses, subscription rates, and editors.

Agni
236 Bay State Road
Boston, MA 02215
Semiannually, $17
Sven Birkerts

American Short Fiction
P.O. Box 301209
Austin, TX 78703
Quarterly, $30
Stacey Swann

The Antioch Review
P.O. Box 148
Yellow Springs, OH 45387-0148
Quarterly, $40
Robert S. Fogarty

Apalachee Review
P.O. Box 10469
Tallahassee, FL 32302
Semiannually, $15
Laura Newton

Appalachian Heritage
CPO 2166
Berea, KY 40404
Quarterly, $18
George Brosi

Arkansas Review
P.O. Box 1890
Arkansas State University
State University, AR 72467
Triannually, $20
Tom Williams

Arts & Letters
Campus Box 89
Georgia College & State University
Milledgeville, GA 31061-0490
Semiannually, $15
Martin Lammon

Atlanta
260 W. Peachtree Street
Suite 300
Atlanta, GA 30303
Monthly, $14.95
Rebecca Burns

The Atlantic Monthly
600 New Hampshire Avenue NW
Washington, DC 20037
Monthly, $19.50
C. Michael Curtis

Backwards City Review
P.O. Box 41317
Greensboro, NC 27404-1317
Semiannually, $12

Bayou
Department of English
University of New Orleans
Lakefront
New Orleans, LA 70148
Semiannually, $10
Joanna Leake

Bellevue Literary Review
Department of Medicine
New York University School of
    Medicine
550 1st Avenue, OBV-612
New York, NY 10016
Semiannually, $12
Ronna Weinberg

Black Warrior Review
University of Alabama
P.O. Box 862936
Tuscaloosa, AL 35486
Semiannually, $16
Fiction Editor

Boulevard
6614 Clayton Road, PMB 325
Richmond Heights, MO 63117
Triannually, $15
Richard Burgin

The Carolina Quarterly
Greenlaw Hall CB# 3520
University of North Carolina
Chapel Hill, NC 27599-3520
Triannually, $18
Fiction Editor

The Chattahoochee Review
Georgia Perimeter College
2101 Womack Road
Dunwoody, GA 30338-4497
Quarterly, $20
Marc Fitten

Cimarron Review
205 Morrill Hall
Oklahoma State University
Stillwater, OK 74078-4069
Quarterly, $24
E. P. Walkiewicz

The Cincinnati Review
Department of English and
    Comparative Literature
University of Cincinnati
P.O. Box 210069
Cincinnati, OH 45221-0069
Semiannually, $15
Brock Clarke

Colorado Review
Department of English
Colorado State University
Fort Collins, CO 80523
Triannually, $24
Stephanie G'Schwind

Conjunctions
21 East 10th Street
New York, NY 10003
Semiannually, $18
Bradford Morrow

Crazyhorse
Department of English
College of Charleston
66 George St.
Charleston, SC 29424
Semiannually, $15
Anthony Varallo

Crucible
Barton College
P.O. Box 5000
Wilson, NC 27893-7000
Annually, $7
Terence L. Grimes

Denver Quarterly
University of Denver
Denver, CO 80208
Quarterly, $20
Bin Ramke

Ecotone
Department of Creative Writing
UNC Wilmington
601 South College Road
Wilmington, NC 28403-3297
Semiannually, $18
Nina de Gramont

Epoch
251 Goldwin Smith Hall
Cornell University
Ithaca, NY 14853-3201
Triannually, $11
Michael Koch

Five Points
Georgia State University
P.O. Box 3999
Atlanta, GA 30302-3999
Triannually, $20
Megan Sexton

Gargoyle
3819 North 13th Street
Arlington, VA 22201
Annually, $15
Lucinda Ebersole and Richard
    Peabody

The Georgia Review
Gilbert Hall
University of Georgia
Athens, GA 30602-9009
Quarterly, $24
Stephen Corey

The Gettysburg Review
Gettysburg College
Gettysburg, PA 17325-1491
Quarterly, $24
Peter Stitt

Glimmer Train Stories
1211 NW Glisan Street, Suite 207
Portland, OR 97209-3054
Quarterly, $36
Susan Burmeister-Brown
    and Linda B. Swanson-Davies

The Greensboro Review
MFA Writing Program
3302 Hall for Humanities and
    Research Administration
UNC Greensboro
Greensboro, NC 27402-6170
Semiannually, $10
Jim Clark

Gulf Coast
Department of English
University of Houston
Houston, TX 77204-3013
Semiannually, $14
Fiction Editor

Harper's Magazine
666 Broadway, 11th Floor
New York, NY 10012
Monthly, $18
Ben Metcalf

Harpur Palate
English Department
Binghamton University
P.O. Box 6000
Binghamton, NY 13902-6000
Semiannually, $16
Fiction Editor

Hayden's Ferry Review
Box 875002
Arizona State University
Tempe, AZ 85287
Semiannually, $14
Fiction Editor

Hobart
submit@hobartpulp.com
Biannually, $17
Aaron Burch

The Idaho Review
Boise State University
Department of English
1910 University Drive
Boise, ID 83725
Annually, $10
Mitch Wieland

Image
3307 Third Avenue, W.
Seattle, WA 98119
Quarterly, $39.95
Gregory Wolfe

Indiana Review
Ballantine Hall 465
Indiana University
1020 E. Kirkwood Drive
Bloomington, IN 47405-7103
Semiannually, $17
Paula Carter

The Iowa Review
308 EPB
University of Iowa
Iowa City, IA 52242-1408
Triannually, $24
David Hamilton

The Journal
Ohio State University
Department of English

164 W. 17th Avenue
Columbus, OH 43210
Semiannually, $12
Kathy Fagan and Michelle Herman

Kalliope
Florida Community College–
    Jacksonville
11901 Beach Boulevard
Jacksonville, FL 32246
Semiannually, $20
Fiction Editor

The Kenyon Review
www.kenyonreview.org
Quarterly, $30
David H. Lynn

The Literary Review
Fairleigh Dickinson University
285 Madison Avenue
Madison, NJ 07940
Quarterly, $18
René Steinke

Long Story
18 Eaton Street
Lawrence, MA 01843
Annually, $7
R. P. Burnham

Louisiana Literature
SLU-10792
Southeastern Louisiana University
Hammond, LA 70402
Semiannually, $12
Jack Bedell

The Louisville Review
Spalding University
851 South 4th Street
Louisville, KY 40203
Semiannually, $14
Fiction Editor

McSweeney's
849 Valencia Street
San Francisco, CA 94110
Quarterly, $55
Dave Eggers

Meridian
University of Virginia
P.O. Box 400145
Charlottesville, VA 22904-4145
Semiannually, $10
Anna Shearer

Mid-American Review
Department of English
Bowling Green State University
Bowling Green, OH 43403
Semiannually, $15
Karen Craigo and Michael
   Czyzniejewski

Mississippi Review
University of Southern Mississippi
Box 5144
Hattiesburg, MS 39406
Semiannually, $15
Frederick Barthelme

The Missouri Review
357 McReynolds Hall
University of Missouri
Columbia, MO 65211
Triannually, $24
Speer Morgan

Natural Bridge
Department of English
University of Missouri-St. Louis
One University Boulevard
St. Louis, MO 63121
Semiannually, $15
Editor

New England Review
Middlebury College
Middlebury, VT 05753
Quarterly, $25
Stephen Donadio

New Letters
University of Missouri at Kansas
   City
5101 Rockhill Road
Kansas City, MO 64110
Quarterly, $22
Robert Stewart

New Orleans Review
P.O. Box 195
Loyola University
New Orleans, LA 70118
Semiannually, $14
Christopher Chambers, Editor

The New Yorker
4 Times Square
New York, NY 10036
Weekly, $47
Deborah Treisman, Fiction
   Editor

Nightsun
Department of English
Frostburg State University
101 Braddock Road
Frostburg, MD 21532
Annually, $9
Fiction Editor

Nimrod International Journal
University of Tulsa
600 South College
Tulsa, OK 74104
Semiannually, $17.50
Francine Ringold

Ninth Letter
Department of English
University of Illinois
608 South Wright Street
Urbana, IL 61801
Biannually, $19.95
Philip Graham

The North American Review
University of Northern Iowa
1222 W. 27th Street
Cedar Falls, IA 50614-0516
Five times a year, $22
Grant Tracey

North Carolina Literary Review
English Department
2201 Bate Building
East Carolina University
Greenville, NC 27858-4353
Annually, $10
Margaret Bauer

Northwest Review
1286 University of Oregon
Eugene, OR 97403
Triannually, $22
John Witte

One Story
www.one-story.com
Monthly, $21
Hannah Tinti

Ontario Review
9 Honey Brook Drive
Princeton, NJ 08540
Semiannually, $16
Raymond J. Smith

Open City
270 Lafayette Street
Suite 1412
New York, NY 10012

Triannually, $30
Thomas Beller, Joanna Yas

Other Voices
University of Illinois at Chicago
Department of English (M/C 162)
601 S. Morgan Street
Chicago, IL 60607-7120
Quarterly, $26
Lois Hauselman

The Oxford American
201 Donaghey Avenue, Main 107
Conway, AR 72035
Quarterly, $14.95
Marc Smirnoff

The Paris Review
62 White Street
New York, NY 10013
Quarterly, $40
Philip Gourevitch

Parting Gifts
March Street Press
3413 Wilshire Drive
Greensboro, NC 27408
Semiannually, $12
Robert Bixby

Pembroke Magazine
UNC-P, Box 1510
Pembroke, NC 28372-1510
Annually, $10
Shelby Stephenson

The Pinch
Department of English
University of Memphis
Memphis, TN 38152-6176
Semiannually, $18
Benjamin Jenkins

Pleiades
Department of English and
    Philosophy
Central Missouri State University
Warrensburg, MO 64093
Semiannually, $12
Susan Steinberg

Ploughshares
Emerson College
120 Boylston St.
Boston, MA 02116-4624
Triannually, $24
Don Lee

PMS
University of Alabama at
    Birmingham
Department of English
HB 217, 900 S. 13th Street
1530 3rd Ave., S.
Birmingham, AL 35294-1260
Annually, $7
Linda Frost

Post Road Magazine
www.postroadmag.com
Semiannually, $18
Rebecca Boyd

Potomac Review
Montgomery College
51 Mannakee Street
Macklin Tower Room 212
Rockville, MD 20850
Annually, $10
Julie Wakeman-Linn

The Powhatan Review
1611-C Colley Avenue
Norfolk, VA 23517
Semiannually

Prairie Schooner
201 Andrews Hall
University of Nebraska

Lincoln, NE 68588-0334
Quarterly, $26
Hilda Raz

A Public Space
www.publicspace.org
Quarterly, $36
Brigid Hughes

Quarterly West
University of Utah
255 S. Central Campus Drive
Department of English
LNCO 3500
Salt Lake City, UT 84112-9109
Semiannually, $14
Jenny Colville

The Rambler
P.O. Box 5070
Chapel Hill, NC 27514-5001
Six issues/year, $19.95
Elizabeth Oliver

REAL
College of Liberal Arts
Box 13007
Stephen F. Austin State University
Nacogdoches, TX 75962-3007
Semiannually, $20
John A. McDermott

Redivider
Writing, Literature, and Publishing
    Department
Emerson College
120 Boylston Street
Boston, MA 02116
Semiannually, $10
Chip Cheek

River Styx
3547 Olive Street, Suite 107
St. Louis, MO 63103
Triannually, $20
Richard Newman

Santa Monica Review
Santa Monica College
1900 Pico Boulevard
Santa Monica, CA 90405
Semiannually, $12
Andrew Tonkovich

The Sewanee Review
735 University Avenue
Sewanee, TN 37383-1000
Quarterly, $25
George Core

Shenandoah
Washington and Lee University
Mattingly House
Lexington, VA 24450
Quarterly, $22
R. T. Smith

Sonora Review
Department of English
University of Arizona
Tucson, AZ 85721
Semiannually
D. Seth Horton

The South Carolina Review
Center for Electronic and Digital
   Publishing
Clemson University
Strode Tower, Box 340522
Clemson, SC 29634
Semiannually, $26
Wayne Chapman

South Dakota Review
Department of English
414 Clark Street
University of South Dakota
Vermillion, SD 57069
Quarterly, $30
John R. Milton

The Southeast Review
Department of English
Florida State University
Tallahassee, FL 32306
Semiannually, $12
Bill Yazbec

Southern Humanities Review
9088 Haley Center
Auburn University
Auburn, AL 36849
Quarterly, $15
Dan R. Latimer and Virginia M.
   Kouidis

The Southern Review
Old President's House
Louisiana State University
Baton Rouge, LA 70803
Quarterly, $25
Bret Lott

Southwest Review
307 Fondren Library West
Box 750374
Southern Methodist University
Dallas, TX 75275
Quarterly, $24
Willard Spiegelman

Sou'wester
Department of English
Southern Illinois University at
   Edwardsville
Edwardsville, IL 62026-1438
Semiannually, $15
Allison Funk and Geoff Schmidt

StoryQuarterly
online submissions only:
www.storyquarterly.com
Annually, $10
M.M.M. Hayes

Subtropics
Department of English
University of Florida
P.O. Box 112075
Gainesville, FL 32611
Triannually, $26
David Leavitt

Tampa Review
University of Tampa
401 W. Kennedy Boulevard
Tampa, FL 33606-1490
Semiannually, $15
Richard Mathews

Texas Review
English Department Box 2146
Sam Houston State University
Huntsville, TX 77341-2146
Semiannually, $20
Paul Ruffin

The Threepenny Review
P.O. Box 9131
Berkeley, CA 94709
Quarterly, $25
Wendy Lesser

Timber Creek Review
P.O. Box 16542
Greensboro, NC 27416
Quarterly, $17
John M. Freiermuth

Tin House
P.O. Box 10500
Portland, OR 97296-0500
Quarterly, $29.90
Rob Spillman

TriQuarterly
Northwestern University
629 Noyes Street
Evanston, IL 60208
Triannually, $24
Susan Firestone Hahn

The Virginia Quarterly Review
One West Range
P.O. Box 400223
Charlottesville, VA 22904-4223
Quarterly, $25
Ted Genoways

West Branch
Bucknell Hall
Bucknell University
Lewisburg, PA 17837
Semiannually, $10
Ron Mohring

Wind
P.O. Box 24548
Lexington, KY 40524
Annually, $12
Eric Tuttle

The Yalobusha Review
Department of English
University of Mississippi
P.O. 1848
University, MS 38677
Annually, $10
Neal Walsh

Yemassee
Department of English
University of South Carolina
Columbia, SC 29208
Semiannually, $15
Fiction Editor

Zoetrope: All-Story
The Sentinel Building
916 Kearny Street
San Francisco, CA 94133
Quarterly, $19.95
Michael Ray

PREVIOUS VOLUMES

Copies of previous volumes of *New Stories from the South* can be ordered through your local bookstore or by calling the Sales Department at Algonquin Books of Chapel Hill. Multiple copies for classroom adoptions are available at a special discount. For information, please call 919-967-0108.

NEW STORIES FROM THE SOUTH: THE YEAR'S BEST, 1986

Max Apple, BRIDGING

Madison Smartt Bell, TRIPTYCH 2

Mary Ward Brown, TONGUES OF FLAME

Suzanne Brown, COMMUNION

James Lee Burke, THE CONVICT

Ron Carlson, AIR

Doug Crowell, SAYS VELMA

Leon V. Driskell, MARTHA JEAN

Elizabeth Harris, THE WORLD RECORD HOLDER

Mary Hood, SOMETHING GOOD FOR GINNIE

David Huddle, SUMMER OF THE MAGIC SHOW

Gloria Norris, HOLDING ON

Kurt Rheinheimer, UMPIRE

W. A. Smith, DELIVERY

Wallace Whatley, SOMETHING TO LOSE

Luke Whisnant, WALLWORK

Sylvia Wilkinson, CHICKEN SIMON

NEW STORIES FROM THE SOUTH: THE YEAR'S BEST, 1987

James Gordon Bennett, DEPENDENTS

Robert Boswell, EDWARD AND JILL

NEW STORIES FROM THE SOUTH: THE YEAR'S BEST, 1988

NEW STORIES FROM THE SOUTH: THE YEAR'S BEST, 1989

Rick Bass, WILD HORSES

Madison Smartt Bell, CUSTOMS OF THE COUNTRY

James Gordon Bennett, PACIFIC THEATER

Larry Brown, SAMARITANS

Mary Ward Brown, IT WASN'T ALL DANCING

Kelly Cherry, WHERE SHE WAS

David Huddle, PLAYING

Sandy Huss, COUPON FOR BLOOD

Frank Manley, THE RAIN OF TERROR

Bobbie Ann Mason, WISH

Lewis Nordan, A HANK OF HAIR, A PIECE OF BONE

Kurt Rheinheimer, HOMES

Mark Richard, STRAYS

Annette Sanford, SIX WHITE HORSES

Paula Sharp, HOT SPRINGS

NEW STORIES FROM THE SOUTH: THE YEAR'S BEST, 1990

Tom Bailey, CROW MAN

Rick Bass, THE HISTORY OF RODNEY

Richard Bausch, LETTER TO THE LADY OF THE HOUSE

Larry Brown, SLEEP

Moira Crone, JUST OUTSIDE THE B.T.

Clyde Edgerton, CHANGING NAMES

Greg Johnson, THE BOARDER

Nanci Kincaid, SPITTIN' IMAGE OF A BAPTIST BOY

Reginald McKnight, THE KIND OF LIGHT THAT SHINES ON TEXAS

Lewis Nordan, THE CELLAR OF RUNT CONROY

Lance Olsen, FAMILY

Mark Richard, FEAST OF THE EARTH, RANSOM OF THE CLAY

Ron Robinson, WHERE WE LAND

Bob Shacochis, LES FEMMES CREOLES

Molly Best Tinsley, ZOE

Donna Trussell, FISHBONE

NEW STORIES FROM THE SOUTH: THE YEAR'S BEST, 1991

Rick Bass, IN THE LOYAL MOUNTAINS

Thomas Phillips Brewer, BLACK CAT BONE

Larry Brown, BIG BAD LOVE

Robert Olen Butler, RELIC

Barbara Hudson, THE ARABESQUE

Elizabeth Hunnewell, A LIFE OR DEATH MATTER

Hilding Johnson, SOUTH OF KITTATINNY

Nanci Kincaid, THIS IS NOT THE PICTURE SHOW

Bobbie Ann Mason, WITH JAZZ

Jill McCorkle, WAITING FOR HARD TIMES TO END

Robert Morgan, POINSETT'S BRIDGE

Reynolds Price, HIS FINAL MOTHER

Mark Richard, THE BIRDS FOR CHRISTMAS

Susan Starr Richards, THE SCREENED PORCH

Lee Smith, INTENSIVE CARE

Peter Taylor, COUSIN AUBREY

NEW STORIES FROM THE SOUTH: THE YEAR'S BEST, 1992

Alison Baker, CLEARWATER AND LATISSIMUS

Larry Brown, A ROADSIDE RESURRECTION

Mary Ward Brown, A NEW LIFE

James Lee Burke, TEXAS CITY, 1947

Robert Olen Butler, A GOOD SCENT FROM A STRANGE MOUNTAIN

Nanci Kincaid, A STURDY PAIR OF SHOES THAT FIT GOOD

Patricia Lear, AFTER MEMPHIS

Dan Leone, YOU HAVE CHOSEN CAKE

Reginald McKnight, QUITTING SMOKING

Karen Minton, LIKE HANDS ON A CAVE WALL

Elizabeth Seydel Morgan, ECONOMICS

Pamela Erbe, SWEET TOOTH

Barry Hannah, NICODEMUS BLUFF

Nanci Kincaid, PRETENDING THE BED WAS A RAFT

Nancy Krusoe, LANDSCAPE AND DREAM

Robert Morgan, DARK CORNER

Reynolds Price, DEEDS OF LIGHT

Leon Rooke, THE HEART MUST FROM ITS BREAKING

John Sayles, PEELING

George Singleton, OUTLAW HEAD & TAIL

Melanie Sumner, MY OTHER LIFE

Robert Love Taylor, MY MOTHER'S SHOES

NEW STORIES FROM THE SOUTH: THE YEAR'S BEST, 1995

R. Sebastian Bennett, RIDING WITH THE DOCTOR

Wendy Brenner, I AM THE BEAR

James Lee Burke, WATER PEOPLE

Robert Olen Butler, BOY BORN WITH TATTOO OF ELVIS

Ken Craven, PAYING ATTENTION

Tim Gautreaux, THE BUG MAN

Ellen Gilchrist, THE STUCCO HOUSE

Scott Gould, BASES

Barry Hannah, DRUMMER DOWN

MMM Hayes, FIXING LU

Hillary Hebert, LADIES OF THE MARBLE HEARTH

Jesse Lee Kercheval, GRAVITY

Caroline A. Langston, IN THE DISTANCE

Lynn Marie, TEAMS

Susan Perabo, GRAVITY

Dale Ray Phillips, EVERYTHING QUIET LIKE CHURCH

Elizabeth Spencer, THE RUNAWAYS

New Stories from the South: The Year's Best, 1996

Robert Olen Butler, jealous husband returns in form of
   parrot

Moira Crone, gauguin

J. D. Dolan, mood music

Ellen Douglas, grant

William Faulkner, rose of lebanon

Kathy Flann, a happy, safe thing

Tim Gautreaux, died and gone to vegas

David Gilbert, cool moss

Marcia Guthridge, the host

Jill McCorkle, paradise

Robert Morgan, the balm of gilead tree

Tom Paine, general markman's last stand

Susan Perabo, some say the world

Annette Sanford, goose girl

Lee Smith, the happy memories club

New Stories from the South: The Year's Best, 1997

preface *by Robert Olen Butler*

Gene Able, marrying aunt sadie

Dwight Allen, the green suit

Edward Allen, ashes north

Robert Olen Butler, help me find my spaceman lover

Janice Daugharty, along a wider river

Ellen Douglas, julia and nellie

Pam Durban, gravity

Charles East, pavane for a dead princess

Rhian Margaret Ellis, every building wants to fall

Tim Gautreaux, little frogs in a ditch

Elizabeth Gilbert, the finest wife

Lucy Hochman, simpler components

Beauvais McCaddon, the half-pint

NEW STORIES FROM THE SOUTH: THE YEAR'S BEST, 1998

NEW STORIES FROM THE SOUTH: THE YEAR'S BEST, 1999

New Stories from the South: The Year's Best, 2000

NEW STORIES FROM THE SOUTH: THE YEAR'S BEST, 2001

New Stories from the South: The Year's Best, 2002

PREFACE *by Larry Brown*

Dwight Allen, END OF THE STEAM AGE

Russell Banks, THE OUTER BANKS

Brad Barkley, BENEATH THE DEEP, SLOW MOTION

Doris Betts, ABOVEGROUND

William Gay, CHARTING THE TERRITORIES OF THE RED

Aaron Gwyn, OF FALLING

Ingrid Hill, THE MORE THEY STAY THE SAME

David Koon, THE BONE DIVERS

Andrea Lee, ANTHROPOLOGY

Romulus Linney, TENNESSEE

Corey Mesler, THE GROWTH AND DEATH OF BUDDY GARDNER

Lucia Nevai, FAITH HEALER

Julie Orringer, PILGRIMS

Dulane Upshaw Ponder, THE RAT SPOON

Bill Roorbach, BIG BEND

George Singleton, SHOW-AND-TELL

Kate Small, MAXIMUM SUNLIGHT

R. T. Smith, I HAVE LOST MY RIGHT

Max Steele, THE UNRIPE HEART

New Stories from the South: The Year's Best, 2003

PREFACE *by Roy Blount Jr.*

Dorothy Allison, COMPASSION

Steve Almond, THE SOUL MOLECULE

Brock Clarke, FOR THOSE OF US WHO NEED SUCH THINGS

Lucy Corin, RICH PEOPLE

John Dufresne, JOHNNY TOO BAD

Donald Hays, DYING LIGHT

Ingrid Hill, THE BALLAD OF RAPPY VALCOUR

Bret Anthony Johnston, CORPUS

Michael Knight, ELLEN'S BOOK

NEW STORIES FROM THE SOUTH: THE YEAR'S BEST, 2004